EX LIBRIS

VINTAGE **CLASSICS**

TONI MORRISON

Toni Morrison was awarded the Nobel Prize in Literature in 1993. She was the author of many novels, including *The Bluest Eye*, *Sula*, *Beloved*, *Paradise* and *Love*. She received the National Book Critics Circle Award and a Pulitzer Prize for her fiction and was awarded the Presidential Medal of Freedom, America's highest civilian honour, in 2012 by Barack Obama. Toni Morrison died on 5 August 2019 at the age of eighty-eight.

'Toni Morrison makes me believe in God. She makes me believe in a divine being, because luck and genetics don't seem to come close to explaining her'
Guardian

'When Morrison writes at her best, you can feel the workings of history through her prose'
Hilary Mantel, *Spectator*

'The nearest thing America has to a national novelist'
New York Times

'Toni Morrison is not just an important contemporary novelist but a major figure in our national literature'
New York Review of Books

'I imagine if our greatest American novelist, William Faulkner, were alive today he would herald Toni Morrison's emergence as a kindred spirit... Discovering a writer like Toni Morrison is the rarest of pleasures'
Washington Post

ALSO BY TONI MORRISON

Fiction

The Bluest Eye

Sula

Song of Solomon

Tar Baby

Jazz

Paradise

Love

A Mercy

Home

God Help the Child

Non-Fiction

The Dancing Mind

*Playing in the Dark: Whiteness
and the Literary Imagination*

The Origin of Others

*Mouth Full of Blood:
Essays, Speeches, Meditations*

TONI MORRISON

Beloved

WITH A FOREWORD BY
Toni Morrison

AND

AN INTRODUCTION BY
Bernardine Evaristo

VINTAGE

1 3 5 7 9 10 8 6 4 2

Vintage
20 Vauxhall Bridge Road,
London SW1V 2SA

Vintage Classics is part of the Penguin Random House group of companies
whose addresses can be found at global.penguinrandomhouse.com

Penguin
Random House
UK

This edition reissued in Vintage Classics in 2022
First published in Vintage in 1997
First published in hardback by Chatto & Windus in 1987

penguin.co.uk/vintage-classics

A CIP catalogue record for this book is available from the British Library

ISBN 9781784876432

Typeset in 10.75/13.25 pt Bell MT
by Integra Software Services Pvt. Ltd, Pondicherry

Printed and bound in Great Britain by Clays Ltd, Elcograf S.p.A.

The authorised representative in the EEA is Penguin Random House Ireland,
Morrison Chambers, 32 Nassau Street, Dublin D02 YH68.

Penguin Random House is committed to a sustainable future for our
business, our readers and our planet. This book is made from Forest
Stewardship Council® certified paper.

*Sixty Million
and more*

I will call them my people,
which were not my people;
and her beloved,
which was not beloved.

ROMANS 9:25

INTRODUCTION

As soon as I read *The Bluest Eye* in 1981, I was hooked on Toni Morrison's writing. How I loved her lush prose in this, her first novel, and the quietly intense dramatic storytelling style that centred young black females, especially the storyline around colourism, with Pecola, the dark-skinned black girl longing for blue eyes in a country that elevated white beauty and deemed blackness ugly. I still have that now extremely mashed-up copy of *The Bluest Eye* on my bookshelf, alongside every other book she published.

I first read *Beloved*, Morrison's fifth novel, soon after it was published in 1987, and found it more difficult than her earlier works. Yet, even when it seemed oblique in parts, there was enough drama and tension to captivate me. There is a giant leap, however, in the scope and sophistication of this novel compared to *The Bluest Eye*, which is a shorter and simpler read. This past week I re-read *Beloved* in order to write this essay and I spent a few days on my sofa, summer rain falling outside, relishing the deep pleasure I have always experienced in savouring her fiction. I read slowly, allowing its gorgeous language, vivid descriptions and sensory atmospheres to sink in.

Reading Morrison always feels like coming home, as her writing connects me to my emotions, my imagination and my soul.

She was clear in her intention with this novel, which was to resurrect America's slave narrative through the stories of the individuals who had endured it. Let us remember that slavery in America lasted 264 years, from 1619 to 1863, and that this aspect of American history is also British history, because from 1607 until the American Revolution of 1783, the country was a British colony and known as British America. Even after it had despatched its colonial master, British slavers continued to transport Africans to America as slaves. In Britain we never seem to take responsibility for American slavery, yet it is as foundational to British history as this country's own multinational business in the trade and enslavement of Africans who were taken to the Caribbean as slaves. My point is, let's not make any bones about it; *Beloved*, the novel, is about the legacy of Britain's extremely profitable investment in enslaving Africans and transporting them to America. We cannot take the moral high ground and distance ourselves from it. In reading this novel, not only was I connecting to black history, but also to the more unsavoury aspects of British history.

Beloved was inspired by the true story of a woman called Margaret Garner, who escaped slavery in 1856, only to be hunted down by slave catchers. She killed her small daughter with a knife, rather than have her raised as a slave. Shocking and tragic, this act should be seen as an indictment against the horrors she knew awaited her girl child, rather than as a moral judgement upon Garner. This notorious, national news story was Morrison's starting point. The novel itself elaborates on the question of why a woman would choose to do this, and the consequences. The book plunges us into the legacy of slavery through the lives of people who had been enslaved and were now living during the period known as Reconstruction (1863-77), which took place after Abolition, when the country was acclimatising to a new infrastructural reality and recalibrating its identity, especially that of its former slaves and slave-owners. The novel's protagonist, Sethe, is a former slave who lives in a haunted house with her eighteen-year-old daughter, Denver. When two other people join the household, Paul D and a strange young woman called Beloved, their intertwining relationships seethe with unresolved desires and resentments. Fragmented and repressed memories creep into the minds of the characters so that the past is constantly contaminating the present. They have endured the daily terrors of slavery and emerged from it profoundly scarred. One hopes for catharsis, and the novel demonstrates that it's only when the past is confronted that these characters can begin to release its shackles and move forwards.

Great literature such as *Beloved* has the potential to reveal more of its riches through re-reading.

When I was younger, I didn't fully appreciate the depth of the interior life of Morrison's characters. My own experiences were still quite nascent and my world view of human behaviour overwhelmingly simplistic, as my principles were founded on the polarities of good versus bad. Yet I believe that I still absorbed Morrison's much more mature comprehension of people as multidimensional, even though I probably didn't recognise it as such. Great stories have the potential to soak into our very being and subconsciously shape us through osmosis; a book such as this one has the potential to transform our perceptions about who we are in the world. Reading *Beloved* at an early stage in my adult life expanded my emotional knowledge beyond my own limitations and enabled me to engage with the extremes and profundity of human experience Morrison imaginatively recreates.

The mechanics of Morrison's craft were impenetrable to my younger self – a poet and dramatist who had not yet written any fiction. Fast forward a few decades and I can see beneath the surface and deconstruct her technique. From the very beginning of the novel, she is unrelenting in describing the cruelty of slavery and its impact on the lives of the enslaved. Barely a page goes by without another shocking revelation, another punch in the gut. It's hard not to be appalled at the suffering we witness, and to feel empathy for those whose post-traumatic stress stops them finding peace in their post-enslaved lives. Morrison utilises multiple perspectives that fade in and out of an often elliptical text with temporal interruptions through which we witness characters relive the past. The non-chronological structure sees the past and present slyly segueing into each other so that the reader has to constantly adjust to shifting time sequences. Yes, the text can be oblique and ambiguous, but that was Morrison's intention. She asks us to do some of the work. In 1984, in an interview in a book called *Black Women Writers at Work* edited by Claudia Tate, Morrison said:

> My writing expects, demands participatory reading . . . It's not just about telling the story; it's about involving the reader. The reader supplies the emotions. The reader supplies even some of the color, some of the sound.

My language has to have holes and spaces so that the
reader can come into it.

Some of the most startling moments in the novel are made
even more graphic because Morrison holds back just enough
to force the reader to visualise what's happening in our imagination. We are required to go from passive to active, which
deepens our engagement with the story. We are no longer just
in the audience; we're helping to construct the narrative for
ourselves.

Writers often do the deep thinking for us. Morrison was no
exception. She provided substantial insight into slavery while
illustrating the crimes done unto black people in the service
of capitalism. This was through the exploitation of an unpaid
labour force over hundreds of years, and she showed us the
impact of this on those who were stripped of their basic human
rights, and who weren't always able to retain their dignity. She
helps us see that, when people in power are desensitised to the
humanity of their fellow human beings through a racist
ideology that relegates them to a kind of semi-sentient sub-
human, then they, the powerful overlords, are capable of perpetu-
ating the worst atrocities, even as they self-justify their
behaviour as morally commendable.

Morrison, the supreme craftswoman, was called an 'African-
American or black writer'. It's exactly what she was and the
culture from which she wrote. For her, it was not limiting or
liminal, but limitless. She enjoyed the endless possibilities of
being black in this world, of being African or descended from
Africans. The appellation was and is a political statement, yet
while white writers are rarely identified as such, nobody would

ever consider them to have somehow reduced their intellectual
and creative options when their perspective, subject matter and
storytelling are all, in effect, steeped in white narratives. The
truth is, in white majority cultures, white literature is the norm.
Morrison also said in 1984:

> When I view the world, perceive it and write about it,
> it's the world of black people. It's not that I won't write
> about white people. I just know that when I'm trying to
> develop the various themes I write about, the people who
> best manifest those themes for me are the black people
> I invent.

How inspiring it was for me to hear those words from an elder
who was validating black voices in literature. When Morrison
and her generation proudly proclaimed their black, female identities, they empowered their younger sisters over the pond to
do the same.

The vast Atlantic lay between me and my lodestar, but
Morrison was instrumental in my own development as a young
writer and became a role model. She interrogated cultural
memory and society through fiction that delved into and encap-
sulated African American psyches and strategies for survival,
while blending a supreme mastery of craft with psychological
complexity and uncompromisingly political writing. Her books
were the gold standard. At first I aspired to write like her, a
typical rite of passage when we want to emulate those we most
admire, and inevitably fall flat on our faces because our writing
is derivative, a pale imitation of the real thing. We should
acknowledge that writers' sensibilities don't just appear out of

nowhere. We are moulded by our circumstances. With this in mind, Morrison's practice came out of her childhood, country, culture, generation, era, educational background, religion, dialect, idiolect, literary influences and oral tradition – including the African-American folk tales her parents told her and the songs they passed on – and her imagination, emotional literacy and intellectual curiosity. A life, in fact, that bore little relation to my own upbringing as a black Londoner thirty years her junior. How could I possibly recreate her genius? She was inimitable. What I eventually came to understand is that, instead of trying to imitate our literary heroines, we need to learn from them the importance of cultivating our own practice and aesthetics; to create a unique literature generated by our own individuality. One such example is that, while I could never write like Morrison, I did learn, or perhaps absorb, that she didn't write perfect English in her novels. Not for her those perfectly modulated, grammatically correct sentences that are sometimes seen as the zenith of great writing, at least in the UK. Instead, she wrote what I call 'interesting English', employing a narrative style that subtly echoed the cadences, syntax and orality of her own culture, and slipping into the vernacular of her characters when appropriate. The lesson I learned from her as a young writer was that I did not have to adhere to any literary traditions that alienated me, but could do my own thing.

Morrison won the Pulitzer Prize for *Beloved* in 1987 and it was made into a major Hollywood film by Jonathan Demme in 1998, starring Oprah Winfrey, Danny Glover and Thandie Newton. It has been taught in schools and at universities globally for decades. In 1993, she received the Nobel Prize in

Literature, the first and only black woman to be awarded it, which propelled her onto the world stage and sealed her reputation as our queen of letters.

Beloved is considered Morrison's greatest work, but all her work is great. I hope that this book will inspire you to read her other novels which show that her talent was sustained, varied and impressively impactful. They all might now be set in the past, but Toni Morrison was a writer for all time.

Bernardine Evaristo
2022

FOREWORD

In 1983 I lost my job – or left it. One, the other, or both. In any case, I had been part-time for a while, coming into the publishing house one day a week to do the correspondence-telephoning-meetings that were part of the job; editing manuscripts at home.

Leaving was a good idea for two reasons. One, I had written four novels and it seemed clear to everyone that writing was my central work. The question of priorities – how can you edit and write at the same time – seemed to me both queer and predictable; it sounded like 'How can you both teach and create?' 'How can a painter or a sculptor or an actor do her work and guide others?' But to many this edit–write combination was conflicting.

The second reason was less ambiguous. The books I had edited were not earning scads of money, even when 'scads' didn't mean what it means now. My list was to me spectacular: writers with outrageous talent (Toni Cade Bambara, June Jordan, Gayle Jones, Lucille Clifton, Henry Dumas, Leon Forrest); scholars with original ideas and hands-on research (William Hinton's *Shen Fan*, Ivan Van Sertima's *They Came Before Columbus*, Karen

DeCrow's *Sexist Justice*, Chinweizu's *The West and the Rest of Us*); public figures eager to set the record straight (Angela Davis, Muhammad Ali, Huey Newton). And when there was a book that I thought needed doing, I found an author to write it. My enthusiasm, shared by some, was muted by others, reflecting the indifferent sales figures. I may be wrong about this, but even in the late seventies, acquiring authors who were certain sellers outranked editing manuscripts or supporting emerging or aging authors through their careers. Suffice it to say, I convinced myself that it was time for me to live like a grown-up writer: off royalties and writing only. I don't know what comic book that notion came from, but I grabbed it.

A few days after my last day at work, sitting in front of my house on the pier jutting out into the Hudson River, I began to feel an edginess instead of the calm I had expected. I ran through my index of problem areas and found nothing new or pressing. I couldn't fathom what was so unexpectedly troubling on a day that perfect, watching a river that serene. I had no agenda and couldn't hear the telephone if it rang. I heard my heart, though, stomping away in my chest like a colt. I went back to the house to examine this apprehension, even panic. I knew what fear felt like; this was different. Then it slapped me: I was happy, free in a way I had never been, ever. It was the oddest sensation. Not ecstasy, not satisfaction, not a surfeit of pleasure or accomplishment. It was a purer delight, a rogue anticipation with certainty. Enter *Beloved*.

I think now it was the shock of liberation that drew my thoughts to what 'free' could possibly mean to women. In the eighties, the debate was still roiling: equal pay, equal treatment, access to professions, schools ... and choice without stigma.

To marry or not. To have children or not. Inevitably these thoughts led me to the different history of black women in this country – a history in which marriage was discouraged, impossible, or illegal; in which birthing children was required, but 'having' them, being responsible for them – being, in other words, their parent – was as out of the question as freedom. Assertions of parenthood under conditions peculiar to the logic of institutional enslavement were criminal.

The idea was riveting, but the canvas overwhelmed me. Summoning characters who could manifest the intellect and the ferocity such logic would provoke proved beyond my imagination until I remembered one of the books I had published back when I had a job. A newspaper clipping in *The Black Book* summarized the story of Margaret Garner, a young mother who, having escaped slavery, was arrested for killing one of her children (and trying to kill the others) rather than let them be returned to the owner's plantation. She became a cause célèbre in the fight against the Fugitive Slave laws, which mandated the return of escapees to their owners. Her sanity and lack of repentance caught the attention of Abolitionists as well as newspapers. She was certainly single-minded and, judging by her comments, she had the intellect, the ferocity, and the willingness to risk everything for what was to her the necessity of freedom.

The historical Margaret Garner is fascinating, but, to a novelist, confining. Too little imaginative space there for my purposes. So I would invent her thoughts, plumb them for a subtext that was historically true in essence, but not strictly factual in order to relate her history to contemporary issues about freedom, responsibility, and women's 'place.' The heroine would represent the unapologetic acceptance of shame and terror; assume the consequences of choosing infanticide; claim her own freedom. The terrain, slavery, was formidable and pathless. To invite readers (and myself) into the repellant landscape (hidden, but not completely; deliberately buried, but not forgotten) was to pitch a tent in a cemetery inhabited by highly vocal ghosts.

I sat on the porch, rocking in a swing, looking at giant stones piled up to take the river's occasional fist. Above the stones is a path through the lawn, but interrupted by an iron-wood gazebo situated under a cluster of trees and in deep shade.

She walked out of the water, climbed the rocks, and leaned against the gazebo. Nice hat.

So she was there from the beginning, and except for me, everybody (the characters) knew it – a sentence that later became 'The women in the house knew it.' The figure most central to the story would have to be her, the murdered, not the murderer, the one who lost everything and had no say in any of it. She could not linger outside; she would have to enter the house. A real house, not a cabin. One with an address, one where former slaves lived on their own. There would be no lobby into this house, and there would be no 'introduction' into it or into the novel. I wanted the reader to be kidnapped, thrown ruthlessly into an alien environment as the first step into a shared experience with the book's population – just as the characters were snatched from one place to another, from any place to any other, without preparation or defense.

It was important to name this house, but not the way 'Sweet Home' or other plantations were named. There would be no adjectives suggesting coziness or grandeur or the laying claim to an instant, aristocratic past. Only numbers here to identify the house while simultaneously separating it from a street or city – marking its difference from the houses of other blacks in the neighborhood; allowing it a hint of the superiority, the pride, former slaves would take in having an address of their own. Yet a house that has, literally, a personality – which we call 'haunted' when that personality is blatant.

In trying to make the slave experience intimate, I hoped the sense of things being both under control and out of control would be persuasive throughout; that the order and quietude of everyday life would be violently disrupted by the chaos of the needy dead; that the herculean effort to forget would be threatened by memory desperate to stay alive. To render enslavement as a personal experience, language must get out of the way.

I husband that moment on the pier, the deceptive river, the instant awareness of possibility, the loud heart kicking, the solitude, the danger. And the girl with the nice hat. Then the focus.

Toni Morrison

Beloved

I

124 was spiteful. Full of a baby's venom. The women in the house knew it and so did the children. For years each put up with the spite in his own way, but by 1873 Sethe and her daughter Denver were its only victims. The grandmother, Baby Suggs, was dead, and the sons, Howard and Buglar, had run away by the time they were thirteen years old—as soon as merely looking in a mirror shattered it (that was the signal for Buglar); as soon as two tiny hand prints appeared in the cake (that was it for Howard). Neither boy waited to see more; another kettleful of chickpeas smoking in a heap on the floor; soda crackers crumbled and strewn in a line next to the door-sill. Nor did they wait for one of the relief periods: the weeks, months even, when nothing was disturbed. No. Each one fled at once—the moment the house committed what was for him the one insult not to be borne or witnessed a second time. Within two months, in the dead of winter, leaving their grandmother, Baby Suggs; Sethe, their mother; and their little sister, Denver, all by themselves in the gray and white house on Bluestone Road. It didn't have a number then, because Cincinnati didn't stretch that far. In fact, Ohio had been calling

itself a state only seventy years when first one brother and
then the next stuffed quilt packing into his hat, snatched up
his shoes, and crept away from the lively spite the house felt
for them.

Baby Suggs didn't even raise her head. From her sickbed
she heard them go but that wasn't the reason she lay still. It
was a wonder to her that her grandsons had taken so long to
realize that every house wasn't like the one on Bluestone Road.
Suspended between the nastiness of life and the meanness of
the dead, she couldn't get interested in leaving life or living
it, let alone the fright of two creeping-off boys. Her past had
been like her present—intolerable—and since she knew death
was anything but forgetfulness, she used the little energy left
her for pondering color.

"Bring a little lavender in, if you got any. Pink, if you don't."

And Sethe would oblige her with anything from fabric to
her own tongue. Winter in Ohio was especially rough if you
had an appetite for color. Sky provided the only drama, and
counting on a Cincinnati horizon for life's principal joy was
reckless indeed. So Sethe and the girl Denver did what they
could, and what the house permitted, for her. Together they
waged a perfunctory battle against the outrageous behavior of
that place; against turned-over slop jars, smacks on the behind,
and gusts of sour air. For they understood the source of the
outrage as well as they knew the source of light.

Baby Suggs died shortly after the brothers left, with no
interest whatsoever in their leave-taking or hers, and right
afterward Sethe and Denver decided to end the persecution by
calling forth the ghost that tried them so. Perhaps a conversation, they thought, an exchange of views or something would

help. So they held hands and said, "Come on. Come on. You may as well just come on."

The sideboard took a step forward but nothing else did.

"Grandma Baby must be stopping it," said Denver. She was ten and still mad at Baby Suggs for dying.

Sethe opened her eyes. "I doubt that," she said.

"Then why don't it come?"

"You forgetting how little it is," said her mother. "She wasn't even two years old when she died. Too little to understand. Too little to talk much even."

"Maybe she don't want to understand," said Denver.

"Maybe. But if she'd only come, I could make it clear to her." Sethe released her daughter's hand and together they pushed the sideboard back against the wall. Outside a driver whipped his horse into the gallop local people felt necessary when they passed 124.

"For a baby she throws a powerful spell," said Denver.

"No more powerful than the way I loved her," Sethe answered and there it was again. The welcoming cool of unchiseled headstones; the one she selected to lean against on tiptoe, her knees wide open as any grave. Pink as a fingernail it was, and sprinkled with glittering chips. Ten minutes, he said. You got ten minutes I'll do it for free.

Ten minutes for seven letters. With another ten could she have gotten "Dearly" too? She had not thought to ask him and it bothered her still that it might have been possible—that for twenty minutes, a half hour, say, she could have had the whole thing, every word she heard the preacher say at the funeral (and all there was to say, surely) engraved on her baby's head-stone: Dearly Beloved. But what she got, settled for, was the one word that mattered. She thought it would be enough, rutting among the headstones with the engraver, his young son looking on, the anger in his face so old; the appetite in it quite new. That should certainly be enough. Enough to answer one more preacher, one more abolitionist and a town full of disgust.

Counting on the stillness of her own soul, she had forgotten the other one: the soul of her baby girl. Who would have thought that a little old baby could harbor so much rage? Rutting among the stones under the eyes of the engraver's son was not enough. Not only did she have to live out her years in a house palsied by the baby's fury at having its throat cut, but those ten minutes she spent pressed up against dawn-colored stone studded with star chips, her knees wide open as the grave, were longer than life, more alive, more pulsating than the baby blood that soaked her fingers like oil.

"We could move," she suggested once to her mother-in-law.

"What'd be the point?" asked Baby Suggs. "Not a house in the country ain't packed to its rafters with some dead Negro's grief. We lucky this ghost is a baby. My husband's spirit was to come back in here? or yours? Don't talk to me. You lucky. You got three left. Three pulling at your skirts and just one raising hell from the other side. Be thankful, why don't you? I had eight. Every one of them gone away from me. Four taken, four chased, and all, I expect, worrying somebody's house into evil." Baby Suggs rubbed her eyebrows. "My firstborn. All I can remember of her is how she loved the burned bottom of bread. Can you beat that? Eight children and that's all I remember."

"That's all you let yourself remember," Sethe had told her, but she was down to one herself—one alive, that is—the boys

chased off by the dead one, and her memory of Buglar was
fading fast. Howard at least had a head shape nobody could
forget. As for the rest, she worked hard to remember as close
to nothing as was safe. Unfortunately her brain was devious.
She might be hurrying across a field, running practically, to
get to the pump quickly and rinse the chamomile sap from her
legs. Nothing else would be in her mind. The picture of the
men coming to nurse her was as lifeless as the nerves in her
back where the skin buckled like a washboard. Nor was there
the faintest scent of ink or the cherry gum and oak bark from
which it was made. Nothing. Just the breeze cooling her face
as she rushed toward water. And then sopping the chamomile
away with pump water and rags, her mind fixed on getting
every last bit of sap off—on her carelessness in taking a shortcut
across the field just to save a half mile, and not noticing how
high the weeds had grown until the itching was all the way
to her knees. Then something. The plash of water, the sight
of her shoes and stockings awry on the path where she had
flung them; or Here Boy lapping in the puddle near her feet,
and suddenly there was Sweet Home rolling, rolling, rolling
out before her eyes, and although there was not a leaf on that
farm that did not make her want to scream, it rolled itself out
before her in shameless beauty. It never looked as terrible as
it was and it made her wonder if hell was a pretty place too.
Fire and brimstone all right, but hidden in lacy groves. Boys
hanging from the most beautiful sycamores in the world. It
shamed her—remembering the wonderful soughing trees
rather than the boys. Try as she might to make it otherwise,
the sycamores beat out the children every time and she could
not forgive her memory for that.

When the last of the chamomile was gone, she went around to the front of the house, collecting her shoes and stockings on the way. As if to punish her further for her terrible memory, sitting on the porch not forty feet away was Paul D, the last of the Sweet Home men. And although she could never mistake his face for another's, she said, "Is that you?"

"What's left." He stood up and smiled. "How you been, girl, besides barefoot?"

When she laughed it came out loose and young. "Messed up my legs back yonder. Chamomile."

He made a face as though tasting a teaspoon of something bitter. "I don't want to even hear 'bout it. Always did hate that stuff."

Sethe balled up her stockings and jammed them into her pocket. "Come on in."

"Porch is fine, Sethe. Cool out here." He sat back down and looked at the meadow on the other side of the road, knowing the eagerness he felt would be in his eyes.

"Eighteen years," she said softly.

"Eighteen," he repeated. "And I swear I been walking every one of em. Mind if I join you?" He nodded toward her feet and began unlacing his shoes.

"You want to soak them? Let me get you a basin of water." She moved closer to him to enter the house.

"No, uh uh. Can't baby feet. A whole lot more tramping they got to do yet."

"You can't leave right away, Paul D. You got to stay awhile."

"Well, long enough to see Baby Suggs, anyway. Where is she?"

"Dead."

"Aw no. When?"

"Eight years now. Almost nine."

"Was it hard? I hope she didn't die hard."

Sethe shook her head. "Soft as cream. Being alive was the hard part. Sorry you missed her though. Is that what you came by for?"

"That's some of what I came for. The rest is you. But if all the truth be known, I go anywhere these days. Anywhere they let me sit down."

"You looking good."

"Devil's confusion. He lets me look good long as I feel bad." He looked at her and the word "bad" took on another meaning.

Sethe smiled. This is the way they were—had been. All of the Sweet Home men, before and after Halle, treated her to a mild brotherly flirtation, so subtle you had to scratch for it.

Except for a heap more hair and some waiting in his eyes, he looked the way he had in Kentucky. Peachstone skin; straight-backed. For a man with an immobile face it was amazing how ready it was to smile, or blaze or be sorry with you. As though all you had to do was get his attention and right away he produced the feeling you were feeling. With less than a blink, his face seemed to change—underneath it lay the activity.

"I wouldn't have to ask about him, would I? You'd tell me if there was anything to tell, wouldn't you?" Sethe looked down at her feet and saw again the sycamores.

"I'd tell you. Sure I'd tell you. I don't know any more now than I did then." Except for the churn, he thought, and you don't need to know that. "You must think he's still alive."

"No. I think he's dead. It's not being sure that keeps him alive."

"What did Baby Suggs think?"

"Same, but to listen to her, all her children is dead. Claimed she felt each one go the very day and hour."

"When she say Halle went?"

"Eighteen fifty-five. The day my baby was born."

"You had that baby, did you? Never thought you'd make it." He chuckled. "Running off pregnant."

"Had to. Couldn't be no waiting." She lowered her head and thought, as he did, how unlikely it was that she had made it. And if it hadn't been for that girl looking for velvet, she never would have.

"All by yourself too." He was proud of her and annoyed by her. Proud she had done it; annoyed that she had not needed Halle or him in the doing.

"Almost by myself. Not all by myself. A whitegirl helped me."

"Then she helped herself too, God bless her."

"You could stay the night, Paul D."

"You don't sound too steady in the offer."

Sethe glanced beyond his shoulder toward the closed door. "Oh it's truly meant. I just hope you'll pardon my house. Come on in. Talk to Denver while I cook you something."

Paul D tied his shoes together, hung them over his shoulder and followed her through the door straight into a pool of red and undulating light that locked him where he stood.

"You got company?" he whispered, frowning.

"Off and on," said Sethe.

"Good God." He backed out the door onto the porch. "What kind of evil you got in here?"

"It's not evil, just sad. Come on. Just step through."

He looked at her then, closely. Closer than he had when she first rounded the house on wet and shining legs, holding her shoes and stockings up in one hand, her skirts in the other. Halle's girl—the one with iron eyes and backbone to match. He had never seen her hair in Kentucky. And though her face was eighteen years older than when last he saw her, it was softer now. Because of the hair. A face too still for comfort; irises the same color as her skin, which, in that still face, used to make him think of a mask with mercifully punched-out eyes. Halle's woman. Pregnant every year including the year she sat by the fire telling him she was going to run. Her three children she had already packed into a wagonload of others in a caravan of Negroes crossing the river. They were to be left with Halle's mother near Cincinnati. Even in that tiny shack, leaning so close to the fire you could smell the heat in her dress, her eyes did not pick up a flicker of light. They were like two wells into which he had trouble gazing. Even punched out they needed to be covered, lidded, marked with some sign to warn folks of what that emptiness held. So he looked instead at the fire while she told him, because her husband was not there for the telling. Mr. Garner was dead and his wife had a lump in her neck the size of a sweet potato and unable to speak to anyone. She leaned as close to the fire as her pregnant belly allowed and told him, Paul D, the last of the Sweet Home men.

There had been six of them who belonged to the farm, Sethe the only female. Mrs. Garner, crying like a baby, had sold his brother to pay off the debts that surfaced the minute she was widowed. Then schoolteacher arrived to put things in order. But what he did broke three more Sweet Home men and punched the glittering iron out of Sethe's eyes, leaving two open wells that did not reflect firelight.

Now the iron was back but the face, softened by hair, made him trust her enough to step inside her door smack into a pool of pulsing red light.

She was right. It was sad. Walking through it, a wave of grief soaked him so thoroughly he wanted to cry. It seemed a long way to the normal light surrounding the table, but he made it—dry-eyed and lucky.

"You said she died soft. Soft as cream," he reminded her.

"That's not Baby Suggs," she said.

"Who then?"

"My daughter. The one I sent ahead with the boys."

"She didn't live?"

"No. The one I was carrying when I run away is all I got left. Boys gone too. Both of em walked off just before Baby Suggs died."

Paul D looked at the spot where the grief had soaked him. The red was gone but a kind of weeping clung to the air where it had been.

Probably best, he thought. If a Negro got legs he ought to use them. Sit down too long, somebody will figure out a way to tie them up. Still ... if her boys were gone ...

"No man? You here by yourself?"

"Me and Denver," she said.

"That all right by you?"

"That's all right by me."

She saw his skepticism and went on. "I cook at a restaurant in town. And I sew a little on the sly."

Paul D smiled then, remembering the bedding dress. Sethe was thirteen when she came to Sweet Home and already iron-eyed. She was a timely present for Mrs. Garner who had lost

Baby Suggs to her husband's high principles. The five Sweet Home men looked at the new girl and decided to let her be. They were young and so sick with the absence of women they had taken to calves. Yet they let the iron-eyed girl be, so she could choose in spite of the fact that each one would have beaten the others to mush to have her. It took her a year to choose—a long, tough year of thrashing on pallets eaten up with dreams of her. A year of yearning, when rape seemed the solitary gift of life. The restraint they had exercised possible only because they were Sweet Home men—the ones Mr. Garner bragged about while other farmers shook their heads in warning at the phrase.

"Y'all got boys," he told them. "Young boys, old boys, picky boys, stroppin boys. Now at Sweet Home, my niggers is men every one of em. Bought em thataway, raised em thataway. Men every one."

"Beg to differ, Garner. Ain't no nigger men."

"Not if you scared, they ain't." Garner's smile was wide. "But if you a man yourself, you'll want your niggers to be men too."

"I wouldn't have no nigger men round my wife."

It was the reaction Garner loved and waited for. "Neither would I," he said. "Neither would I," and there was always a pause before the neighbor, or stranger, or peddler, or brother-in-law or whoever it was got the meaning. Then a fierce argument, sometimes a fight, and Garner came home bruised and pleased, having demonstrated one more time what a real Kentuckian was: one tough enough and smart enough to make and call his own niggers men.

And so they were: Paul D Garner, Paul F Garner, Paul A Garner, Halle Suggs and Sixo, the wild man. All in their twenties, minus women, fucking cows, dreaming of rape, thrashing on pallets, rubbing their thighs and waiting for the new girl—the one who took Baby Suggs' place after Halle bought her with five years of Sundays. Maybe that was why she chose him. A twenty-year-old man so in love with his mother he gave up five years of Sabbaths just to see her sit down for a change was a serious recommendation.

She waited a year. And the Sweet Home men abused cows while they waited with her. She chose Halle and for their first bedding she sewed herself a dress on the sly.

"Won't you stay on awhile? Can't nobody catch up on eighteen years in a day."

Out of the dimness of the room in which they sat, a white staircase climbed toward the blue-and-white wallpaper of the second floor. Paul D could see just the beginning of the paper; discreet flecks of yellow sprinkled among a blizzard of snow-drops all backed by blue. The luminous white of the railing and steps kept him glancing toward it. Every sense he had told him the air above the stairwell was charmed and very thin. But the girl who walked down out of that air was round and brown with the face of an alert doll.

Paul D looked at the girl and then at Sethe who smiled saying, "Here she is my Denver. This is Paul D, honey, from Sweet Home."

"Good morning, Mr. D."

"Garner, baby. Paul D Garner."

"Yes sir."

"Glad to get a look at you. Last time I saw your mama, you were pushing out the front of her dress."

"Still is," Sethe smiled, "provided she can get in it."

Denver stood on the bottom step and was suddenly hot and shy. It had been a long time since anybody (good-willed white-woman, preacher, speaker or newspaperman) sat at their table, their sympathetic voices called liar by the revulsion in their eyes. For twelve years, long before Grandma Baby died, there had been no visitors of any sort and certainly no friends. No coloredpeople. Certainly no hazelnut man with too long hair and no notebook, no charcoal, no oranges, no questions. Someone her mother wanted to talk to and would even consider talking to while barefoot. Looking, in fact acting, like a girl instead of the quiet, queenly woman Denver had known all her life. The one who never looked away, who when a man got stomped to death by a mare right in front of Sawyer's restaurant did not look away; and when a sow began eating her own litter did not look away then either. And when the baby's spirit picked up Here Boy and slammed him into the wall hard enough to break two of his legs and dislocate his eye, so hard he went into convulsions and chewed up his tongue, still her mother had not looked away. She had taken a hammer, knocked the dog unconscious, wiped away the blood and saliva, pushed his eye back in his head and set his leg bones. He recovered, mute and off-balance, more because of his untrustworthy eye than his bent legs, and winter, summer, drizzle or dry, nothing could persuade him to enter the house again.

Now here was this woman with the presence of mind to repair a dog gone savage with pain rocking her crossed ankles and looking away from her own daughter's body. As though the size of it was more than vision could bear. And neither she nor he had on shoes. Hot, shy, now Denver was lonely. All that leaving: first her brothers, then her grandmother—serious

losses since there were no children willing to circle her in a
game or hang by their knees from her porch railing. None of
that had mattered as long as her mother did not look away as
she was doing now, making Denver long, downright long, for
a sign of spite from the baby ghost.

"She's a fine-looking young lady," said Paul D. "Fine-looking.
Got her daddy's sweet face."

"You know my father?"

"Knew him. Knew him well."

"Did he, Ma'am?" Denver fought an urge to realign her
affection.

"Of course he knew your daddy. I told you, he's from Sweet
Home."

Denver sat down on the bottom step. There was nowhere
else gracefully to go. They were a twosome, saying "Your daddy"
and "Sweet Home" in a way that made it clear both belonged
to them and not to her. That her own father's absence was not
hers. Once the absence had belonged to Grandma Baby—a son,
deeply mourned because he was the one who had bought her
out of there. Then it was her mother's absent husband. Now
it was this hazelnut stranger's absent friend. Only those who
knew him ("knew him well") could claim his absence for themselves. Just as only those who lived in Sweet Home could
remember it, whisper it and glance sideways at one another
while they did. Again she wished for the baby ghost—its anger
thrilling her now where it used to wear her out. Wear her out.

"We have a ghost in here," she said, and it worked. They
were not a twosome anymore. Her mother left off swinging
her feet and being girlish. Memory of Sweet Home dropped

away from the eyes of the man she was being girlish for. He looked quickly up the lightning-white stairs behind her.

"So I hear," he said. "But sad, your mama said. Not evil."

"No sir," said Denver, "not evil. But not sad either."

"What then?"

"Rebuked. Lonely and rebuked."

"Is that right?" Paul D turned to Sethe.

"I don't know about lonely," said Denver's mother. "Mad, maybe, but I don't see how it could be lonely spending every minute with us like it does."

"Must be something you got it wants."

Sethe shrugged. "It's just a baby."

"My sister," said Denver. "She died in this house."

Paul D scratched the hair under his jaw. "Reminds me of that headless bride back behind Sweet Home. Remember that, Sethe? Used to roam them woods regular."

"How could I forget? Worrisome ..."

"How come everybody run off from Sweet Home can't stop talking about it? Look like if it was so sweet you would have stayed."

"Girl, who you talking to?"

Paul D laughed. "True, true. She's right, Sethe. It wasn't sweet and it sure wasn't home." He shook his head.

"But it's where we were," said Sethe. "All together. Comes back whether we want it to or not." She shivered a little. A light ripple of skin on her arm, which she caressed back into sleep. "Denver," she said, "start up that stove. Can't have a friend stop by and don't feed him."

"Don't go to any trouble on my account," Paul D said.

"Bread ain't trouble. The rest I brought back from where I work. Least I can do, cooking from dawn to noon, is bring dinner home. You got any objections to pike?"

"If he don't object to me I don't object to him."

At it again, thought Denver. Her back to them, she jostled the kindlin and almost lost the fire. "Why don't you spend the night, Mr. Garner? You and Ma'am can talk about Sweet Home all night long."

Sethe took two swift steps to the stove, but before she could yank Denver's collar, the girl leaned forward and began to cry.

"What is the matter with you? I never knew you to behave this way."

"Leave her be," said Paul D. "I'm a stranger to her."

"That's just it. She got no cause to act up with a stranger. Oh baby, what is it? Did something happen?"

But Denver was shaking now and sobbing so she could not speak. The tears she had not shed for nine years wetting her far too womanly breasts.

"I can't no more. I can't no more."

"Can't what? What can't you?"

"I can't live here. I don't know where to go or what to do, but I can't live here. Nobody speaks to us. Nobody comes by. Boys don't like me. Girls don't either."

"Honey, honey."

"What's she talking 'bout nobody speaks to you?" asked Paul D.

"It's the house. People don't—"

"It's not! It's not the house. It's us! And it's you!"

"Denver!"

"Leave off, Sethe. It's hard for a young girl living in a haunted house. That can't be easy."

"It's easier than some other things."

"Think, Sethe. I'm a grown man with nothing new left to see or do and I'm telling you it ain't easy. Maybe you all ought to move. Who owns this house?"

Over Denver's shoulder Sethe shot Paul D a look of snow. "What you care?"

"They won't let you leave?"

"No."

"Sethe."

"No moving. No leaving. It's all right the way it is."

"You going to tell me it's all right with this child half out of her mind?"

Something in the house braced, and in the listening quiet that followed Sethe spoke.

"I got a tree on my back and a haint in my house, and nothing in between but the daughter I am holding in my arms. No more running—from nothing. I will never run from another thing on this earth. I took one journey and I paid for the ticket, but let me tell you something, Paul D Garner: it cost too much! Do you hear me? It cost too much. Now sit down and eat with us or leave us be."

Paul D fished in his vest for a little pouch of tobacco—concentrating on its contents and the knot of its string while Sethe led Denver into the keeping room that opened off the large room he was sitting in. He had no smoking papers, so he fiddled with the pouch and listened through the open door to Sethe quieting her daughter. When she came back she avoided his look and went straight to a small table next to the stove. Her back was to him and he could see all the hair he wanted without the distraction of her face.

"What tree on your back?"

"Huh." Sethe put a bowl on the table and reached under it for flour.

"What tree on your back? Is something growing on your back? I don't see nothing growing on your back."

"It's there all the same."

"Who told you that?"

"Whitegirl. That's what she called it. I've never seen it and never will. But that's what she said it looked like. A chokecherry tree. Trunk, branches, and even leaves. Tiny little chokecherry leaves. But that was eighteen years ago. Could have cherries too now for all I know."

Sethe took a little spit from the tip of her tongue with her forefinger. Quickly, lightly she touched the stove. Then she trailed her fingers through the flour, parting, separating small hills and ridges of it, looking for mites. Finding none, she poured soda and salt into the crease of her folded hand and tossed both into the flour. Then she reached into a can and scooped half a handful of lard. Deftly she squeezed the flour through it, then with her left hand sprinkling water, she formed the dough.

"I had milk," she said. "I was pregnant with Denver but I had milk for my baby girl. I hadn't stopped nursing her when I sent her on ahead with Howard and Buglar."

Now she rolled the dough out with a wooden pin. "Anybody could smell me long before he saw me. And when he saw me he'd see the drops of it on the front of my dress. Nothing I could do about that. All I knew was I had to get my milk to my baby girl. Nobody was going to nurse her like me. Nobody was going to get it to her fast enough, or take it away when she had enough and didn't know it. Nobody knew that she couldn't pass her air if you held her up on your shoulder, only if she was lying on my knees. Nobody knew that but me and nobody had her milk but me. I told that to the women in the wagon. Told them to put sugar water in cloth to suck from so when I got there in a few days she wouldn't have forgot me. The milk would be there and I would be there with it."

"Men don't know nothing much," said Paul D, tucking his pouch back into his vest pocket, "but they do know a suckling can't be away from its mother for long."

"Then they know what it's like to send your children off when your breasts are full."

"We was talking 'bout a tree, Sethe."

"After I left you, those boys came in there and took my milk. That's what they came in there for. Held me down and took it. I told Mrs. Garner on em. She had that lump and couldn't speak but her eyes rolled out tears. Them boys found out I told on em. Schoolteacher made one open up my back, and when it closed it made a tree. It grows there still."

"They used cowhide on you?"

"And they took my milk."

"They beat you and you was pregnant?"

"And they took my milk!"

The fat white circles of dough lined the pan in rows. Once more Sethe touched a wet forefinger to the stove. She opened the oven door and slid the pan of biscuits in. As she raised up from the heat she felt Paul D behind her and his hands under her breasts. She straightened up and knew, but could not feel, that his cheek was pressing into the branches of her chokecherry tree.

Not even trying, he had become the kind of man who could walk into a house and make the women cry. Because with him, in his presence, they could. There was something blessed in his manner. Women saw him and wanted to weep—to tell him that their chest hurt and their knees did too. Strong women and wise saw him and told him things they only told each other: that way past the Change of Life, desire in them had suddenly become enormous, greedy, more savage than when they were fifteen, and that it embarrassed them and made them sad; that secretly they longed to die—to be quit of it—that sleep was more precious to them than any waking day. Young girls sidled up to him to confess or describe how well-dressed the visitations were that had followed them straight from their dreams. Therefore, although he did not understand why this was so, he was not surprised when Denver dripped tears into the stovefire. Nor, fifteen minutes later, after telling him about her stolen milk, her mother wept as well. Behind her, bending down, his body an arc of kindness, he held her breasts in the palms of his hands. He rubbed his cheek on her back and learned that way her sorrow, the roots of it; its wide trunk and intricate branches. Raising his fingers to the hooks of her dress, he knew without seeing them or hearing any sigh that the tears were coming fast. And when the top of her dress was around her hips and he saw the sculpture her back had become, like the decorative work of an ironsmith too passionate for display, he could think but not say, "Aw, Lord, girl." And he would tolerate no peace until he had touched every ridge and leaf of it with his mouth, none of which Sethe could feel because her back skin had been dead for years. What she knew was that the responsibility for her breasts, at last, was in somebody else's hands.

Would there be a little space, she wondered, a little time, some way to hold off eventfulness, to push busyness into the corners of the room and just stand there a minute or two, naked from shoulder blade to waist, relieved of the weight of her breasts, smelling the stolen milk again and the pleasure of baking bread? Maybe this one time she could stop dead still in the middle of a cooking meal—not even leave the stove—and feel the hurt her back ought to. Trust things and remember things because the last of the Sweet Home men was there to catch her if she sank?

The stove didn't shudder as it adjusted to its heat. Denver wasn't stirring in the next room. The pulse of red light hadn't come back and Paul D had not trembled since 1856 and then for eighty-three days in a row. Locked up and chained down, his hands shook so bad he couldn't smoke or even scratch properly. Now he was trembling again but in the legs this time. It took him a while to realize that his legs were not shaking because of worry, but because the floorboards were and the grinding, shoving floor was only part of it. The house itself was pitching. Sethe slid to the floor and struggled to get back into her dress. While down on all fours, as though she were holding her house down on the ground, Denver burst from the keeping room, terror in her eyes, a vague smile on her lips.

"God damn it! Hush up!" Paul D was shouting, falling, reaching for anchor. "Leave the place alone! Get the hell out!" A table rushed toward him and he grabbed its leg. Somehow he managed to stand at an angle and, holding the table by two legs, he bashed it about, wrecking everything, screaming back at the screaming house. "You want to fight, come on! God damn it! She got enough without you. She got enough!"

The quaking slowed to an occasional lurch, but Paul D did not stop whipping the table around until everything was rock quiet. Sweating and breathing hard, he leaned against the wall in the space the sideboard left. Sethe was still crouched next to the stove, clutching her salvaged shoes to her chest. The three of them, Sethe, Denver, and Paul D, breathed to the same beat, like one tired person. Another breathing was just as tired.

It was gone. Denver wandered through the silence to the stove. She ashed over the fire and pulled the pan of biscuits from the oven. The jelly cupboard was on its back, its contents lying in a heap in the corner of the bottom shelf. She took out a jar, and, looking around for a plate, found half of one by the door. These things she carried out to the porch steps, where she sat down.

The two of them had gone up there. Stepping lightly, easy-footed, they had climbed the white stairs, leaving her down below. She pried the wire from the top of the jar and then the lid. Under it was cloth and under that a thin cake of wax. She removed it all and coaxed the jelly onto one half of the half a plate. She took a biscuit and pulled off its black top. Smoke curled from the soft white insides.

She missed her brothers. Buglar and Howard would be twenty-two and twenty-three now. Although they had been polite to her during the quiet time and gave her the whole top of the bed, she remembered how it was before: the pleasure they had sitting clustered on the white stairs—she between the knees of Howard or Buglar—while they made up die-witch! stories with proven ways of killing her dead. And Baby Suggs telling her things in the keeping room. She smelled like bark in the day and leaves at night, for Denver would not sleep in her old room after her brothers ran away.

Now her mother was upstairs with the man who had gotten rid of the only other company she had. Denver dipped a bit of bread into the jelly. Slowly, methodically, miserably she ate it.

Not quite in a hurry, but losing no time, Sethe and Paul D climbed the white stairs. Overwhelmed as much by the downright luck of finding her house and her in it as by the certainty of giving her his sex, Paul D dropped twenty-five years from his recent memory. A stair step before him was Baby Suggs' replacement, the new girl they dreamed of at night and fucked cows for at dawn while waiting for her to choose. Merely kissing the wrought iron on her back had shook the house, had made it necessary for him to beat it to pieces. Now he would do more.

She led him to the top of the stairs, where light came straight from the sky because the second-story windows of that house had been placed in the pitched ceiling and not the walls. There were two rooms and she took him into one of them, hoping he wouldn't mind the fact that she was not prepared; that though she could remember desire, she had forgotten how it worked; the clutch and helplessness that resided in the hands; how blindness was altered so that what leapt to the eye were places to lie down, and all else—doorknobs, straps, hooks, the sadness that crouched in corners, and the passing of time—was interference.

It was over before they could get their clothes off. Half-dressed and short of breath, they lay side by side resentful of one another and the skylight above them. His dreaming of her had been too long and too long ago. Her deprivation had been not having any dreams of her own at all. Now they were sorry and too shy to make talk.

Sethe lay on her back, her head turned from him. Out of the corner of his eye, Paul D saw the float of her breasts and disliked it, the spread-away, flat roundness of them that he could definitely live without, never mind that downstairs he had held them as though they were the most expensive part of himself. And the wrought-iron maze he had explored in the kitchen like a gold miner pawing through pay dirt was in fact a revolting clump of scars. Not a tree, as she said. Maybe shaped like one, but nothing like any tree he knew because trees were inviting; things you could trust and be near; talk to if you wanted to as he frequently did since way back when he took the midday meal in the fields of Sweet Home. Always in the same place if he could, and choosing the place had been hard because Sweet Home had more pretty trees than any farm around. His choice he called Brother, and sat under it, alone sometimes, sometimes with Halle or the other Pauls, but more often with Sixo, who was gentle then and still speaking English. Indigo with a flame-red tongue, Sixo experimented with night-cooked potatoes, trying to pin down exactly when to put smoking-hot rocks in a hole, potatoes on top, and cover the whole thing with twigs so that by the time they broke for the meal, hitched the animals, left the field and got to Brother, the potatoes would be at the peak of perfection. He might get up in the middle of the night, go all the way out there, start the earth-over by starlight; or he would make the stones less hot and put the next day's potatoes on them right after the meal. He never got it right, but they ate those undercooked, overcooked, dried-out or raw potatoes anyway, laughing, spitting and giving him advice.

Time never worked the way Sixo thought, so of course he never got it right. Once he plotted down to the minute a thirty-mile trip to see a woman. He left on a Saturday when the moon was in the place he wanted it to be, arrived at her cabin before church on Sunday and had just enough time to say good morning before he had to start back again so he'd make the field call on time Monday morning. He had walked for seventeen hours, sat down for one, turned around and walked seventeen more. Halle and the Pauls spent the whole day covering Sixo's fatigue from Mr. Garner. They ate no potatoes that day, sweet or white. Sprawled near Brother, his flame-red tongue hidden from them, his indigo face closed, Sixo slept through dinner like a corpse. Now *there* was a man, and *that* was a tree. Himself lying in the bed and the "tree" lying next to him didn't compare.

Paul D looked through the window above his feet and folded his hands behind his head. An elbow grazed Sethe's shoulder. The touch of cloth on her skin startled her. She had forgotten he had not taken off his shirt. Dog, she thought, and then remembered that she had not allowed him the time for taking it off. Nor herself time to take off her petticoat, and considering she had begun undressing before she saw him on the porch, that her shoes and stockings were already in her hand and she had never put them back on; that he had looked at her wet bare feet and asked to join her; that when she rose to cook he had undressed her further; considering how quickly they had started getting naked, you'd think by now they would be. But maybe a man was nothing but a man, which is what Baby Suggs always said. They encouraged you to put some of your weight in their hands and soon as you felt how light and lovely that was, they studied your scars and tribulations, after which they did what he had done: ran her children out and tore up the house.

She needed to get up from there, go downstairs and piece it all back together. This house he told her to leave as though a house was a little thing—a shirtwaist or a sewing basket you could walk off from or give away any old time. She who had never had one but this one; she who left a dirt floor to come to this one; she who had to bring a fistful of salsify into Mrs. Garner's kitchen every day just to be able to work in it, feel like some part of it was hers, because she wanted to love the work she did, to take the ugly out of it, and the only way she could feel at home on Sweet Home was if she picked some pretty growing thing and took it with her. The day she forgot was the day butter wouldn't come or the brine in the barrel blistered her arms.

At least it seemed so. A few yellow flowers on the table, some myrtle tied around the handle of the flatiron holding the door open for a breeze calmed her, and when Mrs. Garner and she sat down to sort bristle, or make ink, she felt fine. Fine. Not scared of the men beyond. The five who slept in quarters near her, but never came in the night. Just touched their raggedy hats when they saw her and stared. And if she brought food to them in the fields, bacon and bread wrapped in a piece of clean sheeting, they never took it from her hands. They stood

back and waited for her to put it on the ground (at the foot of
a tree) and leave. Either they did not want to take anything
from her, or did not want her to see them eat. Twice or three
times she lingered. Hidden behind honeysuckle she watched
them. How different they were without her, how they laughed
and played and urinated and sang. All but Sixo, who laughed
once—at the very end. Halle, of course, was the nicest. Baby
Suggs' eighth and last child, who rented himself out all over
the county to buy her away from there. But he too, as it turned
out, was nothing but a man.

"A man ain't nothing but a man," said Baby Suggs. "But a
son? Well now, that's *somebody*."

It made sense for a lot of reasons because in all of Baby's
life, as well as Sethe's own, men and women were moved around
like checkers. Anybody Baby Suggs knew, let alone loved, who
hadn't run off or been hanged, got rented out, loaned out,
bought up, brought back, stored up, mortgaged, won, stolen
or seized. So Baby's eight children had six fathers. What she
called the nastiness of life was the shock she received upon
learning that nobody stopped playing checkers just because the
pieces included her children. Halle she was able to keep the
longest. Twenty years. A lifetime. Given to her, no doubt, to
make up for *hearing* that her two girls, neither of whom had
their adult teeth, were sold and gone and she had not been
able to wave goodbye. To make up for coupling with a straw
boss for four months in exchange for keeping her third child,
a boy, with her—only to have him traded for lumber in the
spring of the next year and to find herself pregnant by the
man who promised not to and did. That child she could not
love and the rest she would not. "God take what He would,"

she said. And He did, and He did, and He did and then gave her Halle who gave her freedom when it didn't mean a thing.

Sethe had the amazing luck of six whole years of marriage to that "somebody" son who had fathered every one of her children. A blessing she was reckless enough to take for granted, lean on, as though Sweet Home really was one. As though a handful of myrtle stuck in the handle of a pressing iron propped against the door in a whitewoman's kitchen could make it hers. As though mint sprig in the mouth changed the breath as well as its odor. A bigger fool never lived.

Sethe started to turn over on her stomach but changed her mind. She did not want to call Paul D's attention back to her, so she settled for crossing her ankles.

But Paul D noticed the movement as well as the change in her breathing. He felt obliged to try again, slower this time, but the appetite was gone. Actually it was a good feeling—not wanting her. Twenty-five years and blip! The kind of thing Sixo would do—like the time he arranged a meeting with Patsy the Thirty-Mile Woman. It took three months and two thirty-four-mile round trips to do it. To persuade her to walk one-third of the way toward him, to a place he knew. A deserted stone structure that Redmen used way back when they thought the land was theirs. Sixo discovered it on one of his night creeps, and asked its permission to enter. Inside, having felt what it felt like, he asked the Redmen's Presence if he could bring his woman there. It said yes and Sixo painstakingly instructed her how to get there, exactly when to start out, how his welcoming or warning whistles would sound. Since neither could go anywhere on business of their own, and since the Thirty-Mile Woman was already fourteen and scheduled for

somebody's arms, the danger was real. When he arrived, she
had not. He whistled and got no answer. He went into the
Redmen's deserted lodge. She was not there. He returned to
the meeting spot. She was not there. He waited longer. She
still did not come. He grew frightened for her and walked down
the road in the direction she should be coming from. Three or
four miles, and he stopped. It was hopeless to go on that way,
so he stood in the wind and asked for help. Listening close for
some sign, he heard a whimper. He turned toward it, waited
and heard it again. Uncautious now, he hollered her name. She
answered in a voice that sounded like life to him—not death.
"Not move!" he shouted. "Breathe hard I can find you." He did.
She believed she was already at the meeting place and was
crying because she thought he had not kept his promise. Now
it was too late for the rendezvous to happen at the Redmen's
house, so they dropped where they were. Later he punctured
her calf to simulate snakebite so she could use it in some way
as an excuse for not being on time to shake worms from tobacco
leaves. He gave her detailed directions about following the
stream as a shortcut back, and saw her off. When he got to
the road it was very light and he had his clothes in his hands.
Suddenly from around a bend a wagon trundled toward him.
Its driver, wide-eyed, raised a whip while the woman seated
beside him covered her face. But Sixo had already melted into
the woods before the lash could unfurl itself on his indigo
behind.

He told the story to Paul F, Halle, Paul A and Paul D in
the peculiar way that made them cry-laugh. Sixo went among
trees at night. For dancing, he said, to keep his bloodlines open,
he said. Privately, alone, he did it. None of the rest of them

had seen him at it, but they could imagine it, and the picture they pictured made them eager to laugh at him—in daylight, that is, when it was safe.

But that was before he stopped speaking English because there was no future in it. Because of the Thirty-Mile Woman Sixo was the only one not paralyzed by yearning for Sethe. Nothing could be as good as the sex with her Paul D had been imagining off and on for twenty-five years. His foolishness made him smile and think fondly of himself as he turned over on his side, facing her. Sethe's eyes were closed, her hair a mess. Looked at this way, minus the polished eyes, her face was not so attractive. So it must have been her eyes that kept him both guarded and stirred up. Without them her face was manageable—a face he could handle. Maybe if she would keep them closed like that ... But no, there was her mouth. Nice. Halle never knew what he had.

Although her eyes were closed, Sethe knew his gaze was on her face, and a paper picture of just how bad she must look raised itself up before her mind's eye. Still, there was no mockery coming from his gaze. Soft. It felt soft in a waiting kind of way. He was not judging her—or rather he was judging but not comparing her. Not since Halle had a man looked at her that way: not loving or passionate, but interested, as though he were examining an ear of corn for quality. Halle was more like a brother than a husband. His care suggested a family relationship rather than a man's laying claim. For years they saw each other in full daylight only on Sundays. The rest of the time they spoke or touched or ate in darkness. Predawn darkness and the afterlight of sunset. So looking at each other intently was a Sunday-morning pleasure and Halle examined her as though storing up what he saw in sunlight for the shadow he saw the rest of the week. And he had so little time. After his Sweet Home work and on Sunday afternoons was the debt work he owed for his mother. When he asked her to be his wife, Sethe happily agreed and then was stuck not knowing the next step. There should be a ceremony, shouldn't there? A preacher, some dancing, a party, a something. She and Mrs. Garner were the only women there, so she decided to ask her.

"Halle and me want to be married, Mrs. Garner."

"So I heard." She smiled. "He talked to Mr. Garner about it. Are you already expecting?"

"No, ma'am."

"Well, you will be. You know that, don't you?"

"Yes, ma'am."

"Halle's nice, Sethe. He'll be good to you."

"But I mean we want to get married."

"You just said so. And I said all right."

"Is there a wedding?"

Mrs. Garner put down her cooking spoon. Laughing a little, she touched Sethe on the head, saying, "You are one sweet child." And then no more.

Sethe made a dress on the sly and Halle hung his hitching rope from a nail on the wall of her cabin. And there on top of a mattress on top of the dirt floor of the cabin they coupled for the third time, the first two having been in the tiny cornfield Mr. Garner kept because it was a crop animals could use as well as humans. Both Halle and Sethe were under the impression that they were hidden. Scrunched down among the stalks they couldn't see anything, including the corn tops waving over their heads and visible to everyone else.

Sethe smiled at her and Halle's stupidity. Even the crows knew and came to look. Uncrossing her ankles, she managed not to laugh aloud.

The jump, thought Paul D, from a calf to a girl wasn't all that mighty. Not the leap Halle believed it would be. And taking her in the corn rather than her quarters, a yard away from the cabins of the others who had lost out, was a gesture of tenderness. Halle wanted privacy for her and got public display. Who could miss a ripple in a cornfield on a quiet cloudless day? He, Sixo and both of the Pauls sat under Brother pouring water from a gourd over their heads, and through eyes streaming with well water, they watched the confusion of tassels in the field below. It had been hard, hard, hard sitting there erect as dogs, watching corn stalks dance at noon. The water running over their heads made it worse.

Paul D sighed and turned over. Sethe took the opportunity afforded by his movement to shift as well. Looking at Paul D's back, she remembered that some of the corn stalks broke, folded down over Halle's back, and among the things her fingers clutched were husk and cornsilk hair.

How loose the silk. How jailed down the juice.

The jealous admiration of the watching men melted with the feast of new corn they allowed themselves that night. Plucked from the broken stalks that Mr. Garner could not doubt was the fault of the raccoon. Paul F wanted his roasted; Paul A wanted his boiled and now Paul D couldn't remember how finally they'd cooked those ears too young to eat. What he did remember was parting the hair to get to the tip, the edge of his fingernail just under, so as not to graze a single kernel.

The pulling down of the tight sheath, the ripping sound always convinced her it hurt.

As soon as one strip of husk was down, the rest obeyed and the ear yielded up to him its shy rows, exposed at last. How loose the silk. How quick the jailed-up flavor ran free.

No matter what all your teeth and wet fingers anticipated, there was no accounting for the way that simple joy could shake you.

How loose the silk. How fine and loose and free.

Denver's secrets were sweet. Accompanied every time by wild veronica until she discovered cologne. The first bottle was a gift, the next she stole from her mother and hid among boxwood until it froze and cracked. That was the year winter came in a hurry at suppertime and stayed eight months. One of the War years when Miss Bodwin, the whitewoman, brought Christmas cologne for her mother and herself, oranges for the boys and another good wool shawl for Baby Suggs. Talking of a war full of dead people, she looked happy—flush-faced, and although her voice was heavy as a man's, she smelled like a roomful of flowers—excitement that Denver could have all for herself in the boxwood. Back beyond 124 was a narrow field that stopped itself at a wood. On the yonder side of these woods, a stream. In these woods, between the field and the stream, hidden by post oaks, five boxwood bushes, planted in a ring, had started stretching toward each other four feet off the ground to form a round, empty room seven feet high, its walls fifty inches of murmuring leaves.

Bent low, Denver could crawl into this room, and once there she could stand all the way up in emerald light.

It began as a little girl's houseplay, but as her desires changed, so did the play. Quiet, private and completely secret except for the noisome cologne signal that thrilled the rabbits before it confused them. First a playroom (where the silence was softer), then a refuge (from her brothers' fright), soon the place became the point. In that bower, closed off from the hurt of the hurt world, Denver's imagination produced its own hunger and its own food, which she badly needed because loneliness wore her out. *Wore her out.* Veiled and protected by the live green walls, she felt ripe and clear, and salvation was as easy as a wish.

Once when she was in the boxwood, an autumn long before Paul D moved into the house with her mother, she was made suddenly cold by a combination of wind and the perfume on her skin. She dressed herself, bent down to leave and stood up in snowfall: a thin and whipping snow very like the picture her mother had painted as she described the circumstances of Denver's birth in a canoe straddled by a whitegirl for whom she was named.

Shivering, Denver approached the house, regarding it, as she always did, as a person rather than a structure. A person that wept, sighed, trembled and fell into fits. Her steps and her gaze were the cautious ones of a child approaching a nervous, idle relative (someone dependent but proud). A breastplate of darkness hid all the windows except one. Its dim glow came from Baby Suggs' room. When Denver looked in, she saw her mother on her knees in prayer, which was not unusual. What was unusual (even for a girl who had lived all her life in a house peopled by the living activity of the dead) was that a white dress knelt down next to her mother and had its sleeve around her mother's waist. And it was the tender embrace of the dress sleeve that made Denver remember the details of her birth—that and the thin, whipping snow she was standing in, like the fruit of common flowers. The dress and her mother together looked like two friendly grown-up women—one (the dress) helping out the other. And the magic of her birth, its miracle in fact, testified to that friendliness as did her own name.

Easily she stepped into the told story that lay before her eyes on the path she followed away from the window. There was only one door to the house and to get to it from the back you had to walk all the way around to the front of 124, past the storeroom, past the cold house, the privy, the shed, on around to the porch. And to get to the part of the story she liked best, she had to start way back: hear the birds in the thick woods, the crunch of leaves underfoot; see her mother making her way up into the hills where no houses were likely to be. How Sethe was walking on two feet meant for standing still. How they were so swollen she could not see her arch or feel her ankles. Her leg shaft ended in a loaf of flesh scalloped by five toenails. But she could not, would not, stop, for when she did the little antelope rammed her with horns and pawed the ground of her womb with impatient hooves. While she was walking, it seemed to graze, quietly—so she walked, on two feet meant, in this sixth month of pregnancy, for standing still. Still, near a kettle; still, at the churn; still, at the tub and ironing board. Milk, sticky and sour on her dress, attracted every small flying thing from gnats to grasshoppers. By the time she reached the hill skirt she had long ago stopped waving them off. The clanging in her head, begun as a churchbell heard from a distance, was by then a tight cap of pealing bells around her ears. She sank and had to look down to see whether she was in a hole or kneeling. Nothing was alive but her nipples and the little antelope. Finally, she was horizontal—or must have been because blades of wild onion were scratching her temple and her cheek. Concerned as she was for the life of her children's mother, Sethe told Denver, she remembered thinking: Well, at least I don't have to take another step. A dying thought if ever there was one, and she waited for the little antelope to protest, and why she thought of an antelope Sethe could not imagine since she had never seen one. She guessed it must have been an invention held on to from before Sweet Home, when she was very young. Of that place where she was born (Carolina maybe? or was it Louisiana?) she remembered only song and dance. Not even her own mother, who was pointed out to her by the eight-year-old child who watched over the young ones—pointed out as the one among many backs turned away from her, stooping in a watery field. Patiently Sethe waited for this particular back to gain the row's end and stand. What she saw was a cloth hat as opposed to a straw one, singularity enough in that world of cooing women each of whom was called Ma'am.

"Seth—thuh."

"Ma'am."

"Hold on to the baby."

"Yes, Ma'am."

"Seth—thuh."

"Ma'am."

"Get some kindlin in here."

"Yes, Ma'am."

Oh but when they sang. And oh but when they danced and sometimes they danced the antelope. The men as well as the ma'ams, one of whom was certainly her own. They shifted shapes and became something other. Some unchained, demanding other whose feet knew her pulse better than she did. Just like this one in her stomach.

"I believe this baby's ma'am is gonna die in wild onions on the bloody side of the Ohio River." That's what was on her mind and what she told Denver. Her exact words. And it didn't seem such a bad idea, all in all, in view of the step she would not have to take, but the thought of herself stretched out dead while the little antelope lived on—an hour? a day? a day and a night?—in her lifeless body grieved her so she made the groan that made the person walking on a path not ten yards away halt and stand right still. Sethe had not heard the walking, but suddenly she heard the standing still and then she smelled the hair. The voice, saying, "Who's in there?" was all she needed to know that she was about to be discovered by a whiteboy. That he too had mossy teeth, an appetite. That on a ridge of pine near the Ohio River, trying to get to her three children, one of whom was starving for the food she carried; that after her husband had disappeared; that after her milk had been stolen, her back pulped, her children orphaned, she was not to have an easeful death. No.

She told Denver that a *something* came up out of the earth into her—like a freezing, but moving too, like jaws inside. "Look like I was just cold jaws grinding," she said. Suddenly she was eager for his eyes, to bite into them; to gnaw his cheek.

"I was hungry," she told Denver, "just as hungry as I could be for his eyes. I couldn't wait."

So she raised up on her elbow and dragged herself, one pull, two, three, four, toward the young white voice talking about "Who that back in there?"

"'Come see,' I was thinking. 'Be the last thing you behold,' and sure enough here come the feet so I thought well that's where I'll have to start God do what He would, I'm gonna eat his feet off. I'm laughing now, but it's true. I wasn't just set to do it. I was hungry to do it. Like a snake. All jaws and hungry.

"It wasn't no whiteboy at all. Was a girl. The raggediest-looking trash you ever saw saying, 'Look there. A nigger. If that don't beat all.'"

And now the part Denver loved the best:

Her name was Amy and she needed beef and pot liquor like nobody in this world. Arms like cane stalks and enough hair for four or five heads. Slow-moving eyes. She didn't look at anything quick. Talked so much it wasn't clear how she could breathe at the same time. And those cane-stalk arms, as it turned out, were as strong as iron.

"You 'bout the scariest-looking something I ever seen. What you doing back up in here?"

Down in the grass, like the snake she believed she was, Sethe opened her mouth, and instead of fangs and a split tongue, out shot the truth.

"Running," Sethe told her. It was the first word she had spoken all day and it came out thick because of her tender tongue.

"Them the feet you running on? My Jesus my." She squatted down and stared at Sethe's feet. "You got anything on you, gal, pass for food?"

"No." Sethe tried to shift to a sitting position but couldn't.

"I like to die I'm so hungry." The girl moved her eyes slowly, examining the greenery around her. "Thought there'd be huckleberries. Look like it. That's why I come up in here. Didn't expect to find no nigger woman. If they was any, birds ate em. You like huckleberries?"

"I'm having a baby, miss."

Amy looked at her. "That mean you don't have no appetite? Well I got to eat me something."

Combing her hair with her fingers, she carefully surveyed the landscape once more. Satisfied nothing edible was around, she stood up to go and Sethe's heart stood up too at the thought of being left alone in the grass without a fang in her head.

"Where you on your way to, miss?"

She turned and looked at Sethe with freshly lit eyes. "Boston. Get me some velvet. It's a store there called Wilson. I seen the pictures of it and they have the prettiest velvet. They don't believe I'm a get it, but I am."

Sethe nodded and shifted her elbow. "Your ma'am know you on the lookout for velvet?"

The girl shook her hair out of her face. "My mama worked for these here people to pay for her passage. But then she had me and since she died right after, well, they said I had to work for em to pay it off. I did, but now I want me some velvet."

They did not look directly at each other, not straight into the eyes anyway. Yet they slipped effortlessly into yard chat about nothing in particular—except one lay on the ground.

"Boston," said Sethe. "Is that far?"

"Ooooh, yeah. A hundred miles. Maybe more."

"Must be velvet closer by."

"Not like in Boston. Boston got the best. Be so pretty on me. You ever touch it?"

"No, miss. I never touched no velvet." Sethe didn't know if it was the voice, or Boston or velvet, but while the whitegirl talked, the baby slept. Not one butt or kick, so she guessed her luck had turned.

"Ever see any?" she asked Sethe. "I bet you never even seen any."

"If I did I didn't know it. What's it like, velvet?"

Amy dragged her eyes over Sethe's face as though she would never give out so confidential a piece of information as that to a perfect stranger.

"What they call you?" she asked.

However far she was from Sweet Home, there was no point in giving out her real name to the first person she saw. "Lu," said Sethe. "They call me Lu."

"Well, Lu, velvet is like the world was just born. Clean and new and so smooth. The velvet I seen was brown, but in Boston they got all colors. Carmine. That means red but when you talk about velvet you got to say 'carmine.'" She raised her eyes to the sky and then, as though she had wasted enough time away from Boston, she moved off saying, "I gotta go."

Picking her way through the brush she hollered back to Sethe, "What you gonna do, just lay there and foal?"

"I can't get up from here," said Sethe.

"What?" She stopped and turned to hear.

"I said I can't get up."

Amy drew her arm across her nose and came slowly back to where Sethe lay. "It's a house back yonder," she said.

"A house?"

"Mmmmm. I passed it. Ain't no regular house with people in it though. A lean-to, kinda."

"How far?"

"Make a difference, does it? You stay the night here snake get you."

"Well he may as well come on. I can't stand up let alone walk and God help me, miss, I can't crawl."

"Sure you can, Lu. Come on," said Amy and, with a toss of hair enough for five heads, she moved toward the path.

So she crawled and Amy walked alongside her, and when Sethe needed to rest, Amy stopped too and talked some more about Boston and velvet and good things to eat. The sound of that voice, like a sixteen-year-old boy's, going on and on and on, kept the little antelope quiet and grazing. During the whole hateful crawl to the lean-to, it never bucked once.

Nothing of Sethe's was intact by the time they reached it except the cloth that covered her hair. Below her bloody knees, there was no feeling at all; her chest was two cushions of pins. It was the voice full of velvet and Boston and good things to eat that urged her along and made her think that maybe she wasn't, after all, just a crawling graveyard for a six-month baby's last hours.

The lean-to was full of leaves, which Amy pushed into a pile for Sethe to lie on. Then she gathered rocks, covered them with more leaves and made Sethe put her feet on them, saying: "I know a woman had her feet cut off they was so swole." And she made sawing gestures with the blade of her hand across Sethe's ankles. "Zzz Zzz Zzz Zzz."

"I used to be a good size. Nice arms and everything. Wouldn't think it, would you? That was before they put me in the root cellar. I was fishing off the Beaver once. Catfish in Beaver River sweet as chicken. Well I was just fishing there and a nigger floated right by me. I don't like drowned people, you? Your feet remind me of him. All swole like."

Then she did the magic: lifted Sethe's feet and legs and massaged them until she cried salt tears.

"It's gonna hurt, now," said Amy. "Anything dead coming back to life hurts."

A truth for all times, thought Denver. Maybe the white dress holding its arm around her mother's waist was in pain. If so, it could mean the baby ghost had plans. When she opened the door, Sethe was just leaving the keeping room.

"I saw a white dress holding on to you," Denver said.

"White? Maybe it was my bedding dress. Describe it to me."

"Had a high neck. Whole mess of buttons coming down the back."

"Buttons. Well, that lets out my bedding dress. I never had a button on nothing."

"Did Grandma Baby?"

Sethe shook her head. "She couldn't handle them. Even on her shoes. What else?"

"A bunch at the back. On the sit-down part."

"A bustle? It had a bustle?"

"I don't know what it's called."

"Sort of gathered-like? Below the waist in the back?"

"Um hm."

"A rich lady's dress. Silk?"

"Cotton, look like."

"Lisle probably. White cotton lisle. You say it was holding on to me. How?"

"Like you. It looked just like you. Kneeling next to you while you were praying. Had its arm around your waist."

"Well, I'll be."

"What were you praying for, Ma'am?"

"Not *for* anything. I don't pray anymore. I just talk."

"What were you talking about?"

"You won't understand, baby."

"Yes, I will."

"I was talking about time. It's so hard for me to believe in it. Some things go. Pass on. Some things just stay. I used to think it was my rememory. You know. Some things you forget. Other things you never do. But it's not. Places, places are still there. If a house burns down, it's gone, but the place—the picture of it—stays, and not just in my rememory, but out there, in the world. What I remember is a picture floating around out there outside my head. I mean, even if I don't think it, even if I die, the picture of what I did, or knew, or saw is still out there. Right in the place where it happened."

"Can other people see it?" asked Denver.

"Oh, yes. Oh, yes, yes, yes. Someday you be walking down the road and you hear something or see something going on. So clear. And you think it's you thinking it up. A thought picture. But no. It's when you bump into a rememory that belongs to somebody else. Where I was before I came here, that place is real. It's never going away. Even if the whole farm—every tree and grass blade of it dies. The picture is still there and what's more, if you go there—you who never was there—if you go there and stand in the place where it was, it will happen again; it will be there for you, waiting for you. So, Denver, you can't never go there. Never. Because even though it's all over—over and done with—it's going to always be there waiting for you. That's how come I had to get all my children out. No matter what."

Denver picked at her fingernails. "If it's still there, waiting, that must mean that nothing ever dies."

Sethe looked right in Denver's face. "Nothing ever does," she said.

"You never told me all what happened. Just that they whipped you and you run off, pregnant. With me."

"Nothing to tell except schoolteacher. He was a little man. Short. Always wore a collar, even in the fields. A schoolteacher, she said. That made her feel good that her husband's sister's husband had book learning and was willing to come farm Sweet Home after Mr. Garner passed. The men could have done it, even with Paul F sold. But it was like Halle said. She didn't want to be the only white person on the farm and a woman too. So she was satisfied when the schoolteacher agreed to come. He brought two boys with him. Sons or nephews. I don't know. They called him Onka and had pretty manners, all of em. Talked soft and spit in handkerchiefs. Gentle in a lot of ways. You know, the kind who know Jesus by His first name, but out of politeness never use it even to His face. A pretty good farmer, Halle said. Not strong as Mr. Garner but smart enough. He liked the ink I made. It was her recipe, but he preferred how I mixed it and it was important to him because at night he sat down to write in his book. It was a book about us but we didn't know that right away. We just thought it was his manner to ask us questions. He commenced to carry round a notebook and write down what we said. I still think it was them questions that tore Sixo up. Tore him up for all time."

She stopped.

Denver knew that her mother was through with it—for now anyway. The single slow blink of her eyes; the bottom lip sliding up slowly to cover the top; and then a nostril sigh, like the snuff of a candle flame—signs that Sethe had reached the point beyond which she would not go.

"Well, I think the baby got plans," said Denver.

"What plans?"

"I don't know, but the dress holding on to you got to mean something."

"Maybe," said Sethe. "Maybe it does have plans."

Whatever they were or might have been, Paul D messed them up for good. With a table and a loud male voice he had rid 124 of its claim to local fame. Denver had taught herself to take pride in the condemnation Negroes heaped on them; the assumption that the haunting was done by an evil thing looking for more. None of them knew the downright pleasure of enchantment, of not suspecting but *knowing* the things behind things. Her brothers had known, but it scared them; Grandma Baby knew, but it saddened her. None could appreciate the safety of ghost company. Even Sethe didn't love it. She just took it for granted—like a sudden change in the weather.

But it was gone now. Whooshed away in the blast of a hazelnut man's shout, leaving Denver's world flat, mostly, with the exception of an emerald closet standing seven feet high in the woods. Her mother had secrets—things she wouldn't tell; things she halfway told. Well, Denver had them too. And hers were sweet—sweet as lily-of-the-valley cologne.

*

Sethe had given little thought to the white dress until Paul
D came, and then she remembered Denver's interpretation:
plans. The morning after the first night with Paul D, Sethe
smiled just thinking about what the word could mean. It was
a luxury she had not had in eighteen years and only that
once. Before and since, all her effort was directed not on
avoiding pain but on getting through it as quickly as possible.
The one set of plans she had made—getting away from Sweet
Home—went awry so completely she never dared life by
making more.

Yet the morning she woke up next to Paul D, the word her
daughter had used a few years ago did cross her mind and she
thought about what Denver had seen kneeling next to her, and
thought also of the temptation to trust and remember that
gripped her as she stood before the cooking stove in his arms.
Would it be all right? Would it be all right to go ahead and
feel? Go ahead and *count on something*?

She couldn't think clearly, lying next to him listening to his
breathing, so carefully, carefully, she had left the bed.

Kneeling in the keeping room where she usually went to talk-
think it was clear why Baby Suggs was so starved for color.
There wasn't any except for two orange squares in a quilt that
made the absence shout. The walls of the room were slate-
colored, the floor earth-brown, the wooden dresser the color
of itself, curtains white, and the dominating feature, the quilt
over an iron cot, was made up of scraps of blue serge, black,
brown and gray wool—the full range of the dark and the muted
that thrift and modesty allowed. In that sober field, two patches
of orange looked wild—like life in the raw.

Sethe looked at her hands, her bottle-green sleeves, and thought how little color there was in the house and how strange that she had not missed it the way Baby did. Deliberate, she thought, it must be deliberate, because the last color she remembered was the pink chips in the headstone of her baby girl. After that she became as color conscious as a hen. Every dawn she worked at fruit pies, potato dishes and vegetables while the cook did the soup, meat and all the rest. And she could not remember remembering a molly apple or a yellow squash. Every dawn she saw the dawn, but never acknowledged or remarked its color. There was something wrong with that. It was as though one day she saw red baby blood, another day the pink gravestone chips, and that was the last of it.

124 was so full of strong feeling perhaps she was oblivious to the loss of anything at all. There was a time when she scanned the fields every morning and every evening for her boys. When she stood at the open window, unmindful of flies, her head cocked to her left shoulder, her eyes searching to the right for them. Cloud shadow on the road, an old woman, a wandering goat untethered and gnawing bramble—each one looked at first like Howard—no, Buglar. Little by little she stopped and their thirteen-year-old faces faded completely into their baby ones, which came to her only in sleep. When her dreams roamed outside 124, anywhere they wished, she saw them sometimes in beautiful trees, their little legs barely visible in the leaves. Sometimes they ran along the railroad track laughing, too loud, apparently, to hear her because they never did turn around. When she woke the house crowded in on her: there was the door where the soda crackers were lined up in a row; the white stairs her baby girl loved to climb; the corner

where Baby Suggs mended shoes, a pile of which were still in the cold room; the exact place on the stove where Denver burned her fingers. And of course the spite of the house itself. There was no room for any other thing or body until Paul D arrived and broke up the place, making room, shifting it, moving it over to someplace else, then standing in the place he had made.

So, kneeling in the keeping room the morning after Paul D came, she was distracted by the two orange squares that signaled how barren 124 really was.

He was responsible for that. Emotions sped to the surface in his company. Things became what they were: drabness looked drab; heat was hot. Windows suddenly had view. And wouldn't you know he'd be a singing man.

> *Little rice, little bean,*
> *No meat in between.*
> *Hard work ain't easy,*
> *Dry bread ain't greasy.*

He was up now and singing as he mended things he had broken the day before. Some old pieces of song he'd learned on the prison farm or in the War afterward. Nothing like what they sang at Sweet Home, where yearning fashioned every note.

The songs he knew from Georgia were flat-headed nails for pounding and pounding and pounding.

> *Lay my head on the railroad line,*
> *Train come along, pacify my mind.*

If I had my weight in lime,
I'd whip my captain till he went stone blind.
Five-cent nickel,
Ten-cent dime,
Busting rocks is busting time.

But they didn't fit, these songs. They were too loud, had too much power for the little house chores he was engaged in—resetting table legs; glazing.

He couldn't go back to "Storm upon the Waters" that they sang under the trees of Sweet Home, so he contented himself with mmmmmmmmm, throwing in a line if one occurred to him, and what occurred over and over was "Bare feet and chamomile sap,/Took off my shoes; took off my hat."

It was tempting to change the words (Gimme back my shoes; gimme back my hat), because he didn't believe he could live with a woman—any woman—for over two out of three months. That was about as long as he could abide one place. After Delaware and before that Alfred, Georgia, where he slept underground and crawled into sunlight for the sole purpose of breaking rock, walking off when he got ready was the only way he could convince himself that he would no longer have to sleep, pee, eat or swing a sledge hammer in chains.

But this was not a normal woman in a normal house. As soon as he had stepped through the red light he knew that, compared to 124, the rest of the world was bald. After Alfred he had shut down a generous portion of his head, operating on the part that helped him walk, eat, sleep, sing. If he could do those things—with a little work and a little sex thrown in—he asked for no more, for more required him to dwell on Halle's face and Sixo laughing. To recall trembling in a box built into the ground. Grateful for the daylight spent doing mule work in a quarry because he did not tremble when he had a hammer in his hands. The box had done what Sweet Home had not, what working like an ass and living like a dog had not: drove him crazy so he would not lose his mind.

By the time he got to Ohio, then to Cincinnati, then to Halle Suggs' mother's house, he thought he had seen and felt it all. Even now as he put back the window frame he had smashed, he could not account for the pleasure in his surprise at seeing Halle's wife alive, barefoot with uncovered hair—walking around the corner of the house with her shoes and stockings in her hands. The closed portion of his head opened like a greased lock.

"I was thinking of looking for work around here. What you think?"

"Ain't much. River mostly. And hogs."

"Well, I never worked on water, but I can pick up anything heavy as me, hogs included."

"Whitepeople better here than Kentucky but you may have to scramble some."

"It ain't whether I scramble; it's where. You saying it's all right to scramble here?"

"Better than all right."

"Your girl, Denver. Seems to me she's of a different mind."

"Why you say that?"

"She's got a waiting way about her. Something she's expecting and it ain't me."

"I don't know what it could be."

"Well, whatever it is, she believes I'm interrupting it."

"Don't worry about her. She's a charmed child. From the beginning."

"Is that right?"

"Uh huh. Nothing bad can happen to her. Look at it. Everybody I knew dead or gone or dead and gone. Not her. Not my Denver. Even when I was carrying her, when it got clear that I wasn't going to make it—which meant she wasn't going to make it either—she pulled a whitegirl out of the hill. The last thing you'd expect to help. And when the schoolteacher found us and came busting in here with the law and a shotgun—"

"Schoolteacher found you?"

"Took a while, but he did. Finally."

"And he didn't take you back?"

"Oh, no. I wasn't going back there. I don't care who found who. Any life but not that one. I went to jail instead. Denver was just a baby so she went right along with me. Rats bit everything in there but her."

Paul D turned away. He wanted to know more about it, but jail talk put him back in Alfred, Georgia.

"I need some nails. Anybody around here I can borrow from or should I go to town?"

"May as well go to town. You'll need other things."

One night and they were talking like a couple. They had skipped love and promise and went directly to "You saying it's all right to scramble here?"

To Sethe, the future was a matter of keeping the past at bay. The "better life" she believed she and Denver were living was simply not that other one.

The fact that Paul D had come out of "that other one" into her bed was better too; and the notion of a future with him, or for that matter without him, was beginning to stroke her mind. As for Denver, the job Sethe had of keeping her from the past that was still waiting for her was all that mattered.

Pleasantly troubled, Sethe avoided the keeping room and Denver's sidelong looks. As she expected, since life was like that—it didn't do any good. Denver ran a mighty interference and on the third day flat-out asked Paul D how long he was going to hang around.

The phrase hurt him so much he missed the table. The coffee cup hit the floor and rolled down the sloping boards toward the front door.

"Hang around?" Paul D didn't even look at the mess he had made.

"Denver! What's got into you?" Sethe looked at her daughter, feeling more embarrassed than angry.

Paul D scratched the hair on his chin. "Maybe I should make tracks."

"No!" Sethe was surprised by how loud she said it.

"He know what he needs," said Denver.

"Well, you don't," Sethe told her, "and you must not know what you need either. I don't want to hear another word out of you."

"I just asked if—"

"Hush! *You* make tracks. Go somewhere and sit down."

Denver picked up her plate and left the table but not before adding a chicken back and more bread to the heap she was carrying away. Paul D leaned over to wipe the spilled coffee with his blue handkerchief.

"I'll get that." Sethe jumped up and went to the stove. Behind it various cloths hung, each in some stage of drying. In silence she wiped the floor and retrieved the cup. Then she poured him another cupful, and set it carefully before him. Paul D touched its rim but didn't say anything—as though even "thank you" was an obligation he could not meet and the coffee itself a gift he could not take.

Sethe resumed her chair and the silence continued. Finally she realized that if it was going to be broken she would have to do it.

"I didn't train her like that."

Paul D stroked the rim of the cup.

"And I'm as surprised by her manners as you are hurt by em."

Paul D looked at Sethe. "Is there history to her question?"

"History? What you mean?"

"I mean, did she have to ask that, or want to ask it, of anybody else before me?"

Sethe made two fists and placed them on her hips. "You as bad as she is."

"Come on, Sethe."

"Oh, I am coming on. I am!"

"You know what I mean."

"I do and I don't like it."

"Jesus," he whispered.

"Who?" Sethe was getting loud again.

"Jesus! I said Jesus! All I did was sit down for supper! and I get cussed out twice. Once for being here and once for asking why I was cussed in the first place!"

"She didn't cuss."

"No? Felt like it."

"Look here. I apologize for her. I'm real—"

"You can't do that. You can't apologize for nobody. She got to do that."

"Then I'll see that she does." Sethe sighed.

"What I want to know is, is she asking a question that's on your mind too?"

"Oh no. No, Paul D. Oh no."

"Then she's of one mind and you another? If you can call whatever's in her head a mind, that is."

"Excuse me, but I can't hear a word against her. I'll chastise her. You leave her alone."

Risky, thought Paul D, very risky. For a used-to-be-slave woman to love anything that much was dangerous, especially if it was her children she had settled on to love. The best thing, he knew, was to love just a little bit; everything, just a little bit, so when they broke its back, or shoved it in a croaker sack, well, maybe you'd have a little love left over for the next one. "Why?" he asked her. "Why you think you have to take up for her? Apologize for her? She's grown."

"I don't care what she is. Grown don't mean nothing to a mother. A child is a child. They get bigger, older, but grown? What's that supposed to mean? In my heart it don't mean a thing."

"It means she has to take it if she acts up. You can't protect her every minute. What's going to happen when you die?"

"Nothing! I'll protect her while I'm live and I'll protect her when I ain't."

"Oh well, I'm through," he said. "I quit."

"That's the way it is, Paul D. I can't explain it to you no better than that, but that's the way it is. If I have to choose— well, it's not even a choice."

"That's the point. The whole point. I'm not asking you to choose. Nobody would. I thought—well, I thought you could— there was some space for me."

"She's asking me."

"You can't go by that. You got to say it to her. Tell her it's not about choosing somebody over her—it's making space for somebody along with her. You got to say it. And if you say it and mean it, then you also got to know you can't gag me. There's no way I'm going to hurt her or not take care of what she need if I can, but I can't be told to keep my mouth shut if she's acting ugly. You want me here, don't put no gag on me."

"Maybe I should leave things the way they are," she said.

"How are they?"

"We get along."

"What about inside?"

"I don't go inside."

"Sethe, if I'm here with you, with Denver, you can go anywhere you want. Jump, if you want to, 'cause I'll catch you, girl. I'll catch you 'fore you fall. Go as far inside as you need to, I'll hold your ankles. Make sure you get back out. I'm not saying this because I need a place to stay. That's the last thing I need. I told you, I'm a walking man, but I been heading in this direction for seven years. Walking all around this place. Upstate, downstate, east, west; I been in territory ain't got no

name, never staying nowhere long. But when I got here and
sat out there on the porch, waiting for you, well, I knew it
wasn't the place I was heading toward; it was you. We can
make a life, girl. A life."

"I don't know. I don't know."

"Leave it to me. See how it goes. No promises, if you don't
want to make any. Just see how it goes. All right?"

"All right."

"You willing to leave it to me?"

"Well—some of it."

"Some?" he smiled. "Okay. Here's some. There's a carnival
in town. Thursday, tomorrow, is for coloreds and I got two
dollars. Me and you and Denver gonna spend every penny of
it. What you say?"

"No" is what she said. At least what she started out saying
(what would her boss say if she took a day off?), but even when
she said it she was thinking how much her eyes enjoyed looking
in his face.

The crickets were screaming on Thursday and the sky, stripped
of blue, was white hot at eleven in the morning. Sethe was
badly dressed for the heat, but this being her first social outing
in eighteen years, she felt obliged to wear her one good dress,
heavy as it was, and a hat. Certainly a hat. She didn't want to
meet Lady Jones or Ella with her head wrapped like she was
going to work. The dress, a good-wool castoff, was a Christmas
present to Baby Suggs from Miss Bodwin, the whitewoman
who loved her. Denver and Paul D fared better in the heat
since neither felt the occasion required special clothing.
Denver's bonnet knocked against her shoulder blades; Paul D

wore his vest open, no jacket and his shirt sleeves rolled above
his elbows. They were not holding hands, but their shadows
were. Sethe looked to her left and all three of them were gliding
over the dust holding hands. Maybe he was right. A life.
Watching their hand-holding shadows, she was embarrassed
at being dressed for church. The others, ahead and behind
them, would think she was putting on airs, letting them know
that she was different because she lived in a house with two
stories; tougher, because she could do and survive things they
believed she should neither do nor survive. She was glad Denver
had resisted her urgings to dress up—rebraid her hair at least.
But Denver was not doing anything to make this trip a pleasure.
She agreed to go—sullenly—but her attitude was "Go 'head.
Try and make me happy." The happy one was Paul D. He said
howdy to everybody within twenty feet. Made fun of the
weather and what it was doing to him, yelled back at the crows,
and was the first to smell the doomed roses. All the time, no
matter what they were doing—whether Denver wiped perspiration from her forehead or stooped to retie her shoes; whether
Paul D kicked a stone or reached over to meddle a child's face
leaning on its mother's shoulder—all the time the three
shadows that shot out of their feet to the left held hands.
Nobody noticed but Sethe and she stopped looking after she
decided that it was a good sign. A life. Could be.

Up and down the lumberyard fence old roses were dying.
The sawyer who had planted them twelve years ago to give his
workplace a friendly feel—something to take the sin out of
slicing trees for a living—was amazed by their abundance; how
rapidly they crawled all over the stake-and-post fence that separated the lumberyard from the open field next to it where

homeless men slept, children ran and, once a year, carnival people pitched tents. The closer the roses got to death, the louder their scent, and everybody who attended the carnival associated it with the stench of the rotten roses. It made them a little dizzy and very thirsty but did nothing to extinguish the eagerness of the coloredpeople filing down the road. Some walked on the grassy shoulders, others dodged the wagons creaking down the road's dusty center. All, like Paul D, were in high spirits, which the smell of dying roses (that Paul D called to everybody's attention) could not dampen. As they pressed to get to the rope entrance they were lit like lamps. Breathless with the excitement of seeing whitepeople loose: doing magic, clowning, without heads or with two heads, twenty feet tall or two feet tall, weighing a ton, completely tattooed, eating glass, swallowing fire, spitting ribbons, twisted into knots, forming pyramids, playing with snakes and beating each other up.

All of this was advertisement, read by those who could and heard by those who could not, and the fact that none of it was true did not extinguish their appetite a bit. The barker called them and their children names ("Pickaninnies free!") but the food on his vest and the hole in his pants rendered it fairly harmless. In any case it was a small price to pay for the fun they might not ever have again. Two pennies and an insult were well spent if it meant seeing the spectacle of whitefolks making a spectacle of themselves. So, although the carnival was a lot less than mediocre (which is why it agreed to a Colored Thursday), it gave the four hundred black people in its audience thrill upon thrill upon thrill.

One-Ton Lady spit at them, but her bulk shortened her aim and they got a big kick out of the helpless meanness in her little eyes. Arabian Nights Dancer cut her performance to three minutes instead of the usual fifteen she normally did—earning the gratitude of the children, who could hardly wait for Abu Snake Charmer, who followed her.

Denver bought horehound, licorice, peppermint and lemonade at a table manned by a little whitegirl in ladies' high-topped shoes. Soothed by sugar, surrounded by a crowd of people who did not find her the main attraction, who, in fact, said, "Hey, Denver," every now and then, pleased her enough to consider the possibility that Paul D wasn't all that bad. In fact there was something about him—when the three of them stood together watching Midget dance—that made the stares of other Negroes kind, gentle, something Denver did not remember seeing in their faces. Several even nodded and smiled at her mother, no one, apparently, able to withstand sharing the pleasure Paul D was having. He slapped his knees when Giant danced with Midget; when Two-Headed Man talked to himself. He bought everything Denver asked for and much she did not. He teased Sethe into tents she was reluctant to enter. Stuck pieces of candy she didn't want between her lips. When Wild African Savage shook his bars and said wa wa, Paul D told everybody he knew him back in Roanoke. Paul D made a few acquaintances; spoke to them about what work he might find. Sethe returned the smiles she got. Denver was swaying with delight. And on the way home, although leading them now, the shadows of three people still held hands.

A fully dressed woman walked out of the water. She barely gained the dry bank of the stream before she sat down and leaned against a mulberry tree. All day and all night she sat there, her head resting on the trunk in a position abandoned enough to crack the brim in her straw hat. Everything hurt but her lungs most of all. Sopping wet and breathing shallow she spent those hours trying to negotiate the weight of her eyelids. The day breeze blew her dress dry; the night wind wrinkled it. Nobody saw her emerge or came accidentally by. If they had, chances are they would have hesitated before approaching her. Not because she was wet, or dozing or had what sounded like asthma, but because amid all that she was smiling. It took her the whole of the next morning to lift herself from the ground and make her way through the woods past a giant temple of boxwood to the field and then the yard of the slate-gray house. Exhausted again, she sat down on the first handy place—a stump not far from the steps of 124. By then keeping her eyes open was less of an effort. She could manage it for a full two minutes or more. Her neck, its circumference no wider than a parlor-service saucer, kept bending and her chin brushed the bit of lace edging her dress.

Women who drink champagne when there is nothing to celebrate can look like that: their straw hats with broken brims are often askew; they nod in public places; their shoes are undone. But their skin is not like that of the woman breathing near the steps of 124. She had new skin, lineless and smooth, including the knuckles of her hands.

By late afternoon when the carnival was over, and the Negroes were hitching rides home if they were lucky—walking if they were not—the woman had fallen asleep again. The rays of the sun struck her full in the face, so that when Sethe, Denver and Paul D rounded the curve in the road all they saw was a black dress, two unlaced shoes below it, and Here Boy nowhere in sight.

"Look," said Denver. "What is that?"

And, for some reason she could not immediately account for, the moment she got close enough to see the face, Sethe's bladder filled to capacity. She said, "Oh, excuse me," and ran around to the back of 124. Not since she was a baby girl, being cared for by the eight-year-old girl who pointed out her mother to her, had she had an emergency that unmanageable. She never made the outhouse. Right in front of its door she had to lift her skirts, and the water she voided was endless. Like a horse, she thought, but as it went on and on she thought, No, more like flooding the boat when Denver was born. So much water Amy said, "Hold on, Lu. You going to sink us you keep that up." But there was no stopping water breaking from a breaking womb and there was no stopping now. She hoped Paul D wouldn't take it upon himself to come looking for her and be obliged to see her squatting in front of her own privy making a mudhole too deep to be witnessed without shame. Just about the time she started wondering if the carnival would accept another freak, it stopped. She tidied herself and ran around to the porch. No one was there. All three were inside—Paul D and Denver standing before the stranger, watching her drink cup after cup of water.

"She said she was thirsty," said Paul D. He took off his cap. "Mighty thirsty look like."

The woman gulped water from a speckled tin cup and held it out for more. Four times Denver filled it, and four times the woman drank as though she had crossed a desert. When she was finished a little water was on her chin, but she did not wipe it away. Instead she gazed at Sethe with sleepy eyes. Poorly fed, thought Sethe, and younger than her clothes suggested— good lace at the throat, and a rich woman's hat. Her skin was flawless except for three vertical scratches on her forehead so fine and thin they seemed at first like hair, baby hair before it bloomed and roped into the masses of black yarn under her hat.

"You from around here?" Sethe asked her.

She shook her head no and reached down to take off her shoes. She pulled her dress up to the knees and rolled down her stockings. When the hosiery was tucked into the shoes, Sethe saw that her feet were like her hands, soft and new. She must have hitched a wagon ride, thought Sethe. Probably one of those West Virginia girls looking for something to beat a life of tobacco and sorghum. Sethe bent to pick up the shoes.

"What might your name be?" asked Paul D.

"Beloved," she said, and her voice was so low and rough each one looked at the other two. They heard the voice first— later the name.

"Beloved. You use a last name, Beloved?" Paul D asked her.

"Last?" She seemed puzzled. Then "No," and she spelled it for them, slowly as though the letters were being formed as she spoke them.

Sethe dropped the shoes; Denver sat down and Paul D smiled. He recognized the careful enunciation of letters by those, like himself, who could not read but had memorized the letters of their name. He was about to ask who her people were but thought better of it. A young coloredwoman drifting was drifting from ruin. He had been in Rochester four years ago and seen five women arriving with fourteen female children. All their men—brothers, uncles, fathers, husbands, sons—had been picked off one by one by one. They had a single piece of paper directing them to a preacher on DeVore Street. The War had been over four or five years then, but nobody white or black seemed to know it. Odd clusters and strays of Negroes wandered the back roads and cowpaths from Schenectady to Jackson. Dazed but insistent, they searched each other out for word of a cousin, an aunt, a friend who once said, "Call on me. Anytime you get near Chicago, just call on me." Some of them were running from family that could not support them, some to family; some were running from dead crops, dead kin, life threats, and took-over land. Boys younger than Buglar and Howard; configurations and blends of families of women and children, while elsewhere, solitary, hunted and hunting for, were men, men, men. Forbidden public transportation, chased by debt and filthy "talking sheets," they followed secondary routes, scanned the horizon for signs and counted heavily on each other. Silent, except for social courtesies, when they met one another they neither described nor asked about the sorrow that drove them from one place to another. The whites didn't bear speaking on. Everybody knew.

So he did not press the young woman with the broken hat about where from or how come. If she wanted them to know and was strong enough to get through the telling, she would. What occupied them at the moment was what it might be that she needed. Underneath the major question, each harbored another. Paul D wondered at the newness of her shoes. Sethe was deeply touched by her sweet name; the remembrance of glittering headstone made her feel especially kindly toward her. Denver, however, was shaking. She looked at this sleepy beauty and wanted more.

Sethe hung her hat on a peg and turned graciously toward the girl. "That's a pretty name, Beloved. Take off your hat, why don't you, and I'll make us something. We just got back from the carnival over near Cincinnati. Everything in there is something to see."

Bolt upright in the chair, in the middle of Sethe's welcome, Beloved had fallen asleep again.

"Miss. Miss." Paul D shook her gently. "You want to lay down a spell?"

She opened her eyes to slits and stood up on her soft new feet which, barely capable of their job, slowly bore her to the keeping room. Once there, she collapsed on Baby Suggs' bed. Denver removed her hat and put the quilt with two squares of color over her feet. She was breathing like a steam engine.

"Sounds like croup," said Paul D, closing the door.

"Is she feverish? Denver, could you tell?"

"No. She's cold."

"Then she is. Fever goes from hot to cold."

"Could have the cholera," said Paul D.

"Reckon?"

"All that water. Sure sign."

"Poor thing. And nothing in this house to give her for it. She'll just have to ride it out. That's a hateful sickness if ever there was one."

"She's not sick!" said Denver, and the passion in her voice made them smile.

Four days she slept, waking and sitting up only for water. Denver tended her, watched her sound sleep, listened to her labored breathing and, out of love and a breakneck possessiveness that charged her, hid like a personal blemish Beloved's incontinence. She rinsed the sheets secretly, after Sethe went to the restaurant and Paul D went scrounging for barges to help unload. She boiled the underwear and soaked it in bluing, praying the fever would pass without damage. So intent was her nursing, she forgot to eat or visit the emerald closet.

"Beloved?" Denver would whisper. "Beloved?" and when the black eyes opened a slice all she could say was "I'm here. I'm still here."

Sometimes, when Beloved lay dreamy-eyed for a very long time, saying nothing, licking her lips and heaving deep sighs, Denver panicked. "What is it?" she would ask.

"Heavy," murmured Beloved. "This place is heavy."

"Would you like to sit up?"

"No," said the raspy voice.

It took three days for Beloved to notice the orange patches in the darkness of the quilt. Denver was pleased because it kept her patient awake longer. She seemed totally taken with those faded scraps of orange, even made the effort to lean on her elbow and stroke them. An effort that quickly exhausted her, so Denver rearranged the quilt so its cheeriest part was in the sick girl's sight line.

Patience, something Denver had never known, overtook her. As long as her mother did not interfere, she was a model of compassion, turning waspish, though, when Sethe tried to help.

"Did she take a spoonful of anything today?" Sethe inquired.

"She shouldn't eat with cholera."

"You sure that's it? Was just a hunch of Paul D's."

"I don't know, but she shouldn't eat anyway just yet."

"I think cholera people puke all the time."

"That's even more reason, ain't it?"

"Well she shouldn't starve to death either, Denver."

"Leave us alone, Ma'am. I'm taking care of her."

"She say anything?"

"I'd let you know if she did."

Sethe looked at her daughter and thought, Yes, she has been lonesome. Very lonesome.

"Wonder where Here Boy got off to?" Sethe thought a change of subject was needed.

"He won't be back," said Denver.

"How you know?"

"I just know." Denver took a square of sweet bread off the plate.

Back in the keeping room, Denver was about to sit down when Beloved's eyes flew wide open. Denver felt her heart race. It wasn't that she was looking at that face for the first time with no trace of sleep in it, or that the eyes were big and black. Nor was it that the whites of them were much too white—blue-white. It was that deep down in those big black eyes there was no expression at all.

"Can I get you something?"

Beloved looked at the sweet bread in Denver's hands and Denver held it out to her. She smiled then and Denver's heart stopped bouncing and sat down—relieved and easeful like a traveler who had made it home.

From that moment and through everything that followed, sugar could always be counted on to please her. It was as though sweet things were what she was born for. Honey as well as the wax it came in, sugar sandwiches, the sludgy molasses gone hard and brutal in the can, lemonade, taffy and any type of dessert Sethe brought home from the restaurant. She gnawed a cane stick to flax and kept the strings in her mouth long after the syrup had been sucked away. Denver laughed, Sethe smiled and Paul D said it made him sick to his stomach.

Sethe believed it was a recovering body's need—after an illness—for quick strength. But it was a need that went on and on into glowing health because Beloved didn't go anywhere. There didn't seem anyplace for her to go. She didn't mention one, or have much of an idea of what she was doing in that part of the country or where she had been. They believed the fever had caused her memory to fail just as it kept her slow-moving. A young woman, about nineteen or twenty, and slender, she moved like a heavier one or an older one, holding on to furniture, resting her head in the palm of her hand as though it was too heavy for a neck alone.

"You just gonna feed her? From now on?" Paul D, feeling ungenerous, and surprised by it, heard the irritability in his voice.

"Denver likes her. She's no real trouble. I thought we'd wait till her breath was better. She still sounds a little lumbar to me."

"Something funny 'bout that gal," Paul D said, mostly to himself.

"Funny how?"

"Acts sick, sounds sick, but she don't look sick. Good skin, bright eyes and strong as a bull."

"She's not strong. She can hardly walk without holding on to something."

"That's what I mean. Can't walk, but I seen her pick up the rocker with one hand."

"You didn't."

"Don't tell *me*. Ask Denver. She was right there with her."

"Denver! Come in here a minute."

Denver stopped rinsing the porch and stuck her head in the window.

"Paul D says you and him saw Beloved pick up the rocking chair single-handed. That so?"

Long, heavy lashes made Denver's eyes seem busier than they were; deceptive, even when she held a steady gaze as she did now on Paul D. "No," she said. "I didn't see no such thing."

Paul D frowned but said nothing. If there had been an open latch between them, it would have closed.

Rainwater held on to pine needles for dear life and Beloved could not take her eyes off Sethe. Stooping to shake the damper, or snapping sticks for kindlin, Sethe was licked, tasted, eaten by Beloved's eyes. Like a familiar, she hovered, never leaving the room Sethe was in unless required and told to. She rose early in the dark to be there, waiting, in the kitchen when Sethe came down to make fast bread before she left for work. In lamplight, and over the flames of the cooking stove, their two shadows clashed and crossed on the ceiling like black swords. She was in the window at two when Sethe returned, or the doorway; then the porch, its steps, the path, the road, till finally, surrendering to the habit, Beloved began inching down Bluestone Road further and further each day to meet Sethe and walk her back to 124. It was as though every afternoon she doubted anew the older woman's return.

Sethe was flattered by Beloved's open, quiet devotion. The same adoration from her daughter (had it been forthcoming) would have annoyed her; made her chill at the thought of having raised a ridiculously dependent child. But the company of this sweet, if peculiar, guest pleased her the way a zealot pleases his teacher.

Time came when lamps had to be lit early because night
arrived sooner and sooner. Sethe was leaving for work in the
dark; Paul D was walking home in it. On one such evening
dark and cool, Sethe cut a rutabaga into four pieces and left
them stewing. She gave Denver a half peck of peas to sort and
soak overnight. Then she sat herself down to rest. The heat
of the stove made her drowsy and she was sliding into sleep
when she felt Beloved touch her. A touch no heavier than a
feather but loaded, nevertheless, with desire. Sethe stirred and
looked around. First at Beloved's soft new hand on her shoulder,
then into her eyes. The longing she saw there was bottomless.
Some plea barely in control. Sethe patted Beloved's fingers and
glanced at Denver, whose eyes were fixed on her pea-sorting
task.

"Where your diamonds?" Beloved searched Sethe's face.

"Diamonds? What would I be doing with diamonds?"

"On your ears."

"Wish I did. I had some crystal once. A present from a lady
I worked for."

"Tell me," said Beloved, smiling a wide happy smile. "Tell
me your diamonds."

It became a way to feed her. Just as Denver discovered and
relied on the delightful effect sweet things had on Beloved,
Sethe learned the profound satisfaction Beloved got from storytelling. It amazed Sethe (as much as it pleased Beloved) because
every mention of her past life hurt. Everything in it was painful
or lost. She and Baby Suggs had agreed without saying so that
it was unspeakable; to Denver's inquiries Sethe gave short
replies or rambling incomplete reveries. Even with Paul D, who
had shared some of it and to whom she could talk with at least

a measure of calm, the hurt was always there—like a tender place in the corner of her mouth that the bit left.

But, as she began telling about the earrings, she found herself wanting to, liking it. Perhaps it was Beloved's distance from the events itself, or her thirst for hearing it—in any case it was an unexpected pleasure.

Above the patter of the pea sorting and the sharp odor of cooking rutabaga, Sethe explained the crystal that once hung from her ears.

"That lady I worked for in Kentucky gave them to me when I got married. What they called married back there and back then. I guess she saw how bad I felt when I found out there wasn't going to be no ceremony, no preacher. Nothing. I thought there should be something—something to say it was right and true. I didn't want it to be just me moving over a bit of pallet full of corn husks. Or just me bringing my night bucket into his cabin. I thought there should be some ceremony. Dancing maybe. A little sweet william in my hair." Sethe smiled. "I never saw a wedding, but I saw Mrs. Garner's wedding gown in the press, and heard her go on about what it was like. Two pounds of currants in the cake, she said, and four whole sheep. The people were still eating the next day. That's what I wanted. A meal maybe, where me and Halle and all the Sweet Home men sat down and ate something special. Invite some of the other coloredpeople from over by Covington or High Trees—those places Sixo used to sneak off to. But it wasn't going to be nothing. They said it was all right for us to be husband and wife and that was it. All of it.

"Well, I made up my mind to have at the least a dress that wasn't the sacking I worked in. So I took to stealing fabric, and wound up with a dress you wouldn't believe. The top was from two pillow cases in her mending basket. The front of the skirt was a dresser scarf a candle fell on and burnt a hole in, and one of her old sashes we used to test the flatiron on. Now the back was a problem for the longest time. Seem like I couldn't find a thing that wouldn't be missed right away. Because I had to take it apart afterwards and put all the pieces back where they were. Now Halle was patient, waiting for me to finish it. He knew I wouldn't go ahead without having it. Finally I took the mosquito netting from a nail out the barn. We used it to strain jelly through. I washed it and soaked it best I could and tacked it on for the back of the skirt. And there I was, in the worst-looking gown you could imagine. Only my wool shawl kept me from looking like a haint peddling. I wasn't but four-teen years old, so I reckon that's why I was so proud of myself.

"Anyhow, Mrs. Garner must have seen me in it. I thought I was stealing smart, and she knew everything I did. Even our honeymoon: going down to the cornfield with Halle. That's where we went first. A Saturday afternoon it was. He begged sick so he wouldn't have to go work in town that day. Usually he worked Saturdays and Sundays to pay off Baby Suggs' freedom. But he begged sick and I put on my dress and we walked into the corn holding hands. I can still smell the ears roasting yonder where the Pauls and Sixo was. Next day Mrs. Garner crooked her finger at me and took me upstairs to her bedroom. She opened up a wooden box and took out a pair of crystal earrings. She said, 'I want you to have these, Sethe.' I said, 'Yes, ma'am.' 'Are your ears pierced?' she said. I said, 'No, ma'am.' 'Well do it,' she said, 'so you can wear them. I want you to have them and I want you and Halle to be happy.' I thanked her but I never did put them on till I got away from there. One day after I walked into this here house Baby Suggs unknotted my underskirt and took em out. I sat right here by the stove with Denver in my arms and let her punch holes in my ears for to wear them."

"I never saw you in no earrings," said Denver. "Where are they now?"

"Gone," said Sethe. "Long gone," and she wouldn't say another word. Until the next time when all three of them ran through the wind back into the house with rainsoaked sheets and petticoats. Panting, laughing, they draped the laundry over the chairs and table. Beloved filled herself with water from the bucket and watched while Sethe rubbed Denver's hair with a piece of toweling.

"Maybe we should unbraid it?" asked Sethe.

"Uh uh. Tomorrow." Denver crouched forward at the thought of a fine-tooth comb pulling her hair.

"Today is always here," said Sethe. "Tomorrow, never."

"It hurts," Denver said.

"Comb it every day, it won't."

"Ouch."

"Your woman she never fix up your hair?" Beloved asked.

Sethe and Denver looked up at her. After four weeks they still had not got used to the gravelly voice and the song that seemed to lie in it. Just outside music it lay, with a cadence not like theirs.

"Your woman she never fix up your hair?" was clearly a question for Sethe, since that's who she was looking at.

"My woman? You mean my mother? If she did, I don't remember. I didn't see her but a few times out in the fields and once when she was working indigo. By the time I woke up in the morning, she was in line. If the moon was bright they worked by its light. Sunday she slept like a stick. She must of nursed me two or three weeks—that's the way the others did. Then she went back in rice and I sucked from another woman whose job it was. So to answer you, no. I reckon not. She never fixed my hair nor nothing. She didn't even sleep in the same cabin most nights I remember. Too far from the line-up, I guess. One thing she did do. She picked me up and carried me behind the smokehouse. Back there she opened up her dress front and lifted her breast and pointed under it. Right on her rib was a circle and a cross burnt right in the skin. She said, 'This is your ma'am. This,' and she pointed. 'I am the only one got this mark now. The rest dead. If something happens to me and you can't tell me by my face, you can know me by this mark.' Scared me so. All I could think of was how important this was and how I needed to have something important to say back, but I couldn't think of anything so I just said what I thought. 'Yes, Ma'am,' I said. 'But how will you know me? How will you know me? Mark me, too,' I said. 'Mark the mark on me too.'" Sethe chuckled.

"Did she?" asked Denver.

"She slapped my face."

"What for?"

"I didn't understand it then. Not till I had a mark of my own."

"What happened to her?"

"Hung. By the time they cut her down nobody could tell whether she had a circle and a cross or not, least of all me and I did look." Sethe gathered hair from the comb and leaning back tossed it into the fire. It exploded into stars and the smell infuriated them. "Oh, my Jesus," she said and stood up so suddenly the comb she had parked in Denver's hair fell to the floor.

"Ma'am? What's the matter with you, Ma'am?"

Sethe walked over to a chair, lifted a sheet and stretched it as wide as her arms would go. Then she folded, refolded and double-folded it. She took another. Neither was completely dry but the folding felt too fine to stop. She had to do something with her hands because she was remembering something she had forgotten she knew. Something privately shameful that had seeped into a slit in her mind right behind the slap on her face and the circled cross.

"Why they hang your ma'am?" Denver asked. This was the first time she had heard anything about her mother's mother. Baby Suggs was the only grandmother she knew.

"I never found out. It was a lot of them," she said, but what was getting clear and clearer as she folded and refolded damp laundry was the woman called Nan who took her hand and yanked her away from the pile before she could make out the mark. Nan was the one she knew best, who was around all day, who nursed babies, cooked, had one good arm and half of another. And who used different words. Words Sethe understood then but could neither recall nor repeat now. She believed that must be why she remembered so little before Sweet Home except singing and dancing and how crowded it was. What Nan told her she had forgotten, along with the language she told it in. The same language her ma'am spoke, and which would never come back. But the message—that was and had been there all along. Holding the damp white sheets against her chest, she was picking meaning out of a code she no longer understood. Nighttime. Nan holding her with her good arm, waving the stump of the other in the air. "Telling you. I am telling you, small girl Sethe," and she did that. She told Sethe that her mother and Nan were together from the sea. Both were taken up many times by the crew. "She threw them all away but you. The one from the crew she threw away on the island. The others from more whites she also threw away. Without names, she threw them. You she gave the name of the black man. She put her arms around him. The others she did not put her arms around. Never. Never. Telling you. I am telling you, small girl Sethe."

As small girl Sethe, she was unimpressed. As grown-up woman Sethe she was angry, but not certain at what. A mighty wish for Baby Suggs broke over her like surf. In the quiet following its splash, Sethe looked at the two girls sitting by the stove: her sickly, shallow-minded boarder, her irritable, lonely daughter. They seemed little and far away.

"Paul D be here in a minute," she said.

Denver sighed with relief. For a minute there, while her mother stood folding the wash lost in thought, she clamped her teeth and prayed it would stop. Denver hated the stories her mother told that did not concern herself, which is why Amy was all she ever asked about. The rest was a gleaming, powerful world made more so by Denver's absence from it. Not being in it, she hated it and wanted Beloved to hate it too, although there was no chance of that at all. Beloved took every opportunity to ask some funny question and get Sethe going. Denver noticed how greedy she was to hear Sethe talk. Now she noticed something more. The questions Beloved asked: "Where your diamonds?" "Your woman she never fix up your hair?" And most perplexing: Tell me your earrings.

How did she know?

Beloved was shining and Paul D didn't like it. Women did what strawberry plants did before they shot out their thin vines: the quality of the green changed. Then the vine threads came, then the buds. By the time the white petals died and the mint-colored berry poked out, the leaf shine was gilded tight and waxy. That's how Beloved looked—gilded and shining. Paul D took to having Sethe on waking, so that later, when he went down the white stairs where she made bread under Beloved's gaze, his head was clear.

In the evening when he came home and the three of them were all there fixing the supper table, her shine was so pronounced he wondered why Denver and Sethe didn't see it. Or maybe they did. Certainly women could tell, as men could, when one of their number was aroused. Paul D looked carefully at Beloved to see if she was aware of it but she paid him no attention at all—frequently not even answering a direct question put to her. She would look at him and not open her mouth. Five weeks she had been with them, and they didn't know any more about her than they did when they found her asleep on the stump.

They were seated at the table Paul D had broken the day he arrived at 124. Its mended legs stronger than before. The cabbage was all gone and the shiny ankle bones of smoked pork were pushed in a heap on their plates. Sethe was dishing up bread pudding, murmuring her hopes for it, apologizing in advance the way veteran cooks always do, when something in Beloved's face, some petlike adoration that took hold of her as she looked at Sethe, made Paul D speak.

"Ain't you got no brothers or sisters?"

Beloved diddled her spoon but did not look at him. "I don't have nobody."

"What was you looking for when you came here?" he asked her.

"This place. I was looking for this place I could be in."

"Somebody tell you about this house?"

"She told me. When I was at the bridge, she told me."

"Must be somebody from the old days," Sethe said. The days when 124 was a way station where messages came and then their senders. Where bits of news soaked like dried beans in spring water—until they were soft enough to digest.

"How'd you come? Who brought you?"

Now she looked steadily at him, but did not answer.

He could feel both Sethe and Denver pulling in, holding their stomach muscles, sending out sticky spiderwebs to touch one another. He decided to force it anyway.

"I asked you who brought you here?"

"I walked here," she said. "A long, long, long, long way. Nobody bring me. Nobody help me."

"You had new shoes. If you walked so long why don't your shoes show it?"

"Paul D, stop picking on her."

"I want to know," he said, holding the knife handle in his fist like a pole.

"I take the shoes! I take the dress! The shoe strings don't fix!" she shouted and gave him a look so malevolent Denver touched her arm.

"I'll teach you," said Denver, "how to tie your shoes," and got a smile from Beloved as a reward.

Paul D had the feeling a large, silver fish had slipped from his hands the minute he grabbed hold of its tail. That it was streaming back off into dark water now, gone but for the glistening marking its route. But if her shining was not for him, who then? He had never known a woman who lit up for nobody in particular, who just did it as a general announcement. Always, in his experience, the light appeared when there was focus. Like the Thirty-Mile Woman, dulled to smoke while he waited with her in the ditch, and starlight when Sixo got there. He never knew himself to mistake it. It was there the instant he looked at Sethe's wet legs, otherwise he never would have been bold enough to enclose her in his arms that day and whisper into her back.

This girl Beloved, homeless and without people, beat all, though he couldn't say exactly why, considering the colored-people he had run into during the last twenty years. During, before and after the War he had seen Negroes so stunned, or hungry, or tired or bereft it was a wonder they recalled or said anything. Who, like him, had hidden in caves and fought owls for food; who, like him, stole from pigs; who, like him, slept in trees in the day and walked by night; who, like him, had buried themselves in slop and jumped in wells to avoid regulators, raiders, paterollers, veterans, hill men, posses and merrymakers. Once he met a Negro about fourteen years old who lived by himself in the woods and said he couldn't remember living anywhere else. He saw a witless coloredwoman jailed and hanged for stealing ducks she believed were her own babies.

Move. Walk. Run. Hide. Steal and move on. Only once had it been possible for him to stay in one spot—with a woman, or a family—for longer than a few months. That once was almost two years with a weaver lady in Delaware, the meanest place for Negroes he had ever seen outside Pulaski County, Kentucky, and of course the prison camp in Georgia.

From all those Negroes, Beloved was different. Her shining, her new shoes. It bothered him. Maybe it was just the fact that he didn't bother her. Or it could be timing. She had appeared and been taken in on the very day Sethe and he had patched up their quarrel, gone out in public and had a right good time—like a family. Denver had come around, so to speak; Sethe was laughing; he had a promise of steady work, 124 was cleared up from spirits. It had begun to look like a life. And damn! a water-drinking woman fell sick, got took in, healed, and hadn't moved a peg since.

He wanted her out, but Sethe had let her in and he couldn't put her out of a house that wasn't his. It was one thing to beat up a ghost, quite another to throw a helpless coloredgirl out in territory infected by the Klan. Desperately thirsty for black blood, without which it could not live, the dragon swam the Ohio at will.

Sitting at table, chewing on his after-supper broom straw, Paul D decided to place her. Consult with the Negroes in town and find her her own place.

No sooner did he have the thought than Beloved strangled on one of the raisins she had picked out of the bread pudding. She fell backward and off the chair and thrashed around holding her throat. Sethe knocked her on the back while Denver pried her hands away from her neck. Beloved, on her hands and knees, vomited up her food and struggled for breath.

When she was quiet and Denver had wiped up the mess, she said, "Go to sleep now."

"Come in my room," said Denver. "I can watch out for you up there."

No moment could have been better. Denver had worried herself sick trying to think of a way to get Beloved to share her room. It was hard sleeping above her, wondering if she was going to be sick again, fall asleep and not wake, or (God, please don't) get up and wander out of the yard just the way she wandered in. They could have their talks easier there: at night when Sethe and Paul D were asleep; or in the daytime before either came home. Sweet, crazy conversations full of half sentences, daydreams and misunderstandings more thrilling than understanding could ever be.

When the girls left, Sethe began to clear the table. She stacked the plates near a basin of water.

"What is it about her vex you so?"

Paul D frowned, but said nothing.

"We had one good fight about Denver. Do we need one about her too?" asked Sethe.

"I just don't understand what the hold is. It's clear why she holds on to you, but I just can't see why you holding on to her."

Sethe turned away from the plates toward him. "What you care who's holding on to who? Feeding her is no trouble. I pick up a little extra from the restaurant is all. And she's nice girl company for Denver. You know that and I know you know it, so what is it got your teeth on edge?"

"I can't place it. It's a feeling in me."

"Well, feel this, why don't you? Feel how it feels to have a bed to sleep in and somebody there not worrying you to death about what you got to do each day to deserve it. Feel how that feels. And if that don't get it, feel how it feels to be a colored-woman roaming the roads with anything God made liable to jump on you. Feel that."

"I know every bit of that, Sethe. I wasn't born yesterday and I never mistreated a woman in my life."

"That makes one in the world," Sethe answered.

"Not two?"

"No. Not two."

"What Halle ever do to you? Halle stood by you. He never left you."

"What'd he leave then if not me?"

"I don't know, but it wasn't you. That's a fact."

"Then he did worse; he left his children."

"You don't know that."

"He wasn't there. He wasn't where he said he would be."

"He was there."

"Then why didn't he show himself? Why did I have to pack my babies off and stay behind to look for him?"

"He couldn't get out the loft."

"Loft? What loft?"

"The one over your head. In the barn."

Slowly, slowly, taking all the time allowed, Sethe moved toward the table.

"He saw?"

"He saw."

"He told you?"

"You told me."

"What?"

"The day I came in here. You said they stole your milk. I never knew what it was that messed him up. That was it, I guess. All I knew was that something broke him. Not a one of them years of Saturdays, Sundays and nighttime extra never touched him. But whatever he saw go on in that barn that day broke him like a twig."

"He saw?" Sethe was gripping her elbows as though to keep them from flying away.

"He saw. Must have."

"He saw them boys do that to me and let them keep on breathing air? He saw? He saw? He saw?"

"Hey! Hey! Listen up. Let me tell you something. A man ain't a goddamn ax. Chopping, hacking, busting every goddamn minute of the day. Things get to him. Things he can't chop down because they're inside."

Sethe was pacing up and down, up and down in the lamplight. "The underground agent said, By Sunday. They took my milk and he saw it and didn't come down? Sunday came and he didn't. Monday came and no Halle. I thought he was dead, that's why; then I thought they caught him, that's why. Then I thought, No, he's not dead because if he was I'd know it, and then you come here after all this time and you didn't say he was dead, because you didn't know either, so I thought, Well, he just found him another better way to live. Because if he was anywhere near here, he'd come to Baby Suggs, if not to me. But I never knew he saw."

"What does that matter now?"

"If he is alive, and saw that, he won't step foot in my door. Not Halle."

"It broke him, Sethe." Paul D looked up at her and sighed. "You may as well know it all. Last time I saw him he was sitting by the churn. He had butter all over his face."

Nothing happened, and she was grateful for that. Usually she could see the picture right away of what she heard. But she could not picture what Paul D said. Nothing came to mind. Carefully, carefully, she passed on to a reasonable question.

"What did he say?"

"Nothing."

"Not a word?"

"Not a word."

"Did you speak to him? Didn't you say anything to him? Something!"

"I couldn't, Sethe. I just ... couldn't."

"Why!"

"I had a bit in my mouth."

Sethe opened the front door and sat down on the porch steps. The day had gone blue without its sun, but she could still make out the black silhouettes of trees in the meadow beyond. She shook her head from side to side, resigned to her rebellious brain. Why was there nothing it refused? No misery, no regret, no hateful picture too rotten to accept? Like a greedy child it snatched up everything. Just once, could it say, No thank you? I just ate and can't hold another bite? I am full God damn it of two boys with mossy teeth, one sucking on my breast the other holding me down, their book-reading teacher watching and writing it up. I am still full of that, God damn it, I can't go back and add more. Add my husband to it, watching, above me in the loft—hiding close by—the one place he thought no one would look for him, looking down on what I couldn't look at at all. And not stopping them—looking and letting it happen. But my greedy brain says, Oh thanks, I'd love more—so I add more. And no sooner than I do, there is no stopping. There is also my husband squatting by the churn smearing the butter as well as its clabber all over his face because the milk they took is on his mind. And as far as he is concerned, the world may as well know it. And if he was that broken then, then he is also and certainly dead now. And if Paul D saw him and could not save or comfort him because the iron bit was in his mouth, then there is still more that Paul D could tell me and my brain would go right ahead and take it and never say, No thank you. I don't want to know or have to remember that. I have other things to do: worry, for example, about tomorrow, about Denver, about Beloved, about age and sickness not to speak of love.

But her brain was not interested in the future. Loaded with the past and hungry for more, it left her no room to imagine, let alone plan for, the next day. Exactly like that afternoon in the wild onions—when one more step was the most she could see of the future. Other people went crazy, why couldn't she? Other people's brains stopped, turned around and went on to something new, which is what must have happened to Halle. And how sweet that would have been: the two of them back by the milk shed, squatting by the churn, smashing cold, lumpy butter into their faces with not a care in the world. Feeling it slippery, sticky—rubbing it in their hair, watching it squeeze through their fingers. What a relief to stop it right there. Close. Shut. Squeeze the butter. But her three children were chewing sugar teat under a blanket on their way to Ohio and no butter play would change that.

Paul D stepped through the door and touched her shoulder. "I didn't plan on telling you that."

"I didn't plan on hearing it."

"I can't take it back, but I can leave it alone," Paul D said.

He wants to tell me, she thought. He wants me to ask him about what it was like for him—about how offended the tongue is, held down by iron, how the need to spit is so deep you cry for it. She already knew about it, had seen it time after time in the place before Sweet Home. Men, boys, little girls, women. The wildness that shot up into the eye the moment the lips were yanked back. Days after it was taken out, goose fat was rubbed on the corners of the mouth but nothing to soothe the tongue or take the wildness out of the eye.

Sethe looked up into Paul D's eyes to see if there was any trace left in them.

"People I saw as a child," she said, "who'd had the bit always looked wild after that. Whatever they used it on them for, it couldn't have worked, because it put a wildness where before there wasn't any. When I look at you, I don't see it. There ain't no wildness in your eye nowhere."

"There's a way to put it there and there's a way to take it out. I know em both and I haven't figured out yet which is worse." He sat down beside her. Sethe looked at him. In that unlit daylight his face, bronzed and reduced to its bones, smoothed her heart down.

"You want to tell me about it?" she asked him.

"I don't know. I never have talked about it. Not to a soul. Sang it sometimes, but I never told a soul."

"Go ahead. I can hear it."

"Maybe. Maybe you can hear it. I just ain't sure I can say it. Say it right, I mean, because it wasn't the bit—that wasn't it."

"What then?" Sethe asked.

"The roosters," he said. "Walking past the roosters looking at them look at me."

Sethe smiled. "In that pine?"

"Yeah." Paul D smiled with her. "Must have been five of them perched up there, and at least fifty hens."

"Mister, too?"

"Not right off. But I hadn't took twenty steps before I seen him. He come down off the fence post there and sat on the tub."

"He loved that tub," said Sethe, thinking, No, there is no stopping now.

"Didn't he? Like a throne. Was me took him out the shell, you know. He'd a died if it hadn't been for me. The hen had walked on off with all the hatched peeps trailing behind her. There was this one egg left. Looked like a blank, but then I saw it move so I tapped it open and here come Mister, bad feet and all. I watched that son a bitch grow up and whup everything in the yard."

"He always was hateful," Sethe said.

"Yeah, he was hateful all right. Bloody too, and evil. Crooked feet flapping. Comb as big as my hand and some kind of red. He sat right there on the tub looking at me. I swear he smiled.

My head was full of what I'd seen of Halle a while back. I wasn't even thinking about the bit. Just Halle and before him Sixo, but when I saw Mister I knew it was me too. Not just them, me too. One crazy, one sold, one missing, one burnt and me licking iron with my hands crossed behind me. The last of the Sweet Home men.

"Mister, he looked so ... free. Better than me. Stronger, tougher. Son a bitch couldn't even get out the shell by hisself but he was still king and I was ..." Paul D stopped and squeezed his left hand with his right. He held it that way long enough for it and the world to quiet down and let him go on.

"Mister was allowed to be and stay what he was. But I wasn't allowed to be and stay what I was. Even if you cooked him you'd be cooking a rooster named Mister. But wasn't no way I'd ever be Paul D again, living or dead. Schoolteacher changed me. I was something else and that something was less than a chicken sitting in the sun on a tub."

Sethe put her hand on his knee and rubbed.

Paul D had only begun, what he was telling her was only the beginning when her fingers on his knee, soft and reassuring, stopped him. Just as well. Just as well. Saying more might push them both to a place they couldn't get back from. He would keep the rest where it belonged: in that tobacco tin buried in his chest where a red heart used to be. Its lid rusted shut. He would not pry it loose now in front of this sweet sturdy woman, for if she got a whiff of the contents it would shame him. And it would hurt her to know that there was no red heart bright as Mister's comb beating in him.

Sethe rubbed and rubbed, pressing the work cloth and the stony curves that made up his knee. She hoped it calmed him

as it did her. Like kneading bread in the half-light of the
restaurant kitchen. Before the cook arrived when she stood in
a space no wider than a bench is long, back behind and to the
left of the milk cans. Working dough. Working, working dough.
Nothing better than that to start the day's serious work of
beating back the past.

Upstairs Beloved was dancing. A little two-step, two-step, make-a-new-step, slide, slide and strut on down.

Denver sat on the bed smiling and providing the music.

She had never seen Beloved this happy. She had seen her pouty lips open wide with the pleasure of sugar or some piece of news Denver gave her. She had felt warm satisfaction radiating from Beloved's skin when she listened to her mother talk about the old days. But gaiety she had never seen. Not ten minutes had passed since Beloved had fallen backward to the floor, pop-eyed, thrashing and holding her throat. Now, after a few seconds lying in Denver's bed, she was up and dancing.

"Where'd you learn to dance?" Denver asked her.

"Nowhere. Look at me do this." Beloved put her fists on her hips and commenced to skip on bare feet. Denver laughed.

"Now you. Come on," said Beloved. "You may as well just come on." Her black skirt swayed from side to side.

Denver grew ice-cold as she rose from the bed. She knew she was twice Beloved's size but she floated up, cold and light as a snowflake.

Beloved took Denver's hand and placed another on Denver's shoulder. They danced then. Round and round the tiny room and it may have been dizziness, or feeling light and icy at once, that made Denver laugh so hard. A catching laugh that Beloved caught. The two of them, merry as kittens, swung to and fro, to and fro, until exhausted they sat on the floor. Beloved let her head fall back on the edge of the bed while she found her breath and Denver saw the tip of the thing she always saw in its entirety when Beloved undressed to sleep. Looking straight at it she whispered, "Why you call yourself Beloved?"

Beloved closed her eyes. "In the dark my name is Beloved."

Denver scooted a little closer. "What's it like over there, where you were before? Can you tell me?"

"Dark," said Beloved. "I'm small in that place. I'm like this here." She raised her head off the bed, lay down on her side and curled up.

Denver covered her lips with her fingers. "Were you cold?"

Beloved curled tighter and shook her head. "Hot. Nothing to breathe down there and no room to move in."

"You see anybody?"

"Heaps. A lot of people is down there. Some is dead."

"You see Jesus? Baby Suggs?"

"I don't know. I don't know the names." She sat up.

"Tell me, how did you get here?"

"I wait; then I got on the bridge. I stay there in the dark, in the daytime, in the dark, in the daytime. It was a long time."

"All this time you were on a bridge?"

"No. After. When I got out."

"What did you come back for?"

Beloved smiled. "To see her face."

"Ma'am's? Sethe?"

"Yes, Sethe."

Denver felt a little hurt, slighted that she was not the main reason for Beloved's return. "Don't you remember we played together by the stream?"

"I was on the bridge," said Beloved. "You see me on the bridge?"

"No, by the stream. The water back in the woods."

"Oh, I was in the water. I saw her diamonds down there. I could touch them."

"What stopped you?"

"She left me behind. By myself," said Beloved. She lifted her eyes to meet Denver's and frowned, perhaps. Perhaps not. The tiny scratches on her forehead may have made it seem so.

Denver swallowed. "Don't," she said. "Don't. You won't leave us, will you?"

"No. Never. This is where I am."

Suddenly Denver, who was sitting cross-legged, lurched forward and grabbed Beloved's wrist. "Don't tell her. Don't let Ma'am know who you are. Please, you hear?"

"Don't tell me what to do. Don't you never never tell me what to do."

"But I'm on your side, Beloved."

"She is the one. She is the one I need. You can go but she is the one I have to have." Her eyes stretched to the limit, black as the all-night sky.

"I didn't do anything to you. I never hurt you. I never hurt anybody," said Denver.

"Me either. Me either."

"What you gonna do?"

"Stay here. I belong here."

"I belong here too."

"Then stay, but don't never tell me what to do. Don't never do that."

"We were dancing. Just a minute ago we were dancing together. Let's."

"I don't want to." Beloved got up and lay down on the bed. Their quietness boomed about on the walls like birds in panic. Finally Denver's breath steadied against the threat of an unbearable loss.

"Tell me," Beloved said. "Tell me how Sethe made you in the boat."

"She never told me all of it," said Denver.

"Tell me."

Denver climbed up on the bed and folded her arms under her apron. She had not been in the tree room once since Beloved sat on their stump after the carnival, and had not remembered that she hadn't gone there until this very desperate moment. Nothing was out there that this sister-girl did not provide in abundance: a racing heart, dreaminess, society, danger, beauty. She swallowed twice to prepare for the telling, to construct out of the strings she had heard all her life a net to hold Beloved.

"She had good hands, she said. The whitegirl, she said, had thin little arms but good hands. She saw that right away, she said. Hair enough for five heads and good hands, she said. I guess the hands made her think she could do it: get us both across the river. But the mouth was what kept her from being scared. She said there ain't nothing to go by with whitepeople. You don't know how they'll jump. Say one thing, do another.

But if you looked at the mouth sometimes you could tell by that. She said this girl talked a storm, but there wasn't no meanness around her mouth. She took Ma'am to that lean-to and rubbed her feet for her, so that was one thing. And Ma'am believed she wasn't going to turn her over. You could get money if you turned a runaway over, and she wasn't sure this girl Amy didn't need money more than anything, especially since all she talked about was getting hold of some velvet."

"What's velvet?"

"It's a cloth, kind of deep and soft."

"Go ahead."

"Anyway, she rubbed Ma'am's feet back to life, and she cried, she said, from how it hurt. But it made her think she could make it on over to where Grandma Baby Suggs was and ..."

"Who is that?"

"I just said it. My grandmother."

"Is that Sethe's mother?"

"No. My father's mother."

"Go ahead."

"That's where the others was. My brothers and ... the baby girl. She sent them on before to wait for her at Grandma Baby's. So she had to put up with everything to get there. And this here girl Amy helped."

Denver stopped and sighed. This was the part of the story she loved. She was coming to it now, and she loved it because it was all about herself; but she hated it too because it made her feel like a bill was owing somewhere and she, Denver, had to pay it. But who she owed or what to pay it with eluded her. Now, watching Beloved's alert and hungry face, how she took in every word, asking questions about the color of things and their size, her downright craving to know, Denver began to see what she was saying and not just to hear it: there is this nineteen-year-old slavegirl—a year older than herself—walking through the dark woods to get to her children who are far away. She is tired, scared maybe, and maybe even lost. Most of all she is by herself and inside her is another baby she has to think about too. Behind her dogs, perhaps; guns probably; and certainly mossy teeth. She is not so afraid at night because she is the color of it, but in the day every sound is a shot or a tracker's quiet step.

Denver was seeing it now and feeling it—through Beloved. Feeling how it must have felt to her mother. Seeing how it must have looked. And the more fine points she made, the more detail she provided, the more Beloved liked it. So she anticipated the questions by giving blood to the scraps her mother and grandmother had told her—and a heartbeat. The monologue became, in fact, a duet as they lay down together, Denver nursing Beloved's interest like a lover whose pleasure was to overfeed the loved. The dark quilt with two orange patches was there with them because Beloved wanted it near her when she slept. It was smelling like grass and feeling like hands—the unrested hands of busy women: dry, warm, prickly. Denver spoke, Beloved listened, and the two did the best they could to create what really happened, how it really was, something only Sethe knew because she alone had the mind for it and the time afterward to shape it: the quality of Amy's voice, her breath like burning wood. The quick-change weather up in those hills—cool at night, hot in the day, sudden fog. How recklessly she behaved with this whitegirl—a recklessness born

of desperation and encouraged by Amy's fugitive eyes and her
tenderhearted mouth.

"You ain't got no business walking round these hills, miss."

"Looka here who's talking. I got more business here 'n you
got. They catch you they cut your head off. Ain't nobody after
me but I know somebody after you." Amy pressed her fingers
into the soles of the slavewoman's feet. "Whose baby that?"

Sethe did not answer.

"You don't even know. Come here, Jesus." Amy sighed and
shook her head. "Hurt?"

"A touch."

"Good for you. More it hurt more better it is. Can't nothing
heal without pain, you know. What you wiggling for?"

Sethe raised up on her elbows. Lying on her back so long
had raised a ruckus between her shoulder blades. The fire in
her feet and the fire on her back made her sweat.

"My back hurt me," she said.

"Your back? Gal, you a mess. Turn over here and let me
see."

In an effort so great it made her sick to her stomach, Sethe
turned onto her right side. Amy unfastened the back of her
dress and said, "Come here, Jesus," when she saw. Sethe guessed
it must be bad because after that call to Jesus Amy didn't speak
for a while. In the silence of an Amy struck dumb for a change,
Sethe felt the fingers of those good hands lightly touch her
back. She could hear her breathing but still the whitegirl said
nothing. Sethe could not move. She couldn't lie on her stomach
or her back, and to keep on her side meant pressure on her
screaming feet. Amy spoke at last in her dreamwalker's voice.

"It's a tree, Lu. A chokecherry tree. See, here's the trunk—
it's red and split wide open, full of sap, and this here's the
parting for the branches. You got a mighty lot of branches.
Leaves, too, look like, and dern if these ain't blossoms. Tiny
little cherry blossoms, just as white. Your back got a whole
tree on it. In bloom. What God have in mind, I wonder. I had
me some whippings, but I don't remember nothing like this.
Mr. Buddy had a right evil hand too. Whip you for looking at
him straight. Sure would. I looked right at him one time and
he hauled off and threw the poker at me. Guess he knew what
I was a-thinking."

Sethe groaned and Amy cut her reverie short—long enough
to shift Sethe's feet so the weight, resting on leaf-covered stones,
was above the ankles.

"That better? Lord what a way to die. You gonna die in
here, you know. Ain't no way out of it. Thank your Maker I
come along so's you wouldn't have to die outside in them
weeds. Snake come along he bite you. Bear eat you up. Maybe
you should of stayed where you was, Lu. I can see by your
back why you didn't ha ha. Whoever planted that tree beat
Mr. Buddy by a mile. Glad I ain't you. Well, spiderwebs is
'bout all I can do for you. What's in here ain't enough. I'll
look outside. Could use moss, but sometimes bugs and things
is in it. Maybe I ought to break them blossoms open. Get
that pus to running, you think? Wonder what God had in
mind. You must of did something. Don't run off nowhere
now."

Sethe could hear her humming away in the bushes as she
hunted spiderwebs. A humming she concentrated on because
as soon as Amy ducked out the baby began to stretch. Good

question, she was thinking. What did He have in mind? Amy
had left the back of Sethe's dress open and now a tail of wind
hit it, taking the pain down a step. A relief that let her feel
the lesser pain of her sore tongue. Amy returned with two
palmfuls of web, which she cleaned of prey and then draped
on Sethe's back, saying it was like stringing a tree for
Christmas.

"We got a old nigger girl come by our place. She don't know
nothing. Sews stuff for Mrs. Buddy—real fine lace but can't
barely stick two words together. She don't know nothing, just
like you. You don't know a thing. End up dead, that's what.
Not me. I'm a get to Boston and get myself some velvet.
Carmine. You don't even know about that, do you? Now you
never will. Bet you never even sleep with the sun in your face.
I did it a couple of times. Most times I'm feeding stock before
light and don't get to sleep till way after dark comes. But I
was in the back of the wagon once and fell asleep. Sleeping
with the sun in your face is the best old feeling. Two times I
did it. Once when I was little. Didn't nobody bother me then.
Next time, in back of the wagon, it happened again and doggone
if the chickens didn't get loose. Mr. Buddy whipped my tail.
Kentucky ain't no good place to be in. Boston's the place to be
in. That's where my mother was before she was give to Mr.
Buddy. Joe Nathan said Mr. Buddy is my daddy but I don't
believe that, you?"

Sethe told her she didn't believe Mr. Buddy was her daddy.

"You know your daddy, do you?"

"No," said Sethe.

"Neither me. All I know is it ain't him." She stood up then,
having finished her repair work, and weaving about the

lean-to, her slow-moving eyes pale in the sun that lit her hair, she sang:

> *"When the busy day is done*
> *And my weary little one*
> *Rocketh gently to and fro;*
> *When the night winds softly blow,*
> *And the crickets in the glen*
> *Chirp and chirp and chirp again;*
> *Where 'pon the haunted green*
> *Fairies dance around their queen,*
> *Then from yonder misty skies*
> *Cometh Lady Button Eyes."*

Suddenly she stopped weaving and rocking and sat down, her skinny arms wrapped around her knees, her good good hands cupping her elbows. Her slow-moving eyes stopped and peered into the dirt at her feet. "That's my mama's song. She taught me it."

> *"Through the muck and mist and gloam*
> *To our quiet cozy home,*
> *Where to singing sweet and low*
> *Rocks a cradle to and fro.*
> *Where the clock's dull monotone*
> *Telleth of the day that's done,*
> *Where the moonbeams hover o'er*
> *Playthings sleeping on the floor,*
> *Where my weary wee one lies*
> *Cometh Lady Button Eyes.*

"Layeth she her hands upon
My dear weary little one,
And those white hands overspread
Like a veil the curly head,
Seem to fondle and caress
Every little silken tress.
Then she smooths the eyelids down
Over those two eyes of brown
In such soothing tender wise
Cometh Lady Button Eyes."

Amy sat quietly after her song, then repeated the last line before she stood, left the lean-to and walked off a little ways to lean against a young ash. When she came back the sun was in the valley below and they were way above it in blue Kentucky light.

"You ain't dead yet, Lu? Lu?"

"Not yet."

"Make you a bet. You make it through the night, you make it all the way." Amy rearranged the leaves for comfort and knelt down to massage the swollen feet again. "Give these one more real good rub," she said, and when Sethe sucked air through her teeth, she said, "Shut up. You got to keep your mouth shut."

Careful of her tongue, Sethe bit down on her lips and let the good hands go to work to the tune of "So bees, sing soft and bees, sing low." Afterward, Amy moved to the other side of the lean-to where, seated, she lowered her head toward her shoulder and braided her hair, saying, "Don't up and die on me in the night, you hear? I don't want to see your ugly black face

hankering over me. If you do die, just go on off somewhere
where I can't see you, hear?"

"I hear," said Sethe. "I'll do what I can, miss."

Sethe never expected to see another thing in this world, so
when she felt toes prodding her hip it took a while to come
out of a sleep she thought was death. She sat up, stiff and
shivery, while Amy looked in on her juicy back.

"Looks like the devil," said Amy. "But you made it through.
Come down here, Jesus, Lu made it through. That's because of
me. I'm good at sick things. Can you walk, you think?"

"I have to let my water some kind of way."

"Let's see you walk on em."

It was not good, but it was possible, so Sethe limped, holding
on first to Amy, then to a sapling.

"Was me did it. I'm good at sick things ain't I?"

"Yeah," said Sethe, "you good."

"We got to get off this here hill. Come on. I'll take you
down to the river. That ought to suit you. Me, I'm going to
the Pike. Take me straight to Boston. What's that all over
your dress?"

"Milk."

"You one mess."

Sethe looked down at her stomach and touched it. The baby
was dead. She had not died in the night, but the baby had. If
that was the case, then there was no stopping now. She would
get that milk to her baby girl if she had to swim.

"Ain't you hungry?" Amy asked her.

"I ain't nothing but in a hurry, miss."

"Whoa. Slow down. Want some shoes?"

"Say what?"

"I figured how," said Amy and so she had. She tore two pieces from Sethe's shawl, filled them with leaves and tied them over her feet, chattering all the while.

"How old are you, Lu? I been bleeding for four years but I ain't having nobody's baby. Won't catch me sweating milk cause ..."

"I know," said Sethe. "You going to Boston."

At noon they saw it; then they were near enough to hear it. By late afternoon they could drink from it if they wanted to. Four stars were visible by the time they found, not a riverboat to stow Sethe away on, or a ferryman willing to take on a fugitive passenger—nothing like that—but a whole boat to steal. It had one oar, lots of holes and two bird nests.

"There you go, Lu. Jesus looking at you."

Sethe was looking at one mile of dark water, which would have to be split with one oar in a useless boat against a current dedicated to the Mississippi hundreds of miles away. It looked like home to her, and the baby (not dead in the least) must have thought so too. As soon as Sethe got close to the river her own water broke loose to join it. The break, followed by the redundant announcement of labor, arched her back.

"What you doing that for?" asked Amy. "Ain't you got a brain in your head? Stop that right now. I said stop it, Lu. You the dumbest thing on this here earth. Lu! Lu!"

Sethe couldn't think of anywhere to go but in. She waited for the sweet beat that followed the blast of pain. On her knees again, she crawled into the boat. It waddled under her and she had just enough time to brace her leaf-bag feet on the bench when another rip took her breath away. Panting under four summer stars, she threw her legs over the sides, because here come the head, as Amy informed her as though she did not know it—as though the rip was a breakup of walnut logs in the brace, or of lightning's jagged tear through a leather sky.

It was stuck. Face up and drowning in its mother's blood. Amy stopped begging Jesus and began to curse His daddy.

"Push!" screamed Amy.

"Pull," whispered Sethe.

And the strong hands went to work a fourth time, none too soon, for river water, seeping through any hole it chose, was spreading over Sethe's hips. She reached one arm back and grabbed the rope while Amy fairly clawed at the head. When a foot rose from the river bed and kicked the bottom of the boat and Sethe's behind, she knew it was done and permitted herself a short faint. Coming to, she heard no cries, just Amy's encouraging coos. Nothing happened for so long they both believed they had lost it. Sethe arched suddenly and the afterbirth shot out. Then the baby whimpered and Sethe looked. Twenty inches of cord hung from its belly and it trembled in the cooling evening air. Amy wrapped her skirt around it and the wet sticky women clambered ashore to see what, indeed, God had in mind.

Spores of bluefern growing in the hollows along the riverbank float toward the water in silver-blue lines hard to see unless you are in or near them, lying right at the river's edge when the sunshots are low and drained. Often they are mistook for insects—but they are seeds in which the whole generation sleeps confident of a future. And for a moment it is easy to believe each one has one—will become all of what is contained in the spore: will live out its days as planned. This moment of certainty lasts no longer than that; longer, perhaps, than the spore itself.

On a riverbank in the cool of a summer evening two women struggled under a shower of silvery blue. They never expected to see each other again in this world and at the moment couldn't care less. But there on a summer night surrounded by bluefern they did something together appropriately and well. A pateroller passing would have sniggered to see two throw-away people, two lawless outlaws—a slave and a barefoot whitewoman with unpinned hair—wrapping a ten-minute-old baby in the rags they wore. But no pateroller came and no preacher. The water sucked and swallowed itself beneath them. There was nothing to disturb them at their work. So they did it appropriately and well.

Twilight came on and Amy said she had to go; that she wouldn't be caught dead in daylight on a busy river with a runaway. After rinsing her hands and face in the river, she stood and looked down at the baby wrapped and tied to Sethe's chest.

"She's never gonna know who I am. You gonna tell her? Who brought her into this here world?" She lifted her chin, looked off into the place where the sun used to be. "You better tell her. You hear? Say Miss Amy Denver. Of Boston."

Sethe felt herself falling into a sleep she knew would be deep. On the lip of it, just before going under, she thought, "That's pretty. Denver. Real pretty."

It was time to lay it all down. Before Paul D came and sat on her porch steps, words whispered in the keeping room had kept her going. Helped her endure the chastising ghost; refurbished the baby faces of Howard and Buglar and kept them whole in the world because in her dreams she saw only their parts in trees; and kept her husband shadowy but *there*—somewhere. Now Halle's face between the butter press and the churn swelled larger and larger, crowding her eyes and making her head hurt. She wished for Baby Suggs' fingers molding her nape, reshaping it, saying, "Lay em down, Sethe. Sword and shield. Down. Down. Both of em down. Down by the riverside. Sword and shield. Don't study war no more. Lay all that mess down. Sword and shield." And under the pressing fingers and the quiet instructive voice, she would. Her heavy knives of defense against misery, regret, gall and hurt, she placed one by one on a bank where clear water rushed on below.

Nine years without the fingers or the voice of Baby Suggs was too much. And words whispered in the keeping room were too little. The butter-smeared face of a man God made none sweeter than demanded more: an arch built or a robe sewn.

Some fixing ceremony. Sethe decided to go to the Clearing, back where Baby Suggs had danced in sunlight.

Before 124 and everybody in it had closed down, veiled over and shut away; before it had become the plaything of spirits and the home of the chafed, 124 had been a cheerful, buzzing house where Baby Suggs, holy, loved, cautioned, fed, chastised and soothed. Where not one but two pots simmered on the stove; where the lamp burned all night long. Strangers rested there while children tried on their shoes. Messages were left there, for whoever needed them was sure to stop in one day soon. Talk was low and to the point—for Baby Suggs, holy, didn't approve of extra. "Everything depends on knowing how much," she said, and "Good is knowing when to stop."

It was in front of *that* 124 that Sethe climbed off a wagon, her newborn tied to her chest, and felt for the first time the wide arms of her mother-in-law, who had made it to Cincinnati. Who decided that, because slave life had "busted her legs, back, head, eyes, hands, kidneys, womb and tongue," she had nothing left to make a living with but her heart—which she put to work at once. Accepting no title of honor before her name, but allowing a small caress after it, she became an unchurched preacher, one who visited pulpits and opened her great heart to those who could use it. In winter and fall she carried it to AME's and Baptists, Holinesses and Sanctifieds, the Church of the Redeemer and the Redeemed. Uncalled, unrobed, unanointed, she let her great heart beat in their presence. When warm weather came, Baby Suggs, holy, followed by every black man, woman and child who could make it through, took her great heart to the Clearing—a wide-open place cut deep in the woods nobody knew for what at the end of a path known only to deer and whoever cleared the land in the first place. In the heat of every Saturday afternoon, she sat in the Clearing while the people waited among the trees.

After situating herself on a huge flat-sided rock, Baby Suggs bowed her head and prayed silently. The company watched her from the trees. They knew she was ready when she put her stick down. Then she shouted, "Let the children come!" and they ran from the trees toward her.

"Let your mothers hear you laugh," she told them, and the woods rang. The adults looked on and could not help smiling.

Then "Let the grown men come," she shouted. They stepped out one by one from among the ringing trees.

"Let your wives and your children see you dance," she told them, and groundlife shuddered under their feet.

Finally she called the women to her. "Cry," she told them. "For the living and the dead. Just cry." And without covering their eyes the women let loose.

It started that way: laughing children, dancing men, crying women and then it got mixed up. Women stopped crying and danced; men sat down and cried; children danced, women laughed, children cried until, exhausted and riven, all and each lay about the Clearing damp and gasping for breath. In the silence that followed, Baby Suggs, holy, offered up to them her great big heart.

She did not tell them to clean up their lives or to go and sin no more. She did not tell them they were the blessed of the earth, its inheriting meek or its glorybound pure.

She told them that the only grace they could have was the grace they could imagine. That if they could not see it, they would not have it.

"Here," she said, "in this here place, we flesh; flesh that weeps, laughs; flesh that dances on bare feet in grass. Love it. Love it hard. Yonder they do not love your flesh. They despise it. They don't love your eyes; they'd just as soon pick em out. No more do they love the skin on your back. Yonder they flay it. And O my people they do not love your hands. Those they only use, tie, bind, chop off and leave empty. Love your hands! Love them. Raise them up and kiss them. Touch others with them, pat them together, stroke them on your face 'cause they don't love that either. *You* got to love it, *you!* And no, they ain't in love with your mouth. Yonder, out there, they will see it broken and break it again. What you say out of it they will not heed. What you scream from it they do not hear. What you put into it to nourish your body they will snatch away and give you leavins instead. No, they don't love your mouth. *You* got to love it. This is flesh I'm talking about here. Flesh that needs to be loved. Feet that need to rest and to dance; backs that need support; shoulders that need arms, strong arms I'm telling you. And O my people, out yonder, hear me, they do not love your neck unnoosed and straight. So love your neck; put a hand on it, grace it, stroke it and hold it up. And all your inside parts that they'd just as soon slop for hogs, you got to love them. The dark, dark liver—love it, love it, and the beat and beating heart, love that too. More than eyes or feet. More than lungs that have yet to draw free air. More than your life-holding womb and your life-giving private parts, hear me now, love your heart. For this is the prize." Saying no more, she stood up then and danced with her twisted hip the rest of what her heart had to say while the others opened their mouths and gave her the music. Long notes held until the four-part harmony was perfect enough for their deeply loved flesh.

Sethe wanted to be there now. At the least to listen to the spaces that the long-ago singing had left behind. At the most to get a clue from her husband's dead mother as to what she should do with her sword and shield now, dear Jesus, now nine years after Baby Suggs, holy, proved herself a liar, dismissed her great heart and lay in the keeping-room bed roused once in a while by a craving for color and not for another thing.

"Those white things have taken all I had or dreamed," she said, "and broke my heartstrings too. There is no bad luck in the world but whitefolks." 124 shut down and put up with the venom of its ghost. No more lamp all night long, or neighbors dropping by. No low conversations after supper. No watched barefoot children playing in the shoes of strangers. Baby Suggs, holy, believed she had lied. There was no grace—imaginary or real—and no sunlit dance in a Clearing could change that. Her faith, her love, her imagination and her great big old heart began to collapse twenty-eight days after her daughter-in-law arrived.

Yet it was to the Clearing that Sethe determined to go—to pay tribute to Halle. Before the light changed, while it was still the green blessed place she remembered: misty with plant steam and the decay of berries.

She put on a shawl and told Denver and Beloved to do likewise. All three set out late one Sunday morning, Sethe leading, the girls trotting behind, not a soul in sight.

When they reached the woods it took her no time to find the path through it because big-city revivals were held there regularly now, complete with food-laden tables, banjos and a tent. The old path was a track now, but still arched over with trees dropping buckeyes onto the grass below.

There was nothing to be done other than what she had done, but Sethe blamed herself for Baby Suggs' collapse. However many times Baby denied it, Sethe knew the grief at 124 started when she jumped down off the wagon, her newborn tied to her chest in the underwear of a whitegirl looking for Boston.

Followed by the two girls, down a bright green corridor of oak and horse chestnut, Sethe began to sweat a sweat just like the other one when she woke, mud-caked, on the banks of the Ohio.

Amy was gone. Sethe was alone and weak, but alive, and so was her baby. She walked a ways downriver and then stood gazing at the glimmering water. By and by a flatbed slid into view, but she could not see if the figures on it were whitepeople or not. She began to sweat from a fever she thanked God for since it would certainly keep her baby warm. When the flatbed was beyond her sight she stumbled on and found herself near three coloredpeople fishing—two boys and an older man. She stopped and waited to be spoken to. One of the boys pointed and the man looked over his shoulder at her—a quick look since all he needed to know about her he could see in no time.

No one said anything for a while. Then the man said, "Headin' 'cross?"

"Yes, sir," said Sethe.

"Anybody know you coming?"

"Yes, sir."

He looked at her again and nodded toward a rock that stuck out of the ground above him like a bottom lip. Sethe walked to it and sat down. The stone had eaten the sun's rays but was nowhere near as hot as she was. Too tired to move, she stayed there, the sun in her eyes making her dizzy. Sweat poured over her and bathed the baby completely. She must have slept sitting up, because when next she opened her eyes the man was standing in front of her with a smoking-hot piece of fried eel in his hands. It was an effort to reach for, more to smell, impossible to eat. She begged him for water and he gave her some of the Ohio in a jar. Sethe drank it all and begged more. The clanging was back in her head but she refused to believe that she had come all that way, endured all she had, to die on the wrong side of the river.

The man watched her streaming face and called one of the boys over.

"Take off that coat," he told him.

"Sir?"

"You heard me."

The boy slipped out of his jacket, whining, "What you gonna do? What I'm gonna wear?"

The man untied the baby from her chest and wrapped it in the boy's coat, knotting the sleeves in front.

"What I'm gonna wear?"

The old man sighed and, after a pause, said, "You want it back, then go head and take it off that baby. Put the baby naked in the grass and put your coat back on. And if you can do it, then go on 'way somewhere and don't come back."

The boy dropped his eyes, then turned to join the other. With eel in her hand, the baby at her feet, Sethe dozed, dry-mouthed and sweaty. Evening came and the man touched her shoulder.

Contrary to what she expected they poled upriver, far away from the rowboat Amy had found. Just when she thought he was taking her back to Kentucky, he turned the flatbed and crossed the Ohio like a shot. There he helped her up the steep bank, while the boy without a jacket carried the baby who wore it. The man led her to a brush-covered hutch with a beaten floor.

"Wait here. Somebody be here directly. Don't move. They'll find you."

"Thank you," she said. "I wish I knew your name so I could remember you right."

"Name's Stamp," he said. "Stamp Paid. Watch out for that there baby, you hear?"

"I hear. I hear," she said, but she didn't. Hours later a woman was right up on her before she heard a thing. A short woman, young, with a croaker sack, greeted her.

"Saw the sign a while ago," she said. "But I couldn't get here no quicker."

"What sign?" asked Sethe.

"Stamp leaves the old sty open when there's a crossing. Knots a white rag on the post if it's a child too."

She knelt and emptied the sack. "My name's Ella," she said, taking a wool blanket, cotton cloth, two baked sweet potatoes and a pair of men's shoes from the sack. "My husband, John, is out yonder a ways. Where you heading?"

Sethe told her about Baby Suggs where she had sent her three children.

Ella wrapped a cloth strip tight around the baby's navel as she listened for the holes—the things the fugitives did not say; the questions they did not ask. Listened too for the unnamed, unmentioned people left behind. She shook gravel from the men's shoes and tried to force Sethe's feet into them. They would not go. Sadly, they split them down the heel, sorry indeed to ruin so valuable an item. Sethe put on the boy's jacket, not daring to ask whether there was any word of the children.

"They made it," said Ella. "Stamp ferried some of that party. Left them on Bluestone. It ain't too far."

Sethe couldn't think of anything to do, so grateful was she, so she peeled a potato, ate it, spit it up and ate more in quiet celebration.

"They be glad to see you," said Ella. "When was this one born?"

"Yesterday," said Sethe, wiping sweat from under her chin. "I hope she makes it."

Ella looked at the tiny, dirty face poking out of the wool blanket and shook her head. "Hard to say," she said. "If anybody was to ask me I'd say, 'Don't love nothing.'" Then, as if to take the edge off her pronouncement, she smiled at Sethe. "You had that baby by yourself?"

"No. Whitegirl helped."

"Then we better make tracks."

Baby Suggs kissed her on the mouth and refused to let her see the children. They were asleep she said and Sethe was too ugly-looking to wake them in the night. She took the newborn and handed it to a young woman in a bonnet, telling her not to clean the eyes till she got the mother's urine.

"Has it cried out yet?" asked Baby.

"A little."

"Time enough. Let's get the mother well."

She led Sethe to the keeping room and, by the light of a spirit lamp, bathed her in sections, starting with her face. Then, while waiting for another pan of heated water, she sat next to her and stitched gray cotton. Sethe dozed and woke to the washing of her hands and arms. After each bathing, Baby covered her with a quilt and put another pan on in the kitchen. Tearing sheets, stitching the gray cotton, she supervised the woman in the bonnet who tended the baby and cried into her cooking. When Sethe's legs were done, Baby looked at her feet and wiped them lightly. She cleaned between Sethe's legs with two separate pans of hot water and then tied her stomach and vagina with sheets. Finally she attacked the unrecognizable feet.

"You feel this?"

"Feel what?" asked Sethe.

"Nothing. Heave up." She helped Sethe to a rocker and lowered her feet into a bucket of salt water and juniper. The rest of the night Sethe sat soaking. The crust from her nipples Baby softened with lard and then washed away. By dawn the silent baby woke and took her mother's milk.

"Pray God it ain't turned bad," said Baby. "And when you through, call me." As she turned to go, Baby Suggs caught a glimpse of something dark on the bed sheet. She frowned and looked at her daughter-in-law bending toward the baby. Roses of blood blossomed in the blanket covering Sethe's shoulders. Baby Suggs hid her mouth with her hand. When the nursing was over and the newborn was asleep—its eyes half open, its tongue dream-sucking—wordlessly the older woman greased the flowering back and pinned a double thickness of cloth to the inside of the newly stitched dress.

It was not real yet. Not yet. But when her sleepy boys and crawling-already? girl were brought in, it didn't matter whether it was real or not. Sethe lay in bed under, around, over, among but especially with them all. The little girl dribbled clear spit into her face, and Sethe's laugh of delight was so loud the crawling-already? baby blinked. Buglar and Howard played with her ugly feet, after daring each other to be the first to touch them. She kept kissing them. She kissed the backs of their necks, the tops of their heads and the centers of their palms, and it was the boys who decided enough was enough when she lifted their shirts to kiss their tight round bellies. She stopped when and because they said, "Pappie come?"

She didn't cry. She said "soon" and smiled so they would think the brightness in her eyes was love alone. It was some time before she let Baby Suggs shoo the boys away so Sethe could put on the gray cotton dress her mother-in-law had started stitching together the night before. Finally she lay back and cradled the crawling-already? girl in her arms. She enclosed her left nipple with two fingers of her right hand and the child opened her mouth. They hit home together.

Baby Suggs came in and laughed at them, telling Sethe how strong the baby girl was, how smart, already crawling. Then she stooped to gather up the ball of rags that had been Sethe's clothes.

"Nothing worth saving in here," she said.

Sethe lifted her eyes. "Wait," she called. "Look and see if there's something still knotted up in the petticoat."

Baby Suggs inched the spoiled fabric through her fingers and came upon what felt like pebbles. She held them out toward Sethe. "Going-away present?"

"Wedding present."

"Be nice if there was a groom to go with it." She gazed into her hand. "What you think happened to him?"

"I don't know," said Sethe. "He wasn't where he said to meet him at. I had to get out. Had to." Sethe watched the drowsy eyes of the sucking girl for a moment then looked at Baby Suggs' face. "He'll make it. If I made it, Halle sure can."

"Well, put these on. Maybe they'll light his way." Convinced her son was dead, she handed the stones to Sethe.

"I need holes in my ears."

"I'll do it," said Baby Suggs. "Soon's you up to it."

Sethe jingled the earrings for the pleasure of the crawling-already? girl, who reached for them over and over again.

In the Clearing, Sethe found Baby's old preaching rock and remembered the smell of leaves simmering in the sun, thunderous feet and the shouts that ripped pods off the limbs of the chestnuts. With Baby Suggs' heart in charge, the people let go.

Sethe had had twenty-eight days—the travel of one whole moon—of unslaved life. From the pure clear stream of spit that the little girl dribbled into her face to her oily blood was twenty-eight days. Days of healing, ease and real-talk. Days of company: knowing the names of forty, fifty other Negroes, their views, habits; where they had been and what done; of feeling their fun and sorrow along with her own, which made it better. One taught her the alphabet; another a stitch. All taught her how it felt to wake up at dawn and *decide* what to do with the day. That's how she got through the waiting for Halle. Bit by bit, at 124 and in the Clearing, along with the others, she had claimed herself. Freeing yourself was one thing; claiming ownership of that freed self was another.

Now she sat on Baby Suggs' rock, Denver and Beloved watching her from the trees. There will never be a day, she thought, when Halle will knock on the door. Not knowing it was hard; knowing it was harder.

Just the fingers, she thought. Just let me feel your fingers again on the back of my neck and I will lay it all down, make a way out of this no way. Sethe bowed her head and sure enough—they were there. Lighter now, no more than the strokes of bird feather, but unmistakably caressing fingers. She had to relax a bit to let them do their work, so light was the touch, childlike almost, more finger kiss than kneading. Still she was grateful for the effort; Baby Suggs' long-distance love was equal to any skin-close love she had known. The desire, let alone the gesture, to meet her needs was good enough to lift her spirits to the place where she could take the next step: ask for some clarifying word; some advice about how to keep on with a brain greedy for news nobody could live with in a world happy to provide it.

She knew Paul D was adding something to her life—something she wanted to count on but was scared to. Now he had added more: new pictures and old rememories that broke her heart. Into the empty space of not knowing about Halle—a space sometimes colored with righteous resentment at what could have been his cowardice, or stupidity or bad luck—that empty place of no definite news was filled now with a brand-new sorrow and who could tell how many more on the way. Years ago—when 124 was alive—she had women friends, men friends from all around to share grief with. Then there was no one, for they would not visit her while the baby ghost filled the house, and she returned their disapproval with the potent pride of the mistreated. But now there was someone to share it, and he had beat the spirit away the very day he entered her house and no sign of it since. A blessing, but in its place he brought another kind of haunting: Halle's face smeared with butter and the clabber too; his own mouth jammed full of iron, and Lord knows what else he could tell her if he wanted to.

The fingers touching the back of her neck were stronger now—the strokes bolder as though Baby Suggs were gathering strength. Putting the thumbs at the nape, while the fingers pressed the sides. Harder, harder, the fingers moved slowly around toward her windpipe, making little circles on the way. Sethe was actually more surprised than frightened to find that she was being strangled. Or so it seemed. In any case, Baby Suggs' fingers had a grip on her that would not let her breathe. Tumbling forward from her seat on the rock, she clawed at the hands that were not there. Her feet were thrashing by the time Denver got to her and then Beloved.

"Ma'am! Ma'am!" Denver shouted. "Ma'ammy!" and turned her mother over on her back.

The fingers left off and Sethe had to swallow huge draughts of air before she recognized her daughter's face next to her own and Beloved's hovering above.

"You all right?"

"Somebody choked me," said Sethe.

"Who?"

Sethe rubbed her neck and struggled to a sitting position. "Grandma Baby, I reckon. I just asked her to *rub* my neck, like she used to and she was doing fine and then just got crazy with it, I guess."

"She wouldn't do that to you, Ma'am. Grandma Baby? Uh uh."

"Help me up from here."

"Look." Beloved was pointing at Sethe's neck.

"What is it? What you see?" asked Sethe.

"Bruises," said Denver.

"On my neck?"

"Here," said Beloved. "Here and here, too." She reached out her hand and touched the splotches, gathering color darker than Sethe's dark throat, and her fingers were mighty cool.

"That don't help nothing," Denver said, but Beloved was leaning in, her two hands stroking the damp skin that felt like chamois and looked like taffeta.

Sethe moaned. The girl's fingers were so cool and knowing. Sethe's knotted, private, walk-on-water life gave in a bit, softened, and it seemed that the glimpse of happiness she caught in the shadows swinging hands on the road to the carnival was a likelihood—if she could just manage the news Paul D brought and the news he kept to himself. Just manage it. Not break, fall or cry each time a hateful picture drifted in front of her face. Not develop some permanent craziness like Baby Suggs' friend, a young woman in a bonnet whose food was full of tears. Like Aunt Phyllis, who slept with her eyes wide open. Like Jackson Till, who slept under the bed. All she wanted was to go on. As she had. Alone with her daughter in a haunted house she managed every damn thing. Why now, with Paul D instead of the ghost, was she breaking up? getting scared? needing Baby? The worst was over, wasn't it? She had already got through, hadn't she? With the ghost in 124 she could bear, do, solve anything. Now a hint of what had happened to Halle and she cut out like a rabbit looking for its mother.

Beloved's fingers were heavenly. Under them and breathing evenly again, the anguish rolled down. The peace Sethe had come there to find crept into her.

We must look a sight, she thought, and closed her eyes to see it: the three women in the middle of the Clearing, at the base of the rock where Baby Suggs, holy, had loved. One seated, yielding up her throat to the kind hands of one of the two kneeling before her.

Denver watched the faces of the other two. Beloved watched the work her thumbs were doing and must have loved what she saw because she leaned over and kissed the tenderness under Sethe's chin.

They stayed that way for a while because neither Denver nor Sethe knew how not to: how to stop and not love the look or feel of the lips that kept on kissing. Then Sethe, grabbing Beloved's hair and blinking rapidly, separated herself. She later believed that it was because the girl's breath was exactly like new milk that she said to her, stern and frowning, "You too old for that."

She looked at Denver, and seeing panic about to become something more, stood up quickly, breaking the tableau apart.

"Come on up! Up!" Sethe waved the girls to their feet. As they left the Clearing they looked pretty much the same as they had when they had come: Sethe in the lead, the girls a ways back. All silent as before, but with a difference. Sethe was bothered, not because of the kiss, but because, just before it, when she was feeling so fine letting Beloved massage away the pain, the fingers she was loving and the ones that had soothed her before they strangled her had reminded her of something that now slipped her mind. But one thing for sure, Baby Suggs had not choked her as first she thought. Denver was right, and walking in the dappled tree-light, clearer-headed now—away from the enchantment of the Clearing—Sethe remembered the touch of those fingers that she knew better than her own. They had bathed her in sections, wrapped her womb, combed her hair, oiled her nipples, stitched her clothes, cleaned her feet, greased her back and dropped just about anything they were doing to massage Sethe's nape when, especially in the early days, her spirits fell down under the weight of the things she remembered and those she did not: schoolteacher writing in ink she herself had made while his nephews played on her; the face of the woman in a felt hat as she rose to stretch in the field. If she lay among all the hands in the world, she would know Baby Suggs' just as she did the good hands of the white-girl looking for velvet. But for eighteen years she had lived in a house full of touches from the other side. And the thumbs that pressed her nape were the same. Maybe that was where it had gone to. After Paul D beat it out of 124, maybe it collected itself in the Clearing. Reasonable, she thought.

Why she had taken Denver and Beloved with her didn't puzzle her now—at the time it seemed impulse, with a vague wish for protection. And the girls had saved her, Beloved so agitated she behaved like a two-year-old.

Like a faint smell of burning that disappears when the fire is cut off or the window opened for a breeze, the suspicion that the girl's touch was also exactly like the baby's ghost dissipated. It was only a tiny disturbance anyway—not strong enough to divert her from the ambition welling in her now: she wanted Paul D. No matter what he told and knew, she wanted him in her life. More than commemorating Halle, that is what she had come to the Clearing to figure out, and now it *was* figured. Trust and rememory, yes, the way she believed it could be when he cradled her before the cooking stove. The weight and angle of him; the true-to-life beard hair on him; arched back, educated hands. His waiting eyes and awful human power. The mind of him that knew her own. Her story was bearable because it was his as well—to tell, to refine and tell again. The things neither knew about the other—the things neither had word-shapes for—well, it would come in time: where they led him off to sucking iron; the perfect death of her crawling-already? baby.

She wanted to get back—fast. Set these idle girls to some work that would fill their wandering heads. Rushing through the green corridor, cooler now because the sun had moved, it occurred to her that the two were alike as sisters. Their obedience and absolute reliability shot through with surprise. Sethe understood Denver. Solitude had made her secretive—self-manipulated. Years of haunting had dulled her in ways you wouldn't believe and sharpened her in ways you wouldn't believe either. The consequence was a timid but hard-headed daughter Sethe would die to protect. The other, Beloved, she knew less, nothing, about—except that there was nothing she wouldn't do for Sethe and that Denver and she liked each other's company. Now she thought she knew why. They spent up or held on to their feelings in harmonious ways. What one had to give the other was pleased to take. They hung back in the trees that ringed the Clearing, then rushed into it with screams and kisses when Sethe choked—anyhow that's how she explained it to herself for she noticed neither competition between the two nor domination by one. On her mind was the supper she wanted to fix for Paul D—something difficult to do, something she would do just so—to launch her newer, stronger life with a tender man. Those litty bitty potatoes browned on all sides, heavy on the pepper; snap beans seasoned with rind; yellow

squash sprinkled with vinegar and sugar. Maybe corn cut from
the cob and fried with green onions and butter. Raised bread,
even.

Her mind, searching the kitchen before she got to it, was
so full of her offering she did not see right away, in the space
under the white stairs, the wooden tub and Paul D sitting in
it. She smiled at him and he smiled back.

"Summer must be over," she said.

"Come on in here."

"Uh uh. Girls right behind me."

"I don't hear nobody."

"I have to cook, Paul D."

"Me too." He stood up and made her stay there while he
held her in his arms. Her dress soaked up the water from his
body. His jaw was near her ear. Her chin touched his shoulder.

"What you gonna cook?"

"I thought some snap beans."

"Oh, yeah."

"Fry up a little corn?"

"Yeah."

There was no question but that she could do it. Just like the
day she arrived at 124—sure enough, she had milk enough for
all.

Beloved came through the door and they ought to have heard
her tread, but they didn't.

Breathing and murmuring, breathing and murmuring.
Beloved heard them as soon as the door banged shut behind
her. She jumped at the slam and swiveled her head toward the
whispers coming from behind the white stairs. She took a step

and felt like crying. She had been so close, then closer. And it was so much better than the anger that ruled when Sethe did or thought anything that excluded herself. She could bear the hours—nine or ten of them each day but one—when Sethe was gone. Bear even the nights when she was close but out of sight, behind walls and doors lying next to him. But now— even the daylight time that Beloved had counted on, disciplined herself to be content with, was being reduced, divided by Sethe's willingness to pay attention to other things. Him mostly. Him who said something to her that made her run out into the woods and talk to herself on a rock. Him who kept her hidden at night behind doors. And him who had hold of her now whispering behind the stairs after Beloved had rescued her neck and was ready now to put her hand in that woman's own.

Beloved turned around and left. Denver had not arrived, or else she was waiting somewhere outside. Beloved went to look, pausing to watch a cardinal hop from limb to branch. She followed the blood spot shifting in the leaves until she lost it and even then she walked on, backward, still hungry for another glimpse.

She turned finally and ran through the woods to the stream. Standing close to its edge she watched her reflection there. When Denver's face joined hers, they stared at each other in the water.

"You did it, I saw you," said Denver.

"What?"

"I saw your face. You made her choke."

"I didn't do it."

"You told me you loved her."

"I fixed it, didn't I? Didn't I fix her neck?"

"After. After you choked her neck."

"I kissed her neck. I didn't choke it. The circle of iron choked it."

"I saw you." Denver grabbed Beloved's arm.

"Look out, girl," said Beloved and, snatching her arm away, ran ahead as fast as she could along the stream that sang on the other side of the woods.

Left alone, Denver wondered if, indeed, she had been wrong. She and Beloved were standing in the trees whispering, while Sethe sat on the rock. Denver knew that the Clearing used to be where Baby Suggs preached, but that was when she was a baby. She had never been there herself to remember it. 124 and the field behind it were all the world she knew or wanted.

Once upon a time she had known more and wanted to. Had walked the path leading to a real other house. Had stood outside the window listening. Four times she did it on her own—crept away from 124 early in the afternoon when her mother and grandmother had their guard down, just before supper, after chores; the blank hour before gears changed to evening occupations. Denver had walked off looking for the house other children visited but not her. When she found it she was too timid to go to the front door so she peeped in the window. Lady Jones sat in a straight-backed chair; several children sat cross-legged on the floor in front of her. Lady Jones had a book. The children had slates. Lady Jones was saying something too soft for Denver to hear. The children were saying it after her. Four times Denver went to look. The fifth time Lady Jones caught her and said, "Come in the front door, Miss Denver. This is not a side show."

So she had almost a whole year of the company of her peers and along with them learned to spell and count. She was seven, and those two hours in the afternoon were precious to her. Especially so because she had done it on her own and was pleased and surprised by the pleasure and surprise it created in her mother and her brothers. For a nickel a month, Lady Jones did what whitepeople thought unnecessary if not illegal: crowded her little parlor with the colored children who had time for and interest in book learning. The nickel, tied to a handkerchief knot, tied to her belt, that she carried to Lady Jones, thrilled her. The effort to handle chalk expertly and avoid the scream it would make; the capital w, the little i, the beauty of the letters in her name, the deeply mournful sentences from the Bible Lady Jones used as a textbook. Denver practiced every morning; starred every afternoon. She was so happy she didn't even know she was being avoided by her classmates—that they made excuses and altered their pace not to walk with her. It was Nelson Lord—the boy as smart as she was—who put a stop to it; who asked her the question about her mother that put chalk, the little i and all the rest that those afternoons held, out of reach forever. She should have laughed when he said it, or pushed him down, but there was no meanness in his face or his voice. Just curiosity. But the thing that leapt up in her when he asked it was a thing that had been lying there all along.

She never went back. The second day she didn't go, Sethe asked her why not. Denver didn't answer. She was too scared to ask her brothers or anyone else Nelson Lord's question because certain odd and terrifying feelings about her mother were collecting around the thing that leapt up inside her. Later on, after Baby Suggs died, she did not wonder why Howard

and Buglar had run away. She did not agree with Sethe that
they left because of the ghost. If so, what took them so long?
They had lived with it as long as she had. But if Nelson Lord
was right—no wonder they were sulky, staying away from
home as much as they could.

Meanwhile the monstrous and unmanageable dreams about
Sethe found release in the concentration Denver began to fix
on the baby ghost. Before Nelson Lord, she had been barely
interested in its antics. The patience of her mother and grandmother in its presence made her indifferent to it. Then it began
to irritate her, wear her out with its mischief. That was when
she walked off to follow the children to Lady Jones' house-school.
Now it held for her all the anger, love and fear she didn't know
what to do with. Even when she did muster the courage to ask
Nelson Lord's question, she could not hear Sethe's answer, nor
Baby Suggs' words, nor anything at all thereafter. For two years
she walked in a silence too solid for penetration but which gave
her eyes a power even she found hard to believe. The black
nostrils of a sparrow sitting on a branch sixty feet above her
head, for instance. For two years she heard nothing at all and
then she heard close thunder crawling up the stairs. Baby Suggs
thought it was Here Boy padding into places he never went.
Sethe thought it was the India-rubber ball the boys played with
bounding down the stairs.

"Is that damn dog lost his mind?" shouted Baby Suggs.

"He's on the porch," said Sethe. "See for yourself."

"Well, what's that I'm hearing then?"

Sethe slammed the stove lid. "Buglar! Buglar! I told you all
not to use that ball in here." She looked at the white stairs and
saw Denver at the top.

"She was trying to get upstairs."

"What?" The cloth she used to handle the stove lid was balled in Sethe's hand.

"The baby," said Denver. "Didn't you hear her crawling?"

What to jump on first was the problem: that Denver heard anything at all or that the crawling-already? baby girl was still at it but more so.

The return of Denver's hearing, cut off by an answer she could not bear to hear, cut on by the sound of her dead sister trying to climb the stairs, signaled another shift in the fortunes of the people of 124. From then on the presence was full of spite. Instead of sighs and accidents there was pointed and deliberate abuse. Buglar and Howard grew furious at the company of the women in the house, and spent in sullen reproach any time they had away from their odd work in town carrying water and feed at the stables. Until the spite became so personal it drove each off. Baby Suggs grew tired, went to bed and stayed there until her big old heart quit. Except for an occasional request for color she said practically nothing—until the afternoon of the last day of her life when she got out of bed, skipped slowly to the door of the keeping room and announced to Sethe and Denver the lesson she had learned from her sixty years a slave and ten years free: that there was no bad luck in the world but whitepeople. "They don't know when to stop," she said, and returned to her bed, pulled up the quilt and left them to hold that thought forever.

Shortly afterward Sethe and Denver tried to call up and reason with the baby ghost, but got nowhere. It took a man, Paul D, to shout it off, beat it off and take its place for himself. And carnival or no carnival, Denver preferred the venomous baby to him any day. During the first days after Paul D moved in, Denver stayed in her emerald closet as long as she could, lonely as a mountain and almost as big, thinking everybody had somebody but her; thinking even a ghost's company was denied her. So when she saw the black dress with two unlaced shoes beneath it she trembled with secret thanks. Whatever her power and however she used it, Beloved was *hers*. Denver was alarmed by the harm she thought Beloved planned for Sethe, but felt helpless to thwart it, so unrestricted was her need to love another. The display she witnessed at the Clearing shamed her because the choice between Sethe and Beloved was without conflict.

Walking toward the stream, beyond her green bush house, she let herself wonder what if Beloved really decided to choke her mother. Would she let it happen? Murder, Nelson Lord had said. "Didn't your mother get locked away for murder? Wasn't you in there with her when she went?"

It was the second question that made it impossible for so long to ask Sethe about the first. The thing that leapt up had been coiled in just such a place: a darkness, a stone, and some other thing that moved by itself. She went deaf rather than hear the answer, and like the little four o'clocks that searched openly for sunlight, then closed themselves tightly when it left, Denver kept watch for the baby and withdrew from everything else. Until Paul D came. But the damage he did came undone with the miraculous resurrection of Beloved.

Just ahead, at the edge of the stream, Denver could see her silhouette, standing barefoot in the water, lifting her black skirts up above her calves, the beautiful head lowered in rapt attention.

Blinking fresh tears Denver approached her—eager for a word, a sign of forgiveness.

Denver took off her shoes and stepped into the water with her. It took a moment for her to drag her eyes from the spectacle of Beloved's head to see what she was staring at.

A turtle inched along the edge, turned and climbed to dry ground. Not far behind it was another one, headed in the same direction. Four placed plates under a hovering motionless bowl. Behind her in the grass the other one moving quickly, quickly to mount her. The impregnable strength of him—earthing his feet near her shoulders. The embracing necks—hers stretching up toward his bending down, the pat pat pat of their touching heads. No height was beyond her yearning neck, stretched like a finger toward his, risking everything outside the bowl just to touch his face. The gravity of their shields, clashing, countered and mocked the floating heads touching.

Beloved dropped the folds of her skirt. It spread around her. The hem darkened in the water.

Out of sight of Mister's sight, away, praise His name, from the smiling boss of roosters, Paul D began to tremble. Not all at once and not so anyone could tell. When he turned his head, aiming for a last look at Brother, turned it as much as the rope that connected his neck to the axle of a buckboard allowed, and, later on, when they fastened the iron around his ankles and clamped the wrists as well, there was no outward sign of trembling at all. Nor eighteen days after that when he saw the ditches; the one thousand feet of earth—five feet deep, five feet wide, into which wooden boxes had been fitted. A door of bars that you could lift on hinges like a cage opened into three walls and a roof of scrap lumber and red dirt. Two feet of it over his head; three feet of open trench in front of him with anything that crawled or scurried welcome to share that grave calling itself quarters. And there were forty-five more. He was sent there after trying to kill Brandywine, the man schoolteacher sold him to. Brandywine was leading him, in a coffle with ten others, through Kentucky into Virginia. He didn't know exactly what prompted him to try—other than Halle, Sixo, Paul A, Paul F and Mister. But the trembling was fixed by the time he knew it was there.

Going into detail

Still no one else knew it, because it began inside. A flutter of a kind, in the chest, then the shoulder blades. It felt like rippling—gentle at first and then wild. As though the further south they led him the more his blood, frozen like an ice pond for twenty years, began thawing, breaking into pieces that, once melted, had no choice but to swirl and eddy. Sometimes it was in his leg. Then again it moved to the base of his spine. By the time they unhitched him from the wagon and he saw nothing but dogs and two shacks in a world of sizzling grass, the roiling blood was shaking him to and fro. But no one could tell. The wrists he held out for the bracelets that evening were steady as were the legs he stood on when chains were attached to the leg irons. But when they shoved him into the box and dropped the cage door down, his hands quit taking instruction. On their own, they traveled. Nothing could stop them or get their attention. They would not hold his penis to urinate or a spoon to scoop lumps of lima beans into his mouth. The miracle of their obedience came with the hammer at dawn.

All forty-six men woke to rifle shot. All forty-six. Three whitemen walked along the trench unlocking the doors one by one. No one stepped through. When the last lock was opened, the three returned and lifted the bars, one by one. And one by one the blackmen emerged—promptly and without the poke of a rifle butt if they had been there more than a day; promptly with the butt if, like Paul D, they had just arrived. When all forty-six were standing in a line in the trench, another rifle shot signaled the climb out and up to the ground above, where one thousand feet of the best hand-forged chain in Georgia stretched. Each man bent and waited. The first man picked up the end and threaded it through the loop on his leg iron. He stood up then, and, shuffling a little, brought the chain tip to the next prisoner, who did likewise. As the chain was passed on and each man stood in the other's place, the line of men turned around, facing the boxes they had come out of. Not one spoke to the other. At least not with words. The eyes had to tell what there was to tell: "Help me this mornin; 's bad"; "I'm a make it"; "New man"; "Steady now steady."

Chain-up completed, they knelt down. The dew, more likely than not, was mist by then. Heavy sometimes and if the dogs were quiet and just breathing you could hear doves. Kneeling in the mist they waited for the whim of a guard, or two, or three. Or maybe all of them wanted it. Wanted it from one prisoner in particular or none—or all.

"Breakfast? Want some breakfast, nigger?"

"Yes, sir."

"Hungry, nigger?"

"Yes, sir."

"Here you go."

Occasionally a kneeling man chose gunshot in his head as the price, maybe, of taking a bit of foreskin with him to Jesus. Paul D did not know that then. He was looking at his palsied hands, smelling the guard, listening to his soft grunts so like the doves', as he stood before the man kneeling in mist on his right. Convinced he was next, Paul D retched—vomiting up nothing at all. An observing guard smashed his shoulder with the rifle and the engaged one decided to skip the new man for the time being lest his pants and shoes got soiled by nigger puke.

"Hiiii!"

It was the first sound, other than "Yes, sir," a black man was allowed to speak each morning, and the lead chain gave it everything he had. "Hiiii!" It was never clear to Paul D how he knew when to shout that mercy. They called him Hi Man and Paul D thought at first the guards told him when to give the signal that let the prisoners rise up off their knees and dance two-step to the music of hand-forged iron. Later he doubted it. He believed to this day that the "Hiiii!" at dawn and the "Hoooo!" when evening came were the responsibility Hi Man assumed because he alone knew what was enough, what was too much, when things were over, when the time had come.

They chain-danced over the fields, through the woods to a trail that ended in the astonishing beauty of feldspar, and there Paul D's hands disobeyed the furious rippling of his blood and paid attention. With a sledge hammer in his hands and Hi Man's lead, the men got through. They sang it out and beat it up, garbling the words so they could not be understood; tricking the words so their syllables yielded up other meanings. They sang the women they knew; the children they had been; the animals they had tamed themselves or seen others tame. They sang of bosses and masters and misses; of mules and dogs and the shamelessness of life. They sang lovingly of graveyards and sisters long gone. Of pork in the woods; meal in the pan; fish on the line; cane, rain and rocking chairs.

And they beat. The women for having known them and no more, no more; the children for having been them but never again. They killed a boss so often and so completely they had to bring him back to life to pulp him one more time. Tasting hot mealcake among pine trees, they beat it away. Singing love songs to Mr. Death, they smashed his head. More than the rest, they killed the flirt whom folks called Life for leading them on. Making them think the next sunrise would be worth it; that another stroke of time would do it at last. Only when she was dead would they be safe. The successful ones—the ones who had been there enough years to have maimed, mutilated, maybe even buried her—kept watch over the others who were still in her cock-teasing hug, caring and looking forward, remembering and looking back. They were the ones whose eyes said, "Help me, 's bad"; or "Look out," meaning *this might be the day I bay or eat my own mess or run*, and it was this last that had to be guarded against, for if one pitched and ran—all, all forty-six, would be yanked by the chain that bound them and no telling who or how many would be killed. A man could risk his own life, but not his brother's. So the eyes said, "Steady now," and "Hang by me."

Eighty-six days and done. Life was dead. Paul D beat her butt all day every day till there was not a whimper in her. Eighty-six days and his hands were still, waiting serenely each rat-rustling night for "Hiiii!" at dawn and the eager clench on the hammer's shaft. Life rolled over dead. Or so he thought.

It rained.

Snakes came down from short-leaf pine and hemlock.

It rained.

Cypress, yellow poplar, ash and palmetto drooped under five days of rain without wind. By the eighth day the doves were nowhere in sight, by the ninth even the salamanders were gone. Dogs laid their ears down and stared over their paws. The men could not work. Chain-up was slow, breakfast abandoned, the two-step became a slow drag over soupy grass and unreliable earth.

It was decided to lock everybody down in the boxes till it either stopped or lightened up so a whiteman could walk, damnit, without flooding his gun and the dogs could quit shivering. The chain was threaded through forty-six loops of the best hand-forged iron in Georgia.

It rained.

In the boxes the men heard the water rise in the trench and looked out for cottonmouths. They squatted in muddy water, slept above it, peed in it. Paul D thought he was screaming; his mouth was open and there was this loud throat-splitting sound—but it may have been somebody else. Then he thought he was crying. Something was running down his cheeks. He lifted his hands to wipe away the tears and saw dark brown slime. Above him rivulets of mud slid through the boards of the roof. When it come down, he thought, gonna crush me like a tick bug. It happened so quick he had no time to ponder. Somebody yanked the chain—once—hard enough to cross his legs and throw him into the mud. He never figured out how he knew—how anybody did—but he did know—he did—and he took both hands and yanked the length of chain at his left, so the next man would know too. The water was above his ankles, flowing over the wooden plank he slept on. And then it wasn't water anymore. The ditch was caving in and mud oozed under and through the bars.

They waited—each and every one of the forty-six. Not screaming, although some of them must have fought like the devil not to. The mud was up to his thighs and he held on to the bars. Then it came—another yank—from the left this time and less forceful than the first because of the mud it passed through.

It started like the chain-up but the difference was the power of the chain. One by one, from Hi Man back on down the line, they dove. Down through the mud under the bars, blind, groping. Some had sense enough to wrap their heads in their shirts, cover their faces with rags, put on their shoes. Others just plunged, simply ducked down and pushed out, fighting up, reaching for air. Some lost direction and their neighbors, feeling the confused pull of the chain, snatched them around. For one lost, all lost. The chain that held them would save all or none, and Hi Man was the Delivery. They talked through that chain like Sam Morse and, Great God, they all came up. Like the unshriven dead, zombies on the loose, holding the chains in their hands, they trusted the rain and the dark, yes, but mostly Hi Man and each other.

Past the sheds where the dogs lay in deep depression; past the two guard shacks, past the stable of sleeping horses, past the hens whose bills were bolted into their feathers, they waded. The moon did not help because it wasn't there. The field was a marsh, the track a trough. All Georgia seemed to be sliding, melting away. Moss wiped their faces as they fought the live-oak branches that blocked their way. Georgia took up all of Alabama and Mississippi then, so there was no state line to cross and it wouldn't have mattered anyway. If they had known about it, they would have avoided not only Alfred and the beautiful feldspar, but Savannah too and headed for the Sea Islands on the river that slid down from the Blue Ridge Mountains. But they didn't know.

Daylight came and they huddled in a copse of redbud trees. Night came and they scrambled up to higher ground, praying the rain would go on shielding them and keeping folks at home. They were hoping for a shack, solitary, some distance from its big house, where a slave might be making rope or heating potatoes at the grate. What they found was a camp of sick Cherokee for whom a rose was named.

Decimated but stubborn, they were among those who chose a fugitive life rather than Oklahoma. The illness that swept them now was reminiscent of the one that had killed half their number two hundred years earlier. In between that calamity and this, they had visited George III in London, published a newspaper, made baskets, led Oglethorpe through forests, helped Andrew Jackson fight Creek, cooked maize, drawn up a constitution, petitioned the King of Spain, been experimented on by Dartmouth, established asylums, wrote their language, resisted settlers, shot bear and translated scripture. All to no avail. The forced move to the Arkansas River, insisted upon by the same president they fought for against the Creek, destroyed another quarter of their already shattered number.

That was it, they thought, and removed themselves from those Cherokee who signed the treaty, in order to retire into the forest and await the end of the world. The disease they suffered now was a mere inconvenience compared to the devastation they remembered. Still, they protected each other as best they could. The healthy were sent some miles away; the sick stayed behind with the dead—to survive or join them.

The prisoners from Alfred, Georgia, sat down in semicircle near the encampment. No one came and still they sat. Hours passed and the rain turned soft. Finally a woman stuck her head out of her house. Night came and nothing happened. At dawn two men with barnacles covering their beautiful skin approached them. No one spoke for a moment, then Hi Man raised his hand. The Cherokee saw the chains and went away. When they returned each carried a handful of small axes. Two children followed with a pot of mush cooling and thinning in the rain.

Buffalo men, they called them, and talked slowly to the prisoners scooping mush and tapping away at their chains. Nobody from a box in Alfred, Georgia, cared about the illness the Cherokee warned them about, so they stayed, all forty-six, resting, planning their next move. Paul D had no idea of what to do and knew less than anybody, it seemed. He heard his co-convicts talk knowledgeably of rivers and states, towns and territories. Heard Cherokee men describe the beginning of the world and its end. Listened to tales of other Buffalo men they knew—three of whom were in the healthy camp a few miles away. Hi Man wanted to join them; others wanted to join him. Some wanted to leave; some to stay on. Weeks later Paul D was the only Buffalo man left—without a plan. All he could think of was tracking dogs, although Hi Man said the rain they left in gave that no chance of success. Alone, the last man with buffalo hair among the ailing Cherokee, Paul D finally woke up and, admitting his ignorance, asked how he might get North. Free North. Magical North. Welcoming, benevolent North. The Cherokee smiled and looked around. The flood rains of a month ago had turned everything to steam and blossoms.

"That way," he said, pointing. "Follow the tree flowers," he said. "Only the tree flowers. As they go, you go. You will be where you want to be when they are gone."

So he raced from dogwood to blossoming peach. When they thinned out he headed for the cherry blossoms, then magnolia, chinaberry, pecan, walnut and prickly pear. At last he reached a field of apple trees whose flowers were just becoming tiny knots of fruit. Spring sauntered north, but he had to run like hell to keep it as his traveling companion. From February to July he was on the lookout for blossoms. When he lost them, and found himself without so much as a petal to guide him, he paused, climbed a tree on a hillock and scanned the horizon for a flash of pink or white in the leaf world that surrounded him. He did not touch them or stop to smell. He merely followed in their wake, a dark ragged figure guided by the blossoming plums.

The apple field turned out to be Delaware where the weaver lady lived. She snapped him up as soon as he finished the sausage she fed him and he crawled into her bed crying. She passed him off as her nephew from Syracuse simply by calling him that nephew's name. Eighteen months and he was looking out again for blossoms only this time he did the looking on a dray.

It was some time before he could put Alfred, Georgia, Sixo, schoolteacher, Halle, his brothers, Sethe, Mister, the taste of iron, the sight of butter, the smell of hickory, notebook paper, one by one, into the tobacco tin lodged in his chest. By the time he got to 124 nothing in this world could pry it open.

She moved him.

Not the way he had beat off the baby's ghost—all bang and shriek with windows smashed and jelly jars rolled in a heap. But she moved him nonetheless, and Paul D didn't know how to stop it because it looked like he was moving himself. Imperceptibly, downright reasonably, he was moving out of 124.

The beginning was so simple. One day, after supper, he sat in the rocker by the stove, bone-tired, river-whipped, and fell asleep. He woke to the footsteps of Sethe coming down the white stairs to make breakfast.

"I thought you went out somewhere," she said.

Paul D moaned, surprised to find himself exactly where he was the last time he looked.

"Don't tell me I slept in this chair the whole night."

Sethe laughed. "Me? I won't say a word to you."

"Why didn't you rouse me?"

"I did. Called you two or three times. I gave it up around midnight and then I thought you went out somewhere."

He stood, expecting his back to fight it. But it didn't. Not a creak or a stiff joint anywhere. In fact he felt refreshed. Some things are like that, he thought, good-sleep places. The base of certain trees here and there; a wharf, a bench, a rowboat once, a haystack usually, not always bed, and here, now, a rocking chair, which was strange because in his experience furniture was the worst place for a good-sleep sleep.

The next evening he did it again and then again. He was accustomed to sex with Sethe just about every day, and to avoid the confusion Beloved's shining caused him he still made it his business to take her back upstairs in the morning, or lie down with her after supper. But he found a way and a reason to spend the longest part of the night in the rocker. He told himself it must be his back—something supportive it needed for a weakness left over from sleeping in a box in Georgia.

It went on that way and might have stayed that way but one evening, after supper, after Sethe, he came downstairs, sat in the rocker and didn't want to be there. He stood up and realized he didn't want to go upstairs either. Irritable and longing for rest, he opened the door to Baby Suggs' room and dropped off to sleep on the bed the old lady died in. That settled it—so it seemed. It became his room and Sethe didn't object—her bed made for two had been occupied by one for eighteen years before Paul D came to call. And maybe it was better this way, with young girls in the house and him not being her true-to-life husband. In any case, since there was no reduction in his before-breakfast or after-supper appetites, he never heard her complain.

It went on that way and might have stayed that way, except one evening, after supper, after Sethe, he came downstairs and lay on Baby Suggs' bed and didn't want to be there.

He believed he was having house-fits, the glassy anger men sometimes feel when a woman's house begins to bind them,

when they want to yell and break something or at least run
off. He knew all about that—felt it lots of times—in the
Delaware weaver's house, for instance. But always he associated
the house-fit with the woman in it. This nervousness had
nothing to do with the woman, whom he loved a little bit more
every day: her hands among vegetables, her mouth when she
licked a thread end before guiding it through a needle or bit
it in two when the seam was done, the blood in her eye when
she defended her girls (and Beloved was hers now) or any
coloredwoman from a slur. Also in this house-fit there was no
anger, no suffocation, no yearning to be elsewhere. He just
could not, would not, sleep upstairs or in the rocker or, now,
in Baby Suggs' bed. So he went to the storeroom.

It went on that way and might have stayed that way except
one evening, after supper, after Sethe, he lay on a pallet in the
storeroom and didn't want to be there. Then it was the cold
house and it was out there, separated from the main part of
124, curled on top of two croaker sacks full of sweet potatoes,
staring at the sides of a lard can, that he realized the moving
was involuntary. He wasn't being nervous; he was being
prevented.

So he waited. Visited Sethe in the morning; slept in the cold
room at night and waited.

She came, and he wanted to knock her down.

In Ohio seasons are theatrical. Each one enters like a prima
donna, convinced its performance is the reason the world has
people in it. When Paul D had been forced out of 124 into a
shed behind it, summer had been hooted offstage and autumn
with its bottles of blood and gold had everybody's attention.

Even at night, when there should have been a restful intermission, there was none because the voices of a dying landscape were insistent and loud. Paul D packed newspaper under himself and over, to give his thin blanket some help. But the chilly night was not on his mind. When he heard the door open behind him he refused to turn and look.

"What you want in here? What you want?" He should have been able to hear her breathing.

"I want you to touch me on the inside part and call me my name."

Paul D never worried about his little tobacco tin anymore. It was rusted shut. So, while she hoisted her skirts and turned her head over her shoulder the way the turtles had, he just looked at the lard can, silvery in moonlight, and spoke quietly.

"When good people take you in and treat you good, you ought to try to be good back. You don't ... Sethe loves you. Much as her own daughter. You know that."

Beloved dropped her skirts as he spoke and looked at him with empty eyes. She took a step he could not hear and stood close behind him.

"She don't love me like I love her. I don't love nobody but her."

"Then what you come in here for?"

"I want you to touch me on the inside part."

"Go on back in that house and get to bed."

"You have to touch me. On the inside part. And you have to call me my name."

As long as his eyes were locked on the silver of the lard can he was safe. If he trembled like Lot's wife and felt some womanish need to see the nature of the sin behind him; feel a sympathy, perhaps, for the cursing cursed, or want to hold it in his arms out of respect for the connection between them, he too would be lost.

"Call me my name."

"No."

"Please call it. I'll go if you call it."

"Beloved." He said it, but she did not go. She moved closer with a footfall he didn't hear and he didn't hear the whisper that the flakes of rust made either as they fell away from the seams of his tobacco tin. So when the lid gave he didn't know it. What he knew was that when he reached the inside part he was saying, "Red heart. Red heart," over and over again. Softly and then so loud it woke Denver, then Paul D himself. "Red heart. Red heart. Red heart."

To go back to the original hunger was impossible. Luckily for Denver, looking was food enough to last. But to be looked at in turn was beyond appetite; it was breaking through her own skin to a place where hunger hadn't been discovered. It didn't have to happen often, because Beloved seldom looked right at her, or when she did, Denver could tell that her own face was just the place those eyes stopped while the mind behind it walked on. But sometimes—at moments Denver could neither anticipate nor create—Beloved rested cheek on knuckles and looked at Denver with attention.

It was lovely. Not to be stared at, not seen, but being pulled into view by the interested, uncritical eyes of the other. Having her hair examined as a part of her self, not as material or a style. Having her lips, nose, chin caressed as they might be if she were a moss rose a gardener paused to admire. Denver's skin dissolved under that gaze and became soft and bright like the lisle dress that had its arm around her mother's waist. She floated near but outside her own body, feeling vague and intense at the same time. Needing nothing. Being what there was.

At such times it seemed to be Beloved who needed some-thing—wanted something. Deep down in her wide black eyes, back behind the expressionlessness, was a palm held out for a penny which Denver would gladly give her, if only she knew how or knew enough about her, a knowledge not to be had by the answers to the questions Sethe occasionally put to her: "You disremember everything? I never knew my mother neither, but I saw her a couple of times. Did you never see yours? What kind of whites was they? You don't remember none?"

Beloved, scratching the back of her hand, would say she remembered a woman who was hers, and she remembered being snatched away from her. Other than that, the clearest memory she had, the one she repeated, was the bridge—standing on the bridge looking down. And she knew one whiteman.

Sethe found that remarkable and more evidence to support her conclusions, which she confided to Denver.

"Where'd you get the dress, them shoes?"

Beloved said she took them.

"Who from?"

Silence and a faster scratching of her hand. She didn't know; she saw them and just took them.

"Uh huh," said Sethe, and told Denver that she believed Beloved had been locked up by some whiteman for his own purposes, and never let out the door. That she must have escaped to a bridge or someplace and rinsed the rest out of her mind. Something like that had happened to Ella except it was two men—a father and son—and Ella remembered every bit of it. For more than a year, they kept her locked in a room for themselves.

"You couldn't think up," Ella had said, "what them two done to me."

Sethe thought it explained Beloved's behavior around Paul D, whom she hated so.

Denver neither believed nor commented on Sethe's speculations, and she lowered her eyes and never said a word about the cold house. She was certain that Beloved was the white dress that had knelt with her mother in the keeping room, the true-to-life presence of the baby that had kept her company most of her life. And to be looked at by her, however briefly, kept her grateful for the rest of the time when she was merely the looker. Besides, she had her own set of questions which had nothing to do with the past. The present alone interested Denver, but she was careful to appear uninquisitive about the things she was dying to ask Beloved, for if she pressed too hard, she might lose the penny that the held-out palm wanted, and lose, therefore, the place beyond appetite. It was better to feast, to have permission to be the looker, because the old hunger—the before-Beloved hunger that drove her into boxwood and cologne for just a taste of a life, to feel it bumpy and not flat—was out of the question. Looking kept it at bay.

So she did not ask Beloved how she knew about the earrings, the night walks to the cold house or the tip of the thing she saw when Beloved lay down or came undone in her sleep. The look, when it came, came when Denver had been careful, had explained things, or participated in things, or told stories to keep her occupied when Sethe was at the restaurant. No given chore was enough to put out the licking fire that seemed always to burn in her. Not when they wrung out sheets so tight the rinse water ran back up their arms. Not when they shoveled snow from the path to the outhouse. Or broke three inches of ice from the rain barrel; scoured and boiled last summer's canning jars, packed mud in the cracks of the hen house and warmed the chicks with their skirts. All the while Denver was obliged to talk about what they were doing—the how and why of it. About people Denver knew once or had seen, giving them more life than life had: the sweet-smelling whitewoman who brought her oranges and cologne and good wool skirts; Lady Jones who taught them songs to spell and count by; a beautiful boy as smart as she was with a birthmark like a nickel on his cheek. A white preacher who prayed for their souls while Sethe peeled potatoes and Grandma Baby sucked air. And she told her about Howard and Buglar: the parts of the bed that belonged to each (the top reserved for herself); that before she transferred to Baby Suggs' bed she never knew them to sleep without holding hands. She described them to Beloved slowly, to keep her attention, dwelling on their habits, the games they taught her and not the fright that drove them increasingly out of the house—anywhere—and finally far away.

This day they are outside. It's cold and the snow is hard as packed dirt. Denver has finished singing the counting song Lady Jones taught her students. Beloved is holding her arms steady while Denver unclasps frozen underwear and towels from the line. One by one she lays them in Beloved's arms until the pile, like a huge deck of cards, reaches her chin. The rest, aprons and brown stockings, Denver carries herself. Made giddy by the cold, they return to the house. The clothes will thaw slowly to a dampness perfect for the pressing iron, which will make them smell like hot rain. Dancing around the room with Sethe's apron, Beloved wants to know if there are flowers in the dark. Denver adds sticks to the stovefire and assures her there are. Twirling, her face framed by the neckband, her waist in the apron strings' embrace, she says she is thirsty.

Denver suggests warming up some cider, while her mind races to something she might do or say to interest and entertain the dancer. Denver is a strategist now and has to keep Beloved by her side from the minute Sethe leaves for work until the hour of her return when Beloved begins to hover at the window, then work her way out the door, down the steps and near the road. Plotting has changed Denver markedly. Where she was once indolent, resentful of every task, now she is spry, executing, even extending the assignments Sethe leaves for them. All to be able to say "We got to" and "Ma'am said for us to." Otherwise Beloved gets private and dreamy, or quiet and sullen, and Denver's chances of being looked at by her go down to nothing. She has no control over the evenings. When her mother is anywhere around, Beloved has eyes only for Sethe. At night, in bed, anything might happen. She might want to be told a story in the dark when Denver can't see her. Or she might get up and go into the cold house where Paul D has begun to sleep. Or she might cry, silently. She might even sleep like a brick, her breath sugary from fingerfuls of molasses or sand-cookie crumbs. Denver will turn toward her then, and if Beloved faces her, she will inhale deeply the sweet air from her mouth. If not, she will have to lean up and over her, every once in a while, to catch a sniff. For anything is better than the original hunger—the time when, after a year of the wonderful little *i*, sentences rolling out like pie dough and the company of other children, there was no sound coming through. Anything is better than the silence when she answered to hands gesturing and was indifferent to the movement of lips. When she saw every little thing and colors leaped smoldering into view. She will forgo the most violent of sunsets, stars as fat as dinner plates and all the blood of autumn and settle for the palest yellow if it comes from her Beloved.

The cider jug is heavy, but it always is, even when empty. Denver can carry it easily, yet she asks Beloved to help her. It is in the cold house next to the molasses and six pounds of cheddar hard as bone. A pallet is in the middle of the floor covered with newspaper and a blanket at the foot. It has been slept on for almost a month, even though snow has come and, with it, serious winter.

It is noon, quite light outside; inside it is not. A few cuts of sun break through the roof and walls but once there they are too weak to shift for themselves. Darkness is stronger and swallows them like minnows.

The door bangs shut. Denver can't tell where Beloved is standing.

"Where are you?" she whispers in a laughing sort of way.

"Here," says Beloved.

"Where?"

"Come find me," says Beloved.

Denver stretches out her right arm and takes a step or two. She trips and falls down onto the pallet. Newspaper crackles under her weight. She laughs again. "Oh, shoot. Beloved?"

No one answers. Denver waves her arms and squinches her eyes to separate the shadows of potato sacks, a lard can and a side of smoked pork from the one that might be human.

"Stop fooling," she says and looks up toward the light to check and make sure this is still the cold house and not something going on in her sleep. The minnows of light still swim there; they can't make it down to where she is.

"You the one thirsty. You want cider or don't you?" Denver's voice is mildly accusatory. Mildly. She doesn't want to offend and she doesn't want to betray the panic that is creeping over her like hairs. There is no sight or sound of Beloved. Denver struggles to her feet amid the crackling newspaper. Holding her palm out, she moves slowly toward the door. There is no latch or knob—just a loop of wire to catch a nail. She pushes the door open. Cold sunlight displaces the dark. The room is just as it was when they entered—except Beloved is not there. There is no point in looking further, for everything in the place can be seen at first sight. Denver looks anyway because the loss is ungovernable. She steps back into the shed, allowing the door to close quickly behind her. Darkness or not, she moves rapidly around, reaching, touching cobwebs, cheese, slanting shelves, the pallet interfering with each step. If she stumbles, she is not aware of it because she does not know where her body stops, which part of her is an arm, a foot or a knee. She feels like an ice cake torn away from the solid surface of the stream, floating on darkness, thick and crashing against the edges of things around it. Breakable, meltable and cold.

It is hard to breathe and even if there were light she wouldn't be able to see anything because she is crying. Just as she thought it might happen, it has. Easy as walking into a room. A magical appearance on a stump, the face wiped out by sunlight, and a magical disappearance in a shed, eaten alive by the dark.

"Don't," she is saying between tough swallows. "Don't. Don't go back."

This is worse than when Paul D came to 124 and she cried helplessly into the stove. This is worse. Then it was for herself. Now she is crying because she has no self. Death is a skipped meal compared to this. She can feel her thickness thinning, dissolving into nothing. She grabs the hair at her temples to get enough to uproot it and halt the melting for a while. Teeth clamped shut, Denver brakes her sobs. She doesn't move to open the door because there is no world out there. She decides to stay in the cold house and let the dark swallow her like the minnows of light above. She won't put up with another leaving, another trick. Waking up to find one brother then another not at the bottom of the bed, his foot jabbing her spine. Sitting at the table eating turnips and saving the liquor for her grandmother to drink; her mother's hand on the keeping-room door and her voice saying, "Baby Suggs is gone, Denver." And when she got around to worrying about what would be the case if Sethe died or Paul D took her away, a dream-come-true comes true just to leave her on a pile of newspaper in the dark.

No footfall announces her, but there she is, standing where before there was nobody when Denver looked. And smiling.

Denver grabs the hem of Beloved's skirt. "I thought you left me. I thought you went back."

Beloved smiles, "I don't want that place. This the place I am." She sits down on the pallet and, laughing, lies back looking at the cracklights above.

Surreptitiously, Denver pinches a piece of Beloved's skirt between her fingers and holds on. A good thing she does because suddenly Beloved sits up.

"What is it?" asks Denver.

"Look," she points to the sunlit cracks.

"What? I don't see nothing." Denver follows the pointi
finger.

Beloved drops her hand. "I'm like this."

Denver watches as Beloved bends over, curls up and rocks.
Her eyes go to no place; her moaning is so small Denver can
hardly hear it.

"You all right? Beloved?"

Beloved focuses her eyes. "Over there. Her face."

Denver looks where Beloved's eyes go; there is nothing but
darkness there.

"Whose face? Who is it?"

"Me. It's me."

She is smiling again.

The last of the Sweet Home men, so named and called by one who would know, believed it. The other four believed it too, once, but they were long gone. The sold one never returned, the lost one never found. One, he knew, was dead for sure; one he hoped was, because butter and clabber was no life or reason to live it. He grew up thinking that, of all the Blacks in Kentucky, only the five of them were men. Allowed, encouraged to correct Garner, even defy him. To invent ways of doing things; to see what was needed and attack it without permission. To buy a mother, choose a horse or a wife, handle guns, even learn reading if they wanted to—but they didn't want to since nothing important to them could be put down on paper.

Was that it? Is that where the manhood lay? In the naming done by a whiteman who was supposed to know? Who gave them the privilege not of working but of deciding how to? No. In their relationship with Garner was true metal: they were believed and trusted, but most of all they were listened to.

He thought what they said had merit, and what they felt was serious. Deferring to his slaves' opinions did not deprive him of authority or power. It was schoolteacher who taught

them otherwise. A truth that waved like a scarecrow in rye:
they were only Sweet Home men at Sweet Home. One step off
that ground and they were trespassers among the human race.
Watchdogs without teeth; steer bulls without horns; gelded
workhorses whose neigh and whinny could not be translated
into a language responsible humans spoke. His strength had
lain in knowing that schoolteacher was wrong. Now he
wondered. There was Alfred, Georgia, there was Delaware,
there was Sixo and still he wondered. If schoolteacher was
right it explained how he had come to be a rag doll—picked
up and put back down anywhere any time by a girl young
enough to be his daughter. Fucking her when he was convinced
he didn't want to. Whenever she turned her behind up, the
calves of his youth (was that it?) cracked his resolve. But it
was more than appetite that humiliated him and made him
wonder if schoolteacher was right. It was being moved, placed
where she wanted him, and there was nothing he was able to
do about it. For his life he could not walk up the glistening
white stairs in the evening; for his life he could not stay in the
kitchen, in the keeping room, in the storeroom at night. And
he tried. Held his breath the way he had when he ducked into
the mud; steeled his heart the way he had when the trembling
began. But it was worse than that, worse than the blood eddy
he had controlled with a sledge hammer. When he stood up
from the supper table at 124 and turned toward the stairs,
nausea was first, then repulsion. He, he. He who had eaten raw
meat barely dead, who under plum trees bursting with blossoms had crunched through a dove's breast before its heart
stopped beating. Because he was a man and a man could do
what he would: be still for six hours in a dry well while night

dropped; fight raccoon with his hands and win; watch another man, whom he loved better than his brothers, roast without a tear just so the roasters would know what a man was like. And it was he, *that* man, who had walked from Georgia to Delaware, who could not go or stay put where he wanted to in 124— shame.

Paul D could not command his feet, but he thought he could still talk and he made up his mind to break out that way. He would tell Sethe about the last three weeks: catch her alone coming from work at the beer garden she called a restaurant and tell it all.

He waited for her. The winter afternoon looked like dusk as he stood in the alley behind Sawyer's Restaurant. Rehearsing, imagining her face and letting the words flock in his head like kids before lining up to follow the leader.

"Well, ah, this is not the, a man can't, see, but aw listen here, it ain't that, it really ain't, Ole Garner, what I mean is, it ain't a weakness, the kind of weakness I can fight 'cause 'cause something is happening to me, that girl is doing it, I know you think I never liked her nohow, but she is doing it to me. Fixing me. Sethe, she's fixed me and I can't break it."

What? A grown man fixed by a girl? But what if the girl was not a girl, but something in disguise? A lowdown something that looked like a sweet young girl and fucking her or not was not the point, it was not being able to stay or go where he wished in 124, and the danger was in losing Sethe because he was not man enough to break out, so he needed her, Sethe, to help him, to know about it, and it shamed him to have to ask the woman he wanted to protect to help him do it, God damn it to hell.

Paul D blew warm breath into the hollow of his cupped hands. The wind raced down the alley so fast it sleeked the fur of four kitchen dogs waiting for scraps. He looked at the dogs. The dogs looked at him.

Finally the back door opened and Sethe stepped through holding a scrap pan in the crook of her arm. When she saw him, she said Oh, and her smile was both pleasure and surprise.

Paul D believed he smiled back but his face was so cold he wasn't sure.

"Man, you make me feel like a girl, coming by to pick me up after work. Nobody ever did that before. You better watch out, I might start looking forward to it." She tossed the largest bones into the dirt rapidly so the dogs would know there was enough and not fight each other. Then she dumped the skins of some things, heads of other things and the insides of still more things—what the restaurant could not use and she would not—in a smoking pile near the animals' feet.

"Got to rinse this out," she said, "and then I'll be right with you."

He nodded as she returned to the kitchen.

The dogs ate without sound and Paul D thought they at least got what they came for, and if she had enough for them—

The cloth on her head was brown wool and she edged it down over her hairline against the wind.

"You get off early or what?"

"I took off early."

"Anything the matter?"

"In a way of speaking," he said and wiped his lips.

"Not cut back?"

"No, no. They got plenty work. I just—"

"Hm?"

"Sethe, you won't like what I'm 'bout to say."

She stopped then and turned her face toward him and the hateful wind. Another woman would have squinted or at least teared if the wind whipped her face as it did Sethe's. Another woman might have shot him a look of apprehension, pleading, anger even, because what he said sure sounded like part one of Goodbye, I'm gone.

Sethe looked at him steadily, calmly, already ready to accept, release or excuse an in-need-or-trouble man. Agreeing, saying okay, all right, in advance, because she didn't believe any of them—over the long haul—could measure up. And whatever the reason, it was all right. No fault. Nobody's fault.

He knew what she was thinking and even though she was wrong—he was not leaving her, wouldn't ever—the thing he had in mind to tell her was going to be worse. So, when he saw the diminished expectation in her eyes, the melancholy without blame, he could not say it. He could not say to this woman who did not squint in the wind, "I am not a man."

"Well, say it, Paul D, whether I like it or not."

Since he could not say what he planned to, he said something he didn't know was on his mind. "I want you pregnant, Sethe. Would you do that for me?"

Now she was laughing and so was he.

"You came by here to ask me that? You are one crazy-headed man. You right; I don't like it. Don't you think I'm too old to start that all over again?" She slipped her fingers in his hand for all the world like the hand-holding shadows on the side of the road.

"Think about it," he said. And suddenly it was a solution: a way to hold on to her, document his manhood and break out of the girl's spell—all in one. He put the tips of Sethe's fingers on his cheek. Laughing, she pulled them away lest somebody passing the alley see them misbehaving in public, in daylight, in the wind.

Still, he'd gotten a little more time, bought it, in fact, and hoped the price wouldn't wreck him. Like paying for an afternoon in the coin of life to come.

They left off playing, let go hands and hunched forward as they left the alley and entered the street. The wind was quieter there but the dried-out cold it left behind kept pedestrians fast-moving, stiff inside their coats. No men leaned against door frames or storefront windows. The wheels of wagons delivering feed or wood screeched as though they hurt. Hitched horses in front of the saloons shivered and closed their eyes. Four women, walking two abreast, approached, their shoes loud on the wooden walkway. Paul D touched Sethe's elbow to guide her as they stepped from the slats to the dirt to let the women pass.

Half an hour later, when they reached the city's edge, Sethe and Paul D resumed catching and snatching each other's fingers, stealing quick pats on the behind. Joyfully embarrassed to be that grown-up and that young at the same time.

Resolve, he thought. That was all it took, and no motherless gal was going to break it up. No lazy, stray pup of a woman could turn him around, make him doubt himself, wonder, plead or confess. Convinced of it, that he could do it, he threw his arm around Sethe's shoulders and squeezed. She let her head touch his chest, and since the moment was valuable to both of them, they stopped and stood that way—not breathing, not even caring if a passerby passed them by. The winter light was low. Sethe closed her eyes. Paul D looked at the black trees lining the roadside, their defending arms raised against attack. Softly, suddenly, it began to snow, like a present come down from the sky. Sethe opened her eyes to it and said, "Mercy." And it seemed to Paul D that it was—a little mercy—something given to them on purpose to mark what they were feeling so they would remember it later on when they needed to.

Down came the dry flakes, fat enough and heavy enough to crash like nickels on stone. It always surprised him, how quiet it was. Not like rain, but like a secret.

"Run!" he said.

"You run," said Sethe. "I been on my feet all day."

"Where I been? Sitting down?" and he pulled her along.

"Stop! Stop!" she said. "I don't have the legs for this."

"Then give em to me," he said and before she knew it he had backed into her, hoisted her on his back and was running down the road past brown fields turning white.

Breathless at last, he stopped and she slid back down on her own two feet, weak from laughter.

"You *need* some babies, somebody to play with in the snow." Sethe secured her headcloth.

Paul D smiled and warmed his hands with his breath. "I sure would like to give it a try. Need a willing partner though."

"I'll say," she answered. "Very, very willing."

It was nearly four o'clock now and 124 was half a mile ahead. Floating toward them, barely visible in the drifting snow, was a figure, and although it was the same figure that had been meeting Sethe for four months, so complete was the attention she and Paul D were paying to themselves they both felt a jolt when they saw her close in.

Beloved did not look at Paul D; her scrutiny was for Sethe. She had no coat, no wrap, nothing on her head, but she held in her hands a long shawl. Stretching out her arms she tried to circle it around Sethe.

"Crazy girl," said Sethe. "You the one out here with nothing on." And stepping away and in front of Paul D, Sethe took the shawl and wrapped it around Beloved's head and shoulders. Saying, "You got to learn more sense than that," she enclosed her in her left arm. Snowflakes stuck now. Paul D felt icy cold in the place Sethe had been before Beloved came. Trailing a yard or so behind the women, he fought the anger that shot through his stomach all the way home. When he saw Denver silhouetted in the lamplight at the window, he could not help thinking, "And whose ally you?"

It was Sethe who did it. Unsuspecting, surely, she solved everything with one blow.

"Now I know you not sleeping out there tonight, are you, Paul D?" She smiled at him, and like a friend in need, the chimney coughed against the rush of cold shooting into it from the sky. Window sashes shuddered in a blast of winter air.

Paul D looked up from the stew meat.

"You come upstairs. Where you belong," she said, "... and stay there."

The threads of malice creeping toward him from Beloved's side of the table were held harmless in the warmth of Sethe's smile.

Once before (and only once) Paul D had been grateful to a woman. Crawling out of the woods, cross-eyed with hunger and loneliness, he knocked at the first back door he came to in the colored section of Wilmington. He told the woman who opened it that he'd appreciate doing her woodpile, if she could spare him something to eat. She looked him up and down.

"A little later on," she said and opened the door wider. She fed him pork sausage, the worst thing in the world for a starving man, but neither he nor his stomach objected. Later, when he saw pale cotton sheets and two pillows in her bedroom, he had to wipe his eyes quickly, quickly so she would not see the thankful tears of a man's first time. Soil, grass, mud, shucking, leaves, hay, cobs, seashells—all that he'd slept on. White cotton sheets had never crossed his mind. He fell in with a groan and the woman helped him pretend he was making love to her and not her bed linen. He vowed that night, full of pork, deep in luxury, that he would never leave her. She would have to kill him to get him out of that bed. Eighteen months later, when he had been purchased by Northpoint Bank and Railroad Company, he was still thankful for that introduction to sheets.

Now he was grateful a second time. He felt as though he had been plucked from the face of a cliff and put down on sure ground. In Sethe's bed he knew he could put up with two crazy girls—as long as Sethe made her wishes known. Stretched out to his full length, watching snowflakes stream past the window over his feet, it was easy to dismiss the doubts that took him to the alley behind the restaurant: his expectations for himself were high, too high. What he might call cowardice other people called common sense.

Tucked into the well of his arm, Sethe recalled Paul D's face in the street when he asked her to have a baby for him. Although she laughed and took his hand, it had frightened her. She thought quickly of how good the sex would be if that is what he wanted, but mostly she was frightened by the thought of having a baby once more. Needing to be good enough, alert enough, strong enough, *that* caring—again. Having to stay alive just that much longer. O Lord, she thought, deliver me. Unless carefree, motherlove was a killer. What did he want her pregnant for? To hold on to her? have a sign that he passed this way? He probably had children everywhere anyway. Eighteen years of roaming, he would have to have dropped a few. No. He resented the children she had, that's what. Child, she corrected herself. Child plus Beloved whom she thought of as her own, and that is what he resented. Sharing her with the girls. Hearing the three of them laughing at something he wasn't in on. The code they used among themselves that he could not break. Maybe even the time spent on their needs and not his. They were a family somehow and he was not the head of it.

Can you stitch this up for me, baby?

Um hm. Soon's I finish this petticoat. She just got the one she came here in and everybody needs a change.

Any pie left?

I think Denver got the last of it.

And not complaining, not even minding that he slept all over and around the house now, which she put a stop to this night out of courtesy.

Sethe sighed and placed her hand on his chest. She knew she was building a case against him in order to build a case against getting pregnant, and it shamed her a little. But she had all the children she needed. If her boys came back one day, and Denver and Beloved stayed on—well, it would be the way it was supposed to be, no? Right after she saw the shadows

holding hands at the side of the road hadn't the picture altered?
And the minute she saw the dress and shoes sitting in the front
yard, she broke water. Didn't even have to see the face burning
in the sunlight. She had been dreaming it for years.

Paul D's chest rose and fell, rose and fell under her hand.

Denver finished washing the dishes and sat down at the table. Beloved, who had not moved since Sethe and Paul D left the room, sat sucking her forefinger. Denver watched her face awhile and then said, "She likes him here."

Beloved went on probing her mouth with her finger. "Make him go away," she said.

"She might be mad at you if he leaves."

Beloved, inserting a thumb in her mouth along with the forefinger, pulled out a back tooth. There was hardly any blood, but Denver said, "Ooooh, didn't that hurt you?"

Beloved looked at the tooth and thought, This is it. Next would be her arm, her hand, a toe. Pieces of her would drop maybe one at a time, maybe all at once. Or on one of those mornings before Denver woke and after Sethe left she would fly apart. It is difficult keeping her head on her neck, her legs attached to her hips when she is by herself. Among the things she could not remember was when she first knew that she could wake up any day and find herself in pieces. She had two dreams: exploding, and being swallowed. When her tooth came out—an odd fragment, last in the row—she thought it was starting.

171

"Must be a wisdom," said Denver. "Don't it hurt?"

"Yes."

"Then why don't you cry?"

"What?"

"If it hurts, why don't you cry?"

And she did. Sitting there holding a small white tooth in the palm of her smooth smooth hand. Cried the way she wanted to when turtles came out of the water, one behind the other, right after the blood-red bird disappeared back into the leaves. The way she wanted to when Sethe went to him standing in the tub under the stairs. With the tip of her tongue she touched the salt water that slid to the corner of her mouth and hoped Denver's arm around her shoulders would keep them from falling apart.

The couple upstairs, united, didn't hear a sound, but below them, outside, all around 124 the snow went on and on and on. Piling itself, burying itself. Higher. Deeper.

In the back of Baby Suggs' mind may have been the thought that if Halle made it, God do what He would, it would be a cause for celebration. If only this final son could do for himself what he had done for her and for the three children John and Ella delivered to her door one summer night. When the children arrived and no Sethe, she was afraid and grateful. Grateful that the part of the family that survived was her own grandchildren—the first and only she would know: two boys and a little girl who was crawling already. But she held her heart still, afraid to form questions: What about Sethe and Halle; why the delay? Why didn't Sethe get on board too? Nobody could make it alone. Not only because trappers picked them off like buzzards or netted them like rabbits, but also because you couldn't run if you didn't know how to go. You could be lost forever, if there wasn't nobody to show you the way.

So when Sethe arrived—all mashed up and split open, but with another grandchild in her arms—the idea of a whoop moved closer to the front of her brain. But since there was still no sign of Halle and Sethe herself didn't know what had happened to him, she let the whoop lie—not wishing to hurt his chances by thanking God too soon.

It was Stamp Paid who started it. Twenty days after Sethe got to 124 he came by and looked at the baby he had tied up in his nephew's jacket, looked at the mother he had handed a piece of fried eel to and, for some private reason of his own, went off with two buckets to a place near the river's edge that only he knew about where blackberries grew, tasting so good and happy that to eat them was like being in church. Just one of the berries and you felt anointed. He walked six miles to the riverbank; did a slide-run-slide down into a ravine made almost inaccessible by brush. He reached through brambles lined with blood-drawing thorns thick as knives that cut through his shirt sleeves and trousers. All the while suffering mosquitoes, bees, hornets, wasps and the meanest lady spiders in the state. Scratched, raked and bitten, he maneuvered through and took hold of each berry with fingertips so gentle not a single one was bruised. Late in the afternoon he got back to 124 and put two full buckets down on the porch. When Baby Suggs saw his shredded clothes, bleeding hands, welted face and neck she sat down laughing out loud.

Buglar, Howard, the woman in the bonnet and Sethe came to look and then laughed along with Baby Suggs at the sight of the sly, steely old black man: agent, fisherman, boatman, tracker, savior, spy, standing in broad daylight whipped finally by two pails of blackberries. Paying them no mind he took a berry and put it in the three-week-old Denver's mouth. The women shrieked.

"She's too little for that, Stamp."

"Bowels be soup."

"Sickify her stomach."

But the baby's thrilled eyes and smacking lips made them follow suit, sampling one at a time the berries that tasted like church. Finally Baby Suggs slapped the boys' hands away from the bucket and sent Stamp around to the pump to rinse himself. She had decided to do something with the fruit worthy of the man's labor and his love. That's how it began.

She made the pastry dough and thought she ought to tell Ella and John to stop on by because three pies, maybe four, were too much to keep for one's own. Sethe thought they might as well back it up with a couple of chickens. Stamp allowed that perch and catfish were jumping into the boat—didn't even have to drop a line.

From Denver's two thrilled eyes it grew to a feast for ninety people. 124 shook with their voices far into the night. Ninety people who ate so well, and laughed so much, it made them angry. They woke up the next morning and remembered the meal-fried perch that Stamp Paid handled with a hickory twig, holding his left palm out against the spit and pop of the boiling grease; the corn pudding made with cream; tired, overfed children asleep in the grass, tiny bones of roasted rabbit still in their hands—and got angry.

Baby Suggs' three (maybe four) pies grew to ten (maybe twelve). Sethe's two hens became five turkeys. The one block of ice brought all the way from Cincinnati—over which they poured mashed watermelon mixed with sugar and mint to make a punch—became a wagonload of ice cakes for a washtub full of strawberry shrug. 124, rocking with laughter, goodwill and food for ninety, made them angry. Too much, they thought. Where does she get it all, Baby Suggs, holy? Why is she and

hers always the center of things? How come she always knows
exactly what to do and when? Giving advice; passing messages;
healing the sick, hiding fugitives, loving, cooking, cooking,
loving, preaching, singing, dancing and loving everybody like
it was her job and hers alone.

Now to take two buckets of blackberries and make ten, maybe
twelve, pies; to have turkey enough for the whole town pretty
near, new peas in September, fresh cream but no cow, ice *and*
sugar, batter bread, bread pudding, raised bread, shortbread—
it made them mad. Loaves and fishes were His powers—they
did not belong to an ex-slave who had probably never carried
one hundred pounds to the scale, or picked okra with a baby
on her back. Who had never been lashed by a ten-year-old
whiteboy as God knows they had. Who had not even escaped
slavery—had, in fact, been *bought out* of it by a doting son and
driven to the Ohio River in a wagon—free papers folded between
her breasts (driven by the very man who had been her master,
who also paid her resettlement fee—name of Garner), and
rented a house with *two* floors *and* a well from the Bodwins—
the white brother and sister who gave Stamp Paid, Ella and
John clothes, goods and gear for runaways because they hated
slavery worse than they hated slaves.

It made them furious. They swallowed baking soda, the
morning after, to calm the stomach violence caused by the
bounty, the reckless generosity on display at 124. Whispered
to each other in the yards about fat rats, doom and uncalled-for
pride.

The scent of their disapproval lay heavy in the air. Baby
Suggs woke to it and wondered what it was as she boiled
hominy for her grandchildren. Later, as she stood in the garden,

chopping at the tight soil over the roots of the pepper plants, she smelled it again. She lifted her head and looked around. Behind her some yards to the left Sethe squatted in the pole beans. Her shoulders were distorted by the greased flannel under her dress to encourage the healing of her back. Near her in a bushel basket was the three-week-old baby. Baby Suggs, holy, looked up. The sky was blue and clear. Not one touch of death in the definite green of the leaves. She could hear birds and, faintly, the stream way down in the meadow. The puppy, Here Boy, was burying the last bones from yesterday's party. From somewhere at the side of the house came the voices of Buglar, Howard and the crawling girl. Nothing seemed amiss— yet the smell of disapproval was sharp. Back beyond the vegetable garden, closer to the stream but in full sun, she had planted corn. Much as they'd picked for the party, there were still ears ripening, which she could see from where she stood. Baby Suggs leaned back into the peppers and the squash vines with her hoe. Carefully, with the blade at just the right angle, she cut through a stalk of insistent rue. Its flowers she stuck through a split in her hat; the rest she tossed aside. The quiet clok clok clok of wood splitting reminded her that Stamp was doing the chore he promised to the night before. She sighed at her work and, a moment later, straightened up to sniff the disapproval once again. Resting on the handle of the hoe, she concentrated. She was accustomed to the knowledge that nobody prayed for her—but this free-floating repulsion was new. It wasn't whitefolks—that much she could tell—so it must be colored ones. And then she knew. Her friends and neighbors were angry at her because she had overstepped, given too much, offended them by excess.

Baby closed her eyes. Perhaps they were right. Suddenly, behind the disapproving odor, way way back behind it, she smelled another thing. Dark and coming. Something she couldn't get at because the other odor hid it.

She squeezed her eyes tight to see what it was but all she could make out was high-topped shoes she didn't like the look of.

Thwarted yet wondering, she chopped away with the hoe. What could it be? This dark and coming thing. What was left to hurt her now? News of Halle's death? No. She had been prepared for that better than she had for his life. The last of her children, whom she barely glanced at when he was born because it wasn't worth the trouble to try to learn features you would never see change into adulthood anyway. Seven times she had done that: held a little foot; examined the fat fingertips with her own—fingers she never saw become the male or female hands a mother would recognize anywhere. She didn't know to this day what their permanent teeth looked like; or how they held their heads when they walked. Did Patty lose her lisp? What color did Famous' skin finally take? Was that a cleft in Johnny's chin or just a dimple that would disappear soon's his jawbone changed? Four girls, and the last time she saw them there was no hair under their arms. Does Ardelia still love the burned bottom of bread? All seven were gone or dead. What would be the point of looking too hard at that youngest one? But for some reason they let her keep him. He was with her—everywhere.

When she hurt her hip in Carolina she was a real bargain (costing less than Halle, who was ten then) for Mr. Garner, who took them both to Kentucky to a farm he called Sweet

Home. Because of the hip she jerked like a three-legged dog when she walked. But at Sweet Home there wasn't a rice field or tobacco patch in sight, and nobody, but nobody, knocked her down. Not once. Lillian Garner called her Jenny for some reason but she never pushed, hit or called her mean names. Even when she slipped in cow dung and broke every egg in her apron, nobody said you-black-bitch-what's-the-matter-with-you and nobody knocked her down.

Sweet Home was tiny compared to the places she had been. Mr. Garner, Mrs. Garner, herself, Halle, and four boys, over half named Paul, made up the entire population. Mrs. Garner hummed when she worked; Mr. Garner acted like the world was a toy he was supposed to have fun with. Neither wanted her in the field—Mr. Garner's boys, including Halle, did all of that—which was a blessing since she could not have managed it anyway. What she did was stand beside the humming Lillian Garner while the two of them cooked, preserved, washed, ironed, made candles, clothes, soap and cider; fed chickens, pigs, dogs and geese; milked cows, churned butter, rendered fat, laid fires … Nothing to it. And nobody knocked her down.

Her hip hurt every single day—but she never spoke of it. Only Halle, who had watched her movements closely for the last four years, knew that to get in and out of bed she had to lift her thigh with both hands, which was why he spoke to Mr. Garner about buying her out of there so she could sit down for a change. Sweet boy. The one person who did something hard for her: gave her his work, his life and now his children, whose voices she could just make out as she stood in the garden wondering what was the dark and coming thing behind the scent of disapproval. Sweet Home was a marked improvement.

No question. And no matter, for the sadness was at her center, the desolated center where the self that was no self made its home. Sad as it was that she did not know where her children were buried or what they looked like if alive, fact was she knew more about them than she knew about herself, having never had the map to discover what she was like.

Could she sing? (Was it nice to hear when she did?) Was she pretty? Was she a good friend? Could she have been a loving mother? A faithful wife? Have I got a sister and does she favor me? If my mother knew me would she like me?

In Lillian Garner's house, exempted from the field work that broke her hip and the exhaustion that drugged her mind; in Lillian Garner's house where nobody knocked her down (or up), she listened to the whitewoman humming at her work; watched her face light up when Mr. Garner came in and thought, It's better here, but I'm not. The Garners, it seemed to her, ran a special kind of slavery, treating them like paid labor, listening to what they said, teaching what they wanted known. And he didn't stud his boys. Never brought them to her cabin with directions to "lay down with her," like they did in Carolina, or rented their sex out on other farms. It surprised and pleased her, but worried her too. Would he pick women for them or what did he think was going to happen when those boys ran smack into their nature? Some danger he was courting and he surely knew it. In fact, his order for them not to leave Sweet Home, except in his company, was not so much because of the law, but the danger of men-bred slaves on the loose.

Baby Suggs talked as little as she could get away with because what was there to say that the roots of her tongue could manage? So the whitewoman, finding her new slave excellent if silent help, hummed to herself while she worked.

When Mr. Garner agreed to the arrangements with Halle, and when Halle looked like it meant more to him that she go free than anything in the world, she let herself be taken 'cross the river. Of the two hard things—standing on her feet till she dropped or leaving her last and probably only living child—she chose the hard thing that made him happy, and never put to him the question she put to herself: What for? What does a sixty-odd-year-old slavewoman who walks like a three-legged dog need freedom for? And when she stepped foot on free ground she could not believe that Halle knew what she didn't; that Halle, who had never drawn one free breath, knew that there was nothing like it in this world. It scared her.

Something's the matter. What's the matter? What's the matter? she asked herself. She didn't know what she looked like and was not curious. But suddenly she saw her hands and thought with a clarity as simple as it was dazzling, "These hands belong to me. These *my* hands." Next she felt a knocking in her chest and discovered something else new: her own heart-beat. Had it been there all along? This pounding thing? She felt like a fool and began to laugh out loud. Mr. Garner looked over his shoulder at her with wide brown eyes and smiled himself. "What's funny, Jenny?"

She couldn't stop laughing. "My heart's beating," she said.

And it was true.

Mr. Garner laughed. "Nothing to be scared of, Jenny. Just keep your same ways, you'll be all right."

She covered her mouth to keep from laughing too loud.

"These people I'm taking you to will give you what help you need. Name of Bodwin. A brother and a sister. Scots. I been knowing them for twenty years or more."

Baby Suggs thought it was a good time to ask him something she had long wanted to know.

"Mr. Garner," she said, "why you all call me Jenny?"

"'Cause that what's on your sales ticket, gal. Ain't that your name? What you call yourself?"

"Nothing," she said. "I don't call myself nothing."

Mr. Garner went red with laughter. "When I took you out of Carolina, Whitlow called you Jenny and Jenny Whitlow is what his bill said. Didn't he call you Jenny?"

"No, sir. If he did I didn't hear it."

"What did you answer to?"

"Anything, but Suggs is what my husband name."

"You got married, Jenny? I didn't know it."

"Manner of speaking."

"You know where he is, this husband?"

"No, sir."

"Is that Halle's daddy?"

"No, sir."

"Why you call him Suggs, then? His bill of sale says Whitlow too, just like yours."

"Suggs is my name, sir. From my husband. He didn't call me Jenny."

"What he call you?"

"Baby."

"Well," said Mr. Garner, going pink again, "if I was you I'd stick to Jenny Whitlow. Mrs. Baby Suggs ain't no name for a freed Negro."

Maybe not, she thought, but Baby Suggs was all she had left of the "husband" she claimed. A serious, melancholy man who taught her how to make shoes. The two of them made a pact: whichever one got a chance to run would take it; together if possible, alone if not, and no looking back. He got his chance, and since she never heard otherwise she believed he made it. Now how could he find or hear tell of her if she was calling herself some bill-of-sale name?

She couldn't get over the city. More people than Carolina and enough whitefolks to stop the breath. Two-story buildings everywhere, and walkways made of perfectly cut slats of wood. Roads wide as Garner's whole house.

"This is a city of water," said Mr. Garner. "Everything travels by water and what the rivers can't carry the canals take. A queen of a city, Jenny. Everything you ever dreamed of, they make it right here. Iron stoves, buttons, ships, shirts, hairbrushes, paint, steam engines, books. A sewer system make your eyes bug out. Oh, this is a city, all right. If you have to live in a city—this is it."

The Bodwins lived right in the center of a street full of houses and trees. Mr. Garner leaped out and tied his horse to a solid iron post.

"Here we are."

Baby picked up her bundle and with great difficulty, caused by her hip and the hours of sitting in a wagon, climbed down. Mr. Garner was up the walk and on the porch before she touched ground, but she got a peep at a Negro girl's face at the open door before she followed a path to the back of the house. She waited what seemed a long time before this same girl opened the kitchen door and offered her a seat by the window.

"Can I get you anything to eat, ma'am?" the girl asked.

"No, darling. I'd look favorable on some water though." The girl went to the sink and pumped a cupful of water. She placed it in Baby Suggs' hand. "I'm Janey, ma'am."

Baby, marveling at the sink, drank every drop of water although it tasted like a serious medicine. "Suggs," she said, blotting her lips with the back of her hand. "Baby Suggs."

"Glad to meet you, Mrs. Suggs. You going to be staying here?"

"I don't know where I'll be. Mr. Garner—that's him what brought me here—he say he arrange something for me." And then, "I'm free, you know."

Janey smiled. "Yes, ma'am."

"Your people live around here?"

"Yes, ma'am. All us live out on Bluestone."

"We scattered," said Baby Suggs, "but maybe not for long."

Great God, she thought, where do I start? Get somebody to write old Whitlow. See who took Patty and Rosa Lee. Somebody name Dunn got Ardelia and went West, she heard. No point in trying for Tyree or John. They cut thirty years ago and, if she searched too hard and they were hiding, finding them would do them more harm than good. Nancy and Famous died in a ship off the Virginia coast before it set sail for Savannah. That much she knew. The overseer at Whitlow's place brought her the news, more from a wish to have his way with her than from the kindness of his heart. The captain waited three weeks in port, to get a full cargo before setting off. Of the slaves in the hold who didn't make it, he said, two were Whitlow pickaninnies name of ...

But she knew their names. She knew, and covered her ears with her fists to keep from hearing them come from his mouth.

Janey heated some milk and poured it in a bowl next to a plate of cornbread. After some coaxing, Baby Suggs came to the table and sat down. She crumbled the bread into the hot milk and discovered she was hungrier than she had ever been in her life and that was saying something.

"They going to miss this?"

"No," said Janey. "Eat all you want; it's ours."

"Anybody else live here?"

"Just me. Mr. Woodruff, he does the outside chores. He comes by two, three days a week."

"Just you two?"

"Yes, ma'am. I do the cooking and washing."

"Maybe your people know of somebody looking for help."

"I be sure to ask, but I know they take women at the slaughterhouse."

"Doing what?"

"I don't know."

"Something men don't want to do, I reckon."

"My cousin say you get all the meat you want, plus twenty-five cents the hour. She make summer sausage."

Baby Suggs lifted her hand to the top of her head. Money? Money? They would pay her money every single day? Money?

"Where is this here slaughterhouse?" she asked.

Before Janey could answer, the Bodwins came in to the kitchen with a grinning Mr. Garner behind. Undeniably brother and sister, both dressed in gray with faces too young for their snow-white hair.

"Did you give her anything to eat, Janey?" asked the brother.

"Yes, sir."

"Keep your seat, Jenny," said the sister, and that good news got better.

When they asked what work she could do, instead of reeling off the hundreds of tasks she had performed, she asked about the slaughterhouse. She was too old for that, they said.

"She's the best cobbler you ever see," said Mr. Garner.

"Cobbler?" Sister Bodwin raised her black thick eyebrows. "Who taught you that?"

"Was a slave taught me," said Baby Suggs.

"New boots, or just repair?"

"New, old, anything."

"Well," said Brother Bodwin, "that'll be something, but you'll need more."

"What about taking in wash?" asked Sister Bodwin.

"Yes, ma'am."

"Two cents a pound."

"Yes, ma'am. But where's the in?"

"What?"

"You said 'take in wash.' Where is the 'in'? Where I'm going to be."

"Oh, just listen to this, Jenny," said Mr. Garner. "These two angels got a house for you. Place they own out a ways."

It had belonged to their grandparents before they moved in town. Recently it had been rented out to a whole parcel of Negroes, who had left the state. It was too big a house for Jenny alone, they said (two rooms upstairs, two down), but it was the best and the only thing they could do. In return for laundry, some seamstress work, a little canning and so on (oh shoes, too), they would permit her to stay there. Provided she was clean. The past parcel of colored wasn't. Baby Suggs agreed to the situation, sorry to see the money go but excited about a house with steps—never mind she couldn't climb them. Mr. Garner told the Bodwins that she was a right fine cook as well as a fine cobbler and showed his belly and the sample on his feet. Everybody laughed.

"Anything you need, let us know," said the sister. "We don't hold with slavery, even Garner's kind."

"Tell em, Jenny. You live any better on any place before mine?"

"No, sir," she said. "No place."

"How long was you at Sweet Home?"

"Ten year, I believe."

"Ever go hungry?"

"No, sir."

"Cold?"

"No, sir."

"Anybody lay a hand on you?"

"No, sir."

"Did I let Halle buy you or not?"

"Yes, sir, you did," she said, thinking, But you got my boy and I'm all broke down. You be renting him out to pay for me way after I'm gone to Glory.

Woodruff, they said, would carry her out there, they said, and all three disappeared through the kitchen door.

"I have to fix the supper now," said Janey.

"I'll help," said Baby Suggs. "You too short to reach the fire."

It was dark when Woodruff clicked the horse into a trot. He was a young man with a heavy beard and a burned place on his jaw the beard did not hide.

"You born up here?" Baby Suggs asked him.

"No, ma'am. Virginia. Been here a couple years."

"I see."

"You going to a nice house. Big too. A preacher and his family was in there. Eighteen children."

"Have mercy. Where they go?"

"Took off to Illinois. Bishop Allen gave him a congregation up there. Big."

"What churches around here? I ain't set foot in one in ten years."

"How come?"

"Wasn't none. I dislike the place I was before this last one, but I did get to church every Sunday some kind of way. I bet the Lord done forgot who I am by now."

"Go see Reverend Pike, ma'am. He'll reacquaint you."

"I won't need him for that. I can make my own acquaintance. What I need him for is to reacquaint me with my children. He can read and write, I reckon?"

"Sure."

"Good, 'cause I got a lot of digging up to do." But the news they dug up was so pitiful she quit. After two years of messages written by the preacher's hand, two years of washing, sewing, canning, cobbling, gardening, and sitting in churches, all she found out was that the Whitlow place was gone and that you couldn't write to "a man named Dunn" if all you knew was that he went West. The good news, however, was that Halle got married and had a baby coming. She fixed on that and her own brand of preaching, having made up her mind about what to do with the heart that started beating the minute she crossed the Ohio River. And it worked out, worked out just fine, until she got proud and let herself be overwhelmed by the sight of her daughter-in-law and Halle's children—one of whom was born on the way—and have a celebration of blackberries that put Christmas to shame. Now she stood in the garden smelling disapproval, feeling a dark and coming thing, and seeing high-topped shoes that she didn't like the look of at all. At all.

When the four horsemen came—schoolteacher, one nephew, one slave catcher and a sheriff—the house on Bluestone Road was so quiet they thought they were too late. Three of them dismounted, one stayed in the saddle, his rifle ready, his eyes trained away from the house to the left and to the right, because likely as not the fugitive would make a dash for it. Although sometimes, you could never tell, you'd find them folded up tight somewhere: beneath floorboards, in a pantry— once in a chimney. Even then care was taken, because the quietest ones, the ones you pulled from a press, a hayloft, or, that once, from a chimney, would go along nicely for two or three seconds. Caught red-handed, so to speak, they would seem to recognize the futility of outsmarting a whiteman and the hopelessness of outrunning a rifle. Smile even, like a child caught dead with his hand in the jelly jar, and when you reached for the rope to tie him, well, even then you couldn't tell. The very nigger with his head hanging and a little jelly-jar smile on his face could all of a sudden roar, like a bull or some such, and commence to do disbelievable things. Grab the rifle at its mouth; throw himself at the one holding it—anything. So you had to keep back a pace, leave the tying to another. Otherwise you ended up killing what you were paid to bring back alive. Unlike a snake or a bear, a dead nigger could not be skinned for profit and was not worth his own dead weight in coin.

Six or seven Negroes were walking up the road toward the house: two boys from the slave catcher's left and some women from his right. He motioned them still with his rifle and they stood where they were. The nephew came back from peeping inside the house, and after touching his lips for silence, pointed his thumb to say that what they were looking for was round back. The slave catcher dismounted then and joined the others. Schoolteacher and the nephew moved to the left of the house; himself and the sheriff to the right. A crazy old nigger was standing in the woodpile with an ax. You could tell he was crazy right off because he was grunting—making low, cat noises like. About twelve yards beyond that nigger was another one—a woman with a flower in her hat. Crazy too, probably, because she too was standing stock-still—but fanning her hands as though pushing cobwebs out of her way. Both, however, were staring at the same place—a shed. Nephew walked over to the old nigger boy and took the ax from him. Then all four started toward the shed.

Inside, two boys bled in the sawdust and dirt at the feet of a nigger woman holding a blood-soaked child to her chest with one hand and an infant by the heels in the other. She did not look at them; she simply swung the baby toward the wall planks, missed and tried to connect a second time, when out of nowhere—in the ticking time the men spent staring at what there was to stare at—the old nigger boy, still mewing, ran through the door behind them and snatched the baby from the arc of its mother's swing.

Right off it was clear, to schoolteacher especially, that there was nothing there to claim. The three (now four—because she'd had the one coming when she cut) pickaninnies they had hoped were alive and well enough to take back to Kentucky, take back and raise properly to do the work Sweet Home desperately needed, were not. Two were lying open-eyed in sawdust; a third pumped blood down the dress of the main one—the woman schoolteacher bragged about, the one he said made fine ink, damn good soup, pressed his collars the way he liked besides having at least ten breeding years left. But now she'd gone wild, due to the mishandling of the nephew who'd overbeat her and made her cut and run. Schoolteacher had chastised that nephew, telling him to think—just think—what would his own horse do if you beat it beyond the point of education. Or Chipper, or Samson. Suppose you beat the hounds past that point thataway. Never again could you trust them in the woods or anywhere else. You'd be feeding them maybe, holding out a piece of rabbit in your hand, and the animal would revert—bite your hand clean off. So he punished that nephew by not letting him come on the hunt. Made him stay there, feed stock, feed himself, feed Lillian, tend crops. See how he liked it; see what happened when you overbeat creatures God had given you the respon-sibility of—the trouble it was, and the loss. The whole lot was lost now. Five. He could claim the baby struggling in the arms of the mewing old man, but who'd tend her? Because the woman—something was wrong with her. She was looking at him now, and if his other nephew could see that look he would learn the lesson for sure: you just can't mishandle creatures and expect success.

The nephew, the one who had nursed her while his brother held her down, didn't know he was shaking. His uncle had warned him against that kind of confusion, but the warning didn't seem to be taking. What she go and do that for? On account of a beating? Hell, he'd been beat a million times and he was white. Once it hurt so bad and made him so mad he'd smashed the well bucket. Another time he took it out on Samson—a few tossed rocks was all. But no beating ever made him ... I mean no way he could have ... What she go and do that for? And that is what he asked the sheriff, who was standing there amazed like the rest of them, but not shaking. He was swallowing hard, over and over again. "What she want to go and do that for?"

The sheriff turned, then said to the other three, "You all better go on. Look like your business is over. Mine's started now."

Schoolteacher beat his hat against his thigh and spit before leaving the woodshed. Nephew and the catcher backed out with him. They didn't look at the woman in the pepper plants with the flower in her hat. And they didn't look at the seven or so faces that had edged closer in spite of the catcher's rifle warning. Enough nigger eyes for now. Little nigger-boy eyes open in sawdust; little nigger-girl eyes staring between the wet fingers that held her face so her head wouldn't fall off; little nigger-baby eyes crinkling up to cry in the arms of the old nigger whose own eyes were nothing but slivers looking down at his feet. But the worst ones were those of the nigger woman who looked like she didn't have any. Since the whites in them had

disappeared and since they were as black as her skin, she looked
blind.

They unhitched from schoolteacher's horse the borrowed
mule that was to carry the fugitive woman back to where she
belonged, and tied it to the fence. Then, with the sun straight
up over their heads, they trotted off, leaving the sheriff behind
among the damnedest bunch of coons they'd ever seen. All
testimony to the results of a little so-called freedom imposed
on people who needed every care and guidance in the world
to keep them from the cannibal life they preferred.

The sheriff wanted to back out too. To stand in the sunlight
outside of that place meant for housing wood, coal, kerosene—
fuel for cold Ohio winters, which he thought of now, while
resisting the urge to run into the August sunlight. Not because
he was afraid. Not at all. He was just cold. And he didn't want
to touch anything. The baby in the old man's arms was crying,
and the woman's eyes with no whites were gazing straight
ahead. They all might have remained that way, frozen till
Thursday, except one of the boys on the floor sighed. As if he
were sunk in the pleasure of a deep sweet sleep, he sighed the
sigh that flung the sheriff into action.

"I'll have to take you in. No trouble now. You've done enough
to last you. Come on now."

She did not move.

"You come quiet, hear, and I won't have to tie you up."

She stayed still and he had made up his mind to go near her
and some kind of way bind her wet red hands when a shadow
behind him in the doorway made him turn. The nigger with
the flower in her hat entered.

*

Baby Suggs noticed who breathed and who did not and went straight to the boys lying in the dirt. The old man moved to the woman gazing and said, "Sethe. You take my armload and gimme yours."

She turned to him, and glancing at the baby he was holding, made a low sound in her throat as though she'd made a mistake, left the salt out of the bread or something.

"I'm going out here and send for a wagon," the sheriff said and got into the sunlight at last.

But neither Stamp Paid nor Baby Suggs could make her put her crawling-already? girl down. Out of the shed, back in the house, she held on. Baby Suggs had got the boys inside and was bathing their heads, rubbing their hands, lifting their lids, whispering, "Beg your pardon, I beg your pardon," the whole time. She bound their wounds and made them breathe camphor before turning her attention to Sethe. She took the crying baby from Stamp Paid and carried it on her shoulder for a full two minutes, then stood in front of its mother.

"It's time to nurse your youngest," she said.

Sethe reached up for the baby without letting the dead one go.

Baby Suggs shook her head. "One at a time," she said and traded the living for the dead, which she carried into the keeping room. When she came back, Sethe was aiming a bloody nipple into the baby's mouth. Baby Suggs slammed her fist on the table and shouted, "Clean up! Clean yourself up!"

They fought then. Like rivals over the heart of the loved, they fought. Each struggling for the nursing child. Baby Suggs lost when she slipped in a red puddle and fell. So Denver took her mother's milk right along with the blood of her sister. And that's the way they were when the sheriff returned, having commandeered a neighbor's cart, and ordered Stamp to drive it.

Outside a throng, now, of black faces stopped murmuring. Holding the living child, Sethe walked past them in their silence and hers. She climbed into the cart, her profile knife-clean against a cheery blue sky. A profile that shocked them with its clarity. Was her head a bit too high? Her back a little too straight? Probably. Otherwise the singing would have begun at once, the moment she appeared in the doorway of the house on Bluestone Road. Some cape of sound would have quickly been wrapped around her, like arms to hold and steady her on the way. As it was, they waited till the cart turned about, headed west to town. And then no words. Humming. No words at all.

Baby Suggs meant to run, skip down the porch steps after the cart, screaming, No. No. Don't let her take that last one too. She meant to. Had started to, but when she got up from the floor and reached the yard the cart was gone and a wagon was rolling up. A red-haired boy and a yellow-haired girl jumped down and ran through the crowd toward her. The boy had a half-eaten sweet pepper in one hand and a pair of shoes in the other.

"Mama says Wednesday." He held them together by their tongues. "She says you got to have these fixed by Wednesday."

Baby Suggs looked at him, and then at the woman holding a twitching lead horse to the road.

"She says Wednesday, you hear? Baby? Baby?"

She took the shoes from him—high-topped and muddy—saying, "I beg your pardon. Lord, I beg your pardon. I sure do."

Out of sight, the cart creaked on down Bluestone Road. Nobody in it spoke. The wagon rock had put the baby to sleep. The hot sun dried Sethe's dress, stiff, like rigor mortis.

That ain't her mouth.

Anybody who didn't know her, or maybe somebody who just got a glimpse of her through the peephole at the restaurant, might think it was hers, but Paul D knew better. Oh well, a little something around the forehead—a quietness—that kind of reminded you of her. But there was no way you could take that for her mouth and he said so. Told Stamp Paid, who was watching him carefully.

"I don't know, man. Don't look like it to me. I know Sethe's mouth and this ain't it." He smoothed the clipping with his fingers and peered at it, not at all disturbed. From the solemn air with which Stamp had unfolded the paper, the tenderness in the old man's fingers as he stroked its creases and flattened it out, first on his knees, then on the split top of the piling, Paul D knew that it ought to mess him up. That whatever was written on it should shake him.

Pigs were crying in the chute. All day Paul D, Stamp Paid and twenty more had pushed and prodded them from canal to shore to chute to slaughterhouse. Although, as grain farmers moved west, St. Louis and Chicago now ate up a lot of the business, Cincinnati was still pig port in the minds of Ohioans. Its main job was to receive, slaughter and ship up the river the hogs that Northerners did not want to live without. For a month or so in the winter any stray man had work, if he could breathe the stench of offal and stand up for twelve hours, skills in which Paul D was admirably trained.

A little pig shit, rinsed from every place he could touch, remained on his boots, and he was conscious of it as he stood there with a light smile of scorn curling his lips. Usually he left his boots in the shed and put his walking shoes on along with his day clothes in the corner before he went home. A route that took him smack dab through the middle of a cemetery as old as sky, rife with the agitation of dead Miami no longer content to rest in the mounds that covered them. Over their heads walked a strange people; through their earth pillows roads were cut; wells and houses nudged them out of eternal rest. Outraged more by their folly in believing land was holy than by the disturbances of their peace, they growled on the banks of Licking River, sighed in the trees on Catherine Street and rode the wind above the pig yards. Paul D heard them but he stayed on because all in all it wasn't a bad job, especially in winter when Cincinnati reassumed its status of slaughter and riverboat capital. The craving for pork was growing into a mania in every city in the country. Pig farmers were cashing in, provided they could raise enough and get them sold farther and farther away. And the Germans who flooded southern Ohio brought and developed swine cooking to its highest form. Pig boats jammed the Ohio River, and their captains' hollering at one another over the grunts of the stock was as common a water sound as that of the ducks flying over their heads. Sheep, cows and fowl too floated up and down that river, and all a Negro had to do was show up and there was work: poking, killing, cutting, skinning, case packing and saving offal.

A hundred yards from the crying pigs, the two men stood behind a shed on Western Row and it was clear why Stamp had been eyeing Paul D this last week of work; why he paused when the evening shift came on, to let Paul D's movements catch up to his own. He had made up his mind to show him this piece of paper—newspaper—with a picture drawing of a woman who favored Sethe except that was not her mouth. Nothing like it.

Paul D slid the clipping out from under Stamp's palm. The print meant nothing to him so he didn't even glance at it. He simply looked at the face, shaking his head no. No. At the mouth, you see. And no at whatever it was those black scratches said, and no to whatever it was Stamp Paid wanted him to know. Because there was no way in hell a black face could appear in a newspaper if the story was about something anybody wanted to hear. A whip of fear broke through the heart chambers as soon as you saw a Negro's face in a paper, since the face was not there because the person had a healthy baby, or outran a street mob. Nor was it there because the person had been killed, or maimed or caught or burned or jailed or whipped or evicted or stomped or raped or cheated, since that could hardly qualify as news in a newspaper. It would have to be something out of the ordinary—something whitepeople would find interesting, truly different, worth a few minutes of teeth sucking if not gasps. And it must have been hard to find news about Negroes worth the breath catch of a white citizen of Cincinnati.

So who was this woman with a mouth that was not Sethe's, but whose eyes were almost as calm as hers? Whose head was turned on her neck in the manner he loved so well it watered his eye to see it.

And he said so. "This ain't her mouth. I know her mouth and this ain't it." Before Stamp Paid could speak he said it and even while he spoke Paul D said it again. Oh, he heard all the old man was saying, but the more he heard, the stranger the lips in the drawing became.

Stamp started with the party, the one Baby Suggs gave, but stopped and backed up a bit to tell about the berries—where they were and what was in the earth that made them grow like that.

"They open to the sun, but not the birds, 'cause snakes down in there and the birds know it, so they just grow—fat and sweet—with nobody to bother em 'cept me because don't nobody go in that piece of water but me and ain't too many legs willing to glide down that bank to get them. Me neither. But I was willing that day. Somehow or 'nother I was willing. And they whipped me, I'm telling you. Tore me up. But I filled two buckets anyhow. And took em over to Baby Suggs' house. It was on from then on. Such a cooking you never see no more. We baked, fried and stewed everything God put down here. Everybody came. Everybody stuffed. Cooked so much there wasn't a stick of kindlin left for the next day. I volunteered to do it. And next morning I come over, like I promised, to do it."

"But this ain't her mouth," Paul D said. "This ain't it at all."

Stamp Paid looked at him. He was going to tell him about how restless Baby Suggs was that morning, how she had a listening way about her; how she kept looking down past the corn to the stream so much he looked too. In between ax swings, he watched where Baby was watching. Which is why they both missed it: they were looking the wrong way—toward water—and all the while it was coming down the road. Four. Riding close together, bunched-up like, and righteous. He was going to tell him that, because he thought it was important: why he and Baby Suggs both missed it. And about the party too, because that explained why nobody ran on ahead; why nobody sent a fleet-footed son to cut 'cross a field soon as they saw the four horses in town hitched for watering while the riders asked questions. Not Ella, not John, not anybody ran down or to Bluestone Road, to say some new whitefolks with the Look just rode in. The righteous Look every Negro learned to recognize along with his ma'am's tit. Like a flag hoisted, this righteousness telegraphed and announced the faggot, the whip, the fist, the lie, long before it went public. Nobody warned them, and he'd always believed it wasn't the exhaustion from a long day's gorging that dulled them, but some other thing— like, well, like meanness—that let them stand aside, or not pay attention, or tell themselves somebody else was probably bearing the news already to the house on Bluestone Road where a pretty woman had been living for almost a month. Young and deft with four children, one of which she delivered herself the day before she got there and who now had the full benefit of Baby Suggs' bounty and her big old heart. Maybe they just wanted to know if Baby really was special, blessed in some way they were not. He was going to tell him that, but Paul D was laughing, saying, "Uh uh. No way. A little semblance round the forehead maybe, but this ain't her mouth."

So Stamp Paid did not tell him how she flew, snatching up her children like a hawk on the wing; how her face beaked, how her hands worked like claws, how she collected them every which way: one on her shoulder, one under her arm, one by the hand, the other shouted forward into the woodshed filled with just sunlight and shavings now because there wasn't any wood. The party had used it all, which is why he was chopping some. Nothing was in that shed, he knew, having been there early that morning. Nothing but sunlight. Sunlight, shavings, a shovel. The ax he himself took out. Nothing else was in there except the shovel—and of course the saw.

"You forgetting I knew her before," Paul D was saying. "Back in Kentucky. When she was a girl. I didn't just make her acquaintance a few months ago. I been knowing her a long time. And I can tell you for sure: this ain't her mouth. May look like it, but it ain't."

So Stamp Paid didn't say it all. Instead he took a breath and leaned toward the mouth that was not hers and slowly read out the words Paul D couldn't. And when he finished, Paul D said with a vigor fresher than the first time, "I'm sorry, Stamp. It's a mistake somewhere 'cause that ain't her mouth."

Stamp looked into Paul D's eyes and the sweet conviction in them almost made him wonder if it had happened at all, eighteen years ago, that while he and Baby Suggs were looking the wrong way, a pretty little slavegirl had recognized a hat, and split to the woodshed to kill her children.

"She was crawling already when I got here. One week, less, and the baby who was sitting up and turning over when I put her on the wagon was crawling already. Devil of a time keeping her off the stairs. Nowadays babies get up and walk soon's you drop em, but twenty years ago when I was a girl, babies stayed babies longer. Howard didn't pick up his own head till he was nine months. Baby Suggs said it was the food, you know. If you ain't got nothing but milk to give em, well they don't do things so quick. Milk was all I ever had. I thought teeth meant they was ready to chew. Wasn't nobody to ask. Mrs. Garner never had no children and we was the only women there."

She was spinning. Round and round the room. Past the jelly cupboard, past the window, past the front door, another window, the sideboard, the keeping-room door, the dry sink, the stove—back to the jelly cupboard. Paul D sat at the table watching her drift into view then disappear behind his back, turning like a slow but steady wheel. Sometimes she crossed her hands behind her back. Other times she held her ears, covered her mouth or folded her arms across her breasts. Once in a while she rubbed her hips as she turned, but the wheel never stopped.

"Remember Aunt Phyllis? From out by Minnowville? Mr. Garner sent one a you all to get her for each and every one of my babies. That'd be the only time I saw her. Many's the time I wanted to get over to where she was. Just to talk. My plan was to ask Mrs. Garner to let me off at Minnowville whilst she went to meeting. Pick me up on her way back. I believe she would a done that if I was to ask her. I never did, 'cause that's the only day Halle and me had with sunlight in it for the both of us to see each other by. So there wasn't nobody. To talk to, I mean, who'd know when it was time to chew up a little something and give it to em. Is that what make the teeth come on out, or should you wait till the teeth came and then solid food? Well, I know now, because Baby Suggs fed her right, and a week later, when I got here, she was crawling already. No stopping her either. She loved those steps so much we painted them so she could see her way to the top."

Sethe smiled then, at the memory of it. The smile broke in two and became a sudden suck of air, but she did not shudder or close her eyes. She wheeled.

"I wish I'd a known more, but, like I say, there wasn't nobody to talk to. Woman, I mean. So I tried to recollect what I'd seen back where I was before Sweet Home. How the women did there. Oh they knew all about it. How to make that thing you use to hang the babies in the trees—so you could see them out of harm's way while you worked the fields. Was a leaf thing too they gave em to chew on. Mint, I believe, or sassafras. Comfrey, maybe. I still don't know how they constructed that basket thing, but I didn't need it anyway, because all my work was in the barn and the house, but I forgot what the leaf was. I could have used that. I tied Buglar when we had all that pork to smoke. Fire everywhere and he was getting into everything. I liked to lost him so many times. Once he got up on the well, right on it. I flew. Snatched him just in time. So when I knew we'd be rendering and smoking and I couldn't see after him, well, I got a rope and tied it round his ankle. Just long enough to play round a little, but not long enough to reach the well or the fire. I didn't like the look of it, but I didn't know what else to do. It's hard, you know what I mean? by yourself and no woman to help you get through. Halle was good, but he was debt-working all over the place. And when he did get down to a little sleep, I didn't want to be bothering him with all that. Sixo was the biggest help. I don't 'spect you rememory this, but Howard got in the milk parlor and Red Cora I believe it was mashed his hand. Turned his thumb backwards. When I got to him, she was getting ready to bite it. I don't know to this day how I got him out. Sixo heard him screaming and come running. Know what he did? Turned the thumb right back and tied it cross his palm to his little finger. See, I never would have thought of that. Never. Taught me a lot, Sixo."

It made him dizzy. At first he thought it was her spinning. Circling him the way she was circling the subject. Round and round, never changing direction, which might have helped his head. Then he thought, No, it's the sound of her voice; it's too near. Each turn she made was at least three yards from where he sat, but listening to her was like having a child whisper into your ear so close you could feel its lips form the words you couldn't make out because they were too close. He caught only pieces of what she said—which was fine, because she hadn't gotten to the main part—the answer to the question he had not asked outright, but which lay in the clipping he showed her. And lay in the smile as well. Because he smiled too, when he showed it to her, so when she burst out laughing at the joke—the mix-up of her face put where some other colored-woman's ought to be—well, he'd be ready to laugh right along with her. "Can you beat it?" he would ask. And "Stamp done lost his mind," she would giggle. "Plumb lost it."

But his smile never got a chance to grow. It hung there, small and alone, while she examined the clipping and then handed it back.

Perhaps it was the smile, or maybe the ever-ready love she saw in his eyes—easy and upfront, the way colts, evangelists and children look at you: with love you don't have to deserve—that made her go ahead and tell him what she had not told Baby Suggs, the only person she felt obliged to explain anything to. Otherwise she would have said what the newspaper said she said and no more. Sethe could recognize only seventy-five printed words (half of which appeared in the newspaper clipping), but she knew that the words she did not understand hadn't any more power than she had to explain. It was the smile and the upfront love that made her try.

"I don't have to tell you about Sweet Home—what it was—but maybe you don't know what it was like for me to get away from there."

Covering the lower half of her face with her palms, she paused to consider again the size of the miracle; its flavor.

"I did it. I got us all out. Without Halle too. Up till then it was the only thing I ever did on my own. Decided. And it came off right, like it was supposed to. We was here. Each and every one of my babies and me too. I birthed them and I got em out and it wasn't no accident. I did that. I had help, of course, lots of that, but still it was me doing it; me saying, *Go on*, and *Now*.

Me having to look out. Me using my own head. But it was more than that. It was a kind of selfishness I never knew nothing about before. It felt good. Good and right. I was big, Paul D, and deep and wide and when I stretched out my arms all my children could get in between. I was *that* wide. Look like I loved em more after I got here. Or maybe I couldn't love em proper in Kentucky because they wasn't mine to love. But when I got here, when I jumped down off that wagon—there wasn't nobody in the world I couldn't love if I wanted to. You know what I mean?"

Paul D did not answer because she didn't expect or want him to, but he did know what she meant. Listening to the doves in Alfred, Georgia, and having neither the right nor the permission to enjoy it because in that place mist, doves, sunlight, copper dirt, moon—everything belonged to the men who had the guns. Little men, some of them, big men too, each one of whom he could snap like a twig if he wanted to. Men who knew their manhood lay in their guns and were not even embarrassed by the knowledge that without gunshot fox would laugh at them. And these "men" who made even vixen laugh could, if you let them, stop you from hearing doves or loving moonlight. So you protected yourself and loved small. Picked the tiniest stars out of the sky to own; lay down with head twisted in order to see the loved one over the rim of the trench before you slept. Stole shy glances at her between the trees at chain-up. Grass blades, salamanders, spiders, woodpeckers, beetles, a kingdom of ants. Anything bigger wouldn't do. A woman, a child, a brother—a big love like that would split you wide open in Alfred, Georgia. He knew exactly what she meant: to get to a place where you could love anything you chose—not to need permission for desire—well now, *that* was freedom.

Circling, circling, now she was gnawing something else instead of getting to the point.

"There was this piece of goods Mrs. Garner gave me. Calico. Stripes it had with little flowers in between. 'Bout a yard—not enough for more 'n a head tie. But I been wanting to make a shift for my girl with it. Had the prettiest colors. I don't even know what you call that color: a rose but with yellow in it. For the longest time I been meaning to make it for her and do you know like a fool I left it behind? No more than a yard, and I kept putting it off because I was tired or didn't have the time. So when I got here, even before they let me get out of bed, I stitched her a little something from a piece of cloth Baby Suggs had. Well, all I'm saying is that's a selfish pleasure I never had before. I couldn't let all that go back to where it was, and I couldn't let her nor any of em live under schoolteacher. That was out."

Sethe knew that the circle she was making around the room, him, the subject, would remain one. That she could never close in, pin it down for anybody who had to ask. If they didn't get it right off—she could never explain. Because the truth was simple, not a long-drawn-out record of flowered shifts, tree cages, selfishness, ankle ropes and wells. Simple: she was squatting in the garden and when she saw them coming and recognized schoolteacher's hat, she heard wings. Little hummingbirds stuck their needle beaks right through her headcloth into her hair and beat their wings. And if she thought anything, it was No. No. Nono. Nonono. Simple. She just flew. Collected every bit of life she had made, all the parts of her that were precious and fine and beautiful, and carried, pushed, dragged them through the veil, out, away, over there where no one could hurt them. Over there. Outside this place, where they would be safe. And the hummingbird wings beat on. Sethe paused in her circle again and looked out the window. She remembered when the yard had a fence with a gate that somebody was always latching and unlatching in the time when 124 was busy as a way station. She did not see the whiteboys who pulled it down, yanked up the posts and smashed the gate leaving 124 desolate and exposed at the very hour when everybody stopped dropping by. The shoulder weeds of Bluestone Road were all that came toward the house.

When she got back from the jail house, she was glad the fence was gone. That's where they had hitched their horses— where she saw, floating above the railing as she squatted in the garden, schoolteacher's hat. By the time she faced him, looked him dead in the eye, she had something in her arms that stopped him in his tracks. He took a backward step with each jump of the baby heart until finally there were none.

"I stopped him," she said, staring at the place where the fence used to be. "I took and put my babies where they'd be safe."

The roaring in Paul D's head did not prevent him from hearing the pat she gave to the last word, and it occurred to him that what she wanted for her children was exactly what was missing in 124: safety. Which was the very first message he got the day he walked through the door. He thought he had made it safe, had gotten rid of the danger; beat the shit out of it; run it off the place and showed it and everybody else the difference between a mule and a plow. And because she had not done it before he got there her own self, he thought it was because she could not do it. That she lived with 124 in helpless, apologetic resignation because she had no choice; that minus husband, sons, mother-in-law, she and her slow-witted daughter had to live there all alone making do. The prickly, mean-eyed Sweet Home girl he knew as Halle's girl was obedient (like Halle), shy (like Halle), and work-crazy (like Halle). He was wrong. This here Sethe was new. The ghost in her house didn't bother her for the very same reason a room-and-board witch with new shoes was welcome. This here Sethe talked about love like any other woman; talked about baby clothes like any other woman, but what she meant could cleave the bone. This here Sethe talked about safety with a handsaw. This here new Sethe didn't know where the world stopped and she began. Suddenly he saw what Stamp Paid wanted him to see: more important than what Sethe had done was what she claimed. It scared him.

"Your love is too thick," he said, thinking, That bitch is looking at me; she is right over my head looking down through the floor at me.

"Too thick?" she said, thinking of the Clearing where Baby Suggs' commands knocked the pods off horse chestnuts. "Love is or it ain't. Thin love ain't love at all."

"Yeah. It didn't work, did it? Did it work?" he asked.

"It worked," she said.

"How? Your boys gone you don't know where. One girl dead, the other won't leave the yard. How did it work?"

"They ain't at Sweet Home. Schoolteacher ain't got em."

"Maybe there's worse."

"It ain't my job to know what's worse. It's my job to know what is and to keep them away from what I know is terrible. I did that."

"What you did was wrong, Sethe."

"I should have gone on back there? Taken my babies back there?"

"There could have been a way. Some other way."

"What way?"

"You got two feet, Sethe, not four," he said, and right then a forest sprang up between them; trackless and quiet.

Later he would wonder what made him say it. The calves of his youth? or the conviction that he was being observed through the ceiling? How fast he had moved from his shame to hers. From his cold-house secret straight to her too-thick love.

Meanwhile the forest was locking the distance between them, giving it shape and heft.

He did not put his hat on right away. First he fingered it, deciding how his going would be, how to make it an exit not an escape. And it was very important not to leave without looking. He stood up, turned and looked up the white stairs. She was there all right. Standing straight as a line with her back to him. He didn't rush to the door. He moved slowly and when he got there he opened it before asking Sethe to put supper aside for him because he might be a little late getting back. Only then did he put on his hat.

Sweet, she thought. He must think I can't bear to hear him say it. That after all I have told him and after telling me how many feet I have, "goodbye" would break me to pieces. Ain't that sweet.

"So long," she murmured from the far side of the trees.

II

124 was loud. Stamp Paid could hear it even from the road. He walked toward the house holding his head as high as possible so nobody looking could call him a sneak, although his worried mind made him feel like one. Ever since he showed that newspaper clipping to Paul D and learned that he'd moved out of 124 that very day, Stamp felt uneasy. Having wrestled with the question of whether or not to tell a man about his woman, and having convinced himself that he should, he then began to worry about Sethe. Had he stopped the one shot she had of the happiness a good man could bring her? Was she vexed by the loss, the free and unasked-for revival of gossip by the man who had helped her cross the river and who was her friend as well as Baby Suggs'?

"I'm too old," he thought, "for clear thinking. I'm too old and I seen too much." He had insisted on privacy during the revelation at the slaughter yard—now he wondered whom he was protecting. Paul D was the only one in town who didn't know. How did information that had been in the newspaper become a secret that needed to be whispered in a pig yard? A secret from whom? Sethe, that's who. He'd gone behind her

back, like a sneak. But sneaking was his job—his life; though
always for a clear and holy purpose. Before the War all he did
was sneak: runaways into hidden places, secret information to
public places. Underneath his legal vegetables were the contra-
band humans that he ferried across the river. Even the pigs he
worked in the spring served his purposes. Whole families lived
on the bones and guts he distributed to them. He wrote their
letters and read to them the ones they received. He knew who
had dropsy and who needed stovewood; which children had a
gift and which needed correction. He knew the secrets of the
Ohio River and its banks; empty houses and full; the best
dancers, the worst speakers, those with beautiful voices and
those who could not carry a tune. There was nothing interesting between his legs, but he remembered when there had
been—when that drive drove the driven—and that was why
he considered long and hard before opening his wooden box
and searching for the eighteen-year-old clipping to show Paul
D as proof.

Afterward—not before—he considered Sethe's feelings in
the matter. And it was the lateness of this consideration that
made him feel so bad. Maybe he should have left it alone; maybe
Sethe would have gotten around to telling him herself; maybe
he was not the high-minded Soldier of Christ he thought he
was, but an ordinary, plain meddler who had interrupted something going along just fine for the sake of truth and forewarning,
things he set much store by. Now 124 was back like it was
before Paul D came to town—worrying Sethe and Denver with
a pack of haunts he could hear from the road. Even if Sethe
could deal with the return of the spirit, Stamp didn't believe
her daughter could. Denver needed somebody normal in her

life. By luck he had been there at her very birth almost—before she knew she was alive—and it made him partial to her. It was seeing her, alive, don't you know, and looking healthy four weeks later that pleased him so much he gathered all he could carry of the best blackberries in the county and stuck two in her mouth first, before he presented the difficult harvest to Baby Suggs. To this day he believed his berries (which sparked the feast and the wood chopping that followed) were the reason Denver was still alive. Had he not been there, chopping firewood, Sethe would have spread her baby brains on the planking. Maybe he should have thought of Denver, if not Sethe, before he gave Paul D the news that ran him off, the one normal somebody in the girl's life since Baby Suggs died. And right there was the thorn.

Deeper and more painful than his belated concern for Denver or Sethe, scorching his soul like a silver dollar in a fool's pocket, was the memory of Baby Suggs—the mountain to his sky. It was the memory of her and the honor that was her due that made him walk straight-necked into the yard of 124, although he heard its voices from the road.

He had stepped foot in this house only once after the Misery (which is what he called Sethe's rough response to the Fugitive Bill) and that was to carry Baby Suggs, holy, out of it. When he picked her up in his arms, she looked to him like a girl, and he took the pleasure she would have knowing she didn't have to grind her hipbone anymore—that at last somebody carried *her*. Had she waited just a little she would have seen the end of the War, its short, flashy results. They could have celebrated together; gone to hear the great sermons preached on the occasion. As it was, he went alone from house to joyous house drinking what was offered. But she hadn't waited and he attended her funeral more put out with her than bereaved. Sethe and her daughter were dry-eyed on that occasion. Sethe had no instructions except "Take her to the Clearing," which he tried to do, but was prevented by some rule the whites had invented about where the dead should rest. Baby Suggs went down next to the baby with its throat cut—a neighborliness that Stamp wasn't sure had Baby Suggs' approval.

The setting-up was held in the yard because nobody besides himself would enter 124—an injury Sethe answered with another by refusing to attend the service Reverend Pike presided over. She went instead to the gravesite, whose silence she competed with as she stood there not joining in the hymns the others sang with all their hearts. That insult spawned another by the mourners: back in the yard of 124, they ate the food they brought and did not touch Sethe's, who did not touch theirs and forbade Denver to. So Baby Suggs, holy, having devoted her freed life to harmony, was buried amid a regular dance of pride, fear, condemnation and spite. Just about everybody in town was longing for Sethe to come on difficult times. Her outrageous claims, her self-sufficiency seemed to demand it, and Stamp Paid, who had not felt a trickle of meanness his whole adult life, wondered if some of the "pride goeth before a fall" expectations of the townsfolk had rubbed off on him anyhow—which would explain why he had not considered Sethe's feelings or Denver's needs when he showed Paul D the clipping.

He hadn't the vaguest notion of what he would do or say when and if Sethe opened the door and turned her eyes on his. He was willing to offer her help, if she wanted any from him, or receive her anger, if she harbored any against him. Beyond that, he trusted his instincts to right what he may have done wrong to Baby Suggs' kin, and to guide him in and through the stepped-up haunting 124 was subject to, as evidenced by the voices he heard from the road. Other than that, he would rely on the power of Jesus Christ to deal with things older, but not stronger, than He Himself was.

What he heard, as he moved toward the porch, he didn't understand. Out on Bluestone Road he thought he heard a conflagration of hasty voices—loud, urgent, all speaking at once so he could not make out what they were talking about or to whom. The speech wasn't nonsensical, exactly, nor was it tongues. But something was wrong with the order of the words and he couldn't describe or cipher it to save his life. All he could make out was the word *mine*. The rest of it stayed outside his mind's reach. Yet he went on through. When he got to the steps, the voices drained suddenly to less than a whisper. It gave him pause. They had become an occasional mutter—like the interior sounds a woman makes when she believes she is alone and unobserved at her work: a *sth* when she misses the needle's eye; a soft moan when she sees another chip in her one good platter; the low, friendly argument with which she greets the hens. Nothing fierce or startling. Just that eternal, private conversation that takes place between women and their tasks.

Stamp Paid raised his fist to knock on the door he had never knocked on (because it was always open to or for him) and could not do it. Dispensing with that formality was all the pay he expected from Negroes in his debt. Once Stamp Paid brought you a coat, got the message to you, saved your life, or fixed the cistern he took the liberty of walking in your door as though it were his own. Since all his visits were beneficial, his step or holler through a doorway got a bright welcome. Rather than forfeit the one privilege he claimed for himself, he lowered his hand and left the porch.

Over and over again he tried it: made up his mind to visit Sethe; broke through the loud hasty voices to the mumbling beyond it and stopped, trying to figure out what to do at the door. Six times in as many days he abandoned his normal route and tried to knock at 124. But the coldness of the gesture—its sign that he was indeed a stranger at the gate—overwhelmed him. Retracing his steps in the snow, he sighed. Spirit willing; flesh weak.

While Stamp Paid was making up his mind to visit 124 for Baby Suggs' sake, Sethe was trying to take her advice: *to lay it all down, sword and shield*. Not just to acknowledge the advice Baby Suggs gave her, but actually to take it. Four days after Paul D reminded her of how many feet she had, Sethe rummaged among the shoes of strangers to find the ice skates she was sure were there. Digging in the heap she despised herself for having been so trusting, so quick to surrender at the stove while Paul D kissed her back. She should have known that he would behave like everybody else in town once he knew. The twenty-eight days of having women friends, a mother-in-law, and all her children together; of being part of a neighborhood; of, in fact, having neighbors at all to call her own—all that was long gone and would never come back. No more dancing in the Clearing or happy feeds. No more discussions, stormy or quiet, about the true meaning of the Fugitive Bill, the

Settlement Fee, God's Ways and Negro pews; antislavery, manumission, skin voting, Republicans, Dred Scott, book learning, Sojourner's high-wheeled buggy, the Colored Ladies of Delaware, Ohio, and the other weighty issues that held them in chairs, scraping the floorboards or pacing them in agony or exhilaration. No anxious wait for the *North Star* or news of a beat-off. No sighing at a new betrayal or handclapping at a small victory.

Those twenty-eight happy days were followed by eighteen years of disapproval and a solitary life. Then a few months of the sun-splashed life that the shadows holding hands on the road promised her; tentative greetings from other coloredpeople in Paul D's company; a bed life for herself. Except for Denver's friend, every bit of it had disappeared. Was that the pattern? she wondered. Every eighteen or twenty years her unlivable life would be interrupted by a short-lived glory?

Well, if that's the way it was—that's the way it was.

She had been on her knees, scrubbing the floor, Denver trailing her with the drying rags, when Beloved appeared saying, "What these do?" On her knees, scrub brush in hand, she looked at the girl and the skates she held up. Sethe couldn't skate a lick but then and there she decided to take Baby Suggs' advice: *lay it all down*. She left the bucket where it was. Told Denver to get out the shawls and started searching for the other skates she was certain were in that heap somewhere. Anybody feeling sorry for her, anybody wandering by to peep in and see how she was getting on (including Paul D) would discover that the woman junkheaped for the third time because she loved her children—that woman was sailing happily on a frozen creek.

Hurriedly, carelessly she threw the shoes about. She found one blade—a man's.

"Well," she said. "We'll take turns. Two skates on one; one skate on one; and shoe slide for the other."

Nobody saw them falling.

Holding hands, bracing each other, they swirled over the ice. Beloved wore the pair; Denver wore one, step-gliding over the treacherous ice. Sethe thought her two shoes would hold and anchor her. She was wrong. Two paces onto the creek, she lost her balance and landed on her behind. The girls, screaming with laughter, joined her on the ice. Sethe struggled to stand and discovered not only that she could do a split, but that it hurt. Her bones surfaced in unexpected places and so did laughter. Making a circle or a line, the three of them could not stay upright for one whole minute, but nobody saw them falling.

Each seemed to be helping the other two stay upright, yet every tumble doubled their delight. The live oak and soughing pine on the banks enclosed them and absorbed their laughter while they fought gravity for each other's hands. Their skirts flew like wings and their skin turned pewter in the cold and dying light.

Nobody saw them falling.

Exhausted finally they lay down on their backs to recover breath. The sky above them was another country. Winter stars, close enough to lick, had come out before sunset. For a moment, looking up, Sethe entered the perfect peace they offered. Then Denver stood up and tried for a long, independent glide. The tip of her single skate hit an ice bump, and as she fell, the flapping of her arms was so wild and hopeless that all three—Sethe, Beloved and Denver herself—laughed till they coughed.

Sethe rose to her hands and knees, laughter still shaking her chest, making her eyes wet. She stayed that way for a while, on all fours. But when her laughter died, the tears did not and it was some time before Beloved or Denver knew the difference. When they did they touched her lightly on the shoulders.

Walking back through the woods, Sethe put an arm around each girl at her side. Both of them had an arm around her waist. Making their way over hard snow, they stumbled and had to hold on tight, but nobody saw them fall.

Inside the house they found out they were cold. They took off their shoes, wet stockings, and put on dry woolen ones. Denver fed the fire. Sethe warmed a pan of milk and stirred cane syrup and vanilla into it. Wrapped in quilts and blankets before the cooking stove, they drank, wiped their noses, and drank again.

"We could roast some taters," said Denver.

"Tomorrow," said Sethe. "Time to sleep."

She poured them each a bit more of the hot sweet milk. The stovefire roared.

"You finished with your eyes?" asked Beloved.

Sethe smiled. "Yes, I'm finished with my eyes. Drink up. Time for bed."

But none of them wanted to leave the warmth of the blankets, the fire and the cups for the chill of an unheated bed. They went on sipping and watching the fire.

When the click came Sethe didn't know what it was. Afterward it was clear as daylight that the click came at the very beginning—a beat, almost, before it started; before she heard three notes; before the melody was even clear. Leaning forward a little, Beloved was humming softly.

It was then, when Beloved finished humming, that Sethe recalled the click—the settling of pieces into places designed and made especially for them. No milk spilled from her cup because her hand was not shaking. She simply turned her head and looked at Beloved's profile: the chin, mouth, nose, forehead, copied and exaggerated in the huge shadow the fire threw on the wall behind her. Her hair, which Denver had braided into twenty or thirty plaits, curved toward her shoulders like arms. From where she sat Sethe could not examine it, not the hairline, nor the eyebrows, the lips, nor ...

"All I remember," Baby Suggs had said, "is how she loved the burned bottom of bread. Her little hands I wouldn't know em if they slapped me."

... the birthmark, nor the color of the gums, the shape of her ears, nor ...

"Here. Look here. This is your ma'am. If you can't tell me by my face, look here."

... the fingers, nor their nails, nor even ...

But there would be time. The click had clicked; things were where they ought to be or poised and ready to glide in.

"I made that song up," said Sethe. "I made it up and sang it to my children. Nobody knows that song but me and my children."

Beloved turned to look at Sethe. "I know it," she said.

A hobnail casket of jewels found in a tree hollow should be fondled before it is opened. Its lock may have rusted or broken away from the clasp. Still you should touch the nail heads, and test its weight. No smashing with an ax head before it is decently exhumed from the grave that has hidden it all this time. No gasp at a miracle that is truly miraculous because the magic lies in the fact that you knew it was there for you all along.

Sethe wiped the white satin coat from the inside of the pan, brought pillows from the keeping room for the girls' heads. There was no tremor in her voice as she instructed them to keep the fire—if not, come on upstairs.

With that, she gathered her blanket around her elbows and ascended the lily-white stairs like a bride. Outside, snow solidified itself into graceful forms. The peace of winter stars seemed permanent.

Fingering a ribbon and smelling skin, Stamp Paid approached 124 again.

My marrow is tired, he thought. I been tired all my days, bone-tired, but now it's in the marrow. Must be what Baby Suggs felt when she lay down and thought about color for the rest of her life. When she told him what her aim was, he thought she was ashamed and too shamed to say so. Her authority in the pulpit, her dance in the Clearing, her powerful Call (she didn't deliver sermons or preach—insisting she was too ignorant for that—she *called* and the hearing heard)—all that had been mocked and rebuked by the bloodspill in her backyard. God puzzled her and she was too ashamed of Him to say so. Instead she told Stamp she was going to bed to think about the colors of things. He tried to dissuade her. Sethe was in jail with her nursing baby, the one he had saved. Her sons were holding hands in the yard, terrified of letting go. Strangers and familiars were stopping by to hear how it went one more time, and suddenly Baby declared peace. She just up and quit.

By the time Sethe was released she had exhausted blue and was well on her way to yellow.

At first he would see her in the yard occasionally, or delivering food to the jail, or shoes in town. Then less and less. He believed then that shame put her in the bed. Now, eight years after her contentious funeral and eighteen years after the Misery, he changed his mind. Her marrow was tired and it was a testimony to the heart that fed it that it took eight years to meet finally the color she was hankering after. The onslaught of her fatigue, like his, was sudden, but lasted for years. After sixty years of losing children to the people who chewed up her life and spit it out like a fish bone; after five years of freedom given to her by her last child, who bought her future with his, exchanged it, so to speak, so she could have one whether he did or not—to lose him too; to acquire a daughter and grand-children and see that daughter slay the children (or try to); to belong to a community of other free Negroes—to love and be loved by them, to counsel and be counseled, protect and be protected, feed and be fed—and then to have that community step back and hold itself at a distance—well, it could wear out even a Baby Suggs, holy.

"Listen here, girl," he told her, "you can't quit the Word. It's given to you to speak. You can't quit the Word, I don't care what all happen to you."

They were standing in Richmond Street, ankle deep in leaves. Lamps lit the downstairs windows of spacious houses and made the early evening look darker than it was. The odor of burning leaves was brilliant. Quite by chance, as he pocketed a penny tip for a delivery, he had glanced across the street and recognized the skipping woman as his old friend. He had not seen her in weeks. Quickly he crossed the street, scuffing red leaves as he went. When he stopped her with a greeting, she returned it with a face knocked clean of interest. She could have been a plate. A carpetbag full of shoes in her hand, she waited for him to begin, lead or share a conversation. If there had been sadness in her eyes he would have understood it; but indifference lodged where sadness should have been.

"You missed the Clearing three Saturdays running," he told her.

She turned her head away and scanned the houses along the street.

"Folks came," he said.

"Folks come; folks go," she answered.

"Here, let me carry that." He tried to take her bag from her but she wouldn't let him.

"I got a delivery someplace long in here," she said. "Name of Tucker."

"Yonder," he said. "Twin chestnuts in the yard. Sick, too."

They walked a bit, his pace slowed to accommodate her skip.

"Well?"

"Well, what?"

"Saturday coming. You going to Call or what?"

"If I call them and they come, what on earth I'm going to say?"

"Say the Word!" He checked his shout too late. Two whitemen burning leaves turned their heads in his direction. Bending low he whispered into her ear, "The Word. The Word."

"That's one other thing took away from me," she said, and that was when he exhorted her, pleaded with her not to quit, no matter what. The Word had been given to her and she had to speak it. Had to.

They had reached the twin chestnuts and the white house that stood behind them.

"See what I mean?" he said. "Big trees like that, both of em together ain't got the leaves of a young birch."

"I see what you mean," she said, but she peered instead at the white house.

"You got to do it," he said. "You got to. Can't nobody Call like you. You have to be there."

"What I have to do is get in my bed and lay down. I want to fix on something harmless in this world."

"What world you talking about? Ain't nothing harmless down here."

"Yes it is. Blue. That don't hurt nobody. Yellow neither."

"You getting in the bed to think about yellow?"

"I likes yellow."

"Then what? When you get through with blue and yellow, then what?"

"Can't say. It's something can't be planned."

"You blaming God," he said. "That's what you doing."

"No, Stamp. I ain't."

"You saying the whitefolks won? That what you saying?"

"I'm saying they came in my yard."

"You saying nothing counts."

"I'm saying they came in my yard."

"Sethe's the one did it."

"And if she hadn't?"

"You saying God give up? Nothing left for us but pour out our own blood?"

"I'm saying they came in my yard."

"You punishing Him, ain't you."

"Not like He punish me."

"You can't do that, Baby. It ain't right."

"Was a time I knew what that was."

"You still know."

"What I know is what I see: a nigger woman hauling shoes."

"Aw, Baby." He licked his lips searching with his tongue for the words that would turn her around, lighten her load. "We have to be steady. 'These things too will pass.' What you looking for? A miracle?"

"No," she said. "I'm looking for what I was put here to look for: the back door," and skipped right to it. They didn't let her in. They took the shoes from her as she stood on the steps and she rested her hip on the railing while the whitewoman went looking for the dime.

Stamp Paid rearranged his way. Too angry to walk her home and listen to more, he watched her for a moment and turned to go before the alert white face at the window next door had come to any conclusion.

Trying to get to 124 for the second time now, he regretted that conversation: the high tone he took; his refusal to see the effect of marrow weariness in a woman he believed was a mountain. Now, too late, he understood her. The heart that pumped out love, the mouth that spoke the Word, didn't count. They came in her yard anyway and she could not approve or condemn Sethe's rough choice. One or the other might have saved her, but beaten up by the claims of both, she went to bed. The whitefolks had tired her out at last.

And him. Eighteen seventy-four and whitefolks were still on the loose. Whole towns wiped clean of Negroes; eighty-seven lynchings in one year alone in Kentucky; four colored schools burned to the ground; grown men whipped like children; children whipped like adults; black women raped by the crew; property taken, necks broken. He smelled skin, skin and hot blood. The skin was one thing, but human blood cooked in a lynch fire was a whole other thing. The stench stank. Stank up off the pages of the *North Star*, out of the mouths of witnesses, etched in crooked handwriting in letters delivered by hand. Detailed in documents and petitions full of *whereas* and presented to any legal body who'd read it, it stank. But none of that had worn out his marrow. None of that. It was the ribbon. Tying his flatbed up on the bank of the Licking River, securing it the best he could, he caught sight of something red on its bottom. Reaching for it, he thought it was a cardinal feather stuck to his boat. He tugged and what came loose in his hand was a red ribbon knotted around a curl of wet woolly hair, clinging still to its bit of scalp. He untied the ribbon and put it in his pocket, dropped the curl in the weeds. On the way home, he stopped, short of breath and dizzy. He waited until the spell passed before continuing on his way. A moment later, his breath left him again. This time he sat down by a fence. Rested, he got to his feet, but before he took a step he turned to look back down the road he was traveling and said, to its frozen mud and the river beyond, "What *are* these people? You tell me, Jesus. What *are* they?"

When he got to his house he was too tired to eat the food his sister and nephews had prepared. He sat on the porch in the cold till way past dark and went to his bed only because his sister's voice calling him was getting nervous. He kept the ribbon; the skin smell nagged him, and his weakened marrow made him dwell on Baby Suggs' wish to consider what in the world was harmless. He hoped she stuck to blue, yellow, maybe green, and never fixed on red.

Mistaking her, upbraiding her, owing her, now he needed to let her know he knew, and to get right with her and her kin. So, in spite of his exhausted marrow, he kept on through the voices and tried once more to knock at the door of 124. This time, although he couldn't cipher but one word, he believed he knew who spoke them. The people of the broken necks, of fire-cooked blood and black girls who had lost their ribbons.

What a roaring.

Sethe had gone to bed smiling, eager to lie down and unravel the proof for the conclusion she had already leapt to. Fondle the day and circumstances of Beloved's arrival and the meaning of that kiss in the Clearing. She slept instead and woke, still smiling, to a snow-bright morning, cold enough to see her breath. She lingered a moment to collect the courage to throw off the blankets and hit a chilly floor. For the first time, she was going to be late for work.

Downstairs she saw the girls sleeping where she'd left them, but back to back now, each wrapped tight in blankets, breathing into their pillows. The pair and a half of skates were lying by the front door, the stockings hung on a nail behind the cooking stove to dry had not.

Sethe looked at Beloved's face and smiled.

Quietly, carefully she stepped around her to wake the fire. First a bit of paper, then a little kindlin—not too much—just a taste until it was strong enough for more. She fed its dance until it was wild and fast. When she went outside to collect more wood from the shed, she did not notice the man's frozen footprints. She crunched around to the back, to the cord piled high with snow. After scraping it clean, she filled her arms with as much dry wood as she could. She even looked straight at the shed, smiling, smiling at the things she would not have to remember now. Thinking, She ain't even mad with me. Not a bit.

Obviously the hand-holding shadows she had seen on the road were not Paul D, Denver and herself, but "us three." The three holding on to each other skating the night before; the three sipping flavored milk. And since that was so—if her daughter could come back home from the timeless place— certainly her sons could, and would, come back from wherever they had gone to.

Sethe covered her front teeth with her tongue against the cold. Hunched forward by the burden in her arms, she walked back around the house to the porch—not once noticing the frozen tracks she stepped in.

Inside, the girls were still sleeping, although they had changed positions while she was gone, both drawn to the fire. Dumping the armload into the woodbox made them stir but not wake. Sethe started the cooking stove as quietly as she could, reluctant to wake the sisters, happy to have them asleep at her feet while she made breakfast. Too bad she would be late for work—too, too bad. Once in sixteen years? That's just too bad.

She had beaten two eggs into yesterday's hominy, formed it into patties and fried them with some ham pieces before Denver woke completely and groaned.

"Back stiff?"

"Ooh yeah."

"Sleeping on the floor's supposed to be good for you."

"Hurts like the devil," said Denver.

"Could be that fall you took."

Denver smiled. "That was fun." She turned to look down at Beloved snoring lightly. "Should I wake her?"

"No, let her rest."

"She likes to see you off in the morning."

"I'll make sure she does," said Sethe, and thought, Be nice to think first, before I talk to her, let her know I know. Think about all I ain't got to remember no more. Do like Baby said: Think on it then lay it down—for good. Paul D convinced me there was a world out there and that I could live in it. Should have known better. *Did* know better. Whatever is going on outside my door ain't for me. The world is in this room. This here's all there is and all there needs to be.

They ate like men, ravenous and intent. Saying little, content with the company of the other and the opportunity to look in her eyes.

When Sethe wrapped her head and bundled up to go to town, it was already midmorning. And when she left the house she neither saw the prints nor heard the voices that ringed 124 like a noose.

Trudging in the ruts left earlier by wheels, Sethe was excited to giddiness by the things she no longer had to remember.

I don't have to remember nothing. I don't even have to explain. She understands it all. I can forget how Baby Suggs' heart collapsed; how we agreed it was consumption without a sign of it in the world. Her eyes when she brought my food, I can forget that, and how she told me that Howard and Buglar

were all right but wouldn't let go each other's hands. Played
that way: stayed that way especially in their sleep. She handed
me the food from a basket; things wrapped small enough to
get through the bars, whispering news: Mr. Bodwin going to
see the judge—in chambers, she kept on saying, in chambers,
like I knew what it meant or she did. The Colored Ladies of
Delaware, Ohio, had drawn up a petition to keep me from being
hanged. That two white preachers had come round and wanted
to talk to me, pray for me. That a newspaperman came too.
She told me the news and I told her I needed something for
the rats. She wanted Denver out and slapped her palms when
I wouldn't let her go. "Where your earrings?" she said. "I'll
hold em for you." I told her the jailer took them, to protect
me from myself. He thought I could do some harm with the
wire. Baby Suggs covered her mouth with her hand.
"Schoolteacher left town," she said. "Filed a claim and rode on
off. They going to let you out for the burial," she said, "not
the funeral, just the burial," and they did. The sheriff came
with me and looked away when I fed Denver in the wagon.
Neither Howard nor Buglar would let me near them, not even
to touch their hair. I believe a lot of folks were there, but I
just saw the box. Reverend Pike spoke in a real loud voice, but
I didn't catch a word—except the first two, and three months
later when Denver was ready for solid food and they let me
out for good, I went and got you a gravestone, but I didn't
have money enough for the carving so I exchanged (bartered,
you might say) what I did have and I'm sorry to this day I
never thought to ask him for the whole thing: all I heard of
what Reverend Pike said. Dearly Beloved, which is what you
are to me and I don't have to be sorry about getting only one

word, and I don't have to remember the slaughterhouse and the Saturday girls who worked its yard. I can forget that what I did changed Baby Suggs' life. No Clearing, no company. Just laundry and shoes. I can forget it all now because as soon as I got the gravestone in place you made your presence known in the house and worried us all to distraction. I didn't understand it then. I thought you were mad with me. And now I know that if you was, you ain't now because you came back here to me and I was right all along: there is no world outside my door. I only need to know one thing. How bad is the scar?

As Sethe walked to work, late for the first time in sixteen years and wrapped in a timeless present, Stamp Paid fought fatigue and the habit of a lifetime. Baby Suggs refused to go to the Clearing because she believed *they* had won; he refused to acknowledge any such victory. Baby had no back door; so he braved the cold and a wall of talk to knock on the one she did have. He clutched the red ribbon in his pocket for strength. Softly at first, then harder. At the last he banged furiously— disbelieving it could happen. That the door of a house with coloredpeople in it did not fly open in his presence. He went to the window and wanted to cry. Sure enough, there they were, not a one of them heading for the door. Worrying his scrap of ribbon to shreds, the old man turned and went down the steps. Now curiosity joined his shame and his debt. Two backs curled away from him as he looked in the window. One had a head he recognized; the other troubled him. He didn't know her and didn't know anybody it could be. Nobody, but nobody visited that house.

After a disagreeable breakfast he went to see Ella and John to find out what they knew. Perhaps there he could find out if, after all these years of clarity, he had misnamed himself and there was yet another debt he owed. Born Joshua, he renamed himself when he handed over his wife to his master's son. Handed her over in the sense that he did not kill anybody, thereby himself, because his wife demanded he stay alive. Otherwise, she reasoned, where and to whom could she return when the boy was through? With that gift, he decided that he didn't owe anybody anything. Whatever his obligations were, that act paid them off. He thought it would make him rambunctious, renegade—a drunkard even, the debtlessness, and in a way it did. But there was nothing to do with it. Work well; work poorly. Work a little; work not at all. Make sense; make none. Sleep, wake up; like somebody, dislike others. It didn't seem much of a way to live and it brought him no satisfaction. So he extended this debtlessness to other people by helping them pay out and off whatever they owed in misery. Beaten runaways? He ferried them and rendered them paid for; gave them their own bill of sale, so to speak. "You paid it; now life owes you." And the receipt, as it were, was a welcome door that he never had to knock on, like John and Ella's in front of which he stood and said, "Who in there?" only once and she was pulling on the hinge.

"Where you been keeping yourself? I told John must be cold if Stamp stay inside."

"Oh, I been out." He took off his cap and massaged his scalp.

"Out where? Not by here." Ella hung two suits of underwear on a line behind the stove.

"Was over to Baby Suggs' this morning."

"What you want in there?" asked Ella. "Somebody invite you in?"

"That's Baby's kin. I don't need no invite to look after her people."

"Sth." Ella was unmoved. She had been Baby Suggs' friend and Sethe's too till the rough time. Except for a nod at the carnival, she hadn't given Sethe the time of day.

"Somebody new in there. A woman. Thought you might know who is she."

"Ain't no new Negroes in this town I don't know about," she said. "What she look like? You sure that wasn't Denver?"

"I know Denver. This girl's narrow."

"You sure?"

"I know what I see."

"Might see anything at all at 124."

"True."

"Better ask Paul D," she said.

"Can't locate him," said Stamp, which was the truth although his efforts to find Paul D had been feeble. He wasn't ready to confront the man whose life he had altered with his graveyard information.

"He's sleeping in the church," said Ella.

"The church!" Stamp was shocked and very hurt.

"Yeah. Asked Reverend Pike if he could stay in the cellar."

"It's cold as charity in there!"

"I expect he knows that."

"What he do that for?"

"He's a touch proud, seem like."

"He don't have to do that! Any number'll take him in."

Ella turned around to look at Stamp Paid. "Can't nobody read minds long distance. All he have to do is ask somebody."

"Why? Why he have to ask? Can't nobody offer? What's going on? Since when a blackman come to town have to sleep in a cellar like a dog?"

"Unrile yourself, Stamp."

"Not me. I'm going to stay riled till somebody gets some sense and leastway act like a Christian."

"It's only a few days he been there."

"Shouldn't be no days! You know all about it and don't give him a hand? That don't sound like you, Ella. Me and you been pulling coloredfolk out the water more'n twenty years. Now you tell me you can't offer a man a bed? A working man, too! A man what can pay his own way."

"He ask, I give him anything."

"Why's that necessary all of a sudden?"

"I don't know him all that well."

"You know he's colored!"

"Stamp, don't tear me up this morning. I don't feel like it."

"It's her, ain't it?"

"Her who?"

"Sethe. He took up with her and stayed in there and you don't want nothing to—"

"Hold on. Don't jump if you can't see bottom."

"Girl, give it up. We been friends too long to act like this."

"Well, who can tell what all went on in there? Look here, I don't know who Sethe is or none of her people."

"What?!"

"All I know is she married Baby Suggs' boy and I ain't sure I know that. Where is *he*, huh? Baby never laid eyes on her till John carried her to the door with a baby I strapped on her chest."

"*I* strapped that baby! And you way off the track with that wagon. Her children know who she was even if you don't."

"So what? I ain't saying she wasn't their ma'ammy, but who's to say they was Baby Suggs' grandchildren? How she get on board and her husband didn't? And tell me this, how she have that baby in the woods by herself? Said a white-woman come out the trees and helped her. Shoot. You believe that? A _white_ woman? Well, I know what kind of white that was."

"Aw, no, Ella."

"Anything white floating around in the woods—if it ain't got a shotgun, it's something I don't want *no* part of!"

"You all was friends."

"Yeah, till she showed herself."

"Ella."

"I ain't got no friends take a handsaw to their own children."

"You in deep water, girl."

"Uh uh. I'm on dry land and I'm going to stay there. You the one wet."

"What's any of what you talking got to do with Paul D?"

"What run him off? Tell me that."

"I run him off."

"You?"

"I told him about—I showed him the newspaper, about the—what Sethe did. Read it to him. He left that very day."

"You didn't tell me that. I thought he knew."

"He didn't know nothing. Except her, from when they was at that place Baby Suggs was at."

"He knew Baby Suggs?"

"Sure he knew her. Her boy Halle too."

"And left when he found out what Sethe did?"

"Look like he might have a place to stay after all."

"What you say casts a different light. I thought—"

But Stamp Paid knew what she thought.

"You didn't come here asking about him," Ella said. "You came about some new girl."

"That's so."

"Well, Paul D must know who she is. Or *what* she is."

"Your mind is loaded with spirits. Everywhere you look you see one."

"You know as well as I do that people who die bad don't stay in the ground."

He couldn't deny it. Jesus Christ Himself didn't, so Stamp ate a piece of Ella's head cheese to show there were no bad feelings and set out to find Paul D. He found him on the steps of Holy Redeemer, holding his wrists between his knees and looking red-eyed.

Sawyer shouted at her when she entered the kitchen, but she just turned her back and reached for her apron. There was no entry now. No crack or crevice available. She had taken pains to keep them out, but knew full well that at any moment they could rock her, rip her from her moorings, send the birds twittering back into her hair. Drain her mother's milk, they had already done. Divided her back into plant life—that too. Driven her fat-bellied into the woods—they had done that. All news of them was rot. They buttered Halle's face; gave Paul D iron to eat; crisped Sixo; hanged her own mother. She didn't want any more news about whitefolks; didn't want to know what Ella knew and John and Stamp Paid, about the world done up the way whitefolks loved it. All news of them should have stopped with the birds in her hair.

Once, long ago, she was soft, trusting. She trusted Mrs. Garner and her husband too. She knotted the earrings into her underskirt to take along, not so much to wear but to hold. Earrings that made her believe she could discriminate among them. That for every schoolteacher there would be an Amy; that for every pupil there was a Garner, or Bodwin, or even a sheriff, whose touch at her elbow was gentle and who looked away when she nursed. But she had come to believe every one of Baby Suggs' last words and buried all recollection of them and luck. Paul D dug it up, gave her back her body, kissed her divided back, stirred her rememory and brought her more news: of clabber, of iron, of roosters' smiling, but when he heard *her* news, he counted her feet and didn't even say goodbye.

"Don't talk to me, Mr. Sawyer. Don't say nothing to me this morning."

"What? What? What? You talking back to me?"

"I'm telling you don't say nothing to me."

"You better get them pies made."

Sethe touched the fruit and picked up the paring knife.

When pie juice hit the bottom of the oven and hissed, Sethe was well into the potato salad. Sawyer came in and said, "Not too sweet. You make it too sweet they don't eat it."

"Make it the way I always did."

"Yeah. Too sweet."

None of the sausages came back. The cook had a way with them and Sawyer's Restaurant never had leftover sausage. If Sethe wanted any, she put them aside soon as they were ready. But there was some passable stew. Problem was, all her pies were sold too. Only rice pudding left and half a pan of ginger-bread that didn't come out right. Had she been paying atten-tion instead of daydreaming all morning, she wouldn't be picking around looking for her dinner like a crab. She couldn't read clock time very well, but she knew when the hands were closed in prayer at the top of the face she was through for the day. She got a metal-top jar, filled it with stew and wrapped the gingerbread in butcher paper. These she dropped in her outer skirt pockets and began washing up. None of it was anything like what the cook and the two waiters walked off with. Mr. Sawyer included midday dinner in the terms of the job—along with $3.40 a week—and she made him understand from the beginning she would take her dinner home. But matches, sometimes a bit of kerosene, a little salt, butter too— these things she took also, once in a while, and felt ashamed because she could afford to buy them; she just didn't want the embarrassment of waiting out back of Phelps store with the others till every white in Ohio was served before the keeper turned to the cluster of Negro faces looking through a hole in his back door. She was ashamed, too, because it was stealing and Sixo's argument on the subject amused her but didn't change the way she felt; just as it didn't change schoolteach-er's mind.

"Did you steal that shoat? You stole that shoat." Schoolteacher was quiet but firm, like he was just going through the motions— not expecting an answer that mattered. Sixo sat there, not even getting up to plead or deny. He just sat there, the streak-of-lean in his hand, the gristle clustered in the tin plate like gemstones— rough, unpolished, but loot nevertheless.

"You stole that shoat, didn't you?"

"No. Sir," said Sixo, but he had the decency to keep his eyes on the meat.

"You telling me you didn't steal it, and I'm looking right at you?"

"No, sir. I didn't steal it."

Schoolteacher smiled. "Did you kill it?"

"Yes, sir. I killed it."

"Did you butcher it?"

"Yes, sir."

"Did you cook it?"

"Yes, sir."

"Well, then. Did you eat it?"

"Yes, sir. I sure did."

"And you telling me that's not stealing?"

"No, sir. It ain't."

"What is it then?"

"Improving your property, sir."

"What?"

"Sixo plant rye to give the high piece a better chance. Sixo take and feed the soil, give you more crop. Sixo take and feed Sixo give you more work."

Clever, but schoolteacher beat him anyway to show him that definitions belonged to the definers—not the defined. After Mr. Garner died with a hole in his ear that Mrs. Garner said was an exploded ear drum brought on by stroke and Sixo said was gunpowder, everything they touched was looked on as stealing. Not just a rifle of corn, or two yard eggs the hen herself didn't even remember, everything. Schoolteacher took away the guns from the Sweet Home men and, deprived of game to round out their diet of bread, beans, hominy,

vegetables and a little extra at slaughter time, they began to
pilfer in earnest, and it became not only their right but their
obligation.

Sethe understood it then, but now with a paying job and an
employer who was kind enough to hire an ex-convict, she
despised herself for the pride that made pilfering better than
standing in line at the window of the general store with all
the other Negroes. She didn't want to jostle them or be jostled
by them. Feel their judgment or their pity, especially now. She
touched her forehead with the back of her wrist and blotted
the perspiration. The workday had come to a close and already
she was feeling the excitement. Not since that other escape
had she felt so alive. Slopping the alley dogs, watching their
frenzy, she pressed her lips. Today would be a day she would
accept a lift, if anybody on a wagon offered it. No one would,
and for sixteen years her pride had not let her ask. But today.
Oh, today. Now she wanted speed, to skip over the long walk
home and *be* there.

When Sawyer warned her about being late again, she barely
heard him. He used to be a sweet man. Patient, tender in his
dealings with his help. But each year, following the death of
his son in the War, he grew more and more crotchety. As
though Sethe's dark face was to blame.

"Un huh," she said, wondering how she could hurry time
along and get to the no-time waiting for her.

She needn't have worried. Wrapped tight, hunched forward,
as she started home her mind was busy with the things she
could forget.

Thank God I don't have to rememory or say a thing because
you know it. All. You know I never would a left you. Never.

It was all I could think of to do. When the train came I had
to be ready. Schoolteacher was teaching us things we couldn't
learn. I didn't care nothing about the measuring string. We all
laughed about that—except Sixo. He didn't laugh at nothing.
But I didn't care. Schoolteacher'd wrap that string all over my
head, 'cross my nose, around my behind. Number my teeth. I
thought he was a fool. And the questions he asked was the
biggest foolishness of all.

Then me and your brothers come up from the second patch.
The first one was close to the house where the quick things
grew: beans, onions, sweet peas. The other one was further
down for long-lasting things, potatoes, pumpkin, okra, pork
salad. Not much was up yet down there. It was early still.
Some young salad maybe, but that was all. We pulled weeds
and hoed a little to give everything a good start. After that
we hit out for the house. The ground raised up from the second
patch. Not a hill exactly but kind of. Enough for Buglar and
Howard to run up and roll down, run up and roll down. That's
the way I used to see them in my dreams, laughing, their short
fat legs running up the hill. Now all I see is their backs walking
down the railroad tracks. Away from me. Always away from
me. But that day they was happy, running up and rolling down.
It was early still—the growing season had took hold but not
much was up. I remember the peas still had flowers. The grass
was long though, full of white buds and those tall red blossoms
people call Diane and something there with the leastest little
bit of blue—light, like a cornflower but pale, pale. Real pale.
I maybe should have hurried because I left you back at the
house in a basket in the yard. Away from where the chickens
scratched but you never know. Anyway I took my time getting

back but your brothers didn't have patience with me staring
at flowers and sky every two or three steps. They ran on ahead
and I let em. Something sweet lives in the air that time of
year, and if the breeze is right, it's hard to stay indoors. When
I got back I could hear Howard and Buglar laughing down
by the quarters. I put my hoe down and cut across the side
yard to get to you. The shade moved so by the time I got back
the sun was shining right on you. Right in your face, but you
wasn't woke at all. Still asleep. I wanted to pick you up in my
arms and I wanted to look at you sleeping too. Didn't know
which; you had the sweetest face. Yonder, not far, was a grape
arbor Mr. Garner made. Always full of big plans, he wanted
to make his own wine to get drunk off. Never did get more
than a kettle of jelly from it. I don't think the soil was right
for grapes. Your daddy believed it was the rain, not the soil.
Sixo said it was bugs. The grapes so little and tight. Sour as
vinegar too. But there was a little table in there. So I picked
up your basket and carried you over to the grape arbor. Cool
in there and shady. I set you down on the little table and
figured if I got a piece of muslin the bugs and things wouldn't
get to you. And if Mrs. Garner didn't need me right there in
the kitchen, I could get a chair and you and me could set out
there while I did the vegetables. I headed for the back door to
get the clean muslin we kept in the kitchen press. The grass
felt good on my feet. I got near the door and I heard voices.
Schoolteacher made his pupils sit and learn books for a spell
every afternoon. If it was nice enough weather, they'd sit on
the side porch. All three of em. He'd talk and they'd write. Or
he would read and they would write down what he said. I
never told nobody this. Not your pap, not nobody. I almost

told Mrs. Garner, but she was so weak then and getting weaker. This is the first time I'm telling it and I'm telling it to you because it might help explain something to you although I know you don't need me to do it. To tell it or even think over it. You don't have to listen either, if you don't want to. But I couldn't help listening to what I heard that day. He was talking to his pupils and I heard him say, "Which one are you doing?" And one of the boys said, "Sethe." That's when I stopped because I heard my name, and then I took a few steps to where I could see what they was doing. Schoolteacher was standing over one of them with one hand behind his back. He licked a forefinger a couple of times and turned a few pages. Slow. I was about to turn around and keep on my way to where the muslin was, when I heard him say, "No, no. That's not the way. I told you to put her human characteristics on the left; her animal ones on the right. And don't forget to line them up." I commenced to walk backward, didn't even look behind me to find out where I was headed. I just kept lifting my feet and pushing back. When I bumped up against a tree my scalp was prickly. One of the dogs was licking out a pan in the yard. I got to the grape arbor fast enough, but I didn't have the muslin. Flies settled all over your face, rubbing their hands. My head itched like the devil. Like somebody was sticking fine needles in my scalp. I never told Halle or nobody. But that very day I asked Mrs. Garner a part of it. She was low then. Not as low as she ended up, but failing. A kind of bag grew under her jaw. It didn't seem to hurt her, but it made her weak. First she'd be up and spry in the morning and by the second milking she couldn't stand up. Next she took to sleeping late. The day I went up there she was in bed the whole day, and I thought to carry her some bean soup and ask her then. When I opened the bedroom door she looked at me from underneath her nightcap. Already it was hard to catch life in her eyes. Her shoes and stockings were on the floor so I knew she had tried to get dressed.

"I brung you some bean soup," I said.

She said, "I don't think I can swallow that."

"Try a bit," I told her.

"Too thick. I'm sure it's too thick."

"Want me to loosen it up with a little water?"

"No. Take it away. Bring me some cool water, that's all."

"Yes, ma'am. Ma'am? Could I ask you something?"

"What is it, Sethe?"

"What do characteristics mean?"

"What?"

"A word. Characteristics."

"Oh." She moved her head around on the pillow. "Features. Who taught you that?"

"I heard the schoolteacher say it."

"Change the water, Sethe. This is warm."

"Yes, ma'am. Features?"

"Water, Sethe. Cool water."

I put the pitcher on the tray with the white bean soup and went downstairs. When I got back with the fresh water I held her head while she drank. It took her a while because that lump made it hard to swallow. She laid back and wiped her mouth. The drinking seemed to satisfy her but she frowned and said, "I don't seem able to wake up, Sethe. All I seem to want is sleep."

"Then do it," I told her. "I'm take care of things."

Then she went on: what about this? what about that? Said she knew Halle was no trouble, but she wanted to know if schoolteacher was handling the Pauls all right and Sixo.

"Yes, ma'am," I said. "Look like it."

"Do they do what he tells them?"

"They don't need telling."

"Good. That's a mercy. I should be back downstairs in a day or two. I just need more rest. Doctor's due back. Tomorrow, is it?"

"You said features, ma'am?"

"What?"

"Features?"

"Umm. Like, a feature of summer is heat. A characteristic is a feature. A thing that's natural to a thing."

"Can you have more than one?"

"You can have quite a few. You know. Say a baby sucks its thumb. That's one, but it has others too. Keep Billy away from Red Cora. Mr. Garner never let her calve every other year. Sethe, you hear me? Come away from that window and listen."

"Yes, ma'am."

"Ask my brother-in-law to come up after supper."

"Yes, ma'am."

"If you'd wash your hair you could get rid of that lice."

"Ain't no lice in my head, ma'am."

"Whatever it is, a good scrubbing is what it needs, not scratching. Don't tell me we're out of soap."

"No, ma'am."

"All right now. I'm through. Talking makes me tired."

"Yes, ma'am."

"And thank you, Sethe."

"Yes, ma'am."

You was too little to remember the quarters. Your brothers slept under the window. Me, you and your daddy slept by the wall. The night after I heard why schoolteacher measured me, I had trouble sleeping. When Halle came in I asked him what he thought about schoolteacher. He said there wasn't nothing to think about. Said, He's white, ain't he? I said, But I mean is he like Mr. Garner?

"What you want to know, Sethe?"

"Him and her," I said, "they ain't like the whites I seen before. The ones in the big place I was before I came here."

"How these different?" he asked me.

"Well," I said, "they talk soft for one thing."

"It don't matter, Sethe. What they say is the same. Loud or soft."

"Mr. Garner let you buy out your mother," I said.

"Yep. He did."

"Well?"

"If he hadn't of, she would of dropped in his cooking stove."

"Still, he did it. Let you work it off."

"Uh huh."

"Wake up, Halle."

"I said, Uh huh."

"He could of said no. He didn't tell you no."

"No, he didn't tell me no. She worked here for ten years. If she worked another ten you think she would've made it out? I pay him for her last years and in return he got you, me and three more coming up. I got one more year of debt work; one more. Schoolteacher in there told me to quit it. Said the reason for doing it don't hold. I should do the extra but here at Sweet Home."

"Is he going to pay you for the extra?"

"Nope."

"Then how you going to pay it off? How much is it?"

"$123.70."

"Don't he want it back?"

"He want something."

"What?"

"I don't know. Something. But he don't want me off Sweet Home no more. Say it don't pay to have my labor somewhere else while the boys is small."

"What about the money you owe?"

"He must have another way of getting it."

"What way?"

"I don't know, Sethe."

"Then the only question is how? How he going get it?"

"No. That's one question. There's one more."

"What's that?"

He leaned up and turned over, touching my cheek with his knuckles. "The question now is, Who's going buy you out? Or me? Or her?" He pointed over to where you was laying.

"What?"

"If all my labor is Sweet Home, including the extra, what I got left to sell?"

He turned over then and went back to sleep and I thought I wouldn't but I did too for a while. Something he said, maybe, or something he didn't say woke me. I sat up like somebody hit me, and you woke up too and commenced to cry. I rocked you some, but there wasn't much room, so I stepped outside the door to walk you. Up and down I went. Up and down. Everything dark but lamplight in the top window of the house. She must've been up still. I couldn't get out of my head the thing that woke me up: "While the boys is small." That's what he said and it snapped me awake. They tagged after me the whole day weeding, milking, getting firewood. For now. For now.

That's when we should have begun to plan. But we didn't. I don't know what we thought—but getting away was a money thing to us. Buy out. Running was nowhere on our minds. All of us? Some? Where to? How to go? It was Sixo who brought it up, finally, after Paul F. Mrs. Garner sold him, trying to keep things up. Already she lived two years off his price. But it ran out, I guess, so she wrote schoolteacher to come take over. Four Sweet Home men and she still believed she needed her brother-in-law and two boys 'cause people said she shouldn't be alone out there with nothing but Negroes. So he came with a big hat and spectacles and a coach box full of paper. Talking soft and watching hard. He beat Paul A. Not hard and not long, but it was the first time anyone had, because Mr. Garner disallowed it. Next time I saw him he had company in the prettiest trees you ever saw. Sixo started watching the sky. He was the only one who crept at night and Halle said that's how he learned about the train.

"That way." Halle was pointing over the stable. "Where he took my ma'am. Sixo say freedom is that way. A whole train is going and if we can get there, don't need to be no buy-out."

"Train? What's that?" I asked him.

They stopped talking in front of me then. Even Halle. But they whispered among themselves and Sixo watched the sky.

Not the high part, the low part where it touched the trees. You could tell his mind was gone from Sweet Home.

The plan was a good one, but when it came time, I was big with Denver. So we changed it a little. A little. Just enough to butter Halle's face, so Paul D tells me, and make Sixo laugh at last.

But I got you out, baby. And the boys too. When the signal for the train come, you all was the only ones ready. I couldn't find Halle or nobody. I didn't know Sixo was burned up and Paul D dressed in a collar you wouldn't believe. Not till later. So I sent you all to the wagon with the woman who waited in the corn. Ha ha. No notebook for my babies and no measuring string neither. What I had to get through later I got through because of you. Passed right by those boys hanging in the trees. One had Paul A's shirt on but not his feet or his head. I walked right on by because only me had your milk, and God do what He would, I was going to get it to you. You remember that, don't you; that I did? That when I got here I had milk enough for all?

One more curve in the road, and Sethe could see her chimney; it wasn't lonely-looking anymore. The ribbon of smoke was from a fire that warmed a body returned to her—just like it never went away, never needed a headstone. And the heart that beat inside it had not for a single moment stopped in her hands.

She opened the door, walked in and locked it tight behind her.

The day Stamp Paid saw the two backs through the window and then hurried down the steps, he believed the undecipherable language clamoring around the house was the mumbling

of the black and angry dead. Very few had died in bed, like
Baby Suggs, and none that he knew of, including Baby, had
lived a livable life. Even the educated colored: the long-school
people, the doctors, the teachers, the paper-writers and busi-
nessmen had a hard row to hoe. In addition to having to use
their heads to get ahead, they had the weight of the whole race
sitting there. You needed two heads for that. Whitepeople
believed that whatever the manners, under every dark skin was
a jungle. Swift unnavigable waters, swinging screaming
baboons, sleeping snakes, red gums ready for their sweet white
blood. In a way, he thought, they were right. The more coloredpeople spent their strength trying to convince them how gentle
they were, how clever and loving, how human, the more they
used themselves up to persuade whites of something Negroes
believed could not be questioned, the deeper and more tangled
the jungle grew inside. But it wasn't the jungle blacks brought
with them to this place from the other (livable) place. It was
the jungle whitefolks planted in them. And it grew. It spread.
In, through and after life, it spread, until it invaded the whites
who had made it. Touched them every one. Changed and altered
them. Made them bloody, silly, worse than even they wanted
to be, so scared were they of the jungle they had made. The
screaming baboon lived under their own white skin; the red
gums were their own.

Meantime, the secret spread of this new kind of white-folks'
jungle was hidden, silent, except once in a while when you
could hear its mumbling in places like 124.

Stamp Paid abandoned his efforts to see about Sethe, after
the pain of knocking and not gaining entrance, and when he
did, 124 was left to its own devices. When Sethe locked the

door, the women inside were free at last to be what they liked, see whatever they saw and say whatever was on their minds.

Almost. Mixed in with the voices surrounding the house, recognizable but undecipherable to Stamp Paid, were the thoughts of the women of 124, unspeakable thoughts, unspoken.

Beloved, she my daughter. She mine. See. She come back to me of her own free will and I don't have to explain a thing. I didn't have time to explain before because it had to be done quick. Quick. She had to be safe and I put her where she would be. But my love was tough and she back now. I knew she would be. Paul D ran her off so she had no choice but to come back to me in the flesh. I bet you Baby Suggs, on the other side, helped. I won't never let her go. I'll explain to her, even though I don't have to. Why I did it. How if I hadn't killed her she would have died and that is something I could not bear to happen to her. When I explain it she'll understand, because she understands everything already. I'll tend her as no mother ever tended a child, a daughter. Nobody will ever get my milk no more except my own children. I never had to give it to nobody else—and the one time I did it was took from me—they held me down and took it. Milk that belonged to my baby. Nan had to nurse whitebabies and me too because Ma'am was in the rice. The little whitebabies got it first and I got what was left. Or none. There was no nursing milk to call my own. I know what it is to be without the milk that belongs to you; to have

to fight and holler for it, and to have so little left. I'll tell
Beloved about that; she'll understand. She my daughter. The
one I managed to have milk for and to get it to her even after
they stole it; after they handled me like I was the cow, no, the
goat, back behind the stable because it was too nasty to stay
in with the horses. But I wasn't too nasty to cook their food
or take care of Mrs. Garner. I tended her like I would have
tended my own mother if she needed me. If they had let her
out the rice field, because I was the one she didn't throw away.
I couldn't have done more for that woman than I would my
own ma'am if she was to take sick and need me and I'd have
stayed with her till she got well or died. And I would have
stayed after that except Nan snatched me back. Before I could
check for the sign. It was her all right, but for a long time I
didn't believe it. I looked everywhere for that hat. Stuttered
after that. Didn't stop it till I saw Halle. Oh, but that's all over
now. I'm here. I lasted. And my girl come home. Now I can
look at things again because she's here to see them too. After
the shed, I stopped. Now, in the morning, when I light the fire
I mean to look out the window to see what the sun is doing
to the day. Does it hit the pump handle first or the spigot? See
if the grass is gray-green or brown or what. Now I know why
Baby Suggs pondered color her last years. She never had time
to see, let alone enjoy it before. Took her a long time to finish
with blue, then yellow, then green. She was well into pink when
she died. I don't believe she wanted to get to red and I understand why because me and Beloved outdid ourselves with it.
Matter of fact, that and her pinkish headstone was the last color
I recall. Now I'll be on the lookout. Think what spring will be
for us! I'll plant carrots just so she can see them, and turnips.

Have you ever seen one, baby? A prettier thing God never made. White and purple with a tender tail and a hard head. Feels good when you hold it in your hand and smells like the creek when it floods, bitter but happy. We'll smell them together, Beloved. Beloved. Because you mine and I have to show you these things, and teach you what a mother should. Funny how you lose sight of some things and memory others. I never will forget that whitegirl's hands. Amy. But I forget the color of all that hair on her head. Eyes must have been gray, though. Seem like I do rememory that. Mrs. Garner's was light brown—while she was well. Got dark when she took sick. A strong woman, used to be. And when she talked off her head, she'd say it. "I used to be strong as a mule, Jenny." Called me "Jenny" when she was babbling, and I can bear witness to that. Tall and strong. The two of us on a cord of wood was as good as two men. Hurt her like the devil not to be able to raise her head off the pillow. Still can't figure why she thought she needed schoolteacher, though. I wonder if she lasted, like I did. Last time I saw her she couldn't do nothing but cry, and I couldn't do a thing for her but wipe her face when I told her what they done to me. Somebody had to know it. Hear it. Somebody. Maybe she lasted. Schoolteacher wouldn't treat her the way he treated me. First beating I took was the last. Nobody going to keep me from my children. Hadn't been for me taking care of her maybe I would have known what happened. Maybe Halle was trying to get to me. I stood by her bed waiting for her to finish with the slop jar. When I got her back in the bed she said she was cold. Hot as blazes and she wanted quilts. Said to shut the window. I told her no. She needed the cover; I needed the breeze. Long as those yellow curtains flapped, I was all

right. Should have heeded her. Maybe what sounded like shots
really was. Maybe I would have seen somebody or something.
Maybe. Anyhow I took my babies to the corn, Halle or no.
Jesus. When I heard that woman's rattle. She said, Any more?
I told her I didn't know. She said, I been here all night. Can't
wait. I tried to make her. She said, Can't do it. Come on. Hoo!
Not a man around. Boys scared. You asleep on my back. Denver
sleep in my stomach. Felt like I was split in two. I told her to
take you all; I had to go back. In case. She just looked at me.
Said, Woman? Bit a piece of my tongue off when they opened
my back. It was hanging by a shred. I didn't mean to. Clamped
down on it, it come right off. I thought, Good God, I'm going
to eat myself up. They dug a hole for my stomach so as not to
hurt the baby. Denver don't like for me to talk about it. She
hates anything about Sweet Home except how she was born.
But you was there and even if you too young to memory it, I
can tell it to you. The grape arbor. You memory that? I ran so
fast. Flies beat me to you. I would have known right away who
you was when the sun blotted out your face the way it did when
I took you to the grape arbor. I would have known at once
when my water broke. The minute I saw you sitting on the
stump, it broke. And when I did see your face it had more than
a hint of what you would look like after all these years. I would
have known who you were right away because the cup after
cup of water you drank proved and connected to the fact that
you dribbled clear spit on my face the day I got to 124. I would
have known right off, but Paul D distracted me. Otherwise I
would have seen my fingernail prints right there on your forehead for all the world to see. From when I held your head up,
out in the shed. And later on, when you asked me about the

earrings I used to dangle for you to play with, I would have recognized you right off, except for Paul D. Seems to me he wanted you out from the beginning, but I wouldn't let him. What you think? And look how he ran when he found out about me and you in the shed. Too rough for him to listen to. Too thick, he said. My love was too thick. What he know about it? Who in the world is he willing to die for? Would he give his privates to a stranger in return for a carving? Some other way, he said. There must have been some other way. Let schoolteacher haul us away, I guess, to measure your behind before he tore it up? I have felt what it felt like and nobody walking or stretched out is going to make you feel it too. Not you, not none of mine, and when I tell you you mine, I also mean I'm yours. I wouldn't draw breath without my children. I told Baby Suggs that and she got down on her knees to beg God's pardon for me. Still, it's so. My plan was to take us all to the other side where my own ma'am is. They stopped me from getting us there, but they didn't stop you from getting here. Ha ha. You came right on back like a good girl, like a daughter, which is what I wanted to be and would have been if my ma'am had been able to get out of the rice long enough before they hanged her and let me be one. You know what? She'd had the bit so many times she smiled. When she wasn't smiling she smiled, and I never saw her own smile. I wonder what they was doing when they was caught. Running, you think? No. Not that. Because she was my ma'am and nobody's ma'am would run off and leave her daughter, would she? Would she, now? Leave her in the yard with a one-armed woman? Even if she hadn't been able to suckle the daughter for more than a week or two and had to turn her over to another woman's tit that never had enough for all. They said it was the bit that made her smile when she didn't want to. Like the Saturday girls working the slaughterhouse yard. When I came out of jail I saw them plain. They came when the shift changed on Saturday when the men got paid and worked behind the fences, back of the outhouse. Some worked standing up, leaning on the toolhouse door. They gave some of their nickels and dimes to the foreman as they left but by then their smiles was over. Some of them drank liquor to keep from feeling what they felt. Some didn't drink a drop—just beat it on over to Phelps to pay for what their children needed, or their ma'ammies. Working a pig yard. That has got to be something for a woman to do, and I got close to it myself when I got out of jail and bought, so to speak, your name. But the Bodwins got me the cooking job at Sawyer's and left me able to smile on my own like now when I think about you.

But you know all that because you smart like everybody said because when I got here you was crawling already. Trying to get up the stairs. Baby Suggs had them painted white so you could see your way to the top in the dark where lamplight didn't reach. Lord, you loved the stairsteps.

I got close. I got close. To being a Saturday girl. I had already worked a stone mason's shop. A step to the slaughterhouse would have been a short one. When I put that headstone up I wanted to lay in there with you, put your head on my shoulder and keep you warm, and I would have if Buglar and Howard and Denver didn't need me, because my mind was homeless then. I couldn't lay down with you then. No matter how much I wanted to. I couldn't lay down nowhere in peace, back then. Now I can. I can sleep like the drowned, have mercy. She come back to me, my daughter, and she is mine.

Beloved is my sister. I swallowed her blood right along with my mother's milk. The first thing I heard after not hearing anything was the sound of her crawling up the stairs. She was my secret company until Paul D came. He threw her out. Ever since I was little she was my company and she helped me wait for my daddy. Me and her waited for him. I love my mother but I know she killed one of her own daughters, and tender as she is with me, I'm scared of her because of it. She missed killing my brothers and they knew it. They told me die-witch! stories to show me the way to do it, if ever I needed to. Maybe it was getting that close to dying made them want to fight the War. That's what they told me they were going to do. I guess they rather be around killing men than killing women, and there sure is something in her that makes it all right to kill her own. All the time, I'm afraid the thing that happened that made it all right for my mother to kill my sister could happen again. I don't know what it is, I don't know who it is, but maybe there is something else terrible enough to make her do it again. I need to know what that thing might be, but I don't want to. Whatever it is, it comes from outside this house, outside the yard, and it can come right on in the yard if it wants to. So I never leave this house and I watch over the yard, so it can't happen again and my mother won't have to kill me too. Not since Miss Lady Jones' house have I left 124 by myself. Never. The only other times—two times in all—I was with my mother. Once to see Grandma Baby put down next to Beloved, she's my sister. The other time Paul D went too and when we came back I thought the house would still be empty from when he threw my sister's ghost out. But no. When I came back to 124, there she was. Beloved. Waiting for me. Tired from her long journey back. Ready to be taken care of; ready for me to protect her. This time I have to keep my mother away from her. That's hard, but I have to. It's all on me. I've seen my mother in a dark place, with scratching noises. A smell coming from her dress. I have been with her where something little watched us from the corners. And touched. Sometimes they touched. I didn't remember it for a long time until Nelson Lord made me. I asked her if it was true but couldn't hear what she said and there was no point in going back to Lady Jones if you couldn't hear what anybody said. So quiet. Made me have to read faces and learn how to figure out what people were thinking, so I didn't need to hear what they said. That's how come me and Beloved could play together. Not talking. On the porch. By the creek. In the secret house. It's all on me, now, but she can count on me. I thought she was trying to kill her that day in the Clearing. Kill her back. But then she kissed her neck and I have to warn her about that. Don't love her too much. Don't. Maybe it's still in her the thing that makes it all right to kill her children. I have to tell her. I have to protect her.

She cut my head off every night. Buglar and Howard told me she would and she did. Her pretty eyes looking at me like I was a stranger. Not mean or anything, but like I was somebody she found and felt sorry for. Like she didn't want to do it but she had to and it wasn't going to hurt. That it was just a thing grown-up people do—like pull a splinter out your hand; touch the corner of a towel in your eye if you get a cinder in it. She looks over at Buglar and Howard—see if they all right. Then she comes over to my side. I know she'll be good at it, careful. That when she cuts it off it'll be done right; it won't hurt. After she does it I lie there for a minute with just my head. Then she carries it downstairs to braid my hair. I try not to cry but it hurts so much to comb it. When she finishes the combing and starts the braiding, I get sleepy. I want to go to sleep but I know if I do I won't wake up. So I have to stay awake while she finishes my hair, then I can sleep. The scary part is waiting for her to come in and do it. Not when she does it, but when I wait for her to. Only place she can't get to me in the night is Grandma Baby's room. The room we sleep in upstairs used to be where the help slept when whitepeople lived here. They had a kitchen outside, too. But Grandma Baby turned it into a woodshed and toolroom when she moved in. And she boarded up the back door that led to it because she said she didn't want to make that journey no more. She built around it to make a storeroom, so if you want to get in 124 you have to come by her. Said she didn't care what folks said about her fixing a two-story house up like a cabin where you cook inside. She said they told her visitors with nice dresses don't want to sit in the same room with the cook stove and the peelings and the grease and the smoke. She wouldn't pay

them no mind, she said. I was safe at night in there with
All I could hear was me breathing but sometimes in the day I
couldn't tell whether it was me breathing or somebody next
to me. I used to watch Here Boy's stomach go in and out, in
and out, to see if it matched mine, holding my breath to get
off his rhythm, releasing it to get on. Just to see whose it
was—that sound like when you blow soft in a bottle only
regular, regular. Am I making that sound? Is Howard? Who
is? That was when everybody was quiet and I couldn't hear
anything they said. I didn't care either because the quiet let
me dream my daddy better. I always knew he was coming.
Something was holding him up. He had a problem with the
horse. The river flooded; the boat sank and he had to make a
new one. Sometimes it was a lynch mob or a windstorm. He
was coming and it was a secret. I spent all of my outside self
loving Ma'am so she wouldn't kill me, loving her even when
she braided my head at night. I never let her know my daddy
was coming for me. Grandma Baby thought he was coming,
too. For a while she thought so, then she stopped. I never did.
Even when Buglar and Howard ran away. Then Paul D came
in here. I heard his voice downstairs, and Ma'am laughing, so
I thought it was him, my daddy. Nobody comes to this house
anymore. But when I got downstairs it was Paul D and he
didn't come for me; he wanted my mother. At first. Then he
wanted my sister, too, but she got him out of here and I'm so
glad he's gone. Now it's just us and I can protect her till my
daddy gets here to help me watch out for Ma'am and anything
come in the yard.

My daddy do anything for runny fried eggs. Dip his bread
in it. Grandma used to tell me his things. She said anytime

she could make him a plate of soft fried eggs was Christmas, made him so happy. She said she was always a little scared of my daddy. He was too good, she said. From the beginning, she said, he was too good for the world. Scared her. She thought, He'll never make it through nothing. Whitepeople must have thought so too, because they never got split up. So she got the chance to know him, look after him, and he scared her the way he loved things. Animals and tools and crops and the alphabet. He could count on paper. The boss taught him. Offered to teach the other boys but only my daddy wanted it. She said the other boys said no. One of them with a number for a name said it would change his mind—make him forget things he shouldn't and memorize things he shouldn't and he didn't want his mind messed up. But my daddy said, If you can't count they can cheat you. If you can't read they can beat you. They thought that was funny. Grandma said she didn't know, but it was because my daddy could count on paper and figure that he bought her away from there. And she said she always wished she could read the Bible like real preachers. So it was good for me to learn how, and I did until it got quiet and all I could hear was my own breathing and one other who knocked over the milk jug while it was sitting on the table. Nobody near it. Ma'am whipped Buglar but he didn't touch it. Then it messed up all the ironed clothes and put its hands in the cake. Look like I was the only one who knew right away who it was. Just like when she came back I knew who she was too. Not right away, but soon as she spelled her name—not her given name, but the one Ma'am paid the stonecutter for—I knew. And when she wondered about Ma'am's earrings—something I didn't know about—well, that just made the cheese more binding: my sister come to help me wait for my daddy.

My daddy was an angel man. He could look at you and tell where you hurt and he could fix it too. He made a hanging thing for Grandma Baby, so she could pull herself up from the floor when she woke up in the morning, and he made a step so when she stood up she was level. Grandma said she was always afraid a whiteman would knock her down in front of her children. She behaved and did everything right in front of her children because she didn't want them to see her knocked down. She said it made children crazy to see that. At Sweet Home nobody did or said they would, so my daddy never saw it there and never went crazy and even now I bet he's trying to get here. If Paul D could do it my daddy could too. Angel man. We should all be together. Me, him and Beloved. Ma'am could stay or go off with Paul D if she wanted to. Unless Daddy wanted her himself, but I don't think he would now, since she let Paul D in her bed. Grandma Baby said people look down on her because she had eight children with different men. Coloredpeople and whitepeople both look down on her for that. Slaves not supposed to have pleasurable feelings on their own; their bodies not supposed to be like that, but they have to have as many children as they can to please whoever owned them. Still, they were not supposed to have pleasure deep down. She said for me not to listen to all that. That I should always listen to my body and love it.

The secret house. When she died I went there. Ma'am wouldn't let me go outside in the yard and eat with the others. We stayed inside. That hurt. I know Grandma Baby would have liked the party and the people who came to it, because she got low not seeing anybody or going anywhere—just grieving and thinking about colors and how she made a mistake. That what she thought about what the heart and the body could do was wrong. The whitepeople came anyway. In her yard. She had done everything right and they came in her yard anyway. And she didn't know what to think. All she had left was her heart and they busted it so even the War couldn't rouse her.

She told me all my daddy's things. How hard he worked to buy her. After the cake was ruined and the ironed clothes all messed up, and after I heard my sister crawling up the stairs to get back to her bed, she told me my things too. That I was charmed. My birth was and I got saved all the time. And that I shouldn't be afraid of the ghost. It wouldn't harm me because I tasted its blood when Ma'am nursed me. She said the ghost was after Ma'am and her too for not doing anything to stop it. But it would never hurt me. I just had to watch out for it because it was a greedy ghost and needed a lot of love, which was only natural, considering. And I do. Love her. I do. She played with me and always came to be with me whenever I needed her. She's mine, Beloved. She's mine.

I am Beloved and she is mine. I see her take flowers away from leaves   she puts them in a round basket   the leaves are not for her   she fills the basket   she opens the grass   I would help her but the clouds are in the way   how can I say things that are pictures   I am not separate from her   there is no place where I stop   her face is my own and I want to be there in the place where her face is and to be looking at it too   a hot thing

   All of it is now   it is always now   there will never be a time when I am not crouching and watching others who are crouching too   I am always crouching   the man on my face is dead his face is not mine   his mouth smells sweet but his eyes are locked
   some who eat nasty themselves   I do not eat   the men without skin bring us their morning water to drink   we have none   at night I cannot see the dead man on my face   daylight comes through the cracks and I can see his locked eyes   I am not big   small rats do not wait for us to sleep   someone is thrashing but there is no room to do it in   if we had more to drink we could make tears   we cannot make sweat or morning

water so the men without skin bring us theirs　one time they
bring us sweet rocks to suck　we are all trying to leave our
bodies behind　the man on my face has done it　it is hard to
make yourself die forever　you sleep short and then return
in the beginning we could vomit　now we do not

　　now we cannot　his teeth are pretty white points　someone
is trembling　I can feel it over here　he is fighting hard to
leave his body which is a small bird trembling　there is no
room to tremble so he is not able to die　my own dead man
is pulled away from my face　I miss his pretty white points

　　We are not crouching now　we are standing but my legs
are like my dead man's eyes　I cannot fall because there is no
room to　the men without skin are making loud noises　I am
not dead　the bread is sea-colored　I am too hungry to eat it
the sun closes my eyes　those able to die are in a pile　I cannot
find my man　the one whose teeth I have loved　a hot thing
the little hill of dead people　a hot thing　the men without
skin push them through with poles　the woman is there with
the face I want　the face that is mine　they fall into the sea
which is the color of the bread　she has nothing in her ears
if I had the teeth of the man who died on my face I would bite
the circle around her neck　bite it away　I know she does not
like it　now there is room to crouch and to watch the crouching
others　it is the crouching that is now　always now　inside
the woman with my face is in the sea　a hot thing

　　In the beginning I could see her　I could not help her
because the clouds were in the way　in the beginning I could
see her　the shining in her ears　she does not like the circle

around her neck   I know this   I look hard at her so she will know that the clouds are in the way   I am sure she saw me I am looking at her see me   she empties out her eyes   I am there in the place where her face is and telling her the noisy clouds were in my way   she wants her earrings   she wants her round basket   I want her face   a hot thing

in the beginning the women are away from the men and the men are away from the women   storms rock us and mix the men into the women and the women into the men   that is when I begin to be on the back of the man   for a long time I see only his neck and his wide shoulders above me   I am small   I love him because he has a song   when he turned around to die I see the teeth he sang through   his singing was soft   his singing is of the place where a woman takes flowers away from their leaves and puts them in a round basket   before the clouds   she is crouching near us   but I do not see her until he locks his eyes and dies on my face   we are that way there is no breath coming from his mouth and the place where breath should be is sweet-smelling   the others do not know he is dead   I know   his song is gone   now I love his pretty little teeth instead

I cannot lose her again   my dead man was in the way like the noisy clouds   when he dies on my face I can see hers   she is going to smile at me   she is going to   her sharp earrings are gone   the men without skin are making loud noises   they push my own man through   they do not push the woman with my face through   she goes in   they do not push her   she goes in   the little hill is gone   she was going to smile at me she was going to   a hot thing

They are not crouching now   we are   they are floating on
the water   they break up the little hill and push it through
I cannot find my pretty teeth   I see the dark face that is going
to smile at me   it is my dark face that is going to smile at me
the iron circle is around our neck   she does not have sharp
earrings in her ears or a round basket   she goes in the water
with my face

I am standing in the rain falling   the others are taken
I am not taken   I am falling like the rain is   I watch him eat
inside I am crouching to keep from falling with the rain
I am going to be in pieces   he hurts where I sleep   he puts
his finger there   I drop the food and break into pieces   she
took my face away
there is no one to want me   to say me my name   I wait
on the bridge because she is under it   there is night and there
is day
again   again   night day   night day   I am waiting   no iron
circle is around my neck   no boats go on this water   no men
without skin   my dead man is not floating here   his teeth are
down there where the blue is and the grass   so is the face I
want   the face that is going to smile at me   it is going to   in
the day diamonds are in the water where she is and turtles
in the night I hear chewing and swallowing and laughter   it
belongs to me   she is the laugh   I am the laugher   I see her
face which is mine   it is the face that was going to smile at
me in the place where we crouched   now she is going to   her
face comes through the water   a hot thing   her face is mine
she is not smiling   she is chewing and swallowing   I have to
have my face   I go in   the grass opens   she opens it   I am

in the water and she is coming   there is no round basket   no
iron circle around her neck   she goes up where the diamonds
are   I follow her   we are in the diamonds which are her
earrings now   my face is coming   I have to have it   I am
looking for the join   I am loving my face so much   my dark
face is close to me   I want to join   she whispers to me   she
whispers   I reach for her   chewing and swallowing   she
touches me   she knows I want to join   she chews and swallows me   I am gone   now I am her face   my own face has
left me   I see me swim away   a hot thing   I see the bottoms
of my feet   I am alone   I want to be the two of us   I want
the join

I come out of blue water   after the bottoms of my feet swim
away from me I come up   I need to find a place to be   the air
is heavy   I am not dead   I am not   there is a house   there
is what she whispered to me   I am where she told me   I am
not dead   I sit   the sun closes my eyes   when I open them I
see the face I lost   Sethe's is the face that left me   Sethe sees
me see her and I see the smile   her smiling face is the place
for me   it is the face I lost   she is my face smiling at me
doing it at last   a hot thing   now we can join   a hot thing

I am Beloved and she is mine. Sethe is the one that picked flowers, yellow flowers in the place before the crouching. Took them away from their green leaves. They are on the quilt now where we sleep. She was about to smile at me when the men without skin came and took us up into the sunlight with the dead and shoved them into the sea. Sethe went into the sea. She went there. They did not push her. She went there. She was getting ready to smile at me and when she saw the dead people pushed into the sea she went also and left me there with no face or hers. Sethe is the face I found and lost in the water under the bridge. When I went in, I saw her face coming to me and it was my face too. I wanted to join. I tried to join, but she went up into the pieces of light at the top of the water. I lost her again, but I found the house she whispered to me and there she was, smiling at last. It's good, but I cannot lose her again. All I want to know is why did she go in the water in the place where we crouched? Why did she do that when she was just about to smile at me? I wanted to join her in the sea but I could not move; I wanted to help her when she was picking the flowers, but the clouds of gunsmoke blinded me and I lost her. Three times I lost her: once with the flowers because of the noisy clouds of smoke; once when she went into the sea instead of smiling at me; once under the bridge when I went in to join her and she came toward me but did not smile. She whispered to me, chewed me, and swam away. Now I have found her in this house. She smiles at me and it is my own face smiling. I will not lose her again. She is mine.

Tell me the truth. Didn't you come from the other side?
Yes. I was on the other side.
You came back because of me?
Yes.
You rememory me?
Yes. I remember you.
You never forgot me?
Your face is mine.
Do you forgive me? Will you stay? You safe here now.
Where are the men without skin?
Out there. Way off.
Can they get in here?
No. They tried that once, but I stopped them. They won't ever come back.
One of them was in the house I was in. He hurt me.
They can't hurt us no more.
Where are your earrings?
They took them from me.
The men without skin took them?
Yes.
I was going to help you but the clouds got in the way.

There're no clouds here.
If they put an iron circle around your neck I will bite it away.
Beloved.
I will make you a round basket.
You're back. You're back.
Will we smile at me?
Can't you see I'm smiling?
I love your face.

We played by the creek.
I was there in the water.
In the quiet time, we played.
The clouds were noisy and in the way.
When I needed you, you came to be with me.
I needed her face to smile.
I could only hear breathing.
The breathing is gone; only the teeth are left.
She said you wouldn't hurt me.
She hurt me.
I will protect you.
I want her face.
Don't love her too much.
I am loving her too much.
Watch out for her; she can give you dreams.
She chews and swallows.
Don't fall asleep when she braids your hair.
She is the laugh; I am the laughter.
I watch the house; I watch the yard.
She left me.
Daddy is coming for us.
A hot thing.

Beloved
You are my sister
You are my daughter
You are my face; you are me
I have found you again; you have come back to me
You are my Beloved
You are mine
You are mine
You are mine

I have your milk
I have your smile
I will take care of you

You are my face; I am you. Why did you leave me who am you?
I will never leave you again
Don't ever leave me again
You will never leave me again
You went in the water
I drank your blood
I brought your milk
You forgot to smile
I loved you
You hurt me
You came back to me
You left me

I waited for you
You are mine
You are mine
You are mine

It was a tiny church no bigger than a rich man's parlor. The pews had no backs, and since the congregation was also the choir, it didn't need a stall. Certain members had been assigned the construction of a platform to raise the preacher a few inches above his congregation, but it was a less than urgent task, since the major elevation, a white oak cross, had already taken place. Before it was the Church of the Holy Redeemer, it was a dry-goods shop that had no use for side windows, just front ones for display. These were papered over while members considered whether to paint or curtain them—how to have privacy without losing the little light that might want to shine on them. In the summer the doors were left open for ventilation. In winter an iron stove in the aisle did what it could. At the front of the church was a sturdy porch where customers used to sit, and children laughed at the boy who got his head stuck between the railings. On a sunny and windless day in January it was actually warmer out there than inside, if the iron stove was cold. The damp cellar was fairly warm, but there was no light lighting the pallet or the washbasin or the nail from which a man's clothes could be hung. And an oil lamp in a cellar was sad, so Paul D sat on the porch steps and got additional warmth from a bottle of liquor jammed in his coat pocket. Warmth and red eyes. He held his wrist between his knees, not to keep his hands still but because he had nothing else to hold on to. His tobacco tin, blown open, spilled contents that floated freely and made him their play and prey.

He couldn't figure out why it took so long. He may as well have jumped in the fire with Sixo and they both could have had a good laugh. Surrender was bound to come anyway, why not meet it with a laugh, shouting Seven-O! Why not? Why the delay? He had already seen his brother wave goodbye from the back of a dray, fried chicken in his pocket, tears in his eyes. Mother. Father. Didn't remember the one. Never saw the other. He was the youngest of three half-brothers (same mother— different fathers) sold to Garner and kept there, forbidden to leave the farm, for twenty years. Once, in Maryland, he met four families of slaves who had all been together for a hundred years: great-grands, grands, mothers, fathers, aunts, uncles, cousins, children. Half white, part white, all black, mixed with Indian. He watched them with awe and envy, and each time he discovered large families of black people he made them identify over and over who each was, what relation, who, in fact, belonged to who.

"That there's my auntie. This here's her boy. Yonder is my pap's cousin. My ma'am was married twice—this my half-sister and these her two children. Now, my wife ..."

Nothing like that had ever been his and growing up at Sweet Home he didn't miss it. He had his brothers, two friends, Baby Suggs in the kitchen, a boss who showed them how to shoot and listened to what they had to say. A mistress who made

their soap and never raised her voice. For twenty years they
had all lived in that cradle, until Baby left, Sethe came, and
Halle took her. He made a family with her, and Sixo was hell-
bent to make one with the Thirty-Mile Woman. When Paul
D waved goodbye to his oldest brother, the boss was dead, the
mistress nervous and the cradle already split. Sixo said the
doctor made Mrs. Garner sick. Said he was giving her to drink
what stallions got when they broke a leg and no gunpowder
could be spared, and had it not been for schoolteacher's new
rules, he would have told her so. They laughed at him. Sixo
had a knowing tale about everything. Including Mr. Garner's
stroke, which he said was a shot in his ear put there by a jealous
neighbor.

"Where's the blood?" they asked him.

There was no blood. Mr. Garner came home bent over his
mare's neck, sweating and blue-white. Not a drop of blood.
Sixo grunted, the only one of them not sorry to see him go.
Later, however, he was mighty sorry; they all were.

"Why she call on him?" Paul D asked. "Why she need the
schoolteacher?"

"She need somebody can figure," said Halle.

"You can do figures."

"Not like that."

"No, man," said Sixo. "She need another white on the place."

"What for?"

"What you think? What you think?"

Well, that's the way it was. Nobody counted on Garner
dying. Nobody thought he could. How 'bout that? Everything
rested on Garner being alive. Without his life each of theirs
fell to pieces. Now ain't that slavery or what is it? At the peak

of his strength, taller than tall men, and stronger than most, they clipped him, Paul D. First his shotgun, then his thoughts, for schoolteacher didn't take advice from Negroes. The information they offered he called backtalk and developed a variety of corrections (which he recorded in his notebook) to reeducate them. He complained they ate too much, rested too much, talked too much, which was certainly true compared to him, because schoolteacher ate little, spoke less and rested not at all. Once he saw them playing—a pitching game—and his look of deeply felt hurt was enough to make Paul D blink. He was as hard on his pupils as he was on them—except for the corrections.

For years Paul D believed schoolteacher broke into children what Garner had raised into men. And it was that that made them run off. Now, plagued by the contents of his tobacco tin, he wondered how much difference there really was between before schoolteacher and after. Garner called and announced them men—but only on Sweet Home, and by his leave. Was he naming what he saw or creating what he did not? That was the wonder of Sixo, and even Halle; it was always clear to Paul D that those two were men whether Garner said so or not. It troubled him that, concerning his own manhood, he could not satisfy himself on that point. Oh, he did manly things, but was that Garner's gift or his own will? What would he have been anyway—before Sweet Home—without Garner? In Sixo's country, or his mother's? Or, God help him, on the boat? Did a whiteman saying it make it so? Suppose Garner woke up one morning and changed his mind? Took the word away. Would they have run then? And if he didn't, would the Pauls have stayed there all their lives? Why did the brothers need the one whole night to decide? To discuss whether they would join

Sixo and Halle. Because they had been isolated in a wonderful
lie, dismissing Halle's and Baby Suggs' life before Sweet Home
as bad luck. Ignorant of or amused by Sixo's dark stories.
Protected and convinced they were special. Never suspecting
the problem of Alfred, Georgia; being so in love with the look
of the world, putting up with anything and everything, just to
stay alive in a place where a moon he had no right to was
nevertheless there. Loving small and in secret. His little love
was a tree, of course, but not like Brother—old, wide and
beckoning.

In Alfred, Georgia, there was an aspen too young to call
sapling. Just a shoot no taller than his waist. The kind of thing
a man would cut to whip his horse. Song-murder and the aspen.
He stayed alive to sing songs that murdered life, and watched
an aspen that confirmed it, and never for a minute did he believe
he could escape. Until it rained. Afterward, after the Cherokee
pointed and sent him running toward blossoms, he wanted
simply to move, go, pick up one day and be somewhere else
the next. Resigned to life without aunts, cousins, children. Even
a woman, until Sethe.

And then she moved him. Just when doubt, regret and every
single unasked question was packed away, long after he believed
he had willed himself into being, at the very time and place he
wanted to take root—she moved him. From room to room.
Like a rag doll.

Sitting on the porch of a dry-goods church, a little bit drunk
and nothing much to do, he could have these thoughts. Slow,
what-if thoughts that cut deep but struck nothing solid a man
could hold on to. So he held his wrists. Passing by that woman's
life, getting in it and letting it get in him had set him up for

this fall. Wanting to live out his life with a whole woman was new, and losing the feeling of it made him want to cry and think deep thoughts that struck nothing solid. When he was drifting, thinking only about the next meal and night's sleep, when everything was packed tight in his chest, he had no sense of failure, of things not working out. Anything that worked at all worked out. Now he wondered what-all went wrong, and starting with the Plan, everything had. It was a good plan, too. Worked out in detail with every possibility of error eliminated.

Sixo, hitching up the horses, is speaking English again and tells Halle what his Thirty-Mile Woman told him. That seven Negroes on her place were joining two others going North. That the two others had done it before and knew the way. That one of the two, a woman, would wait for them in the corn when it was high—one night and half of the next day she would wait, and if they came she would take them to the caravan, where the others would be hidden. That she would rattle, and that would be the sign. Sixo was going, his woman was going, and Halle was taking his whole family. The two Pauls say they need time to think about it. Time to wonder where they will end up; how they will live. What work; who will take them in; should they try to get to Paul F, whose owner, they remember, lived in something called the "trace"? It takes them one evening's conversation to decide.

Now all they have to do is wait through the spring, till the corn is as high as it ever got and the moon as fat.

And plan. Is it better to leave in the dark to get a better start, or go at daybreak to be able to see the way better? Sixo spits at the suggestion. Night gives them more time and the protection of color. He does not ask them if they are afraid. He manages some dry runs to the corn at night, burying blankets and two knives near the creek. Will Sethe be able to swim the creek? they ask him. It will be dry, he says, when the corn is tall. There is no food to put by, but Sethe says she will get a jug of cane syrup or molasses, and some bread when it is near the time to go. She only wants to be sure the blankets are where they should be, for they will need them to tie her baby on her back and to cover them during the journey. There are no clothes other than what they wear. And of course no shoes. The knives will help them eat, but they bury rope and a pot as well. A good plan.

They watch and memorize the comings and goings of school-teacher and his pupils: what is wanted when and where; how long it takes. Mrs. Garner, restless at night, is sunk in sleep all morning. Some days the pupils and their teacher do lessons until breakfast. One day a week they skip breakfast completely and travel ten miles to church, expecting a large dinner upon their return. Schoolteacher writes in his notebook after supper; the pupils clean, mend or sharpen tools. Sethe's work is the most uncertain because she is on call for Mrs. Garner anytime, including nighttime when the pain or the weakness or the downright loneliness is too much for her. So: Sixo and the Pauls will go after supper and wait in the creek for the Thirty-Mile Woman. Halle will bring Sethe and the three children before dawn—before the sun, before the chickens and the milking cow need attention, so by the time smoke should be coming from the cooking stove, they will be in or near the creek with the others. That way, if Mrs. Garner needs Sethe in the night and calls her, Sethe will be there to answer. They only have to wait through the spring.

But. Sethe was pregnant in the spring and by August is so heavy with child she may not be able to keep up with the men, who can carry the children but not her.

But. Neighbors discouraged by Garner when he was alive now feel free to visit Sweet Home and might appear in the right place at the wrong time.

But. Sethe's children cannot play in the kitchen anymore, so she is dashing back and forth between house and quarters— fidgety and frustrated trying to watch over them. They are too young for men's work and the baby girl is nine months old. Without Mrs. Garner's help her work increases as do schoolteacher's demands.

But. After the conversation about the shoat, Sixo is tied up with the stock at night, and locks are put on bins, pens, sheds, coops, the tackroom and the barn door. There is no place to dart into or congregate. Sixo keeps a nail in his mouth now, to help him undo the rope when he has to.

But. Halle is told to work his extra on Sweet Home and has no call to be anywhere other than where schoolteacher tells him. Only Sixo, who has been stealing away to see his woman, and Halle, who has been hired away for years, know what lies outside Sweet Home and how to get there.

It is a good plan. It can be done right under the watchful pupils and their teacher.

But. They had to alter it—just a little. First they change the leaving. They memorize the directions Halle gives them. Sixo, needing time to untie himself, break open the door and not disturb the horses, will leave later, joining them at the creek with the Thirty-Mile Woman. All four will go straight to the corn. Halle, who also needs more time now, because of Sethe, decides to bring her and the children at night; not wait till first light. They will go straight to the corn and not assemble at the creek. The corn stretches to their shoulders—it will never be higher. The moon is swelling. They can hardly harvest, or chop, or clear, or pick, or haul for listening for a rattle that is not bird or snake. Then one midmorning, they hear it. Or Halle does and begins to sing it to the others: "Hush, hush. Somebody's calling my name. Hush, hush. Somebody's calling my name. O my Lord, O my Lord, what shall I do?"

On his dinner break he leaves the field. He has to. He has to tell Sethe that he has heard the sign. For two successive nights she has been with Mrs. Garner and he can't chance it that she will not know that this night she cannot be. The Pauls see him go. From underneath Brother's shade where they are chewing corn cake, they see him, swinging along. The bread tastes good. They lick sweat from their lips to give it a saltier flavor. Schoolteacher and his pupils are already at the house eating dinner. Halle swings along. He is not singing now.

Nobody knows what happened. Except for the churn, that was the last anybody ever saw of Halle. What Paul D knew was that Halle disappeared, never told Sethe anything, and was next seen squatting in butter. Maybe when he got to the gate and asked to see Sethe, schoolteacher heard a tint of anxiety in his voice—the tint that would make him pick up his ever-ready shotgun. Maybe Halle made the mistake of saying "my wife" in some way that would put a light in school-teacher's eye. Sethe says now that she heard shots, but did not look out the window of Mrs. Garner's bedroom. But Halle was not killed or wounded that day because Paul D saw him later, after she had run off with no one's help; after Sixo laughed and his brother disappeared. Saw him greased and flat-eyed as a fish. Maybe schoolteacher shot after him, shot at his feet, to remind him of the trespass. Maybe Halle got in the barn, hid there and got locked in with the rest of schoolteacher's stock. Maybe anything. He disappeared and everybody was on his own.

Paul A goes back to moving timber after dinner. They are to meet at quarters for supper. He never shows up. Paul D leaves for the creek on time, believing, hoping, Paul A has gone on ahead; certain schoolteacher has learned something. Paul D gets to the creek and it is as dry as Sixo promised. He waits there with the Thirty-Mile Woman for Sixo and Paul A. Only Sixo shows up, his wrists bleeding, his tongue licking his lips like a flame.

"You see Paul A?"

"No."

"Halle?"

"No."

"No sign of them?"

"No sign. Nobody in quarters but the children."

"Sethe?"

"Her children sleep. She must be there still."

"I can't leave without Paul A."

"I can't help you."

"Should I go back and look for them?"

"I can't help you."

"What you think?"

"I think they go straight to the corn."

Sixo turns, then, to the woman and they clutch each other and whisper. She is lit now with some glowing, some shining that comes from inside her. Before when she knelt on creek pebbles with Paul D, she was nothing, a shape in the dark breathing lightly.

Sixo is about to crawl out to look for the knives he buried. He hears something. He hears nothing. Forget the knives. Now. The three of them climb up the bank and schoolteacher, his pupils and four other whitemen move toward them. With lamps. Sixo pushes the Thirty-Mile Woman and she runs further on in the creekbed. Paul D and Sixo run the other way toward the woods. Both are surrounded and tied.

The air gets sweet then. Perfumed by the things honeybees love. Tied like a mule, Paul D feels how dewy and inviting the grass is. He is thinking about that and where Paul A might be when Sixo turns and grabs the mouth of the nearest pointing rifle. He begins to sing. Two others shove Paul D and tie him to a tree. Schoolteacher is saying, "Alive. Alive. I want him alive." Sixo swings and cracks the ribs of one, but with bound hands cannot get the weapon in position to use it in any other way. All the whitemen have to do is wait. For his song, perhaps, to end? Five guns are trained on him while they listen. Paul D cannot see them when they step away from lamplight. Finally one of them hits Sixo in the head with his rifle, and when he comes to, a hickory fire is in front of him and he is tied at the waist to a tree. Schoolteacher has changed his mind: "This one will never be suitable." The song must have convinced him.

The fire keeps failing and the whitemen are put out with themselves at not being prepared for this emergency. They came to capture, not kill. What they can manage is only enough for cooking hominy. Dry faggots are scarce and the grass is slick with dew.

By the light of the hominy fire Sixo straightens. He is through with his song. He laughs. A rippling sound like Sethe's sons make when they tumble in hay or splash in rainwater. His feet are cooking; the cloth of his trousers smokes. He laughs. Something is funny. Paul D guesses what it is when Sixo interrupts his laughter to call out, "Seven-O! Seven-O!"

Smoky, stubborn fire. They shoot him to shut him up. Have to.

Shackled, walking through the perfumed things honeybees love, Paul D hears the men talking and for the first time learns his worth. He has always known, or believed he did, his value—as a hand, a laborer who could make profit on a farm—but now he discovers his worth, which is to say he learns his price. The dollar value of his weight, his strength, his heart, his brain, his penis, and his future.

As soon as the whitemen get to where they have tied their horses and mount them, they are calmer, talking among themselves about the difficulty they face. The problems. Voices remind schoolteacher about the spoiling these particular slaves have had at Garner's hands. There's laws against what he done: letting niggers hire out their own time to buy themselves. He even let em have guns! And you think he mated them niggers to get him some more? Hell no! He planned for them to marry! if that don't beat all! Schoolteacher sighs, and says doesn't he know it? He had come to put the place aright. Now it faced greater ruin than what Garner left for it, because of the loss of two niggers, at the least, and maybe three because he is not sure they will find the one called Halle. The sister-in-law is too weak to help out and doggone if now there ain't a full-scale stampede on his hands. He would have to trade this here one for $900 if he could get it, and set out to secure the breeding one, her foal and the other one, if he found him. With the money from "this here one" he could get two young ones, twelve or fifteen years old. And maybe with the breeding one, her three pickaninnies and whatever the foal might be, he and his nephews would have seven niggers and Sweet Home would be worth the trouble it was causing him.

"Look to you like Lillian gonna make it?"

"Touch and go. Touch and go."

"You was married to her sister-in-law, wasn't you?"

"I was."

"She frail too?"

"A bit. Fever took her."

"Well, you don't need to stay no widower in these parts."

"My cogitation right now is Sweet Home."

"Can't say as I blame you. That's some spread."

They put a three-spoke collar on him so he can't lie down and they chain his ankles together. The number he heard with his ear is now in his head. Two. Two? Two niggers lost? Paul D thinks his heart is jumping. They are going to look for Halle, not Paul A. They must have found Paul A and if a whiteman finds you it means you are surely lost.

Schoolteacher looks at him for a long time before he closes the door of the cabin. Carefully, he looks. Paul D does not look back. It is sprinkling now. A teasing August rain that raises expectations it cannot fill. He thinks he should have sung along. Loud, something loud and rolling to go with Sixo's tune, but the words put him off—he didn't understand the words.

Although it shouldn't have mattered because he understood the sound: hatred so loose it was juba.

The warm sprinkle comes and goes, comes and goes. He thinks he hears sobbing that seems to come from Mrs. Garner's window, but it could be anything, anyone, even a she-cat making her yearning known. Tired of holding his head up, he lets his chin rest on the collar and speculates on how he can hobble over to the grate, boil a little water and throw in a handful of meal. That's what he is doing when Sethe comes in, rain-wet and big-bellied, saying she is going to cut. She has just come back from taking her children to the corn. The whites were not around. She couldn't find Halle. Who was caught? Did Sixo get away? Paul A?

He tells her what he knows: Sixo is dead; the Thirty-Mile Woman ran, and he doesn't know what happened to Paul A or Halle. "Where could he be?" she asks.

Paul D shrugs because he can't shake his head.

"You saw Sixo die? You sure?"

"I'm sure."

"Was he woke when it happened? Did he see it coming?"

"He was woke. Woke and laughing."

"Sixo laughed?"

"You should have heard him, Sethe."

Sethe's dress steams before the little fire over which he is boiling water. It is hard to move about with shackled ankles and the neck jewelry embarrasses him. In his shame he avoids her eyes, but when he doesn't he sees only black in them—no whites. She says she is going, and he thinks she will never make it to the gate, but he doesn't dissuade her. He knows he will never see her again, and right then and there his heart stopped.

The pupils must have taken her to the barn for sport right afterward, and when she told Mrs. Garner, they took down the cowhide. Who in hell or on this earth would have thought that she would cut anyway? They must have believed, what with her belly and her back, that she wasn't going anywhere. He wasn't surprised to learn that they had tracked her down in Cincinnati, because, when he thought about it now, her price was greater than his; property that reproduced itself without cost.

Remembering his own price, down to the cent, that school-teacher was able to get for him, he wondered what Sethe's would have been. What had Baby Suggs' been? How much did Halle owe, still, besides his labor? What did Mrs. Garner get for Paul F? More than nine hundred dollars? How much more? Ten dollars? Twenty? Schoolteacher would know. He knew the worth of everything. It accounted for the real sorrow in his voice when he pronounced Sixo unsuitable. Who could be fooled into buying a singing nigger with a gun? Shouting Seven-O! Seven-O! because his Thirty-Mile Woman got away with his blossoming seed. What a laugh. So rippling and full of glee it put out the fire. And it was Sixo's laughter that was on his mind, not the bit in his mouth, when they hitched him to the buckboard. Then he saw Halle, then the rooster, smiling as if to say, You ain't seen nothing yet. How could a rooster know about Alfred, Georgia?

"Howdy."

Stamp Paid was still fingering the ribbon and it made a little motion in his pants pocket.

Paul D looked up, noticed the side pocket agitation and snorted. "I can't read. You got any more newspaper for me, just a waste of time."

Stamp withdrew the ribbon and sat down on the steps.

"No. This here's something else." He stroked the red cloth between forefinger and thumb. "Something else."

Paul D didn't say anything so the two men sat in silence for a few moments.

"This is hard for me," said Stamp. "But I got to do it. Two things I got to say to you. I'm a take the easy one first."

Paul D chuckled. "If it's hard for you, might kill me dead."

"No, no. Nothing like that. I come looking for you to ask your pardon. Apologize."

"For what?" Paul D reached in his coat pocket for his bottle.

"You pick any house, any house where colored live. In all of Cincinnati. Pick any one and you welcome to stay there. I'm apologizing because they didn't offer or tell you. But you welcome anywhere you want to be. My house is your house too. John and Ella, Miss Lady, Able Woodruff, Willie Pike— anybody. You choose. You ain't got to sleep in no cellar, and I apologize for each and every night you did. I don't know how that preacher let you do it. I knowed him since he was a boy."

"Whoa, Stamp. He offered."

"Did? Well?"

"Well. I wanted, I didn't want to, I just wanted to be off by myself a spell. He offered. Every time I see him he offers again."

"That's a load off. I thought everybody gone crazy."

Paul D shook his head. "Just me."

"You planning to do anything about it?"

"Oh, yeah. I got big plans." He swallowed twice from the bottle.

Any planning in a bottle is short, thought Stamp, but he knew from personal experience the pointlessness of telling a drinking man not to. He cleared his sinuses and began to think how to get to the second thing he had come to say. Very few people were out today. The canal was frozen so that traffic too had stopped. They heard the clop of a horse approaching. Its rider sat a high Eastern saddle but everything else about him was Ohio Valley. As he rode by he looked at them and suddenly reined his horse, and came up to the path leading to the church. He leaned forward.

"Hey," he said.

Stamp put his ribbon in his pocket. "Yes, sir?"

"I'm looking for a gal name of Judy. Works over by the slaughterhouse."

"Don't believe I know her. No, sir."

"Said she lived on Plank Road."

"Plank Road. Yes, sir. That's up a ways. Mile, maybe."

"You don't know her? Judy. Works in the slaughterhouse."

"No, sir, but I know Plank Road. 'Bout a mile up thataway."

Paul D lifted his bottle and swallowed. The rider looked at him and then back at Stamp Paid. Loosening the right rein, he turned his horse toward the road, then changed his mind and came back.

"Look here," he said to Paul D. "There's a cross up there, so I guess this here's a church or used to be. Seems to me like you ought to show it some respect, you follow me?"

"Yes, sir," said Stamp. "You right about that. That's just what I come over to talk to him about. Just that."

The rider clicked his tongue and trotted off. Stamp made small circles in the palm of his left hand with two fingers of his right. "You got to choose," he said. "Choose anyone. They let you be if you want em to. My house. Ella. Willie Pike. None of us got much, but all of us got room for one more. Pay a little something when you can, don't when you can't. Think about it. You grown. I can't make you do what you won't, but think about it."

Paul D said nothing.

"If I did you harm, I'm here to rectify it."

"No need for that. No need at all."

A woman with four children walked by on the other side of the road. She waved, smiling. "Hoo-oo. I can't stop. See you at meeting."

"I be there," Stamp returned her greeting. "There's another one," he said to Paul D. "Scripture Woodruff, Able's sister. Works at the brush and tallow factory. You'll see. Stay around here long enough, you'll see ain't a sweeter bunch of colored

anywhere than what's right here. Pride, well, that bothers em
a bit. They can get messy when they think somebody's too
proud, but when it comes right down to it, they good people
and anyone will take you in."

"What about Judy? She take me in?"

"Depends. What you got in mind?"

"You know Judy?"

"Judith. I know everybody."

"Out on Plank Road?"

"Everybody."

"Well? She take me in?"

Stamp leaned down and untied his shoe. Twelve black button-
hooks, six on each side at the bottom, led to four pairs of eyes at
the top. He loosened the laces all the way down, adjusted the
tongue carefully and wound them back again. When he got to the
eyes he rolled the lace tips with his fingers before inserting them.

"Let me tell you how I got my name." The knot was tight
and so was the bow. "They called me Joshua," he said. "I renamed
myself," he said, "and I'm going to tell you why I did it," and
he told him about Vashti. "I never touched her all that time.
Not once. Almost a year. We was planting when it started and
picking when it stopped. Seemed longer. I should have killed
him. She said no, but I should have. I didn't have the patience
I got now, but I figured maybe somebody else didn't have much
patience either—his own wife. Took it in my head to see if she
was taking it any better than I was. Vashti and me was in the
fields together in the day and every now and then she be gone
all night. I never touched her and damn me if I spoke three
words to her a day. I took any chance I had to get near the
great house to see her, the young master's wife. Nothing but

a boy. Seventeen, twenty maybe. I caught sight of her finally, standing in the backyard by the fence with a glass of water. She was drinking out of it and just gazing out over the yard. I went over. Stood back a ways and took off my hat. I said, 'Scuse me, miss. Scuse me?' She turned to look. I'm smiling. 'Scuse me. You seen Vashti? My wife Vashti?' A little bitty thing, she was. Black hair. Face no bigger than my hand. She said, 'What? Vashti?' I say, 'Yes'm, Vashti. My wife. She say she owe you all some eggs. You know if she brung em? You know her if you see her. Wear a black ribbon on her neck.' She got rosy then and I knowed she knowed. He give Vashti that to wear. A cameo on a black ribbon. She used to put it on every time she went to him. I put my hat back on. 'You see her tell her I need her. Thank you. Thank you, ma'am.' I backed off before she could say something. I didn't dare look back till I got behind some trees. She was standing just as I left her, looking in her water glass. I thought it would give me more satisfaction than it did. I also thought she might stop it, but it went right on. Till one morning Vashti came in and sat by the window. A Sunday. We worked our own patches on Sunday. She sat by the window looking out of it. 'I'm back,' she said. 'I'm back, Josh.' I looked at the back of her neck. She had a real small neck. I decided to break it. You know, like a twig— just snap it. I been low but that was as low as I ever got."

"Did you? Snap it?"

"Uh uh. I changed my name."

"How you get out of there? How you get up here?"

"Boat. On up the Mississippi to Memphis. Walked from Memphis to Cumberland."

"Vashti too?"

"No. She died."

"Aw, man. Tie your other shoe!"

"What?"

"Tie your goddamn shoe! It's sitting right in front of you! Tie it!"

"That make you feel better?"

"No." Paul D tossed the bottle on the ground and stared at the golden chariot on its label. No horses. Just a golden coach draped in blue cloth.

"I said I had two things to say to you. I only told you one. I have to tell you the other."

"I don't want to know it. I don't want to know nothing. Just if Judy will take me in or won't she."

"I was there, Paul D."

"You was where?"

"There in the yard. When she did it."

"Judy?"

"Sethe."

"Jesus."

"It ain't what you think."

"You don't know what I think."

"She ain't crazy. She love those children. She was trying to out-hurt the hurter."

"Leave off."

"And spread it."

"Stamp, let me off. I knew her when she was a girl. She scares me and I knew her when she was a girl."

"You ain't scared of Sethe. I don't believe you."

"Sethe scares me. I scare me. And that girl in her house scares me the most."

"Who is that girl? Where she come from?"

"I don't know. Just shot up one day sitting on a stump."

"Huh. Look like you and me the only ones outside 124 lay eyes on her."

"She don't go nowhere. Where'd you see her?"

"Sleeping on the kitchen floor. I peeped in."

"First minute I saw her I didn't want to be nowhere around her. Something funny about her. Talks funny. Acts funny." Paul D dug his fingers underneath his cap and rubbed the scalp over his temple. "She reminds me of something. Something, look like, I'm supposed to remember."

"She never say where she was from? Where's her people?"

"She don't know, or says she don't. All I ever heard her say was something about stealing her clothes and living on a bridge."

"What kind of bridge?"

"Who you asking?"

"No bridges around here I don't know about. But don't nobody live on em. Under em neither. How long she been over there with Sethe?"

"Last August. Day of the carnival."

"That's a bad sign. Was she at the carnival?"

"No. When we got back, there she was—'sleep on a stump. Silk dress. Brand-new shoes. Black as oil."

"You don't say? Huh. Was a girl locked up in the house with a whiteman over by Deer Creek. Found him dead last summer and the girl gone. Maybe that's her. Folks say he had her in there since she was a pup."

"Well, now she's a bitch."

"Is she what run you off? Not what I told you 'bout Sethe?"

A shudder ran through Paul D. A bone-cold spasm that made him clutch his knees. He didn't know if it was bad whiskey, nights in the cellar, pig fever, iron bits, smiling roosters, fired feet, laughing dead men, hissing grass, rain, apple blossoms, neck jewelry, Judy in the slaughterhouse, Halle in the butter, ghost-white stairs, chokecherry trees, cameo pins, aspens, Paul A's face, sausage or the loss of a red, red heart.

"Tell me something, Stamp." Paul D's eyes were rheumy. "Tell me this one thing. How much is a nigger supposed to take? Tell me. How much?"

"All he can," said Stamp Paid. "All he can."

"Why? Why? Why? Why? Why?"

III

124 was quiet. Denver, who thought she knew all about silence, was surprised to learn hunger could do that: quiet you down and wear you out. Neither Sethe nor Beloved knew or cared about it one way or another. They were too busy rationing their strength to fight each other. So it was she who had to step off the edge of the world and die because if she didn't, they all would. The flesh between her mother's forefinger and thumb was thin as china silk and there wasn't a piece of clothing in the house that didn't sag on her. Beloved held her head up with the palms of her hands, slept wherever she happened to be, and whined for sweets although she was getting bigger, plumper by the day. Everything was gone except two laying hens, and somebody would soon have to decide whether an egg every now and then was worth more than two fried chickens. The hungrier they got, the weaker; the weaker they got, the quieter they were—which was better than the furious arguments, the poker slammed up against the wall, all the shouting and crying that followed that one happy January when they played. Denver had joined in the play, holding back a bit out of habit, even though it was the most fun she had ever known.

But once Sethe had seen the scar, the tip of which Denver had been looking at whenever Beloved undressed—the little curved shadow of a smile in the kootchy-kootchy-coo place under her chin—once Sethe saw it, fingered it and closed her eyes for a long time, the two of them cut Denver out of the games. The cooking games, the sewing games, the hair and dressing-up games. Games her mother loved so well she took to going to work later and later each day until the predictable happened: Sawyer told her not to come back. And instead of looking for another job, Sethe played all the harder with Beloved, who never got enough of anything: lullabies, new stitches, the bottom of the cake bowl, the top of the milk. If the hen had only two eggs, she got both. It was as though her mother had lost her mind, like Grandma Baby calling for pink and not doing the things she used to. But different because, unlike Baby Suggs, she cut Denver out completely. Even the song that she used to sing to Denver she sang for Beloved alone: "High Johnny, wide Johnny, don't you leave my side, Johnny."

At first they played together. A whole month and Denver loved it. From the night they ice-skated under a star-loaded sky and drank sweet milk by the stove, to the string puzzles Sethe did for them in afternoon light, and shadow pictures in the gloaming. In the very teeth of winter and Sethe, her eyes fever bright, was plotting a garden of vegetables and flowers— talking, talking about what colors it would have. She played with Beloved's hair, braiding, puffing, tying, oiling it until it made Denver nervous to watch her. They changed beds and exchanged clothes. Walked arm in arm and smiled all the time. When the weather broke, they were on their knees in the backyard designing a garden in dirt too hard to chop. The thirty-eight dollars of life savings went to feed themselves with fancy food and decorate themselves with ribbon and dress goods, which Sethe cut and sewed like they were going somewhere in a hurry. Bright clothes—with blue stripes and sassy prints. She walked the four miles to John Shillito's to buy yellow ribbon, shiny buttons and bits of black lace. By the end of March the three of them looked like carnival women with nothing to do. When it became clear that they were only interested in each other, Denver began to drift from the play, but she watched it, alert for any sign that Beloved was in danger. Finally convinced there was none, and seeing her mother that happy, that smiling—how could it go wrong?—she let down her guard and it did. Her problem at first was trying to find out who was to blame. Her eye was on her mother, for a signal that the thing that was in her was out, and she would kill again. But it was Beloved who made demands. Anything she wanted she got, and when Sethe ran out of things to give her, Beloved invented desire. She wanted Sethe's company for hours to watch the layer of brown leaves waving at them from the bottom of the creek, in the same place where, as a little girl, Denver played in the silence with her. Now the players were altered. As soon as the thaw was complete Beloved gazed at her gazing face, rippling, folding, spreading, disappearing into the leaves below. She flattened herself on the ground, dirtying her bold stripes, and touched the rocking faces with her own. She filled basket after basket with the first things warmer weather let loose in the ground—dandelions, violets, forsythia—presenting them to Sethe, who arranged them, stuck them, wound them all over the house. Dressed in Sethe's dresses, she stroked her skin with the palm of her hand. She imitated

Sethe, talked the way she did, laughed her laugh and used her body the same way down to the walk, the way Sethe moved her hands, sighed through her nose, held her head. Sometimes coming upon them making men and women cookies or tacking scraps of cloth on Baby Suggs' old quilt, it was difficult for Denver to tell who was who.

Then the mood changed and the arguments began. Slowly at first. A complaint from Beloved, an apology from Sethe. A reduction of pleasure at some special effort the older woman made. Wasn't it too cold to stay outside? Beloved gave a look that said, So what? Was it past bedtime, the light no good for sewing? Beloved didn't move; said, "Do it," and Sethe complied. She took the best of everything—first. The best chair, the biggest piece, the prettiest plate, the brightest ribbon for her hair, and the more she took, the more Sethe began to talk, explain, describe how much she had suffered, been through, for her children, waving away flies in grape arbors, crawling on her knees to a lean-to. None of which made the impression it was supposed to. Beloved accused her of leaving her behind. Of not being nice to her, not smiling at her. She said they were the same, had the same face, how could she have left her? And Sethe cried, saying she never did, or meant to—that she had to get them out, away, that she had the milk all the time and had the money too for the stone but not enough. That her plan was always that they would all be together on the other side, forever. Beloved wasn't interested. She said when she cried there was no one. That dead men lay on top of her. That she had nothing to eat. Ghosts without skin stuck their fingers in her and said beloved in the dark and bitch in the light. Sethe pleaded for forgiveness, counting, listing again and again her reasons: that Beloved was more important, meant more to her than her own life. That she would trade places any day. Give up her life, every minute and hour of it, to take back just one of Beloved's tears. Did she know it hurt her when mosquitoes bit her baby? That to leave her on the ground to run into the big house drove her crazy? That before leaving Sweet Home Beloved slept every night on her chest or curled on her back? Beloved denied it. Sethe never came to her, never said a word to her, never smiled and worst of all never waved goodbye or even looked her way before running away from her.

When once or twice Sethe tried to assert herself—be the unquestioned mother whose word was law and who knew what was best—Beloved slammed things, wiped the table clean of plates, threw salt on the floor, broke a windowpane.

She was not like them. She was wild game, and nobody said, Get on out of here, girl, and come back when you get some sense. Nobody said, You raise your hand to me and I will knock you into the middle of next week. Ax the trunk, the limb will die. Honor thy mother and father that thy days may be long upon the land which the Lord thy God giveth thee. I will wrap you round that doorknob, don't nobody work for you and God don't love ugly ways.

No, no. They mended the plates, swept the salt, and little by little it dawned on Denver that if Sethe didn't wake up one morning and pick up a knife, Beloved might. Frightened as she was by the thing in Sethe that could come out, it shamed her to see her mother serving a girl not much older than herself. When she saw her carrying out Beloved's night bucket, Denver raced to relieve her of it. But the pain was unbearable when they ran low on food, and Denver watched her mother go without—pick-eating around the edges of the table and stove: the hominy that stuck on the bottom; the crusts and rinds and peelings of things. Once she saw her run her longest finger deep in an empty jam jar before rinsing and putting it away.

They grew tired, and even Beloved, who was getting bigger, seemed nevertheless as exhausted as they were. In any case she substituted a snarl or a tooth-suck for waving a poker around and 124 was quiet. Listless and sleepy with hunger Denver saw the flesh between her mother's forefinger and thumb fade. Saw Sethe's eyes bright but dead, alert but vacant, paying attention to everything about Beloved—her lineless palms, her forehead, the smile under her jaw, crooked and much too long—everything except her basket-fat stomach. She also saw the sleeves of her own carnival shirtwaist cover her fingers; hems that once showed her ankles now swept the floor. She saw themselves beribboned, decked-out, limp and starving but locked in a love that wore everybody out. Then Sethe spit up something she had not eaten and it rocked Denver like gunshot. The job she started out with, protecting Beloved from Sethe, changed to protecting her mother from Beloved. Now it was obvious that her mother could die and leave them both and what would Beloved do then? Whatever was happening, it only worked with three—not two—and since neither Beloved nor Sethe seemed to care what the next day might bring (Sethe happy when Beloved was; Beloved lapping devotion like cream), Denver knew it was on her. She would have to leave the yard; step off the edge of the world, leave the two behind and go ask somebody for help.

Who would it be? Who could she stand in front of who wouldn't shame her on learning that her mother sat around like a rag doll, broke down, finally, from trying to take care of and make up for. Denver knew *about* several people, from hearing her mother and grandmother talk. But she knew, personally, only two: an old man with white hair called Stamp and Lady Jones. Well, Paul D, of course. And that boy who told her about Sethe. But they wouldn't do at all. Her heart kicked and an itchy burning in her throat made her swallow all her saliva away. She didn't even know which way to go. When Sethe used to work at the restaurant and when she still had money to shop, she turned right. Back when Denver went to Lady Jones' school, it was left.

The weather was warm; the day beautiful. It was April and everything alive was tentative. Denver wrapped her hair and her shoulders. In the brightest of the carnival dresses and wearing a stranger's shoes, she stood on the porch of 124 ready to be swallowed up in the world beyond the edge of the porch. Out there where small things scratched and sometimes touched. Where words could be spoken that would close your ears shut. Where, if you were alone, feeling could overtake you and stick to you like a shadow. Out there where there were places in which things so bad had happened that when you went near them it would happen again. Like Sweet Home where time didn't pass and where, like her mother said, the bad was waiting for her as well. How would she know these places? What was more—much more—out there were whitepeople and how could you tell about them? Sethe said the mouth and sometimes the hands. Grandma Baby said there was no defense—they could prowl at will, change from one mind to another, and even when they thought they were behaving, it was a far cry from what real humans did.

"They got me out of jail," Sethe once told Baby Suggs.

"They also put you in it," she answered.

"They drove you 'cross the river."

"On my son's back."

"They gave you this house."

"Nobody *gave* me nothing."

"I got a job from them."

"He got a cook from them, girl."

"Oh, some of them do all right by us."

"And every time it's a surprise, ain't it?"

"You didn't used to talk this way."

"Don't box with me. There's more of us they drowned than there is all of them ever lived from the start of time. Lay down your sword. This ain't a battle; it's a rout."

Remembering those conversations and her grandmother's last and final words, Denver stood on the porch in the sun and couldn't leave it. Her throat itched; her heart kicked—and then Baby Suggs laughed, clear as anything. "You mean I never told you nothing about Carolina? About your daddy? You don't remember nothing about how come I walk the way I do and about your mother's feet, not to speak of her back? I never told you all that? Is that why you can't walk down the steps? My Jesus my."

But you said there was no defense.

"There ain't."

Then what do I do?

"Know it, and go on out the yard. Go on."

*

It came back. A dozen years had passed and the way came back. Four houses on the right, sitting close together in a line like wrens. The first house had two steps and a rocking chair on the porch; the second had three steps, a broom propped on the porch beam, two broken chairs and a clump of forsythia at the side. No window at the front. A little boy sat on the ground chewing a stick. The third house had yellow shutters on its two front windows and pot after pot of green leaves with white hearts or red. Denver could hear chickens and the knock of a badly hinged gate. At the fourth house the buds of a sycamore tree had rained down on the roof and made the yard look as though grass grew there. A woman, standing at the open door, lifted her hand halfway in greeting, then froze it near her shoulder as she leaned forward to see whom she waved to. Denver lowered her head. Next was a tiny fenced plot with a cow in it. She remembered the plot but not the cow. Under her headcloth her scalp was wet with tension. Beyond her, voices, male voices, floated, coming closer with each step she took. Denver kept her eyes on the road in case they were whitemen; in case she was walking where they wanted to; in case they said something and she would have to answer them. Suppose they flung out at her, grabbed her, tied her. They were getting closer. Maybe she should cross the road—now. Was the woman who half waved at her still there in the open door? Would she come to her rescue, or, angry at Denver for not waving back, would she withhold her help? Maybe she should turn around, get closer to the waving woman's house. Before she could make up her mind, it was too late—they were right in front of her. Two men, Negro. Denver breathed. Both men touched their caps and murmured, "Morning. Morning." Denver believed her eyes spoke gratitude but she never got her mouth open in time to reply. They moved left of her and passed on.

Braced and heartened by that easy encounter, she picked up speed and began to look deliberately at the neighborhood surrounding her. She was shocked to see how small the big things were: the boulder by the edge of the road she once couldn't see over was a sitting-on rock. Paths leading to houses weren't miles long. Dogs didn't even reach her knees. Letters cut into beeches and oaks by giants were eye level now.

She would have known it anywhere. The post and scrap-lumber fence was gray now, not white, but she would have known it anywhere. The stone porch sitting in a skirt of ivy, pale yellow curtains at the windows; the laid brick path to the front door and wood planks leading around to the back, passing under the windows where she had stood on tiptoe to see above the sill. Denver was about to do it again, when she realized how silly it would be to be found once more staring into the parlor of Mrs. Lady Jones. The pleasure she felt at having found the house dissolved, suddenly, in doubt. Suppose she didn't live there anymore? Or remember her former student after all this time? What would she say? Denver shivered inside, wiped the perspiration from her forehead and knocked.

Lady Jones went to the door expecting raisins. A child, probably, from the softness of the knock, sent by its mother with the raisins she needed if her contribution to the supper was to be worth the trouble. There would be any number of plain cakes, potato pies. She had reluctantly volunteered her own special creation, but said she didn't have raisins, so raisins is what the president said would be provided—early enough so there would be no excuses. Mrs. Jones, dreading the fatigue of beating batter, had been hoping she had forgotten. Her bake oven had been cold all week—getting it to the right temperature would be awful. Since her husband died and her eyes grew dim, she had let up-to-snuff housekeeping fall away. She was of two minds about baking something for the church. On the one hand, she wanted to remind everybody of what she was able to do in the cooking line; on the other, she didn't want to have to. When she heard the tapping at the door, she sighed and went to it hoping the raisins had at least been cleaned.

She was older, of course, and dressed like a chippy, but the girl was immediately recognizable to Lady Jones. Everybody's child was in that face: the nickel-round eyes, bold yet mistrustful; the large powerful teeth between dark sculptured lips that did not cover them. Some vulnerability lay across the bridge of the nose, above the cheeks. And then the skin. Flawless, economical—just enough of it to cover the bone and not a bit more. She must be eighteen or nineteen by now, thought Lady Jones, looking at the face young enough to be twelve. Heavy eyebrows, thick baby lashes and the unmistakable love call that shimmered around children until they learned better.

"Why, Denver," she said. "Look at you."

Lady Jones had to take her by the hand and pull her in, because the smile seemed all the girl could manage. Other people said this child was simple, but Lady Jones never believed it. Having taught her, watched her eat up a page, a rule, a figure, she knew better. When suddenly she had stopped coming, Lady Jones thought it was the nickel. She approached the ignorant grandmother one day on the road, a woods preacher who mended shoes, to tell her it was all right if the money was owed. The woman said that wasn't it; the child was deaf, and deaf Lady Jones thought she still was until she offered her a seat and Denver heard that.

"It's nice of you to come see me. What brings you?"

Denver didn't answer.

"Well, nobody needs a reason to visit. Let me make us some tea."

Lady Jones was mixed. Gray eyes and yellow woolly hair, every strand of which she hated—though whether it was the color or the texture even she didn't know. She had married the blackest man she could find, had five rainbow-colored children and sent them all to Wilberforce, after teaching them all she knew right along with the others who sat in her parlor. Her light skin got her picked for a coloredgirls' normal school in Pennsylvania and she paid it back by teaching the unpicked. The children who played in dirt until they were old enough for chores, these she taught. The colored population of Cincinnati had two graveyards and six churches, but since no school or hospital was obliged to serve them, they learned and died at home. She believed in her heart that, except for her husband, the whole world (including her children) despised her and her hair. She had been listening to "all that yellow gone to waste" and "white nigger" since she was a girl in a houseful of silt-black children, so she disliked everybody a little bit because she believed they hated her hair as much as she did. With that education pat and firmly set, she dispensed with rancor, was indiscriminately polite, saving her real affection for the unpicked children of Cincinnati, one of whom sat before her in a dress so loud it embarrassed the needlepoint chair seat.

"Sugar?"

"Yes. Thank you." Denver drank it all down.

"More?"

"No, ma'am."

"Here. Go ahead."

"Yes, ma'am."

"How's your family, honey?"

Denver stopped in the middle of a swallow. There was no way to tell her how her family was, so she said what was at the top of her mind.

"I want work, Miss Lady."

"Work?"

"Yes, ma'am. Anything."

Lady Jones smiled. "What can you do?"

"I can't do anything, but I would learn it for you if you have a little extra."

"Extra?"

"Food. My ma'am, she doesn't feel good."

"Oh, baby," said Mrs. Jones. "Oh, baby."

Denver looked up at her. She did not know it then, but it was the word "baby," said softly and with such kindness, that inaugurated her life in the world as a woman. The trail she followed to get to that sweet thorny place was made up of paper scraps containing the handwritten names of others. Lady Jones gave her some rice, four eggs and some tea. Denver said she couldn't be away from home long because of her mother's condition. Could she do chores in the morning? Lady Jones told her that no one, not herself, not anyone she knew, could pay anybody anything for work they did themselves. "But if you all need to eat until your mother is well, all you have to do is say so." She mentioned her church's committee invented so nobody had to go hungry. That agitated her guest who said, "No, no," as though asking for help from strangers was worse than hunger. Lady Jones said goodbye to her and asked her to come back anytime. "Anytime at all."

Two days later Denver stood on the porch and noticed something lying on the tree stump at the edge of the yard. She went to look and found a sack of white beans. Another time a plate of cold rabbit meat. One morning a basket of eggs sat there. As she lifted it, a slip of paper fluttered down. She picked it up and looked at it. "M. Lucille Williams" was written in big crooked letters. On the back was a blob of flour-water paste. So Denver paid a second visit to the world outside the porch, although all she said when she returned the basket was "Thank you."

"Welcome," said M. Lucille Williams.

Every now and then, all through the spring, names appeared near or in gifts of food. Obviously for the return of the pan or plate or basket; but also to let the girl know, if she cared to, who the donor was, because some of the parcels were wrapped in paper, and though there was nothing to return, the name was nevertheless there. Many had X's with designs about them, and Lady Jones tried to identify the plate or pan or the covering towel. When she could only guess, Denver followed her directions and went to say thank you anyway—whether she had the right benefactor or not. When she was wrong, when the person said, "No, darling. That's not my bowl. Mine's got a blue ring on it," a small conversation took place. All of them knew her grandmother and some had even danced with her in the Clearing. Others remembered the days when 124 was a way station, the place they assembled to catch news, taste oxtail

soup, leave their children, cut out a skirt. One remembered the tonic mixed there that cured a relative. One showed her the border of a pillowslip, the stamens of its pale blue flowers French-knotted in Baby Suggs' kitchen by the light of an oil lamp while arguing the Settlement Fee. They remembered the party with twelve turkeys and tubs of strawberry smash. One said she wrapped Denver when she was a single day old and cut shoes to fit her mother's blasted feet. Maybe they were sorry for her. Or for Sethe. Maybe they were sorry for the years of their own disdain. Maybe they were simply nice people who could hold meanness toward each other for just so long and when trouble rode bareback among them, quickly, easily they did what they could to trip him up. In any case, the personal pride, the arrogant claim staked out at 124 seemed to them to have run its course. They whispered, naturally, wondered, shook their heads. Some even laughed outright at Denver's clothes of a hussy, but it didn't stop them caring whether she ate and it didn't stop the pleasure they took in her soft "Thank you."

At least once a week, she visited Lady Jones, who perked up enough to do a raisin loaf especially for her, since Denver was set on sweet things. She gave her a book of Bible verse and listened while she mumbled words or fairly shouted them. By June Denver had read and memorized all fifty-two pages—one for each week of the year.

As Denver's outside life improved, her home life deteriorated. If the whitepeople of Cincinnati had allowed Negroes into their lunatic asylum they could have found candidates in 124. Strengthened by the gifts of food, the source of which neither Sethe nor Beloved questioned, the women had arrived at a doomsday truce designed by the devil. Beloved sat around, ate, went from bed to bed. Sometimes she screamed, "Rain! Rain!" and clawed her throat until rubies of blood opened there, made brighter by her midnight skin. Then Sethe shouted, "No!" and knocked over chairs to get to her and wipe the jewels away. Other times Beloved curled up on the floor, her wrists between her knees, and stayed there for hours. Or she would go to the creek, stick her feet in the water and whoosh it up her legs. Afterward she would go to Sethe, run her fingers over the woman's teeth while tears slid from her wide black eyes. Then it seemed to Denver the thing was done: Beloved bending over Sethe looked the mother, Sethe the teething child, for other than those times when Beloved needed her, Sethe confined herself to a corner chair. The bigger Beloved got, the smaller Sethe became; the brighter Beloved's eyes, the more those eyes that used never to look away became slits of sleeplessness. Sethe no longer combed her hair or splashed her face with water. She sat in the chair licking her lips like a chastised child while Beloved ate up her life, took it, swelled up with it, grew taller on it. And the older woman yielded it up without a murmur.

Denver served them both. Washing, cooking, forcing, cajoling her mother to eat a little now and then, providing sweet things for Beloved as often as she could to calm her down. It was hard to know what she would do from minute to minute. When the heat got hot, she might walk around the house naked or wrapped in a sheet, her belly protruding like a winning watermelon.

Denver thought she understood the connection between her mother and Beloved: Sethe was trying to make up for the handsaw; Beloved was making her pay for it. But there would never be an end to that, and seeing her mother diminished shamed and infuriated her. Yet she knew Sethe's greatest fear was the same one Denver had in the beginning—that Beloved might leave. That before Sethe could make her understand what it meant—what it took to drag the teeth of that saw under the little chin; to feel the baby blood pump like oil in her hands; to hold her face so her head would stay on; to squeeze her so she could absorb, still, the death spasms that shot through that adored body, plump and sweet with life—Beloved might leave. Leave before Sethe could make her realize that worse than that—far worse—was what Baby Suggs died of, what Ella knew, what Stamp saw and what made Paul D tremble. That anybody white could take your whole self for anything that came to mind. Not just work, kill, or maim you, but dirty you. Dirty you so bad you couldn't like yourself anymore. Dirty you so bad you forgot who you were and couldn't think it up. And though she and others lived through and got over it, she could never let it happen to her own. The best thing she was, was her children. Whites might dirty *her* all right, but not her best thing, her beautiful, magical best thing—the part of her that was clean. No undreamable dreams about whether the headless, feetless torso hanging in the tree with a sign on it was her husband or Paul A; whether the bubbling-hot girls in the colored-school fire set by patriots included her daughter; whether a gang of whites invaded her daughter's private parts, soiled her daughter's thighs and threw her daughter out of the wagon. *She* might have to work the slaughterhouse yard, but not her daughter.

And no one, nobody on this earth, would list her daughter's characteristics on the animal side of the paper. No. Oh no.

Maybe Baby Suggs could worry about it, live with the likelihood of it; Sethe had refused—and refused still.

This and much more Denver heard her say from her corner
chair, trying to persuade Beloved, the one and only person she
felt she had to convince, that what she had done was right
because it came from true love.

Beloved, her fat new feet propped on the seat of a chair in
front of the one she sat in, her unlined hands resting on her
stomach, looked at her. Uncomprehending everything except
that Sethe was the woman who took her face away, leaving her
crouching in a dark, dark place, forgetting to smile.

Her father's daughter after all, Denver decided to do the
necessary. Decided to stop relying on kindness to leave something on the stump. She would hire herself out somewhere,
and although she was afraid to leave Sethe and Beloved alone
all day not knowing what calamity either one of them would
create, she came to realize that her presence in that house had
no influence on what either woman did. She kept them alive
and they ignored her. Growled when they chose; sulked,
explained, demanded, strutted, cowered, cried and provoked
each other to the edge of violence, then over. She had begun
to notice that even when Beloved was quiet, dreamy, minding
her own business, Sethe got her going again. Whispering,
muttering some justification, some bit of clarifying information
to Beloved to explain what it had been like, and why, and how
come. It was as though Sethe didn't really want forgiveness
given; she wanted it refused. And Beloved helped her out.

Somebody had to be saved, but unless Denver got work,
there would be no one to save, no one to come home to, and
no Denver either. It was a new thought, having a self to look

out for and preserve. And it might not have occurred to her if
she hadn't met Nelson Lord leaving his grandmother's house
as Denver entered it to pay a thank you for half a pie. All he
did was smile and say, "Take care of yourself, Denver," but she
heard it as though it were what language was made for. The
last time he spoke to her his words blocked up her ears. Now
they opened her mind. Weeding the garden, pulling vegetables,
cooking, washing, she plotted what to do and how. The Bodwins
were most likely to help since they had done it twice. Once for
Baby Suggs and once for her mother. Why not the third generation as well?

She got lost so many times in the streets of Cincinnati it
was noon before she arrived, though she started out at sunrise.
The house sat back from the sidewalk with large windows
looking out on a noisy, busy street. The Negro woman who
answered the front door said, "Yes?"

"May I come in?"

"What you want?"

"I want to see Mr. and Mrs. Bodwin."

"Miss Bodwin. They brother and sister."

"Oh."

"What you want em for?"

"I'm looking for work. I was thinking they might know of
some."

"You Baby Suggs' kin, ain't you?"

"Yes, ma'am."

"Come on in. You letting in flies." She led Denver toward
the kitchen, saying, "First thing you have to know is what door
to knock on." But Denver only half heard her because she was
stepping on something soft and blue. All around her was thick,

soft and blue. Glass cases crammed full of glistening things. Books on tables and shelves. Pearl-white lamps with shiny metal bottoms. And a smell like the cologne she poured in the emerald house, only better.

"Sit down," the woman said. "You know my name?"

"No, ma'am."

"Janey. Janey Wagon."

"How do you do?"

"Fairly. I heard your mother took sick, that so?"

"Yes, ma'am."

"Who's looking after her?"

"I am. But I have to find work."

Janey laughed. "You know what? I've been here since I was fourteen, and I remember like yesterday when Baby Suggs, holy, came here and sat right there where you are. Whiteman brought her. That's how she got that house you all live in. Other things, too."

"Yes, ma'am."

"What's the trouble with Sethe?" Janey leaned against an indoor sink and folded her arms.

It was a little thing to pay, but it seemed big to Denver. Nobody was going to help her unless she told it—told all of it. It was clear Janey wouldn't and wouldn't let her see the Bodwins otherwise. So Denver told this stranger what she hadn't told Lady Jones, in return for which Janey admitted the Bodwins needed help, although they didn't know it. She was alone there, and now that her employers were getting older, she couldn't take care of them like she used to. More and more she was required to sleep the night there. Maybe she could talk them into letting Denver do the night shift, come right after supper, say, maybe get the breakfast. That way Denver could care for Sethe in the day and earn a little something at night, how's that?

Denver had explained the girl in her house who plagued her mother as a cousin come to visit, who got sick too and bothered them both. Janey seemed more interested in Sethe's condition, and from what Denver told her it seemed the woman had lost her mind. That wasn't the Sethe she remembered. This Sethe had lost her wits, finally, as Janey knew she would—trying to do it all alone with her nose in the air. Denver squirmed under the criticism of her mother, shifting in the chair and keeping her eyes on the inside sink. Janey Wagon went on about pride until she got to Baby Suggs, for whom she had nothing but sweet words. "I never went to those woodland services she had, but she was always nice to me. Always. Never be another like her."

"I miss her too," said Denver.

"Bet you do. Everybody miss her. That was a good woman."

Denver didn't say anything else and Janey looked at her face for a while. "Neither one of your brothers ever come back to see how you all was?"

"No, ma'am."

"Ever hear from them?"

"No, ma'am. Nothing."

"Guess they had a rough time in that house. Tell me, this here woman in your house. The cousin. She got any lines in her hands?"

"No," said Denver.

"Well," said Janey. "I guess there's a God after all."

The interview ended with Janey telling her to come back in a few days. She needed time to convince her employers what they needed: night help because Janey's own family needed her. "I don't want to quit these people, but they can't have all my days and nights too."

What did Denver have to do at night?

"Be here. In case."

In case what?

Janey shrugged. "In case the house burn down." She smiled then. "Or bad weather slop the roads so bad I can't get here early enough for them. Case late guests need serving or cleaning up after. Anything. Don't ask me what whitefolks need at night."

"They used to be good whitefolks."

"Oh, yeah. They good. Can't say they ain't good. I wouldn't trade them for another pair, tell you that."

With those assurances, Denver left, but not before she had seen, sitting on a shelf by the back door, a blackboy's mouth full of money. His head was thrown back farther than a head could go, his hands were shoved in his pockets. Bulging like moons, two eyes were all the face he had above the gaping red mouth. His hair was a cluster of raised, widely spaced dots made of nail heads. And he was on his knees. His mouth, wide as a cup, held the coins needed to pay for a delivery or some other small service, but could just as well have held buttons, pins or crab-apple jelly. Painted across the pedestal he knelt on were the words "At Yo Service."

The news that Janey got hold of she spread among the other coloredwomen. Sethe's dead daughter, the one whose throat she cut, had come back to fix her. Sethe was worn down, speckled, dying, spinning, changing shapes and generally bedeviled. That this daughter beat her, tied her to the bed and pulled out all her hair. It took them days to get the story properly blown up and themselves agitated and then to calm down and assess the situation. They fell into three groups: those that believed the worst; those that believed none of it; and those, like Ella, who thought it through.

"Ella. What's all this I'm hearing about Sethe?"

"Tell me it's in there with her. That's all I know."

"The daughter? The killed one?"

"That's what they tell me."

"How they know that's her?"

"It's sitting there. Sleeps, eats and raises hell. Whipping Sethe every day."

"I'll be. A baby?"

"No. Grown. The age it would have been had it lived."

"You talking about flesh?"

"I'm talking about flesh."

"Whipping her?"

"Like she was batter."

"Guess she had it coming."

"Nobody got that coming."

"But, Ella—"

"But nothing. What's fair ain't necessarily right."

"You can't just up and kill your children."

"No, and the children can't just up and kill the mama."

It was Ella more than anyone who convinced the others that rescue was in order. She was a practical woman who believed there was a root either to chew or avoid for every ailment. Cogitation, as she called it, clouded things and prevented action. Nobody loved her and she wouldn't have liked it if they had, for she considered love a serious disability. Her puberty was spent in a house where she was shared by father and son, whom she called "the lowest yet." It was "the lowest yet" who gave her a disgust for sex and against whom she measured all atrocities. A killing, a kidnap, a rape—whatever, she listened and nodded. Nothing compared to "the lowest yet." She understood Sethe's rage in the shed twenty years ago, but not her reaction to it, which Ella thought was prideful, misdirected, and Sethe herself too complicated. When she got out of jail and made no gesture toward anybody, and lived as though she were alone, Ella junked her and wouldn't give her the time of day.

The daughter, however, appeared to have some sense after all. At least she had stepped out the door, asked for the help she needed and wanted work. When Ella heard 124 was occupied by something-or-other beating up on Sethe, it infuriated her and gave her another opportunity to measure what could very well be the devil himself against "the lowest yet." There was also something very personal in her fury. Whatever Sethe had done, Ella didn't like the idea of past errors taking possession of the present. Sethe's crime was staggering and her pride outstripped even that; but she could not countenance the possibility of sin moving on in the house, unleashed and sassy. Daily life took as much as she had. The future was sunset; the past something to leave behind. And if it didn't stay behind, well, you might have to stomp it out. Slave life; freed life—every day was a test and a trial. Nothing could be counted on in a world where even when you were a solution you were a problem. "Sufficient unto the day is the evil thereof," and nobody needed more; nobody needed a grown-up evil sitting at the table with a grudge. As long as the ghost showed out from its ghostly place—shaking stuff, crying, smashing and such—Ella respected it. But if it took flesh and came in her world, well, the shoe was on the other foot. She didn't mind a little communication between the two worlds, but this was an invasion.

"Shall we pray?" asked the women.

"Uh huh," said Ella. "First. Then we got to get down to business."

The day Denver was to spend her first night at the Bodwins', Mr. Bodwin had some business on the edge of the city and told Janey he would pick the new girl up before supper. Denver sat on the porch steps with a bundle in her lap, her carnival dress sun-faded to a quieter rainbow. She was looking to the right, in the direction Mr. Bodwin would be coming from. She did not see the women approaching, accumulating slowly in groups of twos and threes from the left. Denver was looking to the right. She was a little anxious about whether she would prove satisfactory to the Bodwins, and uneasy too because she woke up crying from a dream about a running pair of shoes. The sadness of the dream she hadn't been able to shake, and the heat oppressed her as she went about the chores. Far too early she wrapped a nightdress and hairbrush into a bundle. Nervous, she fidgeted the knot and looked to the right.

Some brought what they could and what they believed would work. Stuffed in apron pockets, strung around their necks, lying in the space between their breasts. Others brought Christian faith—as shield and sword. Most brought a little of both. They had no idea what they would do once they got there. They just started out, walked down Bluestone Road and came together at the agreed-upon time. The heat kept a few women who promised to go at home. Others who believed the story didn't want any part of the confrontation and wouldn't have come no matter what the weather. And there were those like Lady Jones who didn't believe the story and hated the ignorance of those who did. So thirty women made up that company and walked slowly, slowly toward 124.

It was three in the afternoon on a Friday so wet and hot Cincinnati's stench had traveled to the country: from the canal, from hanging meat and things rotting in jars; from small animals dead in the fields, town sewers and factories. The stench, the heat, the moisture—trust the devil to make his presence known. Otherwise it looked almost like a regular workday. They could have been going to do the laundry at the orphanage or the insane asylum; corn shucking at the mill; or to clean fish, rinse offal, cradle whitebabies, sweep stores, scrape hog skin, press lard, case-pack sausage or hide in tavern kitchens so whitepeople didn't have to see them handle their food.

But not today.

When they caught up with each other, all thirty, and arrived at 124, the first thing they saw was not Denver sitting on the steps, but themselves. Younger, stronger, even as little girls lying in the grass asleep. Catfish was popping grease in the pan and they saw themselves scoop German potato salad onto the plate. Cobbler oozing purple syrup colored their teeth. They sat on the porch, ran down to the creek, teased the men, hoisted children on their hips or, if they were the children, straddled the ankles of old men who held their little hands while giving them a horsey ride. Baby Suggs laughed and skipped among them, urging more. Mothers, dead now, moved their shoulders to mouth harps. The fence they had leaned on and climbed over was gone. The stump of the butternut had split like a fan.

But there they were, young and happy, playing in Baby Suggs' yard, not feeling the envy that surfaced the next day.

Denver heard mumbling and looked to the left. She stood when she saw them. They grouped, murmuring and whispering, but did not step foot in the yard. Denver waved. A few waved back but came no closer. Denver sat back down wondering what was going on. A woman dropped to her knees. Half of the others did likewise. Denver saw lowered heads, but could not hear the lead prayer—only the earnest syllables of agreement that backed it: Yes, yes, yes, oh yes. Hear me. Hear me. Do it, Maker, do it. Yes. Among those not on their knees, who stood holding 124 in a fixed glare, was Ella, trying to see through the walls, behind the door, to what was really in there. Was it true the dead daughter come back? Or a pretend? Was it whipping Sethe? Ella had been beaten every way but down. She remembered the bottom teeth she had lost to the brake and the scars from the belt were thick as rope around her waist. She had delivered, but would not nurse, a hairy white thing, fathered by "the lowest yet." It lived five days never making a sound. The idea of that pup coming back to whip her too set her jaw working, and then Ella hollered.

Instantly the kneelers and the standers joined her. They stopped praying and took a step back to the beginning. In the beginning there were no words. In the beginning was the sound, and they all knew what that sound sounded like.

Edward Bodwin drove a cart down Bluestone Road. It displeased him a bit because he preferred his figure astride Princess. Curved over his own hands, holding the reins made him look the age he was. But he had promised his sister a detour to pick up a new girl. He didn't have to think about the way—he was headed for the house he was born in. Perhaps it was his destination that turned his thoughts to time—the way it dripped or ran. He had not seen the house for thirty years. Not the butternut in front, the stream at the rear nor the block house in between. Not even the meadow across the road. Very few of the interior details did he remember because he was three years old when his family moved into town. But he did remember that the cooking was done behind the house, the well was forbidden to play near, and that women died there: his mother, grandmother, an aunt and an older sister before he was born. The men (his father and grandfather) moved with himself and his baby sister to Court Street sixty-seven years ago. The land, of course, eighty acres of it on both sides of Bluestone, was the central thing, but he felt something sweeter and deeper about the house which is why he rented it for a little something if he could get it, but it didn't trouble him to get no rent at all since the tenants at least kept it from the disrepair total abandonment would permit.

There was a time when he buried things there. Precious things he wanted to protect. As a child every item he owned was available and accountable to his family. Privacy was an adult indulgence, but when he got to be one, he seemed not to need it.

The horse trotted along and Edward Bodwin cooled his beautiful mustache with his breath. It was generally agreed upon by the women in the Society that, except for his hands, it was the most attractive feature he had. Dark, velvety, its beauty was enhanced by his strong clean-shaven chin. But his hair was white, like his sister's—and had been since he was a young man. It made him the most visible and memorable person

at every gathering, and cartoonists had fastened onto the theat-
ricality of his white hair and big black mustache whenever they
depicted local political antagonism. Twenty years ago when
the Society was at its height in opposing slavery, it was as
though his coloring was itself the heart of the matter. The
"bleached nigger" was what his enemies called him, and on a
trip to Arkansas, some Mississippi rivermen, enraged by the
Negro boatmen they competed with, had caught him and shoe-
blackened his face and his hair. Those heady days were gone
now; what remained was the sludge of ill will; dashed hopes
and difficulties beyond repair. A tranquil Republic? Well, not
in his lifetime.

Even the weather was getting to be too much for him. He
was either too hot or freezing, and this day was a blister. He
pressed his hat down to keep the sun from his neck, where
heatstroke was a real possibility. Such thoughts of mortality
were not new to him (he was over seventy now), but they still
had the power to annoy. As he drew closer to the old homestead, the place that continued to surface in his dreams, he was
even more aware of the way time moved. Measured by the
wars he had lived through but not fought in (against the Miami,
the Spaniards, the Secessionists), it was slow. But measured by
the burial of his private things it was the blink of an eye.
Where, exactly, was the box of tin soldiers? The watch chain
with no watch? And who was he hiding them from? His father,
probably, a deeply religious man who knew what God knew
and told everybody what it was. Edward Bodwin thought him
an odd man, in so many ways, yet he had one clear directive:
human life is holy, all of it. And that his son still believed,
although he had less and less reason to. Nothing since was as

stimulating as the old days of letters, petitions, meetings,
debates, recruitment, quarrels, rescue and downright sedition.
Yet it had worked, more or less, and when it had not, he and
his sister made themselves available to circumvent obstacles.
As they had when a runaway slavewoman lived in his homestead
with her mother-in-law and got herself into a world of trouble.
The Society managed to turn infanticide and the cry of savagery
around, and build a further case for abolishing slavery. Good
years, they were, full of spit and conviction. Now he just wanted
to know where his soldiers were and his watchless chain. That
would be enough for this day of unbearable heat: bring back
the new girl and recall exactly where his treasure lay. Then
home, supper, and God willing, the sun would drop once more
to give him the blessing of a good night's sleep.

The road curved like an elbow, and as he approached it he
heard the singers before he saw them.

When the women assembled outside 124, Sethe was breaking
a lump of ice into chunks. She dropped the ice pick into her
apron pocket to scoop the pieces into a basin of water. When
the music entered the window she was wringing a cool cloth
to put on Beloved's forehead. Beloved, sweating profusely, was
sprawled on the bed in the keeping room, a salt rock in her
hand. Both women heard it at the same time and both lifted
their heads. As the voices grew louder, Beloved sat up, licked
the salt and went into the bigger room. Sethe and she exchanged
glances and started toward the window. They saw Denver
sitting on the steps and beyond her, where the yard met the
road, they saw the rapt faces of thirty neighborhood women.
Some had their eyes closed; others looked at the hot, cloudless
sky. Sethe opened the door and reached for Beloved's hand.

Together they stood in the doorway. For Sethe it was as though the Clearing had come to her with all its heat and simmering leaves, where the voices of women searched for the right combination, the key, the code, the sound that broke the back of words. Building voice upon voice until they found it, and when they did it was a wave of sound wide enough to sound deep water and knock the pods off chestnut trees. It broke over Sethe and she trembled like the baptized in its wash.

The singing women recognized Sethe at once and surprised themselves by their absence of fear when they saw what stood next to her. The devil-child was clever, they thought. And beautiful. It had taken the shape of a pregnant woman, naked and smiling in the heat of the afternoon sun. Thunder-black and glistening, she stood on long straight legs, her belly big and tight. Vines of hair twisted all over her head. Jesus. Her smile was dazzling.

Sethe feels her eyes burn and it may have been to keep them clear that she looks up. The sky is blue and clear. Not one touch of death in the definite green of the leaves. It is when she lowers her eyes to look again at the loving faces before her that she sees him. Guiding the mare, slowing down, his black hat wide-brimmed enough to hide his face but not his purpose. He is coming into her yard and he is coming for her best thing. She hears wings. Little hummingbirds stick needle beaks right through her headcloth into her hair and beat their wings. And if she thinks anything, it is no. No no. Nonono. She flies. The ice pick is not in her hand; it is her hand.

Standing alone on the porch, Beloved is smiling. But now her hand is empty. Sethe is running away from her, running, and she feels the emptiness in the hand Sethe has been holding.

Now she is running into the faces of the people out there, joining them and leaving Beloved behind. Alone. Again. Then Denver, running too. Away from her to the pile of people out there. They make a hill. A hill of black people, falling. And above them all, rising from his place with a whip in his hand, the man without skin, looking. He is looking at her.

Bare feet and chamomile sap.
Took off my shoes; took off my hat.
Bare feet and chamomile sap.
Gimme back my shoes; gimme back my hat.

Lay my head on a potato sack,
Devil sneak up behind my back.
Steam engine got a lonesome whine;
Love that woman till you go stone blind.

Stone blind; stone blind.
Sweet Home gal make you lose your mind.

His coming is the reverse route of his going. First the cold house, the storeroom, then the kitchen before he tackles the beds. Here Boy, feeble and shedding his coat in patches, is asleep by the pump, so Paul D knows Beloved is truly gone. Disappeared, some say, exploded right before their eyes. Ella is not so sure. "Maybe," she says, "maybe not. Could be hiding

in the trees waiting for another chance." But when Paul D sees
the ancient dog, eighteen years if a day, he is certain 124 is
clear of her. But he opens the door to the cold house halfway
expecting to hear her. "Touch me. Touch me. On the inside
part and call me my name."

There is the pallet spread with old newspapers gnawed at
the edges by mice. The lard can. The potato sacks too, but
empty now, they lie on the dirt floor in heaps. In daylight he
can't imagine it in darkness with moonlight seeping through
the cracks. Nor the desire that drowned him there and forced
him to struggle up, up into that girl like she was the clear air
at the top of the sea. Coupling with her wasn't even fun. It
was more like a brainless urge to stay alive. Each time she
came, pulled up her skirts, a life hunger overwhelmed him and
he had no more control over it than over his lungs. And afterward, beached and gobbling air, in the midst of repulsion and
personal shame, he was thankful too for having been escorted
to some ocean-deep place he once belonged to.

Sifting daylight dissolves the memory, turns it into dust
motes floating in light. Paul D shuts the door. He looks toward
the house and, surprisingly, it does not look back at him.
Unloaded, 124 is just another weathered house needing repair.
Quiet, just as Stamp Paid said.

"Used to be voices all round that place. Quiet, now," Stamp
said. "I been past it a few times and I can't hear a thing.
Chastened, I reckon, 'cause Mr. Bodwin say he selling it soon's
he can."

"That the name of the one she tried to stab? That one?"

"Yep. His sister say it's full of trouble. Told Janey she was
going to get rid of it."

"And him?" asked Paul D.

"Janey say he against it but won't stop it."

"Who they think want a house out there? Anybody got the money don't want to live out there."

"Beats me," Stamp answered. "It'll be a spell, I guess, before it get took off his hands."

"He don't plan on taking her to the law?"

"Don't seem like it. Janey say all he wants to know is who was the naked blackwoman standing on the porch. He was looking at her so hard he didn't notice what Sethe was up to. All he saw was some coloredwomen fighting. He thought Sethe was after one of them, Janey say."

"Janey tell him any different?"

"No. She say she so glad her boss ain't dead. If Ella hadn't clipped her, she say she would have. Scared her to death have that woman kill her boss. She *and* Denver be looking for a job."

"Who Janey tell him the naked woman was?"

"Told him she didn't see none."

"You believe they saw it?"

"Well, they saw something. I trust Ella anyway, and she say she looked it in the eye. It was standing right next to Sethe. But from the way they describe it, don't seem like it was the girl I saw in there. The girl I saw was narrow. This one was big. She say they was holding hands and Sethe looked like a little girl beside it."

"Little girl with a ice pick. How close she get to him?"

"Right up on him, they say. Before Denver and them grabbed her and Ella put her fist in her jaw."

"He got to know Sethe was after him. He got to."

"Maybe. I don't know. If he did think it, I reckon he decided not to. That be just like him, too. He's somebody never turned us down. Steady as a rock. I tell you something, if she had got to him, it'd be the worst thing in the world for us. You know, don't you, he's the main one kept Sethe from the gallows in the first place."

"Yeah. Damn. That woman is crazy. Crazy."

"Yeah, well, ain't we all?"

They laughed then. A rusty chuckle at first and then more, louder and louder until Stamp took out his pocket handkerchief and wiped his eyes while Paul D pressed the heel of his hand in his own. As the scene neither one had witnessed took shape before them, its seriousness and its embarrassment made them shake with laughter.

"Every time a whiteman come to the door she got to kill somebody?"

"For all she know, the man could be coming for the rent."

"Good thing they don't deliver mail out that way."

"Wouldn't nobody get no letter."

"Except the postman."

"Be a mighty hard message."

"And his last."

When their laughter was spent, they took deep breaths and shook their heads.

"And he still going to let Denver spend the night in his house? Ha!"

"Aw no. Hey. Lay off Denver, Paul D. That's my heart. I'm proud of that girl. She was the first one wrestle her mother down. Before anybody knew what the devil was going on."

"She saved his life then, you could say."

"You could. You could," said Stamp, thinking suddenly of
the leap, the wide swing and snatch of his arm as he rescued
the little curly-headed baby from within inches of a split skull.
"I'm proud of her. She turning out fine. Fine."

It was true. Paul D saw her the next morning when he was
on his way to work and she was leaving hers. Thinner, steady
in the eyes, she looked more like Halle than ever.

She was the first to smile. "Good morning, Mr. D."

"Well, it is now." Her smile, no longer the sneer he remembered, had welcome in it and strong traces of Sethe's mouth.
Paul D touched his cap. "How you getting along?"

"Don't pay to complain."

"You on your way home?"

She said no. She had heard about an afternoon job at the shirt
factory. She hoped that with her night work at the Bodwins' and
another one, she could put away something and help her mother
too. When he asked her if they treated her all right over there,
she said more than all right. Miss Bodwin taught her stuff. He
asked her what stuff and she laughed and said book stuff. "She
says I might go to Oberlin. She's experimenting on me." And he
didn't say, "Watch out. Watch out. Nothing in the world more
dangerous than a white schoolteacher." Instead he nodded and
asked the question he wanted to.

"Your mother all right?"

"No," said Denver. "No. No, not a bit all right."

"You think I should stop by? Would she welcome it?"

"I don't know," said Denver. "I think I've lost my mother,
Paul D."

They were both silent for a moment and then he said, "Uh,
that girl. You know. Beloved?"

"Yes?"

"You think she sure 'nough your sister?"

Denver looked at her shoes. "At times. At times I think she was—more." She fiddled with her shirtwaist, rubbing a spot of something. Suddenly she leveled her eyes at his. "But who would know that better than you, Paul D? I mean, you sure 'nough knew her."

He licked his lips. "Well, if you want my opinion—"

"I don't," she said. "I have my own."

"You grown," he said.

"Yes, sir."

"Well. Well, good luck with the job."

"Thank you. And, Paul D, you don't have to stay 'way, but be careful how you talk to my ma'am, hear?"

"Don't worry," he said and left her then, or rather she left him because a young man was running toward her, saying, "Hey, Miss Denver. Wait up."

She turned to him, her face looking like someone had turned up the gas jet.

He left her unwillingly because he wanted to talk more, make sense out of the stories he had been hearing: whiteman came to take Denver to work and Sethe cut him. Baby ghost came back evil and sent Sethe out to get the man who kept her from hanging. One point of agreement is: first they saw it and then they didn't. When they got Sethe down on the ground and the ice pick out of her hands and looked back to the house, it was gone. Later, a little boy put it out how he had been looking for bait back of 124, down by the stream, and saw, cutting through the woods, a naked woman with fish for hair.

As a matter of fact, Paul D doesn't care how It went or even why. He cares about how he left and why. When he looks at himself through Garner's eyes, he sees one thing. Through Sixo's, another. One makes him feel righteous. One makes him feel ashamed. Like the time he worked both sides of the War. Running away from the Northpoint Bank and Railway to join the 44th Colored Regiment in Tennessee, he thought he had made it, only to discover he had arrived at another colored regiment forming under a commander in New Jersey. He stayed there four weeks. The regiment fell apart before it got started on the question of whether the soldiers should have weapons or not. Not, it was decided, and the white commander had to figure out what to command them to do instead of kill other whitemen. Some of the ten thousand stayed there to clean, haul and build things; others drifted away to another regiment; most were abandoned, left to their own devices with bitterness for pay. He was trying to make up his mind what to do when an agent from Northpoint Bank caught up with him and took him back to Delaware, where he slave-worked a year. Then Northpoint took $300 in exchange for his services in Alabama, where he worked for the Rebellers, first sorting the dead and then smelting iron. When he and his group combed the battlefields, their job was to pull the Confederate wounded away from the Confederate dead. Care, they told them. Take good care. Coloredmen and white, their faces wrapped to their eyes, picked their way through the meadows with lamps, listening in the dark for groans of life in the indifferent silence of the dead. Mostly young men, some children, and it shamed him a little to feel pity for what he imagined were the sons of the guards in Alfred, Georgia.

In five tries he had not had one permanent success. Every one of his escapes (from Sweet Home, from Brandywine, from Alfred, Georgia, from Wilmington, from Northpoint) had been frustrated. Alone, undisguised, with visible skin, memorable hair and no whiteman to protect him, he never stayed uncaught. The longest had been when he ran with the convicts, stayed with the Cherokee, followed their advice and lived in hiding with the weaver woman in Wilmington, Delaware: three years. And in all those escapes he could not help being astonished by the beauty of this land that was not his. He hid in its breast, fingered its earth for food, clung to its banks to lap water and tried not to love it. On nights when the sky was personal, weak with the weight of its own stars, he made himself not love it. Its graveyards and low-lying rivers. Or just a house—solitary under a chinaberry tree; maybe a mule tethered and the light hitting its hide just so. Anything could stir him and he tried hard not to love it.

After a few months on the battlefields of Alabama, he was impressed to a foundry in Selma along with three hundred captured, lent or taken coloredmen. That's where the War's end found him, and leaving Alabama when he had been declared free should have been a snap. He should have been able to walk from the foundry in Selma straight to Philadelphia, taking the main roads, a train if he wanted to, or passage on a boat. But it wasn't like that. When he and two colored soldiers (who had been captured from the 44th he had looked for) walked from Selma to Mobile, they saw twelve dead blacks in the first eighteen miles. Two were women, four were little boys. He thought this, for sure, would be the walk of his life. The Yankees in control left the Rebels out of control. They got to the outskirts of Mobile, where blacks were putting down tracks for the Union that, earlier, they had torn up for the Rebels. One of the men with him, a private called Keane, had been with the Massachusetts 54th. He told Paul D they had been paid less than white soldiers. It was a sore point with him that, as a group, they had refused the offer Massachusetts made to make up the difference in pay. Paul D was so impressed by the idea of being paid money to fight he looked at the private with wonder and envy.

Keane and his friend, a Sergeant Rossiter, confiscated a skiff and the three of them floated in Mobile Bay. There the private hailed a Union gunboat, which took all three aboard. Keane and Rossiter disembarked at Memphis to look for their commanders. The captain of the gunboat let Paul D stay aboard all the way to Wheeling, West Virginia. He made his own way to New Jersey.

By the time he got to Mobile, he had seen more dead people than living ones, but when he got to Trenton the crowds of alive people, neither hunting nor hunted, gave him a measure of free life so tasty he never forgot it. Moving down a busy street full of whitepeople who needed no explanation for his presence, the glances he got had to do with his disgusting clothes and unforgivable hair. Still, nobody raised an alarm. Then came the miracle. Standing in a street in front of a row of brick houses, he heard a whiteman call him ("Say there! Yo!") to help unload two trunks from a coach cab. Afterward the whiteman gave him a coin. Paul D walked around with it for hours—not sure what it could buy (a suit? a meal? a horse?) and if anybody would sell him anything. Finally he saw a greengrocer selling vegetables from a wagon. Paul D pointed

to a bunch of turnips. The grocer handed them to him, took
his one coin and gave him several more. Stunned, he backed
away. Looking around, he saw that nobody seemed interested
in the "mistake" or him, so he walked along, happily chewing
turnips. Only a few women looked vaguely repelled as they
passed. His first earned purchase made him glow, never mind
the turnips were withered dry. That was when he decided that
to eat, walk and sleep anywhere was life as good as it got. And
he did it for seven years till he found himself in southern Ohio,
where an old woman and a girl he used to know had gone.

Now his coming is the reverse of his going. First he stands
in the back, near the cold house, amazed by the riot of late-
summer flowers where vegetables should be growing. Sweet
william, morning glory, chrysanthemums. The odd placement
of cans jammed with the rotting stems of things, the blossoms
shriveled like sores. Dead ivy twines around bean poles and
door handles. Faded newspaper pictures are nailed to the
outhouse and on trees. A rope too short for anything but skip-
jumping lies discarded near the washtub; and jars and jars of
dead lightning bugs. Like a child's house; the house of a very
tall child.

He walks to the front door and opens it. It is stone quiet.
In the place where once a shaft of sad red light had bathed
him, locking him where he stood, is nothing. A bleak and minus
nothing. More like absence, but an absence he had to get
through with the same determination he had when he trusted
Sethe and stepped through the pulsing light. He glances quickly
at the lightning-white stairs. The entire railing is wound with
ribbons, bows, bouquets. Paul D steps inside. The outdoor
breeze he brings with him stirs the ribbons. Carefully, not quite

in a hurry but losing no time, he climbs the luminous stairs. He enters Sethe's room. She isn't there and the bed looks so small he wonders how the two of them had lain there. It has no sheets, and because the roof windows do not open the room is stifling. Brightly colored clothes lie on the floor. Hanging from a wall peg is the dress Beloved wore when he first saw her. A pair of ice skates nestles in a basket in the corner. He turns his eyes back to the bed and keeps looking at it. It seems to him a place he is not. With an effort that makes him sweat he forces a picture of himself lying there, and when he sees it, it lifts his spirit. He goes to the other bedroom. Denver's is as neat as the other is messy. But still no Sethe. Maybe she has gone back to work, gotten better in the days since he talked to Denver. He goes back down the stairs, leaving the image of himself firmly in place on the narrow bed. At the kitchen table he sits down. Something is missing from 124. Something larger than the people who lived there. Something more than Beloved or the red light. He can't put his finger on it, but it seems, for a moment, that just beyond his knowing is the glare of an outside thing that embraces while it accuses.

To the right of him, where the door to the keeping room is ajar, he hears humming. Someone is humming a tune. Something soft and sweet, like a lullaby. Then a few words. Sounds like "high Johnny, wide Johnny. Sweet William bend down low." Of course, he thinks. That's where she is—and she is. Lying under a quilt of merry colors. Her hair, like the dark delicate roots of good plants, spreads and curves on the pillow. Her eyes, fixed on the window, are so expressionless he is not sure she will know who he is. There is too much light here in this room. Things look sold.

"Jackweed raise up high," she sings. "Lambswool over my shoulder, buttercup and clover fly." She is fingering a long clump of her hair.

Paul D clears his throat to interrupt her. "Sethe?"

She turns her head. "Paul D."

"Aw, Sethe."

"I made the ink, Paul D. He couldn't have done it if I hadn't made the ink."

"What ink? Who?"

"You shaved."

"Yeah. Look bad?"

"No. You looking good."

"Devil's confusion. What's this I hear about you not getting out of bed?"

She smiles, lets it fade and turns her eyes back to the window.

"I need to talk to you," he tells her.

She doesn't answer.

"I saw Denver. She tell you?"

"She comes in the daytime. Denver. She's still with me, my Denver."

"You got to get up from here, girl." He is nervous. This reminds him of something.

"I'm tired, Paul D. So tired. I have to rest a while."

Now he knows what he is reminded of and he shouts at her, "Don't you die on me! This is Baby Suggs' bed! Is that what you planning?" He is so angry he could kill her. He checks himself, remembering Denver's warning, and whispers, "What you planning, Sethe?"

"Oh, I don't have no plans. No plans at all."

"Look," he says, "Denver be here in the day. I be here in the night. I'm a take care of you, you hear? Starting now. First off, you don't smell right. Stay there. Don't move. Let me heat up some water." He stops. "Is it all right, Sethe, if I heat up some water?"

"And count my feet?" she asks him.

He steps closer. "Rub your feet."

Sethe closes her eyes and presses her lips together. She is thinking: No. This little place by a window is what I want. And rest. There's nothing to rub now and no reason to. Nothing left to bathe, assuming he even knows how. Will he do it in sections? First her face, then her hands, her thighs, her feet, her back? Ending with her exhausted breasts? And if he bathes her in sections, will the parts hold? She opens her eyes, knowing the danger of looking at him. She looks at him. The peachstone skin, the crease between his ready, waiting eyes and sees it—the thing in him, the blessedness, that has made him the kind of man who can walk in a house and make the women cry. Because with him, in his presence, they could. Cry and tell him things they only told each other: that time didn't stay put; that she called, but Howard and Buglar walked on down the railroad track and couldn't hear her; that Amy was scared to stay with her because her feet were ugly and her back looked so bad; that her ma'am had hurt her feelings and she couldn't find her hat anywhere and "Paul D?"

"What, baby?"

"She left me."

"Aw, girl. Don't cry."

"She was my best thing."

Paul D sits down in the rocking chair and examines the quilt patched in carnival colors. His hands are limp between his knees. There are too many things to feel about this woman. His head hurts. Suddenly he remembers Sixo trying to describe what he felt about the Thirty-Mile Woman. "She is a friend of my mind. She gather me, man. The pieces I am, she gather them and give them back to me in all the right order. It's good, you know, when you got a woman who is a friend of your mind."

He is staring at the quilt but he is thinking about her wrought-iron back; the delicious mouth still puffy at the corner from Ella's fist. The mean black eyes. The wet dress steaming before the fire. Her tenderness about his neck jewelry—its three wands, like attentive baby rattlers, curving two feet into the air. How she never mentioned or looked at it, so he did not have to feel the shame of being collared like a beast. Only this woman Sethe could have left him his manhood like that. He wants to put his story next to hers.

"Sethe," he says, "me and you, we got more yesterday than anybody. We need some kind of tomorrow."

He leans over and takes her hand. With the other he touches her face. "You your best thing, Sethe. You are." His holding fingers are holding hers.

"Me? Me?"

There is a loneliness that can be rocked. Arms crossed, knees drawn up; holding, holding on, this motion, unlike a ship's, smooths and contains the rocker. It's an inside kind—wrapped tight like skin. Then there is a loneliness that roams. No rocking can hold it down. It is alive, on its own. A dry and spreading thing that makes the sound of one's own feet going seem to come from a far-off place.

Everybody knew what she was called, but nobody anywhere knew her name. Disremembered and unaccounted for, she cannot be lost because no one is looking for her, and even if they were, how can they call her if they don't know her name? Although she has claim, she is not claimed. In the place where long grass opens, the girl who waited to be loved and cry shame erupts into her separate parts, to make it easy for the chewing laughter to swallow her all away.

It was not a story to pass on.

They forgot her like a bad dream. After they made up their tales, shaped and decorated them, those that saw her that day on the porch quickly and deliberately forgot her. It took longer for those who had spoken to her, lived with her, fallen in love with her, to forget, until they realized they couldn't remember or repeat a single thing she said, and began to believe that, other than what they themselves were thinking, she hadn't said anything at all. So, in the end, they forgot her too. Remembering seemed unwise. They never knew where or why she crouched, or whose was the underwater face she needed like that. Where the memory of the smile under her chin might have been and was not, a latch latched and lichen attached its apple-green bloom to the metal. What made her think her fingernails could open locks the rain rained on?

It was not a story to pass on.

So they forgot her. Like an unpleasant dream during a troubling sleep. Occasionally, however, the rustle of a skirt hushes when they wake, and the knuckles brushing a cheek in sleep seem to belong to the sleeper. Sometimes the photograph of a close friend or relative—looked at too long—shifts, and something more familiar than the dear face itself moves there. They can touch it if they like, but don't, because they know things will never be the same if they do.

This is not a story to pass on.

Down by the stream in back of 124 her footprints come and go, come and go. They are so familiar. Should a child, an adult place his feet in them, they will fit. Take them out and they disappear again as though nobody ever walked there.

By and by all trace is gone, and what is forgotten is not only the footprints but the water too and what it is down there. The rest is weather. Not the breath of the disremembered and unaccounted for, but wind in the eaves, or spring ice thawing too quickly. Just weather. Certainly no clamor for a kiss.

Beloved.

ALSO BY TONI MORRISON

The Bluest Eye

WITH AN INTRODUCTION BY CANDICE CARTY-WILLIAMS

Pecola Breedlove longs for blond hair and blue eyes, so that she will be as beautiful and beloved as all the blond, blue-eyed children in America. In the autumn of 1941, the marigolds in her garden will not bloom, and her wish will not come true. Pecola's life is about to change in other painful and devastating ways.

A powerful interrogation of what it means to conform to an idea of beauty, *The Bluest Eye* asks vital questions about race, class and gender and remains one of Toni Morrison's most unforgettable works.

'Not only a story but an awe-inspiring poem that confronts beauty itself'
Guardian

VINTAGE

ALSO BY TONI MORRISON

Song of Solomon

WITH AN INTRODUCTION BY MARLON JAMES

Soon after a local eccentric leaps from a rooftop in a
vain attempt at flight, Macon 'Milkman' Dead III is born.
Brought up by his well-off black family to revere the white
world around him, Milkman strives to make sense of his
conflicting identities. Always seeking flight in some way,
he leaves his Michigan home for the South, retracing the
steps of his forebears in search of his own buried heritage,
and is introduced to an entire cast of strivers and seeresses,
liars and assassins; the inhabitants of a fully realised black world.

Evocative and kaleidoscopic, *Song of Solomon* is a
brilliantly imagined coming-of-age tale.

'Toni Morrison's *Song of Solomon* grips as a novel of
extraordinary truth, wisdom and humour'
Sunday Telegraph

VINTAGE